P9-DU

A sandhills ballad
Randolph, Ladette
PS3618.A644 S36 2009

DATE DUE

A Sandhills Ballad

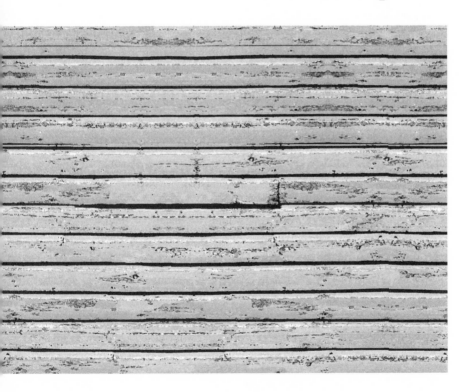

A Sandhills Ballad

Ladette Randolph

UNIVERSITY OF NEW MEXICO PRESS | ALBUQUERQUE

14 13 12 11 10 09   1 2 3 4 5 6

LIBRARY OF CONGRESS CATALOGING-IN-PUBLICATION DATA
Randolph, Ladette.
  A sandhills ballad / Ladette Randolph.
    p. cm.
  ISBN 978-0-8263-4685-8 (ALK. PAPER)
1. Women ranchers—Fiction.
2. Traffic accident victims—Fiction.
3. Psychological fiction. I. Title.
  PS3618.A644S36 2009
  813'.6—dc22
              2008049358

This is a work of fiction. Any similarity to real people
or real situations is purely by coincidence.

Book and jacket design and type composition
  by Kathleen Sparkes.
This book was designed and composed using
  the Warnock PRO OTF family.
Body text is Warnock regular 11.5/15, 26P.

For my mother,
and for my father
who left us too soon

ACKNOWLEDGMENTS

I owe thanks to many people for this book becoming a reality. First, thanks to the Rona Jaffe Foundation for a generous grant that gave me a month away from my desk at University of Nebraska Press and the time I needed to start this novel. The folks at the Arrow Hotel were generous and respectful during my stay in Broken Bow, Nebraska.

I am not a horsewoman, nor am I a rancher. Tom and Janice Yost were kind to talk to me about the rigors and rewards of ranch life. Dallas and Kandy Dodson were incredibly generous, taking an afternoon out of their busy lives, feeding me, driving me around their beautiful ranch on the Niobrara River near Valentine, Nebraska, and patiently answering all my questions. Any errors about ranching and ranch culture are all mine. I was also aided by the published works of Nellie Synder Yost whose stories about her parents gave me insight into the early years of white settlement in Nebraska.

Katherine Brandenburg and other members of the High Street Book Club in Lincoln, Nebraska, took a big risk and agreed to read this book in an early draft. Their feedback was invaluable. I incorporated every bit of their advice. If my revisions have failed to live up to their suggestions, it's my failing alone. They were careful and thoughtful readers.

I owe my sister, Tami Turnbull, thanks for her support and encouragement. She, too, read this manuscript in draft and made many helpful suggestions, as did Beth Barrett and Brenda Robinson of North Platte, Nebraska.

Thanks to Jeff Kleinman and Matt Bokovoy.

Hilda Raz continues to listen and to inspire me to my best work.

Who could ask for a better writing partner than Erin Flanagan. She's been there at every step, and if I falter she picks me up.

I'm deeply grateful to Clark Whitehorn for taking a chance on this book and for talking me through the last revision. As every writer knows, there's nothing more gratifying than finding an editor who gets what you're doing.

My children, Leif, Jordan, and Bronwyn Milliken, have lived their entire lives with an oftentimes distracted mother. They've not only forgiven the lapses but as adults have actively offered their support and feedback. On the worst days, they were there to urge me on.

I'm a lucky woman, and Noel, my partner in life and love, is my first and my best reader always.

This novel is dedicated to my parents, Gerry Randolph and Elaine (Randolph) Anderson. I wish my father had lived to see its publication. For letting me dream unfettered, I offer them all my thanks.

PART ONE

≡CHAPTER 1

≡In that deep sleep she dreamt about the wind. She heard it whistle under the windowsills and through the cracks of an empty house, heard it rattle the loose No Hunting sign on a weathered post, and slam open and shut again the sagging door of an old barn. In the drifting sand she heard the story of her life. When the wind stopped, she woke to silence and to a square of light on the ceiling of a dark room. She stared into the light until she slept again—this time a sleep without dreams.

Sound returned first: a rhythmic whirring, erratic clicks, a consistent tapping interrupted by intermittent beeps, a deep hum she felt more than heard. The light, which she had seen on the ceiling earlier, she now saw was cast by a street lamp outside the window. Through the open blinds she noticed the brick wall of another building.

She saw sitting beside her, his head drooping against his chest, her father, John Rasmussen. His hair was crimped where the crown of his hat usually rested. In the dim light she could make out the gleam of his white forehead in contrast to the ruddy lower half of his face. She knew it was summer by her father's face.

He stirred. "Mary," he said, and she remembered her name. "So you've decided to come back to us?" He leaned forward, bringing his face into the light from outside. "How do you feel?"

"Heavy."

"Do you remember anything?"

"No." She looked slowly around, guessing finally she was in a hospital room.

John reached across the space between them. His hand felt rough in hers, his palm dry and calloused, his fingers thick from work. She felt a small scab on one of his knuckles and through her mind flashed a vivid image of him fixing fence on the ranch. With his free hand, he rubbed his lower lip. He nodded toward the bed. "There's some things you need to know."

Neither of them spoke. Finally, Mary lowered both hands to her legs, and as she did, she felt the fingers of her left hand drop over the edge of her thigh. She looked at John.

He nodded. "They had to take it to get you out of the car." He searched her face, wondering, she guessed, what she was thinking. She thought nothing, felt only a numb detachment as though she were watching herself from a great distance having this conversation with her father. She smoothed the top sheet then and looked away from the empty space where her leg should have been to look more closely at a monitor standing beside the bed. She didn't lift the blanket, didn't want to look any closer at what had happened to her.

John nodded toward the machine. "That thing's kept you with us for the past six weeks." He shifted in his chair, unclasped his hand gently from hers, and moved to stand up. "I need to let the nurses know. And your mother will want to hear. Are you all right if I leave you for a few minutes?"

At Mary's nod, he stood up slowly, stiff from sitting so long in the chair. He was broad-shouldered, slim-hipped, not tall. He wore his customary away-from-the-ranch clothes: new Levi's, a striped western-cut shirt, a tooled leather belt with a shiny silver buckle, and clean cowboy boots. On the stand beside the bed lay his good white summer Stetson. At home would be its counterpart, used only for work, sweat-stained, filthy, its brim curled. Mary preferred the hat at home. She preferred as well his manure-soaked boots and his worn jeans. He looked like a stranger leaving the room in his unfamiliar clothes.

As if he knew what she was thinking, John paused in the doorway and looked back. "Just checking to make sure I wasn't dreaming."

✳

Mary woke again to her mother's voice in the hall. Fresia was scolding Will and Mark, reminding them that Mary still needed to rest. Seconds later, both boys banged through the door of her room. They stopped at the edge of the bed and peered soberly at her with their clear, blue eyes. Freckles spattered their noses.

"Hi guys."

They smiled then and gestured as if to jump on the bed.

"Stay off that bed," Fresia warned. Her skin was browned by the sun, and like John, she wore new Levi's and a western shirt. Her dress boots were fancier than John's, black with green vines and leaves. Her dark hair was pulled away from her face into a loose ponytail that fell across her shoulder as she leaned to hug Mary. Fresia did not speak, but she refused to release her hold on Mary. "You scared us good," she said when she finally pulled away.

Behind Fresia stood Mary's older sister Judy, and her husband Max, along with Fresia's parents, Lydia and Cal Stiles. Mary smiled at all of them. They crowded close to the bed, each of them touching her. Beneath their smiles, she saw something guarded in their faces, but she didn't ask any questions. John looked tired. He closed the door now so they wouldn't bother other patients on the floor. It was not yet 7:00 AM.

"We came as soon as we could," Fresia was saying to John. "We got all the chores done before the sun was up, went out right after you'd . . ."

"Can I see your leg?" Will interrupted. For a split second everyone froze. Fresia grabbed his upper arm then. "William, you won't be..."

"It's all right," Mary said. "I haven't looked at it myself. This is as good a time as any." She paused before pulling away the blanket. She felt her stomach pitch when she saw how the hospital gown fell away at the top of her thigh. She slowly inched up the gown to reveal the gauze-wrapped stump. As she gingerly touched the bandage with the tips of her fingers, it felt as though she were touching someone else's body.

Will and Mark had crowded close to the bed, and Mark looked away from the stump now and into Mary's face. "Can't you uncover it?"

"Mark," Fresia scolded again.

"Not yet, I don't suppose."

After Mary had pulled the sheet back over herself, there was a lull in the room, and her family shifted uncomfortably. They looked from one to another before Fresia finally cleared her throat. She nodded, and everyone left the room except her and Lydia. "It's Brian," Fresia said once the door was closed.

Mary lifted her hand to stop her. She didn't want her to go on. She knew already. The dreams had told her. Before she woke the wind had stopped and the drifting sand had filled the empty house. Sand had drifted against the fencepost and the barn, silencing both the rattling sign and the banging door. Mary looked at her mother and her grandmother, their faces mute with anguish. Now that they had broken the silence, she felt a sudden force of emotion so visceral it was as if she had been pushed hard back down on the bed. She gasped for breath before turning her face away. Fresia and Lydia sat on either side of the bed. Neither spoke as Fresia stroked Mary's hair away from her forehead and Lydia gently rubbed her arm. The sound of Mary's sobs masked the sound of the monitors.

When she was ready, Fresia and Lydia answered all of her questions. The car had been hit by an oncoming truck on Highway 21 just north of Oconto, in early March. The driver had been at the wheel for twenty-six hours. He had fallen asleep and crossed into their lane. Brian was dead by the time the EMTs arrived. He'd been buried weeks before in the little cemetery outside Rose, Nebraska, near the Needham ranch. The rescue team had cut Mary out of the car. Her leg, crushed beyond saving, had been removed at the scene of the accident. As they talked, no matter how she tried, Mary could not reconstruct any memory of that night.

"That's merciful," Lydia said.

There was an official-sounding knock and the door opened. The nurses had changed shifts and it was the new nurse on duty.

"We've been calling you Sleeping Beauty," she joked as she checked Mary's vital signs. "Now we'll have to start calling you by your real name, won't we?" She smiled down at Mary, ignoring her tears, and said to Fresia and Lydia, "Everything looks good." She made a few notes in Mary's chart. "We'll have to be careful, though, not to wear her out." She looked up from the charts at Fresia and Lydia again as she said this. "I know people will be excited to see her, but after this we'll want to limit visitors to two at a time, at least for the next few days."

Both Lydia and Fresia nodded dutifully. They seemed chastened by the nurse's request. On the ranch, they were commanding women in full possession of themselves—strong, capable, and masterful; there was no situation that could get the better of them. But when off the ranch, they sometimes seemed subdued, a little uncertain.

Lydia remembered then the flowers she had brought. "Do you have something we could put these flowers in?" She reached for a bouquet of lavender iris—their stems wrapped in wet paper towels covered with aluminum foil—and held them up for the nurse.

※

Within a day of her waking, the terms phantom limb and phantom pain became a part of Mary's lexicon as the pain in her phantom limb took the form of an excruciatingly tight vise around her missing foot. Nights she woke in agony. During those nights, some of the nurses never let down their guard with her. They remained polite, professional, detached, while others went beyond their duties, staying with Mary after they had administered her medication, sometimes gently massaging the stump, which, when it had been unwrapped, revealed a purple scar, an extra piece of skin folded back over the bone, reminding Mary of the flap of a purse. These nurses did what they could to distract her, telling stories and jokes so she could almost forget the pain until the medication took effect. Many were close to her age, one a new bride herself. Although none of them asked questions, Mary felt their fearful curiosity, their bewildered empathy.

Her team of doctors differed too. The neurosurgeon made his rounds, checked her like one might the engine of a car, made notes in her chart without comment to her, and always left with a curt nod. Others attempted to establish rapport, but they were not all equally successful in the attempt. Among the least graceful of this group was Dr. Jacobs, her orthopedic surgeon. He had a habit of sitting on the edge of Mary's bed, not seeming to sense her discomfort with his overfamiliarity. Despite his awkwardness, it was Dr. Jacobs who helped her finally understand her phantom limb pain.

"The fact that you still have the sensation of a foot is key to your success in learning to adjust to a prosthetic limb." They had been talking earlier about how her fabricated leg had been ordered and that once it came she would begin physical therapy. Dr. Jacobs talked about her having a relationship with the limb. He said she might curse it now but she would eventually see it as a means to freedom. "If you can channel what you now feel as pain into the prosthesis, shoot that sensation down into the prosthetic foot, you'll not only adjust more quickly but what you now understand as pain will, with luck, eventually be perceived simply as feeling."

✳

As the days of her hospitalization went on, Mary became adept at listening to the sounds in the hallway and predicting who might be coming to her room. She discerned the differing squeaks and clicks of the shoes worn by various doctors and nurses. Her brothers were easy to identify, always running ahead of her parents, the soles of their shoes slapping the floor. Her parents' boots made a metallic tap, Fresia's lighter at the heel than John's. Cal and Lydia also wore boots, but theirs sounded very different from her parents. Lydia shuffled slightly, something Mary had never noticed visually but could now hear vividly. Lydia was still very petite and proudly made it known she still wore the same size Levi's she'd worn all of her life. Her gray hair was cropped short. Her icy blue eyes were a startling contrast to her dark and deeply wrinkled skin. Cal walked with a slow, heavy footfall that immediately brought to mind his massive bone structure. He was a tall man, six foot five. Though he stooped a bit now, he was still broad shouldered, squarely built, like a "brick shithouse," as John always said. He had a large head on a thick neck, and he wore a handlebar mustache that made him resemble a walrus. He laughed and talked loudly, his voice deep in his chest. Everything Cal did was big. In recent years he'd developed a belly. He'd grab it sometimes and say salaciously, "I needed a big shed for my tool."

Mary never had trouble believing the near-mythical stories about her grandparents from their younger days. Cal had inherited over twenty thousand acres from his father, Gerald, and the ranch had been in the Stiles family for 115 years. Mary's great-grandfather had been a hard-drinking man, and he had surrounded himself with hard-drinking hands. Her great-grandmother, Katrina, had always worked alongside the hands and was famous in the area for her daredevil ways, her practical jokes, and her tolerance for the antics of Gerald and the cowboys he hired. She was the only girl in a family of eight, the darling of her brothers, and had worked alongside them. When she married Gerald, it was understood she would not be the camp cook, nor would she be, like so many ranch women, stuck inside. For years they hired old wagon cooks retired from the big outfits that had moved herds across the prairies from Texas to Montana each year. Gerald himself had been a part of those cowboy outfits, repping for the 101 out of Nebraska for a decade before marrying Katrina.

Mary never knew Katrina—she'd died before Mary was born—but she remembered Gerald. He died when she was six. She remembered still how all the ranch hands and the neighbors who had helped each year with branding rode two dozen of the ranch's saddle horses in single file to the cemetery. Cal had headed up the procession on foot, leading Gerald's riderless horse, a big, deep-chested iron-gray called Thunder. After Gerald's death, Thunder was turned into the pasture near the barn and given a pensioner's rest, despite the fact that he was only seven when Gerald died. As far as anyone else knew, no one had ridden him since. But Mary had ridden him one night when she was ten. Her friend Katie had been staying over, and they had snuck out of the house on that moonlit night and into the corral where Mary had bridled Thunder and jumped on his bare back while Katie held the gate open. Thunder had taken the bit eagerly, ducking his head for her to slip the bridle over his ears and shifting as he waited for her to tighten the throatlatch. He had run full out on the open prairie, and Mary's pajamas had been wringing wet by the time she returned to Katie, who was angry for having been left alone so long in the dark corral.

The morning after this escapade, Mary had felt ashamed of violating an unspoken code of respect for Gerald. She never rode Thunder again, though for months after that he nickered and bobbed his head toward her each morning when she turned him and the other pension horses out of the corral into the pasture.

Cal and Lydia weren't as dramatic as Gerald and Katrina had been, but there were fabled stories about their youth, too. Like Katrina before her, Lydia had always done ranch work. Once John and Fresia were married and assumed most of the daily operations, Lydia had taken over management of the house. She was as capable and scrappy a woman as Mary had ever known, though Mary sometimes had a little trouble squaring the stories of her grandmother's wild years with the matriarch she had always known. Only in the last five years had Lydia stopped riding roundup each May. Like Katrina before her, there was still a tradition of keeping the door open for former ranch hands, and she'd accepted every one of those troubled cowboys through the years without criticism. She still did, as some of them, damaged physically by the hard work they'd done ranching and mentally by the ravages of alcohol or loneliness, now and then came back to the Stiles ranch to rest or sober up. Cal and Lydia always welcomed them as family and made room at the family table for them.

Things had changed over the years and no hands now lived in the bunkhouse on the ranch. They leased out a few thousand acres of pasture to other ranchers and had cut their herd by more than half. John had more trouble each year finding men willing to work such long hours, and there hadn't been a steady hand for almost three years. Before her marriage to Brian, Mary had been as close to a regular hand as they'd had.

Most of Mary's friends had called or written, but none so far had driven to North Platte to see her. This morning, as Mary sat in a chair beside the window enjoying the sunlight dappling the room, she heard in the hall a light squeak of tennis shoes. She sensed shoving and laughing and knew immediately it was her two best friends from high school, Katie and Janna. Seconds later they knocked and pushed open the door. Their exuberant energy flooded into the room. Their arms were full of stuffed animals, jelly beans, chocolate, and helium balloons. They rushed toward her, hugging and laughing, all the while thrusting their gifts at her. Mary was overcome by their beauty, their health, their wholeness. As they stepped away, she looked at them. They were both wearing shorts and she stared openly at their long shapely legs. She had the sudden feeling this must be the way the old see the young, as a marvel, a gift. She couldn't help herself. They were so beautiful.

After their initial greeting, Katie and Janna pulled away and went to sit on the edge of the bed. Mary watched their expressions grow guarded as they observed her from a distance, reminding her of how she must look, the contusions on her face no longer swollen but still slightly discolored, and her flat, unwashed hair. Katie's expression froze when she saw the uncovered stump peeping out beneath Mary's shorts. Janna saw the stump then, too, but unlike Katie, Janna looked up at Mary with open alarm. Mary smiled grimly and pulled up the hem of her shorts.

"Mary," Janna said, while Katie dragged her eyes away from Mary's. The levity they had brought with them into the room dissipated. They grew watchful, as though they suspected Mary was an imposter, as though they thought perhaps disaster was something contagious.

Janna seemed to remember her manners and smiled wanly, "How are you, Mary?"

Mary shrugged. The old rapport was gone. Whatever their friendship had been in the past, it was not enough to bring them through this together. Even if she had wanted to tell them everything, she guessed they couldn't hear it. "I've been better," she said. She went on to make a bad joke about not being able to run the fifty-yard dash anymore. Katie and Janna's over-boisterous laughter at the joke indicated the extent of their gratitude for being let off the hook. Mary understood how they wanted to get through this visit, to go on with their lives and forget her suffering, to think of her, if ever, with some future regret, part of a sad story they might tell a new acquaintance someday.

They were both home in Anselmo working for the summer, preparing to return to Kearney State College in the fall. Even before the accident, it was clear their lives had been moving in a different direction from hers. Mary had not wanted to go to college. She had seen her future squarely on the ranch. Beneath this glib explanation of their differences, though, was a darker truth, the clear sense that Janna and Katie had a future, while Mary was stranded in limbo watching as the strong continued on without her.

She thought they would have nothing to say to one another, but Janna and Katie were full of plans for the coming year and talked about their hopes after graduation the following spring. As if they had come to the same conclusion as Mary had about her life, neither Katie nor Janna asked what she planned to do next. They sat side by side on the edge of the bed, swinging their beautiful, dangling legs as they talked.

Before they left both girls swooped down to hug Mary again. They each stole quick, sidelong glances at Mary as with great effort she stood up from her chair and balanced on one foot before grabbing her crutches. She walked them to the door, her lurching movements nothing at all like the catlike walk she had been known for before.

"Get better, Mary," Katie said at the door. She said it as though she hoped Mary's leg might grow back soon so Mary could be one of them again.

The Needhams came for the first time a week after Katie and Janna. Unlike her previous visitors, Mary had not sensed their arrival in advance. She hadn't heard them in the hallway at all, so they startled her from sleep. Even now, gathered in her room, they seemed muted as if they had hoped to visit undetected.

Iris was more pale and soft than Mary remembered. Gus, too, was changed, and was grayer, more stooped than before. The four surviving—she had to stumble over the word as she thought it— Needham boys were with them: Kent, Larry, Jeffrey, and Billy. The boys stood at the foot of her bed, pleating between their restless fingers the cowboy hats they held in front of them. They seemed afraid to look at her, and she found herself comforting them, trying to make them all feel more at ease. She insisted they talk about how much hay they were going to put up, how many cattle they planned to sell, and to describe in detail how much weight the cattle had gained since spring. She wanted to hear about the new truck they had bought, Iris's garden, how Jeffrey was doing in his second year at the University of Nebraska. He had clearly made a special trip from Lincoln to come with the rest of the family to see her, though they were too polite to mention this.

Iris had brought homemade cinnamon rolls, saying as she laid them on the stand, "I know how much you like cinnamon rolls." It was the only admission of their former intimacy as they all studiously avoided talking about Brian.

Finally, before they were ready to leave, Gus said softly, "When you're settled back at home, we'd like to come get you some weekend, let you get your things from the house and . . ." he paused for a moment, "take you to see where Brian is resting."

There had been no place for all of them to sit, and the boys had remained standing during their visit, shifting from foot to foot in the crowded hospital room. Mary felt their relief as now, having fulfilled the obligation to visit—and who would know better than she how much they hated uncomfortable social obligations—they were free to leave. Before going, each of the Needham boys hugged Mary. Even Gus brushed her cheek with his dry lips. Iris lingered. She hugged Mary, sobbed once deeply, and then rushed out the door.

After they had left, the air seemed to come back into the room. Mary wondered at their oddness. Who were these people? How had they come to play any role in her life? Out of nowhere, suddenly, strangers who had this claim on her. She doubted momentarily if she had ever known Brian himself. How was it possible he had come from them? She had lived with the Needhams for a year and a half. She had talked over coffee with Iris, roped and branded, cut hay, fixed fence, and rounded up cattle with the boys and Gus, and yet here they were all unable to talk about the thing right in front of them, the thing squeezing the air from the room. Mary wasn't complaining. This was how she had wanted it too. They were all in

14)⟩⟨ Ladette Randolph

agreement that there was no need to talk about how they felt. They knew already how they felt. Some situations couldn't be made better with words. Most things couldn't be made better with words.

❅

Her parents were there the morning the physical therapist brought Mary her prosthetic leg. It had been carefully calibrated to the specifications of her remaining leg. Its finish was a delicate ivory, the surface slightly soft over hard plasticine. Except for its weight and the hinged knee, it resembled the legs of the better baby dolls Mary had played with while growing up. She couldn't help but laugh when she noticed the added details—a small dimple above the knee, delicate toenails. She pictured someone adding these touches, a small kindness meant to help alleviate a great indignity. Although new technology had begun to introduce lightweight steel prostheses into the market, legs with the promise of greater flexibility, Mary had chosen the more traditional prosthesis instead.

Jennifer, the physical therapist, instructed her to pull over her stump an elastic cloth, like a very tight sock. Next, she was fitted with a leather halter to connect the stump to the leg. The stump fit perfectly into a slight hollow at the top of the prosthesis. Jennifer helped her to her feet, and Mary felt for the first time the pressure of her weight on the stump, and how heavy the prosthesis felt as it hung suspended from that small piece of leather. She began to understand then how she would live the rest of her life.

Jennifer demonstrated how the thigh muscles would contract to lift the leg, and how Mary must learn to throw the leg forward, causing the hinge at the knee to release and then catch to mimic a step. Mary rehearsed these unfamiliar movements. After only a few seconds, she was breathless with exhaustion and her stump throbbed with real, rather than phantom, pain.

Jennifer, someone who Mary felt she might have been friends with under other circumstances, finally said, "That's enough for today." She looked at Mary closely as if she understood her frustration. "I know it doesn't feel like you've made any progress, but you've done really well. It'll take time to develop new muscles and build strength. Your stump will need to develop a callous. Eventually, this will all be second nature." Mary did not respond to Jennifer as she unfastened the prosthesis. It felt like an anchor holding her back.

When he came later that afternoon to see how she was doing, Dr. Jacobs told Mary and her parents that some patients went through "mourning rituals" after a limb was amputated.

"Some patients," he explained, "want to see their limbs before they are disposed of. In some cases, they even want to control what happens to the limb. In your situation, Mary, we weren't able to preserve the leg." He looked meaningfully toward her parents then. "It might be necessary to create a ritual nonetheless, some way for Mary to say good-bye to the old leg so she can welcome the new one."

Like her parents, Mary felt herself staring at Dr. Jacobs, trying to process this peculiar idea. It was true, though, and she admitted it to no one, that she felt the urge to weep whenever she thought about her lost leg, thinking of it so vulnerable there where she still pictured it with the car alone on that cold night of the accident. She couldn't remember the cold, but she'd been told about it.

After everyone had left that day, as evening came on, in the dusky light she stole uneasy glances toward where the new leg leaned against the wall beside the bed. In the dimness she felt the leg as a presence in the room. Now and then, if she forgot it was there, she was startled to see it out of the corner of her eye. It seemed at once inhuman and yet human.

This was not the first time she had experienced a presence in the room. In fact, since she had first awakened from the coma she had felt something hovering above the bed, squatting there in a troubling way. Now, uncannily, the presence seemed to have left its place above the bed and shifted to the leg instead. Although it was preferable there, the eerie spirit lent the leg a macabre sort of life.

When she first felt the presence, Mary had thought it was Brian's spirit trying to make contact, but there was something malevolent about it that was impossible to square with her memory of Brian. Lacking other explanations, she had finally decided it was some aspect of God himself lingering above her, watching her, not in the benign way she'd been told about in Sunday School, but with detachment as if she were a curiosity and he was watching for her reaction to suffering.

What Mary couldn't bear in all this was everyone's pity. Pity, though, took a variety of forms. A woman from a neighboring ranch, someone not well known by the Rasmussen family, had sent a card. Unlike the other cards Mary received, all of which universally stated their sympathy and sadness about life's unfairness, Bonnie Klein had written simply, "You must have done something really bad for God to punish you like this."

Mary had not shown Bonnie Klein's card to her parents like she had the other cards she received, knowing they would rush to argue the notion away. She had discovered through this experience that her mother especially was a great defender of God, as though he needed help in explaining what looked to Mary not so much like supreme wisdom as supreme indifference.

Now and then Mary took out Bonnie Klein's card and read the explicit condemnation. Her parents would have found it perverse of her, but to Mary it felt like a welcome pain, for as Bonnie Klein said, Mary believed God was indeed punishing her for some slight against him. One thing Mary knew she didn't need was people making God into such a sugarplum fairy when she knew otherwise. She had barely escaped his ferocious grasp. Brian had not escaped. She didn't know at all why she had been spared to suffer, but one of her theories was that she and Brian had been guilty of loving one another more than loving God. She had never given God much thought, despite her mother's faith and having sat through her share of sermons and Sunday School lessons. None of it had seemed to take. Now, though, she had the nagging sense that she had committed more than her share of those sins the preachers had warned against, and God had finally had enough.

She decided God was telling her he was the missing piece in her life with Brian, and now, in the form of the replacement leg, he meant to make her whole again. She was glad finally to know this, for she'd been meaning to tell God a few things. She didn't want him. She wasn't whole and she would never be whole. She didn't understand him. She didn't want to understand him. She didn't like the Christian metaphor of God's followers being like sheep. After all, everyone knew how stupid sheep were, too stupid to save themselves.

And there was another thing she knew. Ranchers did cruel things to the animals in their care, but they were always necessary cruelties. No rancher worth the name let an animal suffer needlessly. The cow with cancer eye and no hope of living wasn't allowed to suffer and die a natural death. The horse hopelessly tangled in barbed wire, you shot rather than watch suffer. This was how Mary knew God didn't care about her misery. In fact, she suspected he might even enjoy it, and this she found intolerable. She had begun a secret campaign. She wasn't going to repent of her love for Brian, even if it was God's intent that she should. She was locked in a battle over the terms of her life, and she was grateful to Mrs. Klein for confirming her own suspicion that God was the meanest son-of-a-bitch there ever was.

Mary already knew she couldn't win this battle with God. That wasn't the point. It was like those daredevil boys who were determined to ride the orneriest bull or the most spirited horse. They knew they'd be thrown off eventually, but they were going to pit themselves against that wild spirit and give it a run for its money. This was the deal, if God was who everyone said he was, then she and God were now enemies.

Finally she slept, the new leg shimmering in the glow of the streetlight.

❋

Mary did not want to talk about Brian. While no one in her family seemed to feel this was unusual, the hospital staff was clearly concerned. A hospital counselor had come by in the first days after she woke to talk to her about grieving. The counselor had told her there were stages to grief, and that if she wanted to heal, it would be important not to fight each stage but to let it happen. The counselor, an older woman with short gray hair and rosy cheeks, who seemed overly happy to Mary, had told her that she had lost two of her sisters in a car accident twenty years before. Mary supposed this story was meant to encourage her that people can overcome terrible things. Instead, Mary felt this woman was carrying her grief with her like a medal, as though it was her reason for living.

"Would you like to talk about Brian?" the woman asked.

"No," Mary had said. She wanted to keep Brian close and the only way she could see to do that was to not speak of him.

The Grief Woman had come by the next day with a pink flowered notebook. With it she brought a pink pen and laid them both on the bedside stand among the flowers and cards and candy, and both the notebook and the pen fell to the floor twice before the woman finally asked if she couldn't move some of the flowers to another place in the room.

"When you're ready," the woman said timidly before she left, "maybe it will be easier to write in this." Mary had to admit she liked the woman better when she wasn't being so enthusiastic. Still, she ignored the pink journal.

✿

Before she could go home, Mary needed to prove herself capable of certain tasks: walking up and down stairs, climbing in and out of vehicles, and traversing difficult surfaces such as gravel, sand, sloping walks, and rock. For hours each day she practiced these tasks, dismayed again and again by her awkwardness. She lurched and careened in the early stages before mastery and more than a few times would have taken a bad fall had it not been for Jennifer there to support her. Finally, after she'd accomplished all of these tasks, she was made to simulate the very fall she had been trying so hard to avoid so she could learn to get back on her feet again without aid, an agonizing and humiliating process. More than the physical pain of recovery, the psychological pain was the hardest to overcome. Her altered body infuriated and shamed her. The confidence she had always had in her physical grace and strength was gone and in its place was doubtfulness and second-guessing. Despite these challenges, she had been determined to succeed, systematically approaching each task like she might any new chore, concentrating all of her energies toward success.

"You've done a terrific job, Mary," Jennifer said one day. "It helps that you're young and strong." At this, Mary had stomped her prosthetic leg. The therapist had laughed, misinterpreting the gesture as a sign of her feistiness, when Mary had meant it as a reminder to God of her fight with him. She knew it was crazy how she was acting. It wasn't normal. But she couldn't seem to help herself.

❃

"Your room's all fixed up for you," Fresia said when the doctors told her she could leave the next week.

"Blue's wondering where you've been." John was referring to Mary's horse. She'd had Blue since she was six, when Great-grandpa Gerald's favorite mare threw a blue roan colt that reminded him of a horse from his days as a rep cowboy. She could still hear him saying, "Best cutting horse I ever had in my string." He'd been proud of Mary's precocious riding skills and decreed the colt should be hers, one of the last things he did before he died.

"You got him from the Needhams then?" Mary said.

John nodded. "They said they'd keep him as long as we needed. We took the trailer up last weekend. He'll be glad to see you, that's for sure." As John had expected, the mention of Blue was the first happy thought for Mary in a long time, but even Blue couldn't help her overcome her feeling of failure as she imagined returning to her parents' house.

The day before she was scheduled to leave, Ward Hamilton, the new minister from the Church of Christ in Custer City, stopped by the hospital to say hello, explaining to Fresia, who attended a sister church in Merna, that her minister had been unable to come that week and had asked Ward to visit in his stead. Ward Hamilton had used exactly that word—"stead."

He was a tall man, broad shouldered. He exuded good health; his blonde hair shone and his cheeks were flushed pink. He seemed immaculately groomed, his hands uncalloused, his nails perfectly manicured, his hair freshly barbered, his cheeks shaved smooth. For Mary it was the most notable thing about him, his cleanliness. When he smiled, she noticed his teeth were small. Now, as she looked closer, she saw his chin was a bit weak too. His imperfections seemed magnified in contrast to his otherwise boisterous good health.

"Mary Needham," he had said as he entered the room that day, and his use of her full name stated in this way, not as a question but as an announcement, had struck her as odd and formal. He extended his hand toward her as he strode to the chair where she was sitting. That was how she learned of the smoothness of his hands. She had never in her life before felt a man's hands that weren't calloused. It made her feel funny, those womanish hands. Everything about him seemed peculiar to her experience of what a man should be and do.

Mary could tell by John's response that day that he didn't like this tall stranger, but then, everyone knew John would as soon be bit by a rattlesnake as in the same room with a preacher, so Mary supposed it wasn't just Ward that he didn't like. Fresia, more accepting of preachers as a class, said she was grateful to Ward for making the trip all the way to North Platte from Custer City.

"I was happy to," Ward said. "Besides, the drive through the Sandhills this morning was glorious."

The word glorious echoed in the room. No one Mary knew talked this way. Neither she nor her parents responded to his comment for a few seconds until Fresia gestured for Ward to sit down.

After he was seated, Fresia said, "Mary's leaving the hospital tomorrow." Mary noticed Ward's quick glance toward her prosthetic leg exposed below her shorts. "We're so anxious to have her back home with us," Fresia went on.

Ward continued to look at Mary and he said to her then, as though they were alone in the room, as though he were a prophet, "God has been merciful to you, Mary Needham, sparing you as he did. I'm sure you've given a lot of thought to that, and have renewed your commitment to him."

Mary froze as Ward spoke. He said this with such authority she felt a shock of recognition, as if God himself were speaking through him. She felt embarrassed at the possibility this man might be in direct contact with God and aware of everything she had been thinking the past few weeks. Ward's eyes continued to hold hers. He did not smile and in no way indicated it was a merciful God he knew. She pulled in her bottom lip, tempted unreasonably to confess what she now understood had been blasphemy.

John cleared his throat. "How long have you been in Custer City, Ward?"

Ward dragged his eyes slowly away from Mary's to address John's question. "Just a month now."

"Do you have a family, Mr. Hamilton?" Fresia asked, and Mary wished she hadn't addressed him in that deferential way.

"Only a widowed mother."

≡CHAPTER 2

≡She had been driving that day in Rock County, Nebraska, on the lonely stretch of Highway 183 between Taylor and Bancroft when the Chevy pickup ran out of gas. It was her fault. She hadn't thought to check the gauge after the sale in Burwell, where she had gone to bid on fifty scrappy little red Angus yearling heifers from a breeder in Wyoming. It was May and the grass looked good, and they'd decided that year to run a few extra cattle. Plus, they wanted to experiment a little and breed a few red Angus first calf heifers with their Hereford bull. While neighboring ranchers were moving into the exotics market or competing by breeding Herefords and Angus for size, the Stileses—in large part due to Mary's convincing opinions about the cost of inputs versus the gain of a couple hundred pounds, and the potential maternal problems with breeding for size—were thinking in another direction.

John trusted Mary's ability to judge quality stock, and he often sent her alone with his blessing to bid if she found anything worthwhile. No one, least of all Mary, had any idea how it was she did it, but she could look at a group of calves and know if they were sound or not. Each time before she went to a sale, John reminded her to trust her instincts. She had good instincts about other things too. At that morning's sale, she had bought as pretty a bunch of heifers as you could hope to find. It was risky to bid on cattle when you didn't know the grower, but somehow Mary had never made a mistake, and she trusted she hadn't made one now either. She and John would drive up together the next week in the cattle truck to get them.

There wasn't a house to be seen for miles in the Skull Valley there north of Rose when the truck sputtered to a stop. Already she knew John would rib her mercilessly about it, wondering what on earth she'd been doing that far north of Burwell when she was supposed to be heading home after the sale. He would have known, though, without being told what she had been feeling that day, driving for the sheer life of it through the Sandhills in springtime.

She had gotten out of the truck to walk. Not that she thought she would make it to a ranch house on her own in that desolate country, but she figured someone would eventually stop, and she hadn't wanted to wait. As it was, she walked over three miles before a faded red '69 Ford three-quarter ton stopped for her. The driver, an older man, leaned across the passenger-side seat and looked at her through the open window. "That your Chevy back there?"

"Yep."

"You in trouble or just walking?"

"I guess you could say I was in trouble."

He pushed open the door. "Get on in then. We'll see if we can't figure out what's the matter."

Mary got into the passenger seat, but before the man could turn the truck around, she stopped him. "I already know what the trouble is . . . I ran the truck out of gas."

The man nodded once, pushed his cowboy hat back revealing his white forehead, and scratched at his hairline. She thought he might scold her, but instead he grinned and looked across the seat at her. "Even those damn Chevys need gas now and then."

Mary didn't say anything, but she smiled and nodded once, and he headed north down the highway. Mary knew without being told the man driving the truck owned miles and miles of the hills they were driving through. She could see it in the way he looked out across the horizon, the Sandhills green with sand bluestem, six-weeks fescue, and soapweed dotting the roadside. He missed nothing with his focused gaze. His eyes were faded in his dark face. She could tell he knew every inch of that land through every season. Like the man beside her, Mary's father and grandfather had the look of men who were used to seeing across long distances in a wide-open country, men who could spot within a split second out of the corner of an eye if anything was out of place in all of it. This man was as surely one of her own people as Mary had ever seen.

Finally, he turned off the highway onto a dirt road. At another turnoff, a wooden sign said Needham Ranch. He drove another mile on a two-track trail as it wound around behind the shaggy hills until finally a rambling two-story house with a gabled attic and a wraparound porch came into view. There was a corral to the south and load-out chutes. Outbuildings were scattered around the house and a large barn stood farther to the south. From the number and size of the tractors, trucks, and hay rakes, Mary knew it was a large operation.

In one of the corrals, a dozen saddle horses came to stand against the fence to peer at the truck as it pulled into the yard. A little sorrel they were breaking was snubbed to a post in another corral, and in a nearby pasture a few mares grazed with new colts. An old pump stood beside the yard. Along the foundation and in front of the house inside the fence were well-tended flower beds. The only trees Mary had seen for miles were those near the house: large old cottonwoods, elms, and red cedar.

As they pulled into the yard, the man cut the truck's engine and five boys came from five different directions. The man sitting beside her chuckled softly. "Flies to honey," he said as the boys, three of them young men, gathered around the truck. None of them looked at Mary directly, though she felt them stealing sideways glances.

A woman came to the back door of the house, wiping her hands on a dishtowel. She wore a dress covered by a black-and-white gingham apron embroidered with little flowers across the bottom. She had auburn hair, brown eyes, and a pale unlined face. Now as the man got out of the truck Mary did too. An old collie hobbled lamely toward the man, and he stooped to scratch her between the ears. In response, her long tail swished and beat against his pants leg.

The boys still made no sign to indicate they had noticed Mary, but the woman came toward her and stretched out her hand. "I'm Iris Needham."

"Mary Rasmussen."

"I don't suppose Gus introduced himself," Iris said with an accusing look toward Gus. Gus shrugged. "These are our boys," Iris said, and started with the oldest. "Larry, Kent, Brian, Jeffrey, and little Billy." The boys all smiled shyly before looking away from her. They were handsome boys, the three oldest around her age, Mary guessed. "I'm just making dinner," Iris said. "You've come at a good time."

"She isn't here visiting, Iris," Gus said. "Her truck needs gas twenty miles back."

"Gus, that don't mean she can't eat a little, does it?"

"I didn't say it didn't."

This exchange sounded gruff, but Mary sensed no real tension.

"One a you boys have time to take some gas back to her truck?" The boys all shuffled a little as Gus asked this. Mary guessed they were used to taking orders from Gus, and none was willing to volunteer for fear he might suspect they were too interested. Gus pointed to the one Iris had just introduced as Brian. "Brian, you fill up the gas can and go with her. She can follow you back. We'll fill her up—her truck and her stomach," he said, looking at Iris.

Brian left to fill the gas can and within minutes took Gus's place behind the wheel of the Ford. Mary crawled back into the truck beside him. She had always been puzzled by how other people made decisions. She had instincts, that was all, like knowing as soon as she got into the truck beside Brian that what at first she had thought was an accident—running out of gas and being picked up by Gus Needham—hadn't been an accident at all, but her destiny straight up. She'd had fun with a lot of boys, but she'd never gotten set on anyone. Not until Brian. She'd known as soon as they exchanged their first smile across the seat of that old red Ford truck that she had just met the man she was going to marry. She was nineteen.

❇

Within a few weeks after that day in May when they first met, Brian came to the Stiles ranch to take her out to the Blaine County Fair. He was wearing a new white shirt with mother of pearl snaps and his best white summer Stetson. She wore a white dress with little blue flowers and white sandals. Already they looked like they were headed to the altar. Fresia took their picture that day like she could see it too. That night when he was bringing her back home, she told him to turn into one of the pastures. She opened the gate for his truck and led him to a ridge overlooking the Middle Loup. There was a nearly full moon, and the slow water of the river glinted in the light. Stars blanketed the sky. The radio was playing a country music station and when Charlie Rich came on with "Behind Closed Doors," Brian got out and came around to open her door, and they danced together on that ridge. She felt happier than she'd ever felt in her life.

He came back the next Sunday and the next, staying later each time so that he was barely making it home on Monday mornings in time for chores. The third Sunday Brian invited her to drive up to the Needham ranch again. Before she set out, Iris relayed through Brian that Mary should stay the night on Sunday. "She doesn't want you driving home late Sunday night," he said. "She's like that. She'll worry you to death."

When after only having known her a month, Brian asked her to marry him, saying, "Mary, I know we don't really know each other, but it feels like my whole life," she knew what he meant. After she'd told him yes, Brian said in a voice both relieved and puzzled, "Mary, you didn't act surprised just now when I asked you to marry me."

"You're going to have to get used to that," she said to him. "I'll see most things coming before they get here." And that had seemed to make sense to Brian, like most things about her had.

A month before the wedding, she woke once in the middle of the night with a feeling of such foreboding she had to get out of bed. She went to stand in the doorway of her parents' room, as if watching them sleep might comfort her somehow. A full moon shone through the bedroom windows and in its light she could see them sleeping. She hadn't meant to wake them, hadn't realized she'd said aloud, "Brian's going to die," until Fresia sat up in bed.

"What'd you say, Mary?"

"Brian's going to die," she repeated. "We don't have any kind of future together."

"Now why would you say something like that?" John asked as he sat up and turned on the lamp beside the bed.

She told them then about the dream she'd had. "I saw an old windmill. Most of its paddles were missing, and when the wind blew it tried to turn, but it could only groan and limp. It couldn't turn at all. It was a terrible dream."

"It's just a dream, honey," Fresia said, her pretty face creased with sleep and confusion. "It doesn't mean anything."

Mary's talk had disturbed Will and Mark and they had come to stand behind her in the hallway. It was a cool September evening, and the windows were still open to the outside, so that Mary shivered now as Fresia said, "You boys get back to bed. There isn't a thing in the world for you to see here."

Mary heard her brothers shuffle back to bed, but she could feel them listening from their room. There was a strange electricity in the hallway where she stood. John didn't look comfortable. He believed in her instincts after all, counted on them regularly, but he didn't much like it when they took a turn like this.

"It's natural you'd worry. You're getting married, and that's a big step," he said.

Mary shook her head. "It isn't like that. It's something I see."

"This is different, honey," John said. "You're in love, and it's natural you'd worry about losing Brian."

Fresia nodded. "I was afraid, too, before I married your dad. It seemed too perfect. I was sure it wouldn't work out."

"You were?"

"I was."

Mary felt herself relax. If her mother, the calmest person she'd ever known, could have jitters, maybe it was normal. "I love Brian so much," Mary said then. Her parents nodded. She noted their expressions of bewilderment. She wasn't one to share her feelings so openly, but she went on, "I've never wanted anything in my life as much as him. I don't know what I'd do if . . ."

"You stop your fretting now," Fresia said. "Everything's going to be all right. You'll see."

None of them ever spoke again about what had happened that night.

❋

After she had followed Brian back to the Needham ranch that first day, Iris came out to the gas tank where Brian was filling the truck. She was wiping her hands on a dishtowel like she had been earlier. "I've set an extra place for you at the table, Mary. Wouldn't you like to call your parents and let them know you'll be late?"

At supper that evening, Iris asked if she was John Rasmussen's daughter.

"Yes," Mary said between passing bowls of mashed potatoes and gravy, chicken fried steak, new peas, radishes, a salad of greens.

"You're Fresia's girl?" Gus said.

"Yes."

"Why, I didn't think she'd be old enough to have a big girl like you." Gus looked at her face closely then, and said, "I should have known who you were. You look just like your mother did when she was your age."

Mary blushed, embarrassed because all at once those five handsome Needham boys had turned their dark eyes in her direction. They had been stealing glances at her since they had all sat down at the table, but now Gus seemed to have given them permission to look at her straight on. Boys had always liked her, but that night was the first time Mary realized she might be pretty. She hadn't given much thought to it before. She kept her dark hair cropped short. She had slim hips, a flat boyish chest. She didn't gussy up the way other girls did, and, like her mother, she favored jeans and boots and western shirts. That's what she had been wearing that day, her work clothes. But none of it had stopped those boys from looking.

Once during supper, Iris intercepted a glance exchanged between Mary and Brian, and Mary could tell Iris had read everything between them in that glance.

Mary couldn't exactly say right away why Brian had stood out to her, why her instincts chose him. It took her a while to find the words for the difference between him and his brothers, but there was a difference. His eyes were brighter and softer at the same time. He looked a little sad sometimes, like someone who didn't like to see things suffering like you have to on a ranch. He seemed watchful, not like Gus or John or Grandpa Cal, looking toward the distant horizon, but watchful inside. She knew he read things in the world a little differently than everyone around him, and that made him seem lonely. Mary understood that, too.

CHAPTER 3

The day Mary finally left the hospital, Dr. Jacobs, Jennifer, and the nurses who had cared for her during her long stay came to say good-bye. In accordance with hospital policy, Mary was wheeled out in a wheelchair while her entourage followed, everyone carrying the things sent by well-wishers during the weeks of her stay. The hospital staff clapped when she stood up from the wheelchair and climbed into the car's back seat beside Will and Mark. John held the door open as she pulled her leg inside; then he closed it gently behind her before turning to the hospital staff.

"You'll understand my saying we're grateful for all you did for us, but I hope I never see you again." Everyone laughed as he got into the car.

Fresia, in the passenger seat, turned to look back at Mary with a smile. "We're on our way."

During the long drive home, Mary thought about sleeping in her old room alone again. It had been almost two years since she'd left home, and she felt she was going backward, losing time, her life altered beyond recovery. She knew something else. Along with Brian and her leg, she had also lost her instincts. She felt more alone in the world without them, thrown back on flimsier methods of decision making, far from the quicksilver decisions of the past.

When at last they pulled into the driveway, Mary looked at the ranch as though it were a distant memory. The light and heat were intense now at the end of July. The grass had bleached yellow and in the heat of midday even the birds and the insects were silent. Blue ran along the corral fence as they drove past. He tossed his head and snorted, and Mary knew this had been planned to make her homecoming feel less awkward. She suddenly felt a throb of sadness for her parents trying so desperately to please her.

John stopped the car. They all sat for a few seconds in silence, listening to the pinging of the cooling engine. Will and Mark were the first to leave, bolting finally like they had been freed from restraints. As soon as Mary stepped out of the car and felt the earth beneath her foot, she sensed a familiar shift inside. The horizon spread as far as she could see in any direction. Above her, thin clouds moved across the big sky like unraveling wool. She was reduced to a feeling she could only describe as normal. This was how she had perceived herself her entire life against this austere landscape. She instantly saw herself as she always had in relation to the vastness of the sky: small, vulnerable, fragile, momentary, free of scrutiny, silent. She was here now and someday she would be gone. Her disability and her new status as widow were not the beginning of feelings of inconsequence. There was a grim comfort in being reminded of what she had always believed was her true place in the scheme of things. She had no voice here. No one did. The far horizon. The wind. Their voices had nowhere to go. Best to keep quiet.

She saw something about herself and her people in that moment stepping out of the family car onto the ranch where she had lived since her birth—and her mother and her grandfather since theirs—that this was why people here did not waste their breath with talk. The effort to put their thoughts into words was always instantly understood as vanity when speaking into this boundless space. And she knew something else in that moment of recognition, something that startled her. She was no longer one of them. She stood apart now and she had been changed in ways she did not yet comprehend.

"Hey, Mary," John said, "you all right?"

She smiled then, realizing she had been leaning against the open car door. She didn't answer, but she slammed the car door shut and insisted on carrying one of the bags from the trunk.

Will and Mark, who had gone inside the house, now ran back out again to help carry Mary's things. They were followed by Judy and Max, and Cal and Lydia. "We've got dinner on," Lydia was saying. "You hungry for some fried chicken?"

"If it's yours, Grandma."

"Who else's would it be?"

Mark and Will walked on either side of Mary, pulling her toward the house. "There's watermelon and homemade ice cream, too."

"It sounds like a feast," Mary heard herself say, her voice bright. She wondered how long she would be able to keep up this cheerful front. Already she felt exhausted by the need to reassure everyone, but once she was inside the house and smelled the familiar smells of chicken frying and potatoes boiling, felt the breeze coming through the windows of the living room, heard the old metal fan rumbling in the corner of the dining room where the table was set for lunch, she couldn't help it. She wanted to hide the tears, but there was no way she could control herself. Her shoulders heaved with sobs.

"Mary, honey," Fresia said, following quickly. "Here. Let's get your stuff into the bedroom. You boys help Grandma with dinner."

Mary followed her mother upstairs, barely seeing through her tears. "I'm okay, Mama, really," she said once they'd reached the second floor and were headed down the hall to her bedroom at the back of the house. She wiped her face furiously with the backs of her hands. "I just need a Kleenex, that's all."

"No need to explain, Mary," Fresia said.

Mary felt maybe there was a need to explain, but she didn't know how to explain. "I'm just happy, Mama, thankful for my family."

"I know that, honey." Fresia opened the door, and Mary noticed fresh flowers in a vase on the dresser, a new quilt on the bed. The room smelled of pine cleanser and an unfamiliar, overly sweet room deodorizer. The windows were open, and the white cotton curtains blew into the room and then sucked back against the screens, bringing with them the smell of the outdoors. It quieted her, that familiar smell and the way the curtains blew into the room. She was glad they hadn't changed the curtains. It seemed suddenly so important that they hadn't done that.

"Why don't you just rest a little, Mary. Dinner won't be ready for another half hour." Fresia found a box of Kleenex and handed several to Mary.

Mary took the Kleenex, mopped her wet face, then shook her head. "I'm all right. I don't want to be alone right now. I'm glad to be here, that's all."

A flicker of understanding crossed Fresia's face and she smiled a rueful smile.

"Let's go back down together," Mary said, linking her arm through her mother's.

⁂

After lunch, Mary offered to help with the dishes, but Lydia wouldn't hear of it.

"Tomorrow you can help, but not today." Then, as if regretting her quick response, Lydia said more softly, "Why don't you go out and say hello to Blue?"

Blue nickered at her later as Mary walked out of the back door, but she did not go immediately to him. Instead, she rounded the corner of the house and stopped under the enormous cottonwood tree shading the south side, outside her bedroom window. The tree's circumference was over twenty feet. She had walked it off not long before she married Brian. The leaves of the cottonwood rustled.

Their shiny green tops and silvery bottoms spun in the breeze. The tree was ancient, unusual for a cottonwood. It had been old when Grandpa Cal had been a boy growing up on this place, old at the time the house was built. Despite its longevity, Mary felt a proprietary relationship with it. Perhaps because of its proximity to her bedroom window, she had always thought of it as her tree.

When finally she opened the gate of the corral Blue lowered his head and let her scratch between his ears. She ran her hands though his mane, and then buried her face against his warm neck, breathing in deeply his sharp, salty smell. Blue stamped once and then stood quietly as Mary kept her face turned into his neck. She wanted to ask of Blue, as she might have an oracle, what she should do next. His hide twitched in an effort to chase away the swarming flies.

Finally, the flies distracted Mary. She swatted them away and walked toward the barn. Blue stayed outside as she opened the barn's half door. Inside, it was cool and dark. Old straw lay piled in a corner pen. The milking stalls were empty. There hadn't been a milk cow on the place for many years. An old galvanized bucket bearing a cracked rubber nipple on one side hung from a rusty nail, the only indication that months before orphaned calves had been fed here. Swallows swooped in and out of the open haymow door. She wandered into the tack room and its familiar smells of old leather and dust. In the heat, the cedar barn boards emitted a mineral smell. Since the barn was built, nothing had been thrown away, and the whole history of the ranch could be read in the layers of that room.

Gerald's last saddle—custom made, studded with silver—hung, gray with dust, on a beam high above the others. In a corner on a stud sat Katrina's saddle from her days teaching school before marrying Gerald; Lydia's childhood saddle and the saddle Cal bought her when they were married hung on a rope hammock; Cal's saddles from his rodeo days; Fresia's saddles from her days competing in horsemanship; Judy's barrel-racing saddle; the children's saddles passed down through generations. Mary only now remembered her own favorite saddle was probably still at the Needham ranch. She didn't see it hanging here among the others. Bridles and halters hung on pegs and nails. She found the tiny saddle she'd used as a preschooler, recalling her earliest memories of Fresia waiting outside the corral watching while Mary cornered the horse she wanted. She remembered climbing onto the fence to put on the bridle before signaling Fresia for help with the saddle.

She left the tack room then, glancing up at the darting swallows before finally sitting on the edge of a wooden feed trough. Blue watched her from the doorway. He stamped his hooves, twitched his ears, and swished his tail, still battling the flies. Mary looked from where Blue was framed in the sunshine outside the barn and back again into the barn's darkness, feeling herself blinded for an instant before her eyes readjusted. In that brief moment of shifting sight she had been almost content, her mind emptied for a few seconds: no memories of the past, no possible future, only the present, the smell of old cow manure and used straw, the faint smell, perhaps only in her memory, of horse feed, calf milk formula, grain dust, and bag balm.

That night in the darkness of her room, Mary listened to the sounds coming through the open windows. The cicada had quieted earlier, and now the crickets were out. A screech owl whinnied now and then. In the distance, she heard coyotes yipping and the questioning hoot of a barn owl. She would have known, even if she'd been transported here blindfolded, that it was a late summer night in Nebraska. Despite a bone-deep weariness, she couldn't sleep. Every time she closed her eyes, images of the day flashed before her: Cal hugging her against his broad chest; Lydia hovering over lunch despite Fresia telling her to sit down; Fresia scolding Will and Mark; Judy bossing Max; John smiling softly when Mary caught his eye. All of them had spent their lives watching animals. They watched her carefully, none of them fooled by her pretense, but no one spoke of it.

In the corner of the room, illuminated now in the moonlight, leaned her leg, which Mary had named Peggy in an attempt to amuse everyone. In this room she no longer felt the presence she had in the hospital, and she was relieved by that, glad to be rid of what she knew had been an unhealthy projection. But that didn't mean she was finished thinking about God. While it was true before her accident she hadn't thought about God, she had always been grateful for the good things of the earth, and sometimes she had felt the urge to thank whatever or whoever might be responsible for creating those things. She guessed she had once had a simple sort of faith, but she wasn't simple anymore. She had prayed a black prayer in the hospital and she had meant it. This God, whoever he was, had let her down. He had taken a big interest in her life, stripped her bare, and now it seemed he had moved on to other things as though he were bored with her. She felt like she had been left for dead but had perversely recovered, and now she was neither living nor dead. She sensed God was laying low for the time being, but that they would have their reckoning yet.

She traced with her eyes the shadow of the big cottonwood cast on the ceiling of her bedroom. She heard the soft rustle of its leaves. On the breeze she smelled the cottonwood's spicy smell. And then she slept.

≡CHAPTER 4

≡The details of that first day at the Needham ranch played obsessively in Mary's mind as though there were some mystery to solve. Iris's dress, the flowers in the garden: hollyhocks not yet in bloom, poppies blooming beside the back door where Iris had stood. Iris's black pumps. Mary had known immediately that day Iris did not take part in the outside work at the ranch. Her role was to cook and clean. Every ranch operation was a little different in the way its women took part, and Mary was used to a different sort of woman. She couldn't imagine ever seeing her mother or grandmother in a dress in the middle of a regular day.

Fresia had been a beauty, and as a young woman had won state championships in horsemanship and had been a rodeo queen. Her old show costumes—the rhinestones and sequins coming loose from the fabric—still hung in the back of her closet. Just as Katrina and Lydia before her had been full partners on the ranch, Fresia was John's partner. If at first Mary had compared Fresia and Iris, as she grew to know the Needham family it was the differences between John and Gus and their styles of ranch management she came to scrutinize. Unlike Gus Needham, John would not have made a major decision without Fresia's input.

When John married Fresia, Cal and Lydia had welcomed him into the operation as though he were their own son. John's family had owned a small place outside Mason City near the long-gone town of Algernon where all of the Rasmussen family had homesteaded. In the hard years of the Depression, everyone except John's parents and grandparents had left the state for Idaho and Oregon. Although those acres had fallen out of the Rasmussen family's hands after John's parents died, Mary still felt they were theirs somehow. She had loved her father's stories of great aunts and uncles, the orchestra they had formed when they were young, the dances, the singing, the card games. All that remained of the Rasmussens now were a few abandoned buildings and the little family cemetery near Algernon where those who hadn't left were buried.

❋

Before supper was over that first night at the Needham ranch, Mary had learned to distinguish between the five boys. Larry was taller and thinner than the others, though she guessed Billy would grow up to be taller still. Larry was serious, his face a little drawn, and Mary guessed Gus relied on him too much so that he couldn't quite see himself separate from the ranch.

Kent was short and stocky, ruddier complected than the others. He liked to tease his mother. He had a lopsided smile, and his face reddened quickly with any passing emotion. Mary saw correctly that first night he had a quick temper as well.

Brian was slight and not as tall as Larry. His hair was the same auburn as Iris's. His eyes were large and a deeper brown than his brothers', his lashes as long and curly as a girl's.

Jeffrey was still in high school. He had talked about their herd in a way Mary imagined would lead him to the university, as it eventually had. Already at that early age there was a gravity about Jeffrey that Mary found hard to describe but that she found admirable in a boy. Billy, only thirteen when she first met him, was already very handsome, with his father's square jaw and deep-set eyes.

While Mary had been helping Iris do the supper dishes that

first night, Iris surprised her by asking, "How's Fresia?" Mary must have looked startled, for Iris had smiled gently before looking back to the dish she was cleaning. "Everyone knew your mother." Mary noticed then Iris looked out the window toward where Gus was smoking a cigarette by the gate.

Later, Brian told Mary how he and his mother had sat together and drunk coffee at the kitchen table after Mary left, as they liked to do on summer evenings. Iris had told Brian Gus's heart had been broken over thirty years earlier by Fresia Stiles. She told Brian Mary was a dead ringer for her mother at that age, and Iris had laughed as she told Brian she figured Gus must have thought his past had come back to haunt him when he saw Mary standing on Highway 183 that afternoon.

When Mary asked her mother about Gus, Fresia answered with a quizzical smile, "Gus Needham? Why, he was way too old for me." And that was all she ever said about it. Something about that story, though, had made Mary feel even more strongly she was destined to meet Brian Needham, that something in Gus's unrequited passion for her mother had passed on to the next generation.

❋

Mary and Brian had planned at first to get married in the spring a year after they met, but by the time they started thinking about it, they figured they didn't want to wait that long and decided late October would be best.

"October?" Iris had said. "Why, that's a terrible time to marry." For ranchers it wasn't the worst time, but Iris wasn't thinking about what was right for the ranch. She had romantic notions about marriage and had wanted a June wedding. "We'll have just finished branding and be right in the middle of haying in June," Brian had said in irritation.

Iris was further disappointed when Mary and Brian refused to go in for the trappings of a traditional wedding. Mary bought a dress off the rack, a cotton ecru Jessica McClintock. They sent out handwritten invitations instead of printed ones, and decided against a wedding party. All of these decisions had been fine with Fresia, but even Fresia was dismayed when Mary and Brian decided to marry at the Stiles ranch rather than in the Church of Christ at Merna.

The Needhams bought a used single-wide trailer house and parked it three hundred yards from the main house, and it was there Mary and Brian moved after the wedding. They moved in on a cold, dry day at the end of the month, the wind blowing a gale that kicked up so much dust and sand they could hardly see the house when they returned from their honeymoon. They'd taken the horse trailer and camped for two nights with the horses on the Dismal River. Those two days had been perfect, the autumn air crisp at night and the trees in full fall color, but after they returned to the Needham ranch the wind blew for days. Now and then it gusted so hard at night that Mary woke from her sleep, disoriented at first about where she was, and afterward laying awake in fear the wind would topple the trailer house.

Mary didn't care much about a house or any of the things that went into one. She hadn't really known what to make of all those fancy wedding presents: vases and bowls and wall hangings, most of which she and Brian kept boxed up because there was no place for them anyway. They were all still in boxes stored in the second bedroom of the trailer house.

Mary hadn't thought about the trailer where she and Brian had lived together. Now, though, she couldn't get it out of her mind. She saw over and over a forlorn picture of the trailer house standing empty on the prairie. She thought about all of their things still there, silently waiting, about how they had left the house the morning of the accident to visit Brian's cousins in Oconto. She could not remember in what condition she had left the trailer. Had she made their bed? Had she washed their cereal dishes, or were they still sitting dirty in the sink? All this time later had the rooms been left undisturbed, their life together caught in midmotion? Or had Iris gone into the trailer and cleaned up? Mary could see Iris going to the door of the trailer with that intention but stopping short of crossing the threshold, too intimidated by the powerful memories lurking there.

Some of Mary's friends who had come to visit her after she got married thought it was a terrible setup, living in her in-laws' backyard like that and in a dumpy old trailer house to boot, but Mary hadn't thought about it that way at all. Gus and Iris and the boys had always been respectful. They never came to the trailer unless invited, and the truth was, she and Brian didn't spend much time there except nights anyway. They ate most of their meals at the main house, spent most days working outside. It had been exactly what Mary had wanted for her life, a dream in fact.

Gus had let Mary know right away that growing up his mother and six sisters had never once been in the barn. Their father wouldn't allow it, afraid to expose them to the hands' barn talk. He had strong opinions about the place of women in ranching, but Mary wouldn't hear of being restricted to the kitchen with Iris. He'd finally said once, grudgingly, after Mary had been around for a while, that she was like having another hand on the place. She could ride roundup, rope and wrangle, mend fence, and drive a tractor to cut and rake hay and alfalfa as well as any of the boys, and Gus quickly figured out what John had known for years, that she was a good judge of cattle. Flattered as Mary had been by Gus's assessment, she wasn't sure after a while she'd made the right choice by pleasing him. She quickly saw how he would use her hard like he used his boys, how he would press her, like he had everyone else, into his service, his vision, and his plan for the ranch, allowing none of them to contribute so much as an idea.

She had learned this about Gus the hard way when one day she had suggested a change in pasture rotation. Everyone had stopped what they were doing and watched nervously to see what Gus would do. Mary had stood her ground, and although Gus didn't respond in anger like the boys seemed to have expected, Mary never again freely expressed an opinion. It made her uneasy the way his boys worked for him as little more than hired hands.

Brian had come with the trailer the week before they married and took Blue back to the ranch. Blue got on well with Brian's horse Clementine—a high-spirited paint—and they regularly took the horses out together into the hills after a day of work, especially that first summer after they were married. Iris, in her romantic way, understood that they needed to get away from the family now and then. She had occasionally packed a lunch and told them to take it with them to one of the small lakes in nearby Bloody Valley.

Now, looking back, Mary could see that Iris had been living through them a little, her own failed dreams maybe a motive for trying to protect them. That was just a guess, but it was something that kept nagging at Mary. Seeing Iris in memory there in the doorway that first day, Mary saw something lonely in her she hadn't seen before. It was a funny thing to Mary how people so familiar, people she thought she knew so well, she now saw she hadn't known at all. She had to wonder again, as she had when they had visited her in the hospital, if it was like that with everyone she knew best, if maybe those were really the people she knew least.

And Brian, too? Would he seem like a stranger if he were suddenly to appear before her again? Had they ever really known one another? Had the last few months changed her so much that he would no longer recognize her? Mary didn't like it when her mind took her to this point, and she backed away from that question whenever it came to her.

Instead, she preferred to remember those mornings she and Brian ate bacon and eggs at his mother's table while around them his brothers laughed and joked. She liked remembering how while moving cattle, they caught one another's eye, and how without even as much as a nod or a gesture, they knew what the other would do, what they could count on from each other. So much about how they had loved one another was how they had worked together. Work had seemed a natural part of their life, something they didn't have to explain to the other. Their whole life, work and play and love, was one thing. She knew she would never again have a life like that. Brian had been her one and only chance at it.

≡CHAPTER 5

≡Life returned to normal for everyone except Mary. Judy and Max went back to their house and their life together. John and Fresia returned to the work of the ranch, Cal helping out as he could while Lydia managed the house. Will and Mark began the new school year, leaving the house early each morning to catch the school bus at the bottom of the long driveway.

For the first few weeks Mary was up early for breakfast, watching as the boys and her parents left for the day. Lydia continued to pooh-pooh her offers to help in the house. The ranch work she most wanted to be doing no one believed possible anymore, and as the days grew shorter, she began to sleep later, often waking lethargically around ten to a quiet house, Lydia puttering in the addition where she and Cal lived, her radio playing country western music interrupted occasionally by the farm market reports.

While Mary ate her toast and drank her cup of coffee, she tried to read the newspaper or her grandmother's magazines, but her mind wandered so that she found herself turning the pages only to realize after an hour that she couldn't remember a single thing she had read. Lydia brought her sewing projects, tried to teach her to quilt, embroider, knit, all of the things Mary had spurned before. Although she tried to follow Lydia's swift hands and her careful coaching, it was useless. Her fingers fumbled with the close work.

One evening after dinner as they were all sitting around the table, Mary said, "How would it be if I looked into taking a few classes at Mid-Plains Community College?"

John and Fresia exchanged a quick glance. They seemed unaccountably panicked at the suggestion. "You don't need to be worrying about things, Mary," Fresia had said. "You're just fine here."

"You don't want to go all that way to North Platte just to kill time taking those classes," John said.

Mary knew they meant well, their quick protective remarks meant to avoid making her feel like a burden, but their insistence only reminded her of a long life of staying in this house with them.

As the days grew colder and darker that winter, she began to nap in the afternoon. At first she woke with the slam of the kitchen door signaling the boys' return home from school, but eventually she only stirred with the sound and went back to sleep again. She struggled to consciousness like someone fighting to keep from drowning before she sank again into the stupor of sleep until someone woke her for supper. Everyone noticed her listlessness, but no one knew how to confront her. The only definition they had for this sort of behavior was laziness.

It was Judy who finally took it into her hands to help. She burst into Mary's room one afternoon and watched as Mary struggled to wake up. Judy had been angry when she came in—Mary could tell by the tone of her voice—but as she watched Mary's efforts to awaken, she finally sat on the edge of the bed and gently coaxed Mary to open her eyes.

"You're wasting your life," Judy said once Mary sat up.

"What life would that be, Judy?"

Judy rolled her eyes in exasperation. "You've got to start pulling yourself together. Grandma and I have been talking about it, and we think you're depressed." Mary sighed, but Judy went on.

"It's not a surprise you'd be depressed." She said this carefully as though she had rehearsed it. "You need something to focus on outside yourself." Mary pursed her lips at this. "Just listen to me," Judy said. "You need . . . we all need to quit acting like you can't do the things you used to. There's no reason why you can't be outside working again."

Mary pushed the blankets away and reached for her prosthesis. "That's easy for you to say."

"No, Mary, it's not." Judy slumped a little as she said this. She straightened then. "You'll have to relearn some things, but there's no reason why you can't ride again." Mary reached again for her leg, finished with the conversation. "Listen, Mary, you could try, right? I'd help you."

Mary ran a hand over her face, a gesture of frustration she had seen in her mother. "Go home, Judy," she finally said. "Just leave me alone. I don't need you coming around here feeling sorry for me. That's the one thing I know I don't need."

"You idiot. I'm not feeling sorry for you. That's the difference between me and everybody else. They're all willing to let you rot here all your life like a cripple, but I think you need to get off your duff and start making yourself useful." More gently then, Judy added, "I'm not going to just sit by and watch you turn into a freak."

That's how the riding lessons began.

The first afternoon they went out, the sky was gray and a raw wind blew from the northwest.

"What a shitty day," Judy grumbled as she tightened Blue's saddle.

"We've been out in worse." Mary stroked Blue's neck. She felt a flutter of nervousness as she tried to picture herself mounting him.

When Judy started toward the fence, Mary said, "Not like that."

"You have to start over."

"But not like that. Please."

Judy sighed. She went to the barn and returned with a wooden crate. "This better?" Mary nodded, and Judy set the crate on the frozen ground. As she coaxed Blue toward it, Mary heard Judy complaining under her breath. Mary ignored her, and Judy shifted her attention to strategy. She seemed to be working out something in her head as she situated Blue.

"Come over here," she said finally. "Can you lead with your left?"

"I'm not sure."

"Well, try it."

Mary gingerly stepped onto the crate. She wobbled and leaned on Judy's shoulder for support.

"Just try."

Still leaning on Judy's shoulder while Judy steadied Blue, Mary grabbed her left leg and guided her foot into the stirrup. She dropped her foot then. "This isn't going to work."

"I can see that."

"I don't have the strength in my left leg I need." Mary stepped down from the crate and Judy dragged it around. It felt all wrong mounting that way, and Blue shifted uneasily. "Hold, boy," Mary said. As soon as she felt her right foot slip into the stirrup, she lifted her body up with it, and swung the left leg awkwardly over the saddle, holding the saddle horn with her right hand and pushing the leg with her left. Blue started to crow hop, and Mary took the reins from Judy to calm him. She was surprised at how awkward it all was, how much exertion it had taken to complete something that had been second nature to her before. Blue snorted at her unfamiliar seat, but he stood for her.

"Not bad," Judy said, appraising Mary. "Not great, but not bad." She smiled, and Mary couldn't resist returning her smile. "How's it feel?"

"Weird but all right."

Judy started to help Mary tuck her left foot into the stirrup better but stopped herself. "You do it."

Mary used both hands to situate the foot. It took her several seconds of concentrated effort to get it secured, but as soon as she had, she took the reins and attempted to tap Blue with her legs. Only the right leg responded, confusing Blue who turned to the right instead of moving forward. Mary practiced making the left leg squeeze the way she wanted it to until finally she coaxed Blue into a slow walk.

She circled the corral while Judy took the crate back to the barn. By the time Judy returned, Mary had coaxed Blue into a trot and then into a canter. Judy settled on top of the fence to watch as Mary urged him into a loping gallop. Judy laughed as Mary came by.

Mary wanted to wave, but she didn't yet feel confident enough to change anything.

When later it started to rain, Mary let Judy help her down against the fence. Blue had been skittish through the entire exercise, confused by the familiar thing that had suddenly become unfamiliar. Mary thought she knew how he felt.

❋

In early November, long after they had promised, Gus and Iris came to take Mary home for a weekend. There had been a cold snap that week and a subzero wind pulled at their coats as Mary followed them to the new Ford pickup they now drove. Neither Gus nor Iris commented on her prosthesis, but Mary noticed both of them stealing glances as she walked. Between their discomfort and her parents' obvious reluctance to let her go, Mary felt like a little girl going on her first sleepover. John and Fresia hovered even after Mary got into the truck's cab, and they lingered in the driveway waving as the truck pulled away.

Mary wondered briefly why Gus and Iris had brought the truck instead of the Mercury sedan as mile after mile the three of them rode packed together in the bench seat. Iris talked aimlessly to fill the time. Her chatter quickly got on Mary's nerves and Mary was curious at her own impatience. She hadn't remembered thinking of Iris as irritating before this.

Gus, meanwhile, was silent for the duration of the drive. Mary could see how hard these months had been on him. She knew how he had counted on Brian and her to help on the ranch this summer, believing he would have an extra hand again this year, when instead he had been short by two. The stoop of his shoulders was more pronounced than it had been the day they visited her in the hospital.

The boys were all at the house when they arrived, reminding her eerily of her first visit as once more they came from all corners to gather around the truck. They were standoffish toward her like they had been at the hospital, watching closely as Mary got out of the truck, curious she guessed to see how she would maneuver on the new leg.

As if to answer their curiosity, she smiled after closing the passenger-side door. "I've got on my contraption. Do you want to see it?" The boys relaxed. Billy nodded. "Wait 'til we're inside, and I'll show you."

Gus carried Mary's overnight bag in through the back door. Iris had gone in ahead of everyone and had a pot of coffee already brewing. Inside Mary felt a pang of nostalgia as she smelled the familiar smells and glimpsed again the yellow kitchen. She was wearing sweatpants and she easily pulled up the loose bottom to reveal her new left leg. Only the boys were comfortable with this demonstration. Gus and Iris both hung back. Mary had the distinct feeling they didn't approve of the exhibition for some reason, as though she were being unseemly. Mary felt confused suddenly by their obvious disapproval, felt herself a stranger again, and her former feelings of comfort and belonging dissipated. She was taken aback by the sudden sharp anger she felt toward both Gus and Iris.

In their discomfort, she felt a judgment she had long suspected. What they would never ask was why she rather than Brian had been driving the night of the accident. The answer was easy. Brian had been tired and she hadn't been. She knew without any of them saying it that the Needhams believed if Brian had been driving the accident would not have happened.

She had not seen the Needhams in their first moments of grief, but she thought she could imagine how it had gone. Iris would have wept in the bedroom with the door closed, and she would have thought to herself if it had been any of the other boys or Gus, she could have talked to Brian about it. He alone of all of them would not have been embarrassed by her tears or his own. She would have understood in that first instant how lonely her life would be without Brian in it.

Gus would have gotten into his old pickup and driven up into the hills. He would have cut the engine and let the silence fill the cab. He would have looked out across the country where he had lived all his life, into the distance, blue with spring, into the starry night sky, clear and black, and he would have thought about his surprise that Brian's life would not go as his had.

Like Gus, the boys would have found solitary pursuits, and the family would never have spoken directly together of Brian's death. Now, into this silence, Mary had come, a reminder of everything they had lost. She was the one person whose presence forced all of them to confront the pain they wanted to forget.

She slept in a spare room in the house that night, and the next morning, first thing, while the sun was still a pale cold light in the east, they drove together to the cemetery at Rose. The Mercury's doors rang in the cold as they slammed them shut, and they stood in a circle around the stone: Brian Edward Needham. Born December 10, 1953. Died March 5, 1980.

"You weren't able to help us make any decisions, Mary," Iris said. "I hope the stone is all right."

Mary looked up. "Of course it's all right."

The wind blew, and the boys shuffled and stomped their feet in an effort to keep warm. Mary shoved her hands deep into the pockets of her coat as they all stood mute before the stone. She felt keyed up, unable to focus or to feel anything, distracted by the Needhams and their enormous grief. There was clearly no room for her here, no place to join them in their mourning.

She had seen the little graveyard at Rose before. Brian had brought her here shortly after they had met that first summer. For generations this was where the Needham family had been buried. Unlike the abandoned cemetery at Algernon, the ranchers around Rose maintained the grave sites. Mary had felt it meant something the way both she and Brian loved these old cemeteries.

The air grew humid, and it started to snow. Despite her warm coat, Mary shivered with cold. The gloom made it difficult to see into the distance where every one of them longed to look. Billy kicked idly at a tuft of dead snakeweed near the grave site. Everyone except Mary kept their heads lowered, as if afraid to reveal their feelings, afraid to see hers. She felt nothing standing there except a weariness of life so deep she couldn't imagine ever truly living again.

Finally, when they began to steal glances at her, questioning to see if they had spent enough time, Mary smiled at them each in turn, first the boys and then Gus and Iris. They had clearly brought her to the ranch out of a sense of obligation, and she felt they could barely tolerate the fact of her existence, as though if they could erase her, they could perhaps pretend that Brian had never lived among them, as if that erasure would take away their sadness. Even had she wanted to, she knew enough not to speak of Brian in their presence, knew that to violate a code so deep would be the greatest transgression of all. It was as though she had traveled somewhere distant from them and had returned only to find they could not hear the tale she wished to tell.

Through the weekend Kent and Larry were polite and distant. They stayed outside longer at their chores than necessary. Jeffrey was home from the university, and she felt certain he had planned the visit to coincide with hers. He helped her clear her things from the trailer house. Second to Brian, Jeffrey was the one least likely to feel uncomfortable with strong emotions. Billy came and went, helping to carry boxes to the pickup. As Mary had known when she first set eyes on him, Billy had grown so tall he had to stoop to pass through the trailer house door. They laughed a few times when he miscalculated and whacked his head. And as she had predicted from the first, he had grown into a handsome young man. He still had enough of the little boy in him to relax now and then into his former role as little brother with Mary, teasing her a few times about being short.

After they had finished packing the last of her things and were alone in the empty trailer house, Jeffrey turned as he was going out the door for the last time. "I'm sorry this happened to you, Mary."

"I'm sorry it happened to all of us."

On Sunday afternoon Gus and Iris drove Mary back to her parents' house, the bed of the truck loaded with boxes and furniture. John and Gus unloaded her things while Iris and Fresia talked at the kitchen table. As soon as the truck was emptied, Gus and Iris prepared to leave, refusing Lydia's invitation to stay for supper with the excuse that the weather was getting nasty. They all made promises to see one another often, but Mary knew as they spoke this would not happen, that their lives had intersected for a short time and now they would diverge once more.

※

A few weeks later, on Christmas morning, after they'd opened their presents, Judy announced, "You all need to come out to the corral for Mary's surprise." Everyone donned their coats and boots and tromped through the yard toward the corral. A dry snow had fallen a few days before, and the wind blew up a little ground blizzard as they stood beside the corral.

"Wait here," Judy said, coming fully into herself in a situation where she was in charge. She had saddled Blue earlier that morning, and she brought him out of the barn now to Mary who stood in the middle of the corral. Without help from Judy or the crate, Mary mounted Blue with almost as much fluidity as she had when she still had both legs. She heard her parents and grandparents gasp, and she felt a flush of pride that embarrassed her. How little it took now to please all of them. How little they all, including herself, had come to expect of her. She would have to go a long way to regain not only her own confidence but theirs in her. She didn't dwell on this, though, as she walked Blue around the corral, then brought him to a canter and finally into a slow gallop. Lydia clapped and Cal roared with laughter. Mary saw Fresia dab a bit at her eyes. John smiled and shook his head.

"Looks like I've got my second-best hand back," John said after she'd dismounted, a bit more awkwardly than she had hoped. As she smiled at him, Mary knew as well as John that it would take a lot more than this to bring her back into the life of the ranch.

What she could not confess to her parents was how little this physical progress meant to her recovery. There was still a vast empty place in her core, a void where Brian had once fit. She had tried banking against that abyss, but she felt herself slipping over the edge. She didn't know what to do with all the love she still felt for his memory. Among the things she had brought back with her from the Needham ranch was the photo album from their wedding. She kept it hidden under her mattress, and every night she took out the album and lingered over the photographs of Brian. She had thought that with time she would get past the raw pain of the loss, or at least learn to live with it, but instead with time she only felt more lost, more obsessed with the past.

≡CHAPTER 6

≡The day Ward Hamilton made a trip to the Stiles ranch, Cal and Lydia had gone to Broken Bow to visit friends. Mary had stopped choring early so she'd be there when Mark and Will got home from school. He came without calling ahead that afternoon in February during a winter thaw. He parked his newer model Toyota Corolla in the drive, and Mary watched as he fastidiously stepped into the muddy driveway.

She waited in the doorway of the mud porch until he looked up. "Hi," she said.

"Hi yourself." His voice was loud and jovial.

"Are you lost?"

Ward laughed. "I was, but now I'm found."

Mary didn't smile at what she knew was meant as a joke. She stepped aside to let him pass through the door onto the porch. She saw him take note of the gun closet, the old green linoleum they'd been meaning to replace on the porch, the long rack with hooks for coats and hats, several pairs of boots on the floor beneath it, and beyond that into the large kitchen with its round oak table always set for eight.

"Could I take your coat?"

"That's a lot of guns."

Mary shrugged. "Elk hunting."

Ward smiled at her and peeled off what looked like a brand-new tan Carhartt barn coat. Beneath it was a western shirt, still bearing the folds from its cardboard frame, new Wrangler jeans, and new work boots, all items she recognized as regular merchandise from Wheelers. He knelt to unlace and remove his boots.

"You've changed your look," she said.

Ward looked down at himself and back up at her without the least hint of embarrassment. "Well, as they say, when in Rome . . ."

As she started to invite him into the living room, the little boys, just home from school, came in from outside, curious about who had dropped in. Once their curiosity was satisfied, they went into the family room and turned on the television. Mary had just started to invite Ward into the living room when she saw her mother outside the porch window. It was calving season, and Fresia and John had been working night and day. Mary recognized Fresia's look of concern through the window, and she shrugged, signaling she didn't know the reason for Ward's visit.

"Mr. Hamilton," Fresia said as she entered the door to the porch. "What a surprise."

"I was just out your way and I thought I'd stop by."

The Stiles ranch was on the way to nowhere, and it took some maneuvering to find their house from the road, meaning he must have been given detailed directions from someone. Mary wondered why Ward would lie about his visit.

"I apologize for my appearance," Fresia said. "I was out helping John. We have six new calves already." Anyone from the area would understand this meant Fresia had hurried back to the house when she saw a strange car drive up, and John had been left to work alone. Ward, however, did not catch the hint, and Mary heard Fresia's agitation as she said politely, "Go on into the living room and make yourself at home, Mr. Hamilton." Fresia quickly washed her hands in the kitchen sink after hanging her coat and removing her muddy boots. "Mary, will you show him the way?"

Ward followed Mary into the living room where a fire burned in the wood-burning stove. "It's sure cozy in here," Ward commented as he settled into the recliner nearest the stove.

"Would you like a cup of coffee?" Fresia asked as she popped her head into the room.

"Would a cup of tea be too much trouble?"

Fresia glanced quickly toward Mary. "Of course not."

Mary excused herself and followed her mother back into the kitchen where Fresia was already looking desperately through the cupboards. She looked at Mary in relief. "Didn't we have some tea bags stashed somewhere?"

"Let me look, Mama. Go in and talk to Ward."

"But he's come to see you."

"I certainly hope not," Mary said. "You have more in common with him than I do."

"I don't know that I do," Fresia said. They both smiled then at the absurdity of fighting over who had to go talk to their unwelcome guest.

"Okay," Fresia conceded. "Good luck finding that tea."

The teakettle was whistling by the time Mary finally located a squashed box of Lipton far back in the pantry.

"Here you go, Ward," Mary said when she brought the tea to him. "Would you like some sugar to go with your tea?"

"Sugar and cream would be terrific," he said.

Ward seemed well settled into the chair when Mary returned to the living room with the cream and sugar. She had the distinct feeling he was planning to stay for a long time.

"Mr. Hamilton . . ." Fresia began.

"Please, call me Ward."

"Ward. Where are you from originally?"

"I grew up in Indiana. My parents moved there from Boston when I was three."

"And what did your folks do?"

"My father was also a minister."

"You're an only child you told us at the hospital."

"Yes."

Mary was embarrassed at her mother's prying, but Ward seemed undisturbed as he answered, "My father died when I was twelve, so it's just been Mother and me for a long time now."

Mary listened silently from the chair farthest from where Ward and Fresia sat talking. She was grateful for her mother's ease with this sort of thing, but she could tell from the way Fresia sat perched on the edge of the couch that she was forcing herself to this performance.

Ward looked at Mary then. "Mary, you're so far away over there. Wouldn't you like to sit closer?"

"I'm fine where I am." Mary bristled at Ward's attempt to orchestrate where she sat.

The conversation went on, Mary drifting in and out, as Fresia listened and Ward talked. Mary could see how he must love having a congregation. And yet, how odd that he had ended up preaching in a small church in what he must feel was the middle of nowhere.

Ward was telling them stories about his visits to local attractions, describing at length the various places he had seen, the people he had encountered, as though Mary and Fresia had never before set foot in any of these familiar establishments or met the local people. He seemed enthralled with his stories about living in the Wild West. He actually called it that a few times and seemed to consider himself very daring for the adventure. At one point he interrupted himself during a particularly long story about the details of going to a sale at the stock barn to say, "Isn't this an interesting story?" Mary winced. Fresia did not respond at all; she seemed to be in a trance, no doubt thinking about John, whom she had abandoned to work alone in the cold and the falling darkness. Mary knew from experience it was possible one of the cows was having a hard time calving.

Ward seemed immune to Fresia's stress as he continued to talk about his daring for having come to Custer City rather than accepting a ministry with an urban congregation. ". . . But I like the simple folks out here," he was saying now as Mary's attention returned to him. He was beaming with what she supposed was his love for the simple folk.

The hours dragged by and neither Mary nor Fresia noticed how late it had gotten until they heard John at the porch door stomping his boots. The house had grown dark and Fresia stood up quickly to turn on a few lights. "Goodness, where did the afternoon go?" If Lydia had been there she would have been starting supper by now.

Fresia left for the kitchen where Mary knew she was warning John about their guest. Drop-ins were fine, but lingering like this except on a holiday or a special occasion was unheard of. The little boys had been watching television all during the hours of Ward's visit, careful to keep quiet so no one would notice and make them turn it off.

John saw it now. "Turn off that TV, boys." Mary knew his gruffness was not caused so much by the boys as it was evidence of his distaste for Ward Hamilton. As always, after coming in from the cold, John's face was ruddy. He nodded curtly toward Ward. "Mr. Hamilton" was the extent of his greeting. Ward smiled and asked cheerfully if he couldn't get another cup of tea. Mary stood up to serve him.

"I'm afraid I need to start supper, Ward," Fresia said, returning to the living room.

"Don't let me keep you from your work."

"You'll stay and eat with us then, will you?" Fresia said. John shot her a sharp look, which she did her best to ignore.

"I'd love to."

CHAPTER 7

Later, Mary would wonder how it happened that Ward Hamilton's visits to the ranch became a weekly habit. With those first few visits, her heart sank every time she saw his car emerge around the corner of the driveway, and each time she had to fight a frantic urge to hide and avoid answering the door. By April, she felt like a captive in her own house. She'd taken a bad fall on Blue while helping Fresia move cows with new calves and hadn't been able to work outside. No one quite knew what went wrong except that Blue had turned sharply and Mary, off balance, fell hard on her left side. While her parents wanted to blame Blue, Mary couldn't help but feel the mistake had been hers. She'd felt herself start to slip and had overcorrected. The resulting damage to her prosthesis was serious, and she was on crutches again as she waited for the repairs. Everyone around her acted as though it was a minor mishap, that once her leg was back, she'd go on as usual, but Mary couldn't gloss over the incident so glibly. It was bound to happen again. It was the nature of their work. The next time she might not be so lucky.

John had made no secret of his dislike for Ward. He'd wanted to tell Ward to back off his visits, but Fresia had practically begged him to be polite. John's solution had been to avoid the house altogether when Ward was there. Eventually even Fresia began to avoid Ward, making any excuse possible to get out of spending another unproductive day. At first, Mary was convinced Ward would tire of the visits, but when weeks passed and it became clear he was only growing more entrenched, she wasn't sure how to extricate herself.

❦

"Mary," Ward said one day. "You were kept alive for a reason." She listened closely to this, wanting to believe her life had a deeper purpose. Ward went on. "God is creating a tapestry of your life. We see the back of his work with its messy knots and what appears to be a random pattern. Only God can see the front of the work, and one day, when his work is done, you'll see the true beauty of your life emerge."

On his next visit, Ward brought her books to read. They were stories about missionaries who had achieved miraculous things, people so daring in their faith they had gone into dangerous situations with confidence that God would keep them safe. Stories about angels and miracles and belief so powerful it allowed regular people to act heroically. When she had finished those, he brought her books filled with stories of dramatic conversions, always Christians cast in the role of hero. While she had been unable to concentrate to read before, these stories captivated Mary. On some level she came to adore these stories. Someone was always confronted with a problem—an insurmountable fear or loss—only to find strength to overcome it through prayer and God's power in their lives.

Ward tried to teach her to pray, but it didn't seem natural to her. She could mimic the prayers well enough, but she could never convince herself anyone was listening. No matter how she tried, she couldn't quite get her mind around the concept of a God who cared for her. She may have regretted her conclusions in the hospital, but she couldn't completely let go of her sense of God as a slightly malevolent force.

While she had liked the missionary and conversion stories, she did not like as much the next cycle of books Ward brought. These were books about what Ward called the End Times, books by Francis Schaeffer, D. James Kennedy, Tim LaHaye, David Wilkerson, people she'd never heard of, but that wasn't surprising. She'd never been much for reading, and the only books they had in the house were her mother's Bible and a set of encyclopedias Cal and Lydia had bought when Fresia was a girl. Gerald had read paperback Westerns, and there were stacks of them in one of the old bunkhouses.

"We need to get right with God," Ward said each time he gave her a book. "This is a Christian country, but we've gone far astray, and until we're right with God, Jesus won't return." The books warned about how the signs on earth were in keeping with the prophesies of the Bible, how all these signs were a clear indication the world was nearing the end of time when Christ would return to claim his loyal followers. Ward told Mary the culture was decadent. It was a disgrace, and God's heart was broken because of it.

"You're a woman of modesty," Ward said to her one day. "That's what I liked about you most that first day I saw you." Mary was puzzled by his characterization of her. It wasn't how any of her friends would have described her, at least not before the accident.

Unlike the missionary stories, Mary was left troubled by the stories of what Ward called the apocalypse. Each week as she read, she felt there was something wrong with the books. The first time she met Ward with her doubts, he seemed taken aback. He literally sat back against his chair as though she had pushed him. He smiled eventually and leaned forward. He didn't disagree with her like she had expected. Instead, he said things like, "Well, Niebuhr,"—or Merton, or Tillich—"might agree with you on that." Mary didn't know who this Niebuhr, Merton, and Tillich were, but she felt vindicated by the strangers he cited. "Of course," he went on, "that isn't ultimately the point Schaeffer, or Birch, or Dobson is trying to make," and he steered the conversation away from her dispute in a direction she hadn't anticipated. She listened to Ward, finding things in his explanation she didn't like either, but she wasn't quick enough to formulate her arguments on the spot. She found herself thinking about the things Ward had said through the week, waiting more anxiously than she expected for the next time he came to discuss the point further.

"Would you bring me a book by Tillich or Merton?" she asked one day.

Ward didn't say anything right away. "I don't think you're quite ready to read them yet," he answered finally. "They're dangerous, you know. You'd need to have a strong biblical foundation not to be confused by their loose interpretations."

"But I could try, right?"

"Yes. Well. Let me look on my shelves at the parsonage and see what I find."

When she asked again a few weeks later, he said, "You don't want to waste your time reading them."

After Ward left each week, Mary felt a little embarrassed about how she had argued with him. The only way she could explain what was happening was that she was bored. She had never argued so much in her life, never read and discussed anything, yet here she was each week speaking her mind to Ward.

❉

Later that spring, Ward started to bring with him each week a short scripture. He read the passages aloud each time, but unlike previous situations did not discuss with her what he had read. He simply closed his Bible and moved the conversation in another direction. She had been amused at first by the formality of the ritual. Such an odd man, she had thought, but after a while she began to see a message emerge in his readings. He was creating a story through these passages about how God worked in mysterious ways, how he brought strangers together, and how out of tragedy he wanted to create a new life, a new love. He said as much finally one blustery day. The wind battered the windows and whistled around the loose-fitting porch door.

"Mary, as soon as I saw you in the hospital last summer, I knew you were special."

"You don't even know me, Ward."

"But the Lord has revealed your heart to me."

The old Mary would have rolled her eyes at this, but the new Mary hesitated. God remained a mystery to her. As she'd learned in the hospital, his communications with her were cryptic and slightly menacing. Still, she genuinely believed God was trying to tell her something she needed to hear.

That night, after Ward left, she listened to the tapping of the cottonwood branches on her bedroom window. Although she tried, she couldn't hear God speaking to her the way he did to Ward. If God was trying to communicate, his meaning was as unclear to her as the message in those tapping branches.

※

She was in bed reading one of the books Ward had brought her the night she overheard her parents arguing. John was objecting to Ward's visits. Over the past few months, he'd made no effort to hide his contempt for the man. Her parents rarely argued and she was startled by their raised voices.

"Mary doesn't have any other visitors," Fresia was saying. "It's good for her to have a friend." Friend? Mary was surprised to hear Ward described as her friend.

"I don't like him skulking around here all the time."

"He isn't skulking, and anyway Mary doesn't complain. I think it's been good for her."

Mary laid the book face down on the bed. She had taken off her leg for the night, and she grabbed her crutches. As quietly as possible, she went to the door and pressed her ear against it.

"He's filling her head with bullshit," she heard John say. "Have you taken a look at those books he's been giving her? I don't like it. I should have put an end to it a long time ago."

"It isn't our place, John. Besides, it isn't doing any harm," Fresia persisted. "At least she's reading. She seems to look forward to Ward's visits. Goodness knows, they talk a mile a minute when he's here."

"That's not the sort of talk that's going to help her." John was silent for a few seconds, but it was clear to Mary he wasn't finished. "Maybe we ought to look into getting her into some classes at Mid-Plains," he finally said. "She wanted to do that."

"How would she get back and forth?"

"She'd drive, Fresia. She'd drive. We need to let go a little here. People do it all the time with prosthetic limbs."

Fresia was quiet, and Mary could feel her thinking, could almost see the thoughts slowly turning in her mind, but before her mother could answer, Mary had to ask herself how she felt about the suggestion. She hadn't driven since the accident, and although no one had mentioned it, everyone knew it was more than her disability that kept her from driving. Nor was she sure how she felt now about taking classes. She always read the course catalogs when they came to the house. She was interested in range management, cattle futures, breeding for the market—all the courses related to ranching—but since her fall that spring she hadn't felt confident enough to really be of help, and she knew her future in ranching was over. Other than ranching, she couldn't imagine what else she would do with her life. No one knew how to accommodate her disability. Just as an animal that is no longer of use has to be discarded, it struck Mary now that so too did the person who could not contribute. She hated what a burden she was for her parents. Here they were fighting over her, hiding their worry in their argument. The real problem was *her*, not Ward.

John's disapproval of Ward was of the most profound sort, though. She knew without his saying it he felt Ward lacked common sense, and that was all a person had, by John's reckoning. Only a few weeks earlier Ward had made a mistake in judgment that Mary knew her father would never forgive him for, no matter how much time passed, how many other things he might do well. He had driven into the ranch yard, and not reading the situation, honked his car horn loudly when he saw them. John and Fresia had been trying to load a skittish cull bull into the back of the truck for market all morning. The bull had already bolted once from the chute, and they had finally gotten him settled down when Ward made his appearance, the horn setting the bull into another frenzy, leading John to finally give up for the day. Ward never did see what he'd done, and John's overt disgust didn't seem to register. Fresia, like Mary, felt confused in her loyalties, embarrassed for Ward and sympathetic to John.

Nor did John approve of Ward's self-righteousness. Ward had made it quietly clear he didn't approve of Cal's use of profanity or his habit of rolling his own cigarettes, but it came to a head after supper one evening when John offered Ward a beer, something Mary understood as a conciliatory gesture, to which Ward had said primly, "I don't believe in drinking." Perhaps it wasn't what he said so much as how he said it, suggesting John was at fault for asking. After Ward had left that night, Cal commented, "He's sure differ'nt," as clear a condemnation as you'd hear from Cal.

Her parents' voices quieted, no doubt because they feared exactly this possibility that Mary would overhear them. She listened for a long time as their voices continued to murmur behind their bedroom door. John raised his voice only once more before their light went out. "Nothing good will come of it." It was the last word on the matter. Whatever they felt, neither of them later mentioned their concerns to her or asked Ward not to visit anymore.

❇

Ward had been visiting for several weeks, when late that spring, Mary finally convinced him to go for a short walk on the prairie. She was disappointed when it was clear he didn't appreciate the wildflowers in bloom or the greening prairie grasses. A hard, straight wind was blowing, and Ward was preoccupied with trying to keep his hair out of his eyes. Rather than relaxing as the walk progressed, he had grown more agitated. "You should have worn a hat like I told you," Mary finally said irritably. He didn't answer her.

They'd been discussing one of the books he had loaned her. Mainly, Mary was arguing. Ward had grown quiet. It had become something of a struggle between them, him posing new evidence to support a particular biblical standpoint, her finding some new way to question it. Mary wasn't even sure herself why she continued with these debates. She didn't care. Not like Ward did. She'd grown bored with her own insistence on arguing and suddenly regretted having given Ward such a hard time over the past few weeks. While a few old friends had dropped by once or twice after she'd left the hospital, all of them had drifted away through the winter. She couldn't hold it against them. Why wouldn't they move on? In many ways, what Fresia had said about Ward felt true. Maybe he was her friend. Maybe he was her only friend.

Her gratitude toward Ward translated briefly into a confusion of emotion. She looked quickly at him. Despite his obvious frustration with the wind, or maybe because of it, she saw something endearingly childlike about him in his unguardedness, and she felt herself smile. Ward looked at her and stopped himself midway through pushing his hair away from his face. He smiled back.

She led him to a little cutaway beside a pond where they could sit out of the wind. Once they sat down, Ward's frown returned, and he said now in a voice more his own than she had ever heard before, "Look here, Mary. What do I mean to you?"

Mary stammered for a few seconds. "I don't know, Ward," she finally said. "You're the one who keeps driving all the way out here every week."

"Mary, ever since I saw you in the hospital . . . you looked like an angel there, Mary, and the Lord's been speaking to me, and he's let me know he has a plan for us." Ward looked her full in the face. "It's clear we were meant to be together, Mary."

Ward looked at her. Mary flushed and turned away. She could feel him watching her, but she refused to meet his eyes.

"I know maybe it's too soon," Ward said, "but I'm a man, Mary. I'm a human being, and now that it's become clear to me where my future lies, I'm having a hard time being patient. We're going to be together, and I'd like it to be sooner rather than later." Mary still didn't respond, and Ward went on. "I know you don't love me, Mary." He swallowed hard before continuing, "But the scriptures tell us if a man loves his wife and a woman respects her husband, the marriage will be sound." He paused. "Do you think you can at least respect me, Mary?"

As Ward talked, Mary had the most peculiar experience. It was as if she'd become two people. Her second self stood apart from her, aloof, above the confusion of emotions. The second Mary was cool and calm, and Mary sensed her other self was more cunning than she was, more calculating. This new self said to her, "There's no future for you here. No rancher will ever marry you, not the way you are. You have no skills, no job prospects. You're going to be stuck on this ranch, in your parents' house, for the rest of your life. This is the best chance you have for a life. This is your last hope. No one else will have you."

"Can you, Mary?" Ward was saying. "Can you at least respect me?"

She was relieved not to have to hide the fact she wasn't in love with him. "Yes," she heard her second self say for her. "I think I can respect you." Mary was startled to hear herself say this, but her cunning sister self made it clear it was the wise thing to do, a way to buy time, if nothing else, and Mary felt strangely passive as though she could do nothing but follow along with where this new self seemed to be leading.

"That's good," Ward said in a rush as if he had been holding his breath. "That's good."

He leaned over and abruptly kissed her. Mary's eyes opened wide and she pulled away.

Ward shook his head. "You're not ready. I understand that, but I'm confident that with time you'll come to love me like I love you."

Mary didn't know about that, but what she did know was that she wanted her happiness back, and here was Ward offering her a life. He had started to remove his shoes. Mary watched as he went on to peel off his socks, and to roll up the bottoms of his pants.

"Are you going wading?"

Ward didn't answer. Instead, after he finished rolling up his pants, he stood up and rolled up his shirtsleeves. "Take off your shoes."

Mary laughed. "I don't feel like wading."

"We aren't wading. I'm going to baptize you."

"I've already been baptized."

Ward sat down again beside her. He looked into her eyes. "But did you believe in it, Mary? In your heart? Did you experience a true conversion? Did you experience salvation?"

Mary was silenced by his questions. She shrugged.

Ward nodded. "That's what I thought. We need to start this thing right, and Mary, your heart has to be right with God."

Mary didn't think she would be fooling God. After all, wasn't he supposed to know everything? How could this work? She waited for Ward to ask her to confess her faith, and when he didn't she thought about how she had always liked the childish practice of the do over. Here Ward was offering her a second chance, a do over for her life without requiring any sort of evidence from her.

"Come on, Mary," Ward said. "We can't move forward with our life together until you're right with God." What did it matter if she believed or not? What seemed important was that Ward thought she did, and maybe he was right. Maybe there would be something magical in the baptismal water. She nodded and began to remove her shoes.

Ward watched solemnly as she pulled off her socks. She paused, and he reached for her hand to help pull her up. She nodded toward her prosthesis. Ward blushed and looked away as she removed it. Afterward, she laid it on the grass and waited.

For a few seconds Ward seemed confused as to why she remained seated before he finally understood and bent to lift her into his arms. He carried her gingerly on his bare feet through the new gramma grass to the muddy, algae-coated edge of the pond. He stepped into the water, slipping slightly as the mud gave way. The water crept up to his knees, and Mary shivered as the water lapped at her foot. Ward hesitated before moving deeper into the pond until the water came to his waist. He stopped and looked at Mary. She expected him to smile at the absurdity of what they were doing, but his face remained somber.

"Mary Needham," he said then in the same formal voice he had used at the hospital, "do you take Jesus Christ to be your Lord and Savior?"

She hesitated only a second before blithely answering, "Sure." She felt a strange urge to laugh but stopped herself.

Ward nodded. "Then upon the confession of your faith, I now baptize you in the name of the Father, the Son, and the Holy Ghost." With these words, Ward bent and lowered her beneath the water. She felt his feet slip slightly in the mud again before he steadied himself. Her head went under. The frigid water was a shock as it closed over her. She opened her eyes briefly and saw the sun wavering greenish through the murky water of the pond. Then she was coming up out of the cold and the murk into the full sun, and Ward was wrapping his arms around her. He was laughing as she cleared her nose. Her teeth chattered with the cold. All the while Ward held her tight against his warm chest. He was still laughing as he carried her out of the water. Once he had reached the shore he set her down and swaddled her in his jacket before he squeezed the excess water from her hair.

"We'd better get you home and warm you up," he said then, still smiling. Through her dripping hair, Mary smiled, too, though she wondered what sort of pact she was making with the future. "I don't know anything about being a preacher's wife," she said.

"Oh," Ward laughed. "It won't take you long to catch on to that. Until then we'll take it one day at a time."

When they entered the kitchen door later that afternoon, in addition to their disheveled appearance, the change must have been obvious on Ward's face, for John glanced quickly from Ward to Mary, his sharp-eyed look lingering on Mary a few seconds before he turned away. He'd been watching her closely for months, and now he seemed resigned, ready to give up on her. She wished she could tell him about the baptism, her sense that she had a future after all. She wished she could explain to him that it wasn't how it looked. She wanted him to understand how he needed to give it some time, how she had found a way to move forward, and while it wasn't a miracle, it was the best she could do for herself given her circumstances. She couldn't tell him, though, and that spring afternoon Mary felt keenly the loss of her father. She had made a choice that was simply unconscionable to him, bringing into the intimacy of their family the clearest example of a bonehead as he could imagine. Unlike Brian who had been a natural fit, and Max who was like a son to him, Ward was an enigma and a fool, and John was not a man to suffer fools. Knowing this, seeing all of it, Mary felt the most peculiar peace. She wished John could see everything was going to be all right. She wished he could see that she was going to make a life for herself again. She'd be happy again. They would be able to stop worrying about her.

❋

That summer Ward visited almost every night. He had told her they had to wait until after their wedding to have sex, but on those nights, after the family went to bed, he pressed himself against her. He was a virgin himself, he'd told her. He sometimes got carried away and rubbed against her until he shuddered and groaned, always pulling away afterward with an apologetic grin. She found his behavior very odd, but he had explained to her fornication was a sin.

"I'm not a virgin, Ward," Mary had reminded him, and Ward had looked away sadly. She wasn't sure if his sadness was in sympathy for her loss, or in sadness for her imperfection.

"Yes," he said, "but you're a widowed person. It was right within the context of marriage." Mary didn't tell him about the boys before

Brian. Somehow she knew this confession would only confuse matters. She decided instead to giggle with Ward as he left on those evenings, his Bible covering the stain at his crotch.

Sometimes after he left, she panicked a little, for always while Ward was caressing her, her mind wandered and she imagined Brian in his place. She felt a jolt to her psyche every time she opened her eyes and saw Ward instead.

The wedding date was set for a month after the baptism, a little over a year after the accident. The minister at the Church of Christ in Merna would perform the marriage service, but Mary had insisted there be no wedding ceremony, no reception, no guests. This didn't feel like something to share with others. As her second self had made clear, this was a calculated decision, a transaction that she felt sure would develop into something more with time. She was anxious suddenly just to be finished with the waiting, to begin her new life. Now and then she felt a rush of emotion she interpreted as confidence that she would be happy again once she and Ward were married, certain the pain of the past would collapse behind her, relieved her parents would not have to worry about her any longer, sure she could recreate herself.

No one approved of the engagement. Each of her family members tried in their own way to discourage her from the marriage. "At least wait another year," her mother had said.

Judy was more forceful. "What are you thinking?" she said one day, her face filled with disgust and disbelief. Mary shrugged, and Judy mimicked her. "What's this? What sort of an answer is that? You don't love him. I know you don't love him, so why are you doing this?"

"You wouldn't understand."

"Probably not. But, Mary, for Pete's sake, don't do it. The world isn't going to come to an end if you just tell him you can't do it. You shouldn't rush into something this big without knowing why."

"I didn't say *I* didn't understand. I said '*you* wouldn't understand.'"

Judy sighed. "What on earth is the matter with you?"

"Leave me alone, Judy. Just leave me alone. Like I said, you wouldn't understand."

"What's to understand? You've lost your marbles. That's all there is to it. You'll regret it, Mary. You really will."

"I know what I'm doing, Judy. It's going to be okay."

Judy rolled her eyes. "Whatever you say. I won't ever mention it again."

"Sure you won't."

But Mary had been wrong. Judy never did speak of it again. She joined in the silence of the rest of the family, speaking volumes in their reticence, never confronting Mary with the mistake they all felt she was making.

Only Lydia tried one last time to talk to her about it, gently, careful not to offend. "You're young, Mary. You have a long life ahead of you." Mary had nodded at this, waiting for Lydia to finish. Lydia nodded back. "I want you to be happy, more than anything, Mary. I want you to be happy."

Mary looked down. She was surprised to feel tears gather and quickly swiped them away with the back of her hand. "Can anybody say they're happy, Grandma?"

Lydia pursed her lips. "That's not a question."

"Yes it is. Can anyone assure someone else they'll be happy?"

"No, but there are things that make happiness more likely."

"I think it's the right thing to do," Mary finally said.

Lydia shook her head then, a look of undisguised concern on her face. "Oh, Mary."

≋CHAPTER 8

≋"They sighted a funnel over north of Arnold, moving this direction," John said as he adjusted the dial of the truck's radio. The weather bulletin faded in and out as Mary stopped to listen. She balanced the box she was carrying on one hip. Fresia came from the house, the wind forcing her to duck into the truck's cab to retie her hair. Mary kept her hair cropped short and she remained out in the wind, a buoyant feeling coming over her with the announcement of the storm.

"Sounds like we could be in for a bad one," John said. He left the radio on and got out of the truck. Mary took the box she was holding into the parsonage and deposited it with the others stacked in the living room. She didn't have many things, but she had needed her parents' help to make the move. Earlier that morning a few church people had come by with casseroles, salads, and desserts. Their offerings lined the counters in the kitchen. Some had helped move a few things, but most of them hadn't stayed long.

Now as clouds roiled in the west in a green-tinged sky, Mary felt as if the houses of Custer City were huddled together on the stark plains like covered wagons circled for protection from the elements and unforeseen dangers. Custer City was where the Stiles family did much of their business, from buying and selling cattle at the sale barn to grocery shopping and having their taxes figured, but Mary seemed to be seeing it for the first time as she moved into the parsonage a week after marrying Ward. It was mid-May but already the days were hot and dry. There had been no rain for weeks and even the young leaves on the trees wilted in the heat.

The parsonage was a ramshackle affair built before the turn of the century at the same time as the church. Through the years it had been added on to according to the needs of the various ministers' families. The additions to the house had been built by church volunteers of varying skills, and the structure had the feel of a chicken coop with thin walls and low ceilings. Narrow hallways led to ill-conceived wings. The thresholds to the various additions were uneven, requiring either a step up or a step down, sometimes only an inch or two, sometimes as much as half a foot. In the kitchen, despite what looked like a new coat of aqua paint, a dark line of mildew crept up the walls. When the wind gusted, the windows of the house rattled and the roof thrummed. It was the sorriest place Mary had ever seen, and she felt haunted by the lives of the people who had dwelt there before her.

Ward, with castoffs from the congregation, had furnished the house. None of the furniture matched and he had not bothered to hang pictures or curtains. Neither Fresia nor John had commented as they slowly walked through the house after they first arrived, but their faces had registered the same dismay Mary felt. Ward seemed undisturbed by their silence. He left them later, saying he had a church emergency, leading John to grumble beneath his breath, "What kind of emergency could you have the week after you get married?"

Mary had not tried to respond to John's criticism. She wanted to put the best light on her new life, and Fresia, who seemed to share her feelings, brightened now as Mary glanced at her.

"We'll get this place spruced up so you won't even recognize it."

Mary was so grateful for her mother she wanted to weep. It left her with no alternative but to join in and help get herself settled.

She and Ward had spent their honeymoon the week before in Colorado. The one-room cabin Ward rented had been recently remodeled: cheap wood paneling, a pale blue shag carpet, wrinkled blue curtains, and a sagging mattress in a scarred wooden bed frame covered by a polyester throw. Mary's enduring memory from the week, though, was of an owl-shaped clock at the foot of the bed. The eyes of the clock moved back and forth with the ticking of the second hand, visibly tracking time in a way that had unnerved her.

The entire week, Ward had been enthusiastic as each day they drove through the mountains. He took hairpin curves without caution, passed other cars on blind corners, and all the while pointed out sights while driving perilously close to the edge of the road, the steep drop-offs so near that Mary felt she dared not look around at all for fear if she weren't vigilant they would plunge to the bottom.

Almost immediately after the wedding, Mary had felt the enormity of her mistake. During the week of their honeymoon, she discovered she often didn't like herself when she was with Ward. She felt she was self-centered, cranky, demanding. Nothing was quite the way she'd imagined it would be. She hadn't given much thought to the details, hadn't felt any urge to daydream prior to the marriage about life with Ward. Instead, she had felt only that she needed to move on with things, and now she saw how it would be. She and Ward didn't like to do the same things: he liked museums, while she wanted to swim in the mountain streams; he liked afternoons reading; she wanted to hike. Worst of all, Ward seemed indifferent to what she liked and wanted. She felt there was no compromise. And sex? Well, she couldn't seem to stop making comparisons. Marriage hadn't cured his—how could she put it delicately?—tendency toward prematurity. She spent every night, long after Ward had gone to sleep, wrestling with her complaints against him. She watched the eyes of the owl clock in the moonlight until she grew too restless to stay in bed. Several nights she gave up on sleep altogether and paced the room before finally sitting at the open window wrapped in an extra blanket, looking out into the woods around the cabin and wondering at what she had done. Ward had told her she would be tested. "As servants of the Lord, ministers and their families come under greater attack by Satan." Mary wished she could see her situation in his terms. Then at least they would be partners fighting against a common enemy. No matter how she tried, though, she wasn't able to see it that way. She'd been naive to think she could move on so easily into a new life. She felt betrayed by herself, and yet she remained divided in a way that was new to her, her cunning sister self telling her to set aside her feelings, to move on, to grow up.

Mary had hoped before the wedding she might learn to love Ward as he'd promised she would, but love seemed like a gift, a luxury, and she didn't believe such grace was to be granted her. No matter what, though, she'd made a decision to live again. Maybe her life wasn't what she had dreamed of at one time, but she had a place in the world as Ward's wife, whatever that might mean.

Now, as she stood in the kitchen of the parsonage with its single sink set a bit too low, its hodgepodge of cupboards, its ancient linoleum curling at the edges of the floor, she chided herself for complaining. Outside the kitchen window stood a hawthorn tree. It was a young tree, and she found something stalwart and hopeful about it. She admired that tree, how it withstood the wind whipping it about, forcing it almost parallel to the ground. As long as she looked to the east and ignored the storm massing in the west, the sun was hopeful in a wan sort of way. She dared not look too far beyond the hawthorn tree, though, for the large backyard of the parsonage was as bleak as the house itself. Like the house, it had never really been tended. A feeling of transience and failed vision remained in evidence of long-neglected garden plots and poorly executed plantings. Mary felt keenly in this place the great weight of entropy against the feeble endeavors of her predecessors, all of whom, like herself, she knew had been poor. From some lingering communal spirit, she knew they had been lonely as well.

The burden of those collective failures thronged every corner of the house, and they threatened to overwhelm her as she saw how pointless it was for her to be scrubbing the greasy residue gathered at the edge of the countertop. As she cleaned, Mary now and then experienced a peculiar feeling of déjà vu. Along with the sense of oppression was something vaguely familiar about the house, though she couldn't begin to place it. She had a gallon of new yellow paint, though, and she intended to get a second coat on the kitchen walls yet that afternoon. John had bought a can of Kilz, which they'd painted on the walls to eradicate the mildew stains, and the first coat of paint was drying.

Her dreary thoughts that afternoon were interrupted by a knock at the front door. She hung the dishcloth she had been using on the faucet and went to the living room where Fresia, who had been unpacking boxes in the dining room, had already opened the screen door. Standing in the doorway was a pretty young woman, her long blonde hair falling in two braids across her shoulders. She wore jean shorts and a T-shirt, and she was holding a plate of cookies.

"I'm Julie from next door," the young woman was saying to Fresia as Mary entered the room. "You must be Mrs. Hamilton?"

Fresia was momentarily flustered by Julie's mistake. "No . . . no," she said with a gesture toward Mary. "Mary . . . my daughter . . . it's my daughter who's married to Ward."

Mary came into the room then. She smiled as Julie handed her the plate of cookies.

"Can you come in?"

"I'm sorry. I can't. I have a five-month-old at home. I took advantage of her nap to slip over here with the cookies, but I should be getting back."

"Come by sometime with the baby," Mary said.

Julie smiled. "I will. And you're welcome to stop by anytime. But please knock, don't ring the bell. If the baby's asleep, the doorbell . . ." She interrupted herself with a blush. "Sorry. I'm a typical new mom, I guess." Before she left, she said, "I'll keep an eye on the storm for you. Come to my house if you need to take shelter. Your house doesn't have a basement."

"She's nice," Fresia said with undisguised relief after Julie left. "You'll be glad to have a nice neighbor like that." She changed the subject then. "I'm almost finished unpacking the dishes in the dining room. Do you need help in the kitchen?"

❉

In the late afternoon, after the gathering storm finally went around them, as Mary and her parents sat down with glasses of lemonade, three women arrived. Mary knew immediately they were church members, though they had not been among the earlier visitors. They all carried casserole dishes. One of them knocked and without waiting for an answer walked through the unlocked screen door. The other two followed. Fresia glanced quickly at Mary and raised her eyebrows at their impertinence. The larger of the three introduced herself as Mrs. Conroy, no first names here. Her cohorts she introduced as Mrs. Kunz and Mrs. Turner.

Mrs. Conroy looked around the room. "Looks like you've been rearranging."

"Could you stay for some lemonade?" Mary said.

Mrs. Conroy continued in her role as spokeswoman. "We'd like that."

Mary introduced her parents and asked the three women to find a place to sit down before she left for the kitchen. A few minutes later as she was returning with a tray, she overheard Mrs. Kunz say to Fresia, "It was news to all of us, Mr. Hamilton marrying so suddenly, and marrying someone we didn't know. We were relieved to learn she came from the Merna church."

Mary stopped just outside the doorway to the living room, curious suddenly about what they had to say.

Another one, Mrs. Turner, Mary guessed, said, "There are so many nice young ladies in our congregation. . . ." She stopped herself, seeming to remember to whom she was speaking. Mary recognized

Mrs. Conroy's voice as she jumped in to try to cover for her friend's mistake. "That is, if we'd known Mr. Hamilton was looking . . . we had no idea he was interested in marrying. That's all."

Fresia had been making understanding noises during their conversation, but as Mary entered the room, she could see her mother's discomfort. In Mary's absence, John had somehow managed to escape and Mary glimpsed him outside now near the garage.

The three women stayed until Ward returned home at which time they promptly excused themselves. Their demeanor changed completely in Ward's presence; whereas with Mary they had seemed domineering, with Ward they grew demure. They wouldn't dream of wasting his time with gossip and advice, but it was already clear to Mary they felt her time was not important. Fresia saw it too.

After the three women left, Fresia said to Mary once they were alone, "Did we just step back in time?"

Mary knew what her mother meant. Through the day she had felt her life slowly constrict around her as she had settled into the parsonage. It was as though the modern, outside world did not exist here at all, as though they were on a different and separate plane.

Before Fresia and John left for the evening, as she hugged Mary good-bye, Fresia said softly so Ward wouldn't hear, "Don't let those old gabblers get you down."

❉

Once her parents had left, Mary waited for Ward to comment on the house. When he wasn't forthcoming, she finally asked. "You didn't say anything about the house. What do you think?"

"I wasn't going to mention it, but since you brought it up, I have to say I didn't think it was a problem the way things were arranged before."

Ward's criticism struck her like a blow. It was so unexpected it took her a few seconds to recover. "Do you want me to move things back?"

"No, that isn't necessary, but you might ask me next time before making changes."

Mary was unaccountably crushed by his disapproval and felt she should apologize, but she wasn't sure for what.

When Ward first entered the kitchen, he'd stopped short. "I thought I smelled paint." Mary smiled, proud of all she'd accomplished that day. "You didn't ask me."

"Well, no . . . ," Mary said. "The mildew . . . I hate aqua . . ."

"I don't like yellow," Ward interrupted.

Mary had imagined that maybe after supper they would walk together around town, or, like other people she had noticed, sit on their front porch to enjoy the evening and perhaps visit with the neighbors. Instead Ward said he needed to start working on his sermon and went into the far end of the house where he had a small study.

The study was a windowless room lined with bookcases where Ward kept shelves of Bible commentaries and books by Christian writers. She'd noticed many of the same books he'd lent her. A shelf of books by James Dobson. Tim LaHaye's *The Battle for the Mind*; Francis Schaeffer, Duane Gish, D. James Kennedy, Paul Weyrich, John Birch. She felt funny seeing those books. Taken together, they seemed too formidable to argue with. She couldn't imagine how she'd muster the strength now to argue as she had before. Then, too, she'd felt keenly since marrying him that Ward was no longer interested in hearing her thoughts and opinions. On the walls of the study were maps of the Holy Land. The room was dominated by an enormous black desk that clearly could never be moved without first dismantling the walls. That was the story of the parsonage, Mary decided, after seeing that room with its desk like a huge caged animal. Arrivals and departures with nothing to call your own, everything tied to this forsaken place.

After she had cleared the supper dishes, Mary wandered outside alone. At last the wind had died down, leaving in its wake small branches and leaves scattered on yards and sidewalks. The street in front of the parsonage was quiet. In the hush, she heard a baby cry once briefly and guessed it was Julie's baby. She heard, too, the clattering of silverware and the clinking of dishes coming through the open windows of the houses lining the street. These sounds seemed exotic to her. She had never lived close enough to anyone to hear such sounds. It seemed like a violation of sorts to overhear someone's private life in this way, but as she set off to get away from the sounds, she only encountered new ones in the houses on neighboring blocks.

Only in the park in the little town square did she feel she had finally escaped these domestic noises. She was alone except for an old man sitting on a bench. He had nodded at her when she passed him. From across the park she watched now as he tried to entice a squirrel with a piece of fruit. She wondered how lonely you would have to be to want to attract a squirrel's attention. She had the feeling this old man's actions were being mirrored around the world, that old men in China and Germany and Brazil and Australia were sitting in parks coaxing to themselves some wild but proximate beast.

CHAPTER 9

≡"I'd like all of you to meet my new wife and helpmeet, Mary," Ward said from the pulpit that first Sunday after their honeymoon. "As all of you know, we were married last week in a quiet service at the Merna church. Thank you for your generous gifts: the silver serving tray and the new set of Bible commentaries. I'm sure all of you will find Mary as much a treasure as I do, and I know you'll help make her comfortable here."

Ward looked toward her and gestured in a vague way. Mary wasn't sure what she was supposed to do after this introduction. Was she supposed to stand up and wave at everyone? Was she supposed to look around with a cool nod of the head? Her face was flaming, and there would be nothing cool about it. In her indecision she remained rigidly facing forward, knowing somehow this was exactly the wrong thing to do. Why hadn't Ward thought to tell her what would be expected of her? She felt his exposing her in this way was negligent. Ward, however, appeared to see nothing amiss in her conduct; instead, he continued to beam at her from the pulpit.

At the end of what felt like a very long service, Ward stopped for her at the pew, extended his arm, and guided her to the back of the church where together they greeted the departing congregation. Everyone was friendly to Mary, shaking her hand, sometimes hugging her, always saying how lucky she was to have caught Ward. She frantically tried to remember all of their names as Ward introduced them. She remembered Mrs. Turner, Mrs. Kunz, and Mrs. Conroy. Beyond theirs, she couldn't remember a single name. The congregation was small, but by the time the church was empty Mary felt like that group of fewer than a hundred had grown exponentially. Long before the last member of the congregation finally straggled out she was ready to go home. Only she wanted to really go home. To the ranch. Not to the parsonage.

The parsonage was separated from the church by a tall privet hedge regularly trimmed by Berl Frakes, an elderly member of the congregation. Berl was long retired from the railroad, and despite being stooped almost double he volunteered as the maintenance man and groundskeeper for the church. Fresia knew Berl and told Mary there had been a terrible tragedy in his early life. His young wife had died alone in a house fire while he was away. He had never remarried. In addition to maintaining the church grounds, for years Berl had taken care of the yards of all the church's widows.

Her first month in the parsonage Mary watched Berl as each Friday morning he methodically sharpened his hedge clippers and then set to work making the unruly bushes square again. He worked with as much care as if the church hedge were the hedge on a palace grounds. On those occasions when he noticed Mary watching from one of the windows of the parsonage, Berl smiled and nodded. She was always embarrassed to be caught, hoping to keep her spying a secret, but it hadn't taken her long to realize there would be no secrets in the parsonage.

Lydia had sent transplants of iris and sedum and Mary had planted them around the front sidewalk. She'd bought a few sets of moss rose cheap at the hardware store and planted those as well. Berl, a man who didn't miss anything, came by one day while she was watering the young plants.

"I've got some extra holly and a few yews at home. I'd give them to you if you'd like, for your foundation there." She looked as he spoke and saw how stark the cement foundation seemed against the bare ground.

"Are you sure you can spare them?"

"They're going to go to waste if you don't need them."

The next day he came by with the bushes, three of each. She worked with him, and he taught her how much space she needed for the root-ball. He'd brought along peat moss and compost. "I make my own compost," he'd explained. After that they worked together in a comfortable silence. When they'd finished Mary invited him inside for coffee, which Berl declined.

Through those first few weeks of summer, Berl brought Mary any extra plants he'd found and helped her put them in the ground. She finally guessed he might be buying the plants himself at least some of the time. He was so gracious about the gift, he somehow made it seem like she was doing him a favor by taking them off his hands, and she didn't know how to thank him properly.

Since moving day, Mary had come to expect but not yet accept the habit of some of the older church women—who considered themselves church leaders—of walking into her house during the day without waiting for her to answer their knock. She had the distinct feeling they were trying to catch her in the act of doing something she shouldn't and that they were always slightly disappointed to find her instead employed in useful activity: scrubbing the floor, ironing clothes, or washing dishes.

Within a short time she had seen what would be expected of her as the minister's wife. First, she was to be available at all times for any need that might possibly arise in the congregation: last minute babysitting, bringing a meal for the sick, offering a bed for someone else's out of town guests, leading meetings of the women's committees, organizing church dinners, overseeing funeral dinners and wedding receptions.

If her duties were clear, so were her boundaries. She was to have no vote in church policy or to play any role in church controversies. Nor was she to have a part in the private concerns of church members. This role was assigned to Ward only, and he took seriously his congregants' right to privacy, not even sharing with Mary the smallest detail of his counseling sessions with members. Mary understood then the people with whom she spent most of her time would be the people she knew least in Custer City, and yet they would make incredible demands upon her, ask of her the unaskable. In other words, she was to be the church's servant, and in her case this would not be a metaphor as it was when they called Ward the servant of Christ.

Mary learned about most things in the congregation the hard way, like the first week after moving into the parsonage when she went with Ward to the Wednesday night Bible Study. The group was reading from the Old Testament book of Isaiah. Mary struggled to find the scripture until Ward finally noticed, first sending her a scolding look, and then finding it for her. As the group discussed the chapter in question, Mary's mind wandered. She took note of how the basement of the church where they were meeting smelled like mildew. There was a lingering odor from the propane heater. Worn beige linoleum covered the floor. At some point there had been updates in the basement. Faux wood panels covered what must have been the old plaster walls of the foundation. Fiberboard partitions sectioned off Sunday School classrooms. An old upright piano sat in the southeast corner of the main room where the Bible Study group was meeting. Mary was taking in all these details when Ward interrupted her. She couldn't tell if he had done it intentionally or not.

"What do you think, Mary?"

"I . . . I . . . Could you repeat the question?"

"About salvation? For those born before Christ?"

"I don't . . . I never . . . I can't really . . . I've never believed . . . really . . . heaven and hell."

Ed Lundgren, one of the younger men in the congregation, a man around Mary's age, interrupted her stammering to say, "You don't believe in heaven and hell?" He was frowning as he asked this. Ed's close-set eyes narrowed now, and it was clear to Mary she had inadvertently waded into an argument she didn't want to have with this group.

"That didn't quite come out right," she said, looking frantically to Ward. She thought he shook his head slightly at her as everyone waited. When Ward did not come to her rescue, she continued. "I can't quite imagine God would really send someone to hell. I mean, can you? When you really think about it, which I don't. I don't really think about it."

Ed seemed even more agitated by this answer, and now most of the others in the small group also seemed offended. One of the women said, "It's disturbing that the minister's wife . . ."

Ward jumped in then finally. "What Mary's trying to say . . ." He went on to contrive an answer for her that implied a deeper theological sophistication than she had. Although his answer seemed to satisfy some members of the group, Mary sensed among them distrust for her.

Ward stayed after the Bible Study to close up the church, but when he got home Mary was waiting for him. "What were you thinking putting me on the spot like that?"

Ward raised his eyebrows. "I thought you'd learned better than that from what I've been trying to teach you."

"I told you before we got married I wasn't cut out to be a minister's . . ."

"Still, Mary. These are basic doctrinal issues. I thought sure . . ."

"What is it you want from me? I don't understand what you people want."

"Settle down now," Ward said. "I hadn't realized how far we'd need to bring you along, that's all. I hadn't realized it. I thought you'd been taking in everything I'd given you to read."

Mary exhaled quickly through her nose. "Get this, Ward. You aren't going to be 'bringing me along' anywhere. I see how things are here. I get what my role is. I see that. This is the deal, though. I'll show up for things. I'll do that. I'll do whatever they ask of me, but don't start thinking, any of you, that you can mess with my head. It's off limits. No more putting me on the spot like that. No more weird questions. Are we straight on that?"

Ward smiled a peculiar little smile. Mary didn't have a clue what it signified, but she had meant what she'd said. It was a firm line she drew between her public role as minister's wife and her private self.

※

There were two families and a single woman in the congregation Mary liked very much, an elderly couple, Delbert and Alice Ochsner; a young couple with two school-age children, Greg and Kelly Carpenter; and Lana Perkins. Alice, Kelly, and Lana regularly came to Mary's defense and readily volunteered for any of the things the church expected her to help organize. Most days, Mary felt if it hadn't been for those three women she couldn't have continued.

While she increasingly found the congregation strange, in many cases downright unlikable, Mary grew to love the church building. Where the parsonage had been hideously neglected and deformed through the years, the church had, at least at one time, been lavished with every attention. Built in 1889, it reflected the wealth of the large founding congregation and their optimism about the town's future and their own future in it.

As the size of the congregation had dwindled in recent decades, necessary maintenance had become too costly, and the building was decaying. Mary loved it, and she loved it most of all for its squalor. She could not explain why the crumbling plaster in the back corners of the balcony or the slightly earthy, rotting smell in the basement gave her such pleasure, but her spirits lifted each time she entered the building. She made a habit of going each day alone to relish the quiet, always entering through an ancillary door just on the other side of the privet hedge from the parsonage.

The cavernous sanctuary was made even more majestic by a swooping vaulted ceiling. On the plaster was impressed an intricate design, which though crumbling in places was still exquisite. The height of the ceiling dwarfed the huge crystal chandeliers hanging from it. The most pressing piece of church business that first summer Mary was married to Ward was the cleaning of the chandeliers. The crystals were dusty. Many were missing. A committee was in place to raise funds to clean and repair the lights. Now and then as Mary sat in the sanctuary she imagined herself climbing a tall ladder and washing each separate crystal with vinegar water. She sometimes grew dizzy with the thought.

Immense stained-glass windows lined both sides of the sanctuary. Behind the stage and the pulpit was a large rose window. To the west of the stage was an overflow room, and on the stage itself stood a solid walnut choir loft. A worn blue carpet bearing a faint star pattern covered the stage and served as a runner down both aisles of the sanctuary. The walnut pews were original to the church, their varnish thick and in the heat of summer prone to stickiness. The pew hymnals were ancient too, and when opened their bindings cracked and the yellowed pages released a slight smell of mildew.

If the emptiness shook her a little each time she entered the sanctuary, Mary still chose not to turn on the lights, preferring instead to let her eyes adjust to the light filtering through the stained-glass windows. Each time she entered that quiet space, she felt something stir in her, something almost like hope. When it was empty of people, the church felt holy to her. In terms of her faith, Mary wished she had more in common with the other members of the congregation. She wished she had their faith, but the God they talked about in no way resembled the God she'd encountered. And Jesus seemed like a fairy tale to her. Who could she tell these things? She'd failed to meet the church's expectations for a minister's wife, but alone in the empty sanctuary she felt a kind of faith. She didn't have words for what she believed, but in the silence of the empty church, she felt at peace with herself.

❉

On a Thursday afternoon in August, six weeks after her marriage to Ward, Mary was sitting in one of the pews beneath the balcony.

It was a pleasant day outside, and she had propped open the front door to let in the breeze. She liked to observe the sanctuary from the dimness under the balcony. To the right of the stage stood an upright piano. Like the church pews, its finish was dark and cracked. To the left of the stage stood an organ, and between them the altar where the Communion service was held each week. This afternoon, the light from the stained-glass windows refracted in such a way as to illuminate the old piano, and Mary fixed her attention upon it.

She had never been around a piano. Her family didn't own one, and she had never in her life felt a piano's keys. She stood up and walked toward the front of the church, her footfalls echoing in the emptiness. Once there, she timidly rolled back the piano's cover to reveal the keyboard. After a few seconds of observation she laid her fingers on the yellowed ivory keys and felt their surprising slippery coolness before finally pulling out the bench to sit down. For a few minutes, she simply stared at the keyboard. This time, when she laid her fingers on the ivory keys, she pressed down gently. No sound issued from the strings. She grew bolder then and pressed the keys more firmly, depressing one of the pedals as well, and was satisfied when a single note sounded. The note rang in the cavernous sanctuary. It echoed and hung as if suspended from the ceiling, even after Mary released the key.

She looked at the span her fingers made on the keyboard. Then, starting from the bottom, she methodically worked her way key by key to the top, listening as the tones shaded from the deepest notes, barely a growl, to the highest notes, a mere tinkling. She felt beneath her fingertips the contrast between the slickness of the ivory keys and the dull woodenness of the black keys. She began then to play clusters of notes, depressing the keys randomly, experimenting with sounds, and making a gratifying noise. With a little time, she was able to find combinations of notes that conveyed not so much the sound but the feeling she was looking for.

Once the silence had been broken, Mary overcame her hesitance and began to play with abandon. She played great crashing chords in combination with strings of more delicate individual notes. Now and then where she paused, she heard the clamorous sounds she had made echoing and ricocheting in the sanctuary. She imagined those chords collecting in the darkness at the very back of the balcony, unable to escape the church walls.

Her reverie was cut short when at some point she sensed a human presence in the building. She looked up and was startled to see Ward running down the right side aisle toward her. He was gesturing wildly for her to stop, which she did as she soon as she saw him. By the look on his face, Mary thought something terrible must have happened, and she was too concerned to be embarrassed about being caught in what she had believed was a private moment.

"Mary, what are you thinking? Why are you playing the piano like that? This is a place of worship. This is God's house. You can't play like that here."

Mary was mortified to have been caught being so foolish, and she felt the beautiful music she had made suddenly crash about her. All the lovely notes she had imagined hovering in the balcony now tumbled at her feet.

"I . . . I don't know. I just started playing and lost track of everything."

Ward was shaking his head. "You can't do that. What will people think?"

"No one was here. I didn't think it would matter."

Ward smiled a thin smile. "Everyone on the street can hear you. You're the minister's wife, Mary. You can't be so eccentric."

Mary felt her face grow hot with humiliation at the possibility of having been a public spectacle, but while she felt terrible for having done something to embarrass Ward, she also felt the urge to tell him to grow up, to stop worrying about what the ninnies in the church thought of her. She couldn't see how playing a piano, even if it was a made-up song, even if it wasn't a church song, could possibly merit this much concern.

Perhaps Ward sensed her rebellion, for he laughed then. "If you want to play the piano, at least let's get you some lessons. There wasn't anything musical about that cacophony." Mary couldn't understand how they had heard the sounds she had made so differently. How could it have sounded as badly as Ward suggested when it had seemed so magnificent to her?

The idea of piano lessons didn't appeal to Mary, but Ward continued as if thinking out loud, "A minister's wife should know how to play the piano. It would be good if you could play hymns, don't you think?"

Mary shrugged. He went on. "I'll talk to Mrs. Lesley about finding some time for you." Mrs. Lesley was the church pianist. A small, wispy-haired woman, Mrs. Lesley wore button-down house dresses and matching cardigans for every occasion. She was a quiet woman, not one of the church members who regularly dropped in at the parsonage.

❋

When she went the following week to her house, Mary found Mrs. Lesley was even more timid at home than she was at church, and, if possible, more confused than Mary about the purpose of the piano lessons. Her house was clean but filled with clutter. Piles of books, magazines, newspapers, and sheet music covered the tables and lined the floors along the walls, and Mary had to walk through a narrow path to get from the front door into the living room where Mrs. Lesley had a baby grand piano.

"My husband," she explained when Mary commented on it. "He bought it for me before he died." She smiled a bit wanly, and Mary saw something of the young woman she once must have been. Mrs. Lesley's life suddenly struck Mary as enormously mysterious. She seemed arrested, though, stalled at a certain place in her life. Mary couldn't begin to fill in the puzzle of how Mrs. Lesley had ended up as she had.

She wished Ward were the sort of husband that she could ask, but she knew he would meet her inquiries with his usual "Mary, you know I can't discuss the church members with you." It didn't matter if the information she wanted was something innocuous; Ward treated every inquiry as though it were gossip. Nor did Mary feel that Mrs. Lesley was someone who would come to share confidences about her life with Mary. And as if to underscore that point now, Mrs. Lesley inexplicably started a metronome ticking on the side of the piano. It was an awkward and nervous gesture, and Mrs. Lesley herself seemed at a loss as to why she had done it. Despite that, she did not stop the metronome; instead, she flushed self-consciously. "Go ahead and sit down," she instructed, and Mary pulled out the piano bench. "What do you know about the piano?"

"Nothing."

"Do you at least know where middle C is located?"

"No," Mary said, the ticking of the metronome like a scolding finger.

Mrs. Lesley sighed, and Mary regretted her ignorance. "All right then. We'll start from the beginning."

Mary could not say she enjoyed the lessons or even that she made as much progress as either she or Mrs. Lesley had hoped, but the need to practice did allow her regularly to seek out the piano in the church sanctuary where, occasionally, when Ward was out of earshot on a call, she could still play as she wished. She no longer played with as much abandon as she had that first day when Ward had caught her, but if she played softly she could still create what she in a self-mocking way called her celestial music. Self-mocking though she was, the music did feel inspired to Mary. After her experience with Ward, though, she guessed no one else could hear what she heard and she kept the music to herself, practicing enough to satisfy Mrs. Lesley each week, even though the scales and simple songs she played for her lessons were a torment, all earthbound and painfully circumscribed compared to what she believed was her true music.

≡CHAPTER 10

≡"Your tree. How pretty."

On this sunny Tuesday morning late in September the leaves of the linden tree in Julie's yard were falling, the golden leaves so graceful they looked like butterflies in flight. Mary had been kept so busy with church activities she rarely saw Julie Masek except in passing. Julie was sitting on her front steps with her baby, a girl named Molly, who at nine months was pulling herself up to the concrete steps and trying to walk around them. Molly crowed with delight when she saw Mary. They watched together in silence as the leaves fell slowly in the sun. It was a rare windless day, the sky a deep blue. Cumulus clouds floated leisurely across the sky like fat ladies on parade. As Mary continued to watch the leaves fall, she must have looked peculiar for when she finally came back to herself she found Julie watching her closely.

"I got a little distracted there," Mary said with a laugh.

Julie smiled. "It's all right. I've been meaning to tell you how nice your flowers are. It's so much. . . . It's such an improvement."

Both of them turned to look at Mary's front yard. With Berl's help, in one summer, the front yard of the parsonage had been transformed. Fall flowers bloomed—mums and sedum, tall phlox and rudbeckia. The new bushes and now a couple of ornamental trees, though still young, created an inviting landscape. Mary hardly noticed how shabby the exterior of the parsonage was anymore because of it.

"It's a miracle what you've done to that place," Julie went on. "You're quite the gardener."

"Not really. I've never planted flowers before, but it needed something. The inside . . . well, the inside is hopeless. Berl's so good to help me with the outside."

"I've watched you two working over there," Julie said. She seemed to want to say something more but stopped herself. For some reason, Mary lingered. She allowed the silence between them to pass, and with it she felt Julie's caution dissolve. "How are you doing in your new life?" Julie finally asked.

Mary shrugged. She couldn't seem to fake an answer like she knew Ward would want her to. "It's hard."

"I can imagine." Julie paused before saying, "I don't know how you put up with those people."

Mary laughed. "I don't very well. Sometimes I have downright violent fantasies."

Now it was Julie's turn to laugh. "Could you come in for a few minutes?"

"I'd love to."

Like its exterior, the interior of Julie's house was cozy and clean. The furniture was simple but tasteful, the walls painted in warm earth colors. Something sweet was baking in the oven, and Mary felt a wave of homesickness. Her face must have registered her dismay for Mary saw a look of understanding in Julie's eyes.

Julie sat Molly down on the carpet. "Would you mind watching the baby for a few seconds while I check on the apple crisp? It should be finished soon, if you could stay."

"That sounds great."

After Julie left the room, Mary sat down on one of the chairs in the dining room near where Molly was playing. She leaned over, and Molly tried to grab her sweater. Molly smiled at Mary, her gummy mouth open, dimpled hands reaching. "Do you want to come up?" Mary said and Molly smiled wider. Molly was heavier than she looked, but she settled into Mary's lap, her warm little body cuddling in.

"It looks like the two of you have made friends," Julie said when she returned.

"She's adorable. I've never really been around babies much, not since my brothers were born."

Julie bent to flirt with Molly, and Molly's entire body convulsed with pleasure at her mother's attention. "You are pretty sweet, aren't you?"

"If you ever need someone to watch her, I'd be happy to."

"That's kind of you, Mary. Dan and I haven't been out alone since Molly was born. He works so much it's hard to plan." Julie's husband was someone Mary had only seen in passing and had never formally met. He worked at the grain elevator and his hours were long, especially during spring planting and now again at harvest. Mary had noticed that Julie was alone a lot with Molly.

"If you need to run errands or have some time to yourself, Julie, I'd be glad to come over for a few minutes." She knew she didn't want Molly in the parsonage. It wasn't a good place for a baby.

"That means a lot to me," Julie said. She nodded then toward the bowls of apple crisp she had set on the table. "Let's eat."

While they ate, Julie told Mary that she and Dan had only lived in Custer City for a year. They'd moved from Omaha when Dan was offered a job as assistant manager of the local grain co-op.

"I'm still getting adjusted," Julie said. "I miss movies the most. We never see new movies anymore." She smiled toward Molly then. "Now with Molly in the picture we probably wouldn't have been going out if we still lived in Omaha either, but it's nice to think you could if you wanted to." She looked at Mary. "What do you miss most since you moved here?"

"I miss the land," Mary said. She didn't go on to explain further as she saw Julie's puzzled expression.

The homesickness Mary had felt at Julie's house led her later that day to call her parents and invite them to come for dinner that weekend. Mary had seen little of them since the wedding. They always said they wanted to come get her to take her home for a long weekend, but she was so busy with the church that she never felt she could leave. The first time Mary had said this Fresia frowned. "You just tell those people you'll be gone. You don't need to be there at their beck and call all the time. That's the only way they're going to learn that you aren't their slave." Mary thought it was easy for her mother to play tough with the church people, but she didn't have to live among them, and she didn't have to endure Ward's disapproval.

Fresia accepted the dinner invitation, but Mary sensed she and John would dread it in some way. Only after Mary hung up the phone did her confidence fail her. Despite its yellow paint the kitchen of the parsonage was a dismal place, and she was no cook. What sort of meal could she put together out of the food allowance Ward gave her?

"I invited my folks to come for dinner on Friday night," she told Ward as they got ready for bed that night. "I checked the church calendar, and we didn't have anything going on."

"You should have asked me first, but if I don't have anything, I guess it's fine."

"I'm not sure what I'm going to make," Mary said, and Ward laughed. It was a joke between them that she really couldn't cook and hadn't cared enough to learn when she was growing up. Over the past few weeks, she had been gathering recipes from Fresia and Lydia, and studying the cookbook published by the Ladies Aid at the church. Still, there had been a few spectacular disasters in her attempts to learn. "Is there any way I could get a little extra for this week's grocery money so I could make something special?"

Ward grew quiet for a few minutes before making a little tsking sound that she knew meant he wasn't pleased, but he wasn't angry either. Finally he said, "I imagine we could do that."

"Oh, thank you, Ward."

Ward seemed to enjoy the effect of his gesture, and he chuckled again. "So now the big question is, what's for dinner?"

Mary worried all week about that question. Fresia and Lydia were expert cooks, and they would, without meaning to, expect the same of her. Her nervousness took her off guard, the first awareness of the need to perform for her family as an adult. In her life with Brian, there had never been an expectation of Mary keeping house, and it was a role she had never wanted for herself. Lydia had now and then tried to convince Mary to learn a few domestic skills, saying that someday she would wish she had paid attention, but Mary had never been interested. Mary figured this was the "someday" Lydia had been talking about. How quickly those regrets she had been warned about had started to accumulate in her life. Until now, Mary had thought she had all the time in the world.

She finally decided on a simple meal: a beef roast with potatoes, celery, carrots, and onions. She had called Lydia a couple times during the week to get the cooking time and the oven temperature right, and now, late Friday afternoon, the house was filled with the familiar smell of roasting meat. She had scrubbed every room in the parsonage, so she knew it was clean. Still, it defied any attempt at creating coziness. This would be the first time Cal and Lydia had seen the house, and Mary was determined that they not be shocked by it. She put the leaves in the dining room table, brought in extra chairs from the church basement, and pulled out for the first time the wedding china she and Ward had received from his mother and the silver they had received from his aunt and uncle. She took the crystal glasses from her marriage to Brian out of their boxes for the first time, and she ironed a linen tablecloth and napkins. Those gifts had seemed so frivolous to her at the time, but now she was grateful for them. She cut a few flowers from the front garden and put them in a cut-glass vase on the table.

Once the table had been set, and the house was filled with the smells of dinner, Mary felt it was as close to homey as she could make it. When Ward came home that evening he saw the table and took a step back. "This looks lovely, Mary." He sniffed the air. "Something smells good, too."

She was frosting the cake when her family arrived. She looked up to see them at the door, and her heart filled with happiness. They brought with them the smell of the ranch. She wanted to weep with joy; instead, she pulled off her apron and went to greet all of them with hugs. Her brothers quickly took off into the backyard. Fresia went into the kitchen to see what she could do to help finish the meal. John accepted a cup of coffee, and Ward herded him to the living room while Mary showed Cal and Lydia around the house.

Neither of her grandparents said much as they walked through the rooms of the house, Mary reminding them constantly to either step up or step down. Cal was a meticulous carpenter, and Mary knew he couldn't fathom how people had built something like this.

"Well," Cal said at last, "I'll be goddamned. Your mother told us this place was a dump, and I guess it is." Mary winced at his criticism. Already she had come to associate so closely with the parsonage that she felt she had to apologize for it, as though it was hers and not a place she had inherited with her marriage. Lydia, seeming to sense Mary's hurt, said, "Cal, you damn dummy, keep your opinions to yourself."

"I didn't mean no offense," Cal said to Lydia and then hugged Mary roughly to his side.

"None taken, Grandpa."

❋

Later, as they all sat down together at the table, Mary felt again that flush of pleasure she had felt upon first seeing her family at the door. "I'm so . . ." she started to say.

Ward, not hearing her, interrupted in what she thought of as his minister voice, "Mary and I are truly honored to have you in our home," he said, and paused meaningfully. "Shall we bow for prayer?" The festive mood around the table dissipated as everyone bowed their heads. Once Ward had finished, Mary found it impossible to express her feelings for her family naturally and instead began to pass the platters and bowls. When Ward attempted to direct the dinner conversation, playing his accustomed role as facilitator for church gatherings, John shifted in his seat at the end of the table, refusing to meet Ward's eyes. A few times Mary saw him actually clench his jaw while Ward was talking. Like her feelings of protectiveness toward the house, Mary felt herself now wanting to protect Ward from her family's judgment of him.

The food itself was better than Mary had hoped, and although the meal was by no means as good as a meal prepared by Lydia and Fresia, she knew they were sincere when they praised her efforts. When the women gathered in the kitchen to clean up afterward, Mary knew her father and Cal were suffering in the other room. She couldn't see them, but she knew by eavesdropping that Ward was talking about Custer City politics, something for which John and Cal had little interest. Ward was contemplating a run for city council, and she guessed he was talking about that. Mary felt Ward had been a little deformed by a job in which those around him were always eager to listen, quick to affirm whatever he said.

John's disapproval of Ward was still palpable, and he was incapable of overlooking Ward's foibles even for Mary's sake. He had never had to please anyone beyond family in the course of a day's work, and he didn't see that he might have to be flexible on some occasions. Already, four months into her marriage Mary wasn't sure who she was anymore. She guessed the circumstances of a life would always threaten to overwhelm what was most essential to a person.

≡CHAPTER 11

≡By November, the days had grown cold. The sun filtering through thick gray clouds cast a gaunt yellow light over the town. The wind howled around the parsonage, and no matter how many rags she stuffed under the windowsills, Mary could not keep out the drafts. She wore a thick sweater in the house, and when she sat down for any reason she wrapped herself in an afghan Lydia had crocheted.

Into this cold month came a weeklong revival meeting at the church. All week it rained, and both the church and the parsonage felt clammy and cold. The revival was an annual affair that required what had seemed like endless planning. This year's revival speaker, Joel Mason, had been a popular speaker a few years before and was everyone's first choice to invite back. He was a little person and something of a novelty in the revival circuit. Mary was named chair of the Revival Planning Committee, which meant she was responsible for lining up volunteers for their guest's accommodations and meals, as well as volunteers to bring snacks after each evening's meeting.

She had thought she was prepared to meet Joel Mason, but his appearance at first sight was so unsettling she felt herself gape at him. Despite being barely three feet tall, Joel Mason looked remarkably like Clark Gable, including a thin black mustache and thick dark hair he combed back from his face. He had high cheekbones and a strong jaw, lovely white teeth, and intense dark eyes. He was a handsome man, and when he stepped behind the podium and onto the stool he carried with him, it was easy to forget he was so small. His booming bass voice furthered the illusion, making all the more absurd his transformation as with great dignity he stepped off the stool and walked down the church aisle, first gathering his pretty "normal-sized" wife, Jeanette, and their three children, one "normal" and the other two clearly little people.

Joel Mason did not flinch from his condition. In fact, he played up the novelty of being a little person, and the week's theme was how God could work through small people. Each night his talk featured a biblical character who had done great things in spite of his or her smallness of faith or smallness of stature, as in the case of David challenging and defeating Goliath, or the story of Zacchaeus, who so desperately wanted to see Jesus passing by that he climbed up a sycamore tree.

Jeanette was elegant and quiet. On several occasions during that week Mary tried to start a conversation with her, but Mary's questions were either met with only a vacant smile or an answer so oblique Mary was left baffled.

"She's an excellent seamstress," Mary overheard Mabel Conroy say during the week.

"I've heard she makes all of Mr. Mason's suits." This from Bonnie Abel.

"I know for a fact she makes her own clothes and the kids' clothes, too," Viola Klydefelter said.

"They say," Mabel went on, "she can take anything, practically a rag, and turn it into a beautiful outfit, that's how talented she is." This conversation had taken place within earshot of Mary, and she felt sure it was a deliberate attempt to point up her deficiencies. Not only could she not sew, but by their standards she didn't dress well either. After they were married, Ward had let her know it wouldn't be appropriate for her to wear her ranch clothes unless she was working in the yard. She'd bought a few vintage dresses—the only ones she halfway liked—from the secondhand store to satisfy Ward, but she still didn't fit in.

Later in the week, she overheard yet another conversation, this one focused on Jeanette's great talents as a cook. In addition, Jeanette played the piano and sang, providing the special music during the week of the revival. She had taught the three children to sing in harmony, and they sang each evening too. The Custer City Church of Christ was crazy for Joel and Jeanette, but it seemed to Mary they expressed their appreciation for Jeanette especially vehemently, and she finally understood Jeanette Mason was their idea of a perfect minister's wife. Meanwhile, Mary increasingly saw her as a nodding, smiling, piano-playing automaton. "A brain-dead doll," she had finally commented in frustration to Julie one afternoon during the revival week. Julie had laughed gratifyingly.

On the final Sunday of the weeklong meetings, during the big potluck dinner in the church basement, Mary was so tired of the congregation, she sat with a table of visitors, women from the community she had never seen before. She was grateful to talk to someone new and lingered with them more than Ward would have liked, deliberately ignoring his attempts to catch her eye and remind her to move about more and share her time among the church members.

"He reminds me of Oscar. His perkiness, you know," one of the women was saying of Joel Mason.

The other women nodded. At Mary's look of confusion, the woman who had spoken explained, "Oscar's a fellow down at the nursing home—we all work there—a tiny fella, and in a bad way, poor old guy, but he's full of pi . . ." She stopped herself short of finishing her sentence.

"Piss and vinegar," Mary finished for her.

The woman laughed. "Yeah, piss and vinegar." She nodded toward

Mary as though deciding she was all right after all. "You've got to hand it to a guy who makes the best of being dealt a bad hand."

Mary listened as they went on to describe other residents at the rest home and couldn't help but laugh along at their descriptions of the residents' various antics for escape.

"You seem to like the elderly," a woman who'd introduced herself earlier as Mildred Weber finally said. "They're looking for a part-time nurse's assistant."

It hadn't occurred to Mary to look for a job in Custer City, nor would she have described herself as someone who particularly liked or disliked old people, but as soon as Mildred mentioned the job, Mary felt something stir in her. The idea of a little money of her own and a chance to get out of the house for something other than church events sounded good. "I don't have any sort of training," she said finally.

"You don't need any. They'll train you," Mildred said. "It doesn't pay a lot, but it's decent enough work. Think about it. If you're interested, I'll put in a word for you with the Theresa, the head nurse."

Mary needed no more time to think about it, but if she'd learned nothing else since living with Ward, it was to talk to him before making a decision.

❋

As she waited for that long day of a very long week to end, Mary found herself returning again and again to the idea of working at the nursing home. By the time Ward got home after the last person had left the church that evening, Mary was almost giddy with excitement. Perhaps because of it she blurted out more forcefully than she'd intended to that she'd like to do a bit of part-time work.

"Work?" Ward seemed puzzled. "What would people think?"

"Why would anyone care? Besides, if they didn't want me to work, they could pay you better." It was the first time Mary had criticized Ward's paycheck, and she caught her breath slightly after she'd said it.

Ward bristled. "The church isn't in a position to pay me more than they do, I've told you that."

They didn't talk again about the job until later that night as they were getting ready for bed when Mary surprised herself by saying, "Ward, I want that job. I'm going down there tomorrow to apply."

Ward was quiet for a few seconds before saying, "You won't be able to do it. Not with your leg."

"What do you mean?" she said, startled by his dismissive judgment. "Why couldn't I?" She decided to retreat from her combative stance and said with a laugh, "I get around all right on old Peggy."

Ward shrugged. "You'll fail, but you might as well get it out of your system."

Mary tightened her jaw and clamped her mouth shut. She wasn't going to give Ward the satisfaction of a fight.

The next morning Mary called Mildred Weber and told her she would be interested in the job. Mildred must have gone immediately to the head nurse, for within only a few minutes Mary received a call from a Theresa O'Gorman asking her to come in for an interview.

That afternoon, Mary put on her best dress and walked the four blocks in the cold to the nursing home. She felt exhilarated on that walk as she imagined the possibility of having somewhere to be every day, invigorated by the wind and the cold. The gray houses under the gray sky on the gray prairie did not feel like reason to despair like they had only days before. Custer City was simply a place, and for the first time since moving there Mary felt as though she might have a role in this town, some purpose of her own.

As soon as she opened the large glass door at the front of the nursing home, she was greeted by a blast of overheated air. The smell was peculiar, on the surface a sickly sweet disinfectant, and beneath it a putrid odor, thick and foul. She had brought in with her some of the fresh cold air from outdoors, and she breathed the last of it before stepping inside.

Several residents loitered near the front door, and as Mary stood for a moment in the entryway, one elderly woman attempted to slip out of the still-closing door. Fast behind, a tall, slender, dark-haired woman cruised past Mary and confronted the elderly woman.

"Elma, for the love of God. What are you thinking? You know you can't go out by yourself. Do you want to get arrested?"

Mary must have looked startled at the idea, for the dark-haired woman now winked at Mary. To Elma, she said, "Come on. Get back inside here." The young woman adeptly steered Elma away from the door and back into the building.

Once Elma was safely delivered into one of the green vinyl–covered chairs in the lounge area just inside the front door, the young woman returned to Mary. Mary saw then she was a beautiful woman, perhaps the most beautiful woman she had ever seen.

"I'm Claire Rowe. You must be Mary Hamilton." Mary nodded faintly. "We've been watching for you. Come with me."

Mary followed Claire down a corridor, passing rooms along the way with residents in various resigned postures, some laying on beds, obviously unable to move on their own, others strapped into wheelchairs, still others shuffling around aimlessly.

"Have you done this work before?"

"No," Mary said, suddenly unsure if she could possibly stand another minute in this horrifying place.

As though guessing what Mary was thinking, Claire laughed softly before stopping in front of a nurses' station in the middle of the building. "It isn't as bad as it looks at first. You get used to it, and believe it or not, you start to actually like some of these old farts. Hey, Theresa," she shouted then. "Your fresh meat's here."

At this, a short, overweight woman wearing a snug nurse's uniform and round, dark-rimmed glasses, her dark hair cropped in a square around her face, came from inside a back room. "This is the little tyrant," Claire said to Mary by way of introduction.

"And don't you ever forget it," Theresa said without a smile. Mary was unsure if they were joking or not. A call light came on behind the large U-shaped desk, and Claire left without excusing herself.

"She's a pain in the ass," Theresa said, turning to go back into the room from which she had come, beckoning for Mary to follow, "but she's one of the best goddamned nurses I've ever had."

Mary was so taken aback by Theresa's language she stopped short. What sort of place was this? It was as different an environment from the church as she could imagine, and Mary revised her impressions of Custer City, all shaped by her limited contact with the church members, as a prissy place. She was still processing the possibility of other lives in this town when Theresa poked her head out the door. "You coming?"

Inside the office, Theresa closed the door and sat down behind a desk while Mary sat in a turquoise plastic chair across from her. "Mildred says you need some part-time work."

"Yes."

"You ever done anything like this before?"

"No."

"That all you ever say? Yes, no?"

"I don't know what else to say."

Theresa smiled. "I'm just jerking your chain. You'll have to lighten up if you're going to be working here. You can't take yourself seriously or you'll never last. You think you can do that?"

"Do what?"

"Not take yourself too seriously?" Theresa said, rolling her eyes.

"I suppose so."

Theresa shook her head. "Oh, Jesus. I have a bad feeling about this, but we needed someone yesterday, and you're at least a warm body, if a stiff one, so I'm going to have to take a chance on you. If you burn yourself out, well, what am I supposed to do? The thing is, I need asses to be wiped, and mouths to be fed, and bodies to be turned. It's that simple. We don't have enough hands." She seemed to be talking to herself, and Mary sat quietly, waiting for her to finally give her verdict, which she now did. "So, are you in, or not?"

"Sure. What time do you need me?"

"Like I said, I needed you yesterday. Can you start tomorrow? Come every Tuesday, Thursday, and Saturday?"

"Yes. What do I need? Do I need a uniform?"

"We'll get one for you. Don't worry about that. Shoes too, and hose. We'll get you all fixed up. Just talk to Mildred sitting out at the desk in front here. She'll get your sizes, and everything will be here when you come tomorrow. You'll start at 7:00 AM, but come a little early so you can get into your uniform. Our board doesn't believe in making nurse's aides go into debt over uniforms. They're real humane that way." The way Theresa said this suggested that she thought the board was anything but humane, and Mary didn't know what to make of that inference since she was relieved not to have to buy a uniform she couldn't afford.

"Can you find your own way out?"

"I think so."

"That's good. Just so you know, half our residents can't get out of bed on their own, and the other half we have to tie down so they don't run away. All in all, there aren't that many of them that can actually walk around. It's a funny kind of business but you'll get used to it."

Mary nodded. When Theresa suddenly stood up, she realized the interview was over, and just that quickly she had been hired. "We'll see you tomorrow."

Mary stopped by the desk where Mildred was waiting with a smile to take her sizes for the uniform.

On her way out, Mary ran into Claire again. "So, did she beg you to come?"

"She didn't have to."

"When do you start?"

"Tomorrow."

"I'll see you then. Go home and practice breathing through your mouth."

The cold air greeted Mary with a rush as she left the building. For a few seconds she wondered if she had actually been inside, if she had really been hired. It all felt slightly unreal to her. As if to convince herself, she turned around to look back at the building from which she had just emerged. There, standing in the entryway, Elma was waiting for her next opportunity to escape. She looked straight at Mary with blank eyes, and Mary lifted her hand in a wave. Elma didn't respond. She seemed to be living in a parallel world, seeing someone other than Mary, and waiting to leave for a long-overdue appointment. Mary felt a rush of some new emotion as she found herself trying to empathize with Elma's confusion.

CHAPTER 12

≡"What's the occasion?" Ward asked as he hung his coat that night when he came home. Mary was putting a pie into the oven. A pot of beef stew bubbled on the stove.

She closed the oven door and stood up. "I got the job."

"So we're celebrating?"

"I hope this piecrust turns out. I've never made one before."

"When do you start?"

"Tomorrow."

"So soon?"

Mary laughed. "I think they're desperate."

"Do they know about . . . ?" Ward gestured toward her leg.

"I'm sure they noticed, Ward," she said. "Just let it go, will you?" She could tell he didn't like the idea of her working any more than he had the night before, but she was resolved to ignore his disapproval.

Later, as they ate the apple pie, its crust overworked and a bit chewy, Mary said, "Do you suppose I should think about going to nursing school?"

"No point thinking so far ahead."

"But what if I like nursing? Is there a place nearby where I could study?"

Ward frowned. "The nearest place is probably Kearney. That'd be a long drive for you." He didn't add what he must have been thinking—that it was a long way for someone who didn't drive.

After Ward retreated to his study, Mary sat in the living room and looked out the window at the street where she lived. The grayness of Custer City had closed in upon her again. In the glow of the pale streetlight she saw it had started to snow. As the wind howled and the windows shuddered, Mary pulled the afghan closer about her. She wondered as she had never wondered before what her life would have been like if she had been born somewhere else. Even in one of the families from town. Her parents had never encouraged her to go to college, nor did she recall her teachers mentioning it, save one, a history teacher who several times had told Mary she could do better with her life than she seemed destined to do. Mary had always made it clear to everyone who knew her that she wanted only one thing, to be a rancher. She recalled now that she had felt at the time her teacher was being critical of her. She hadn't seen it as encouragement. She was a girl who loved horses, a girl who loved her freedom, a girl who had never thought that she could possibly end up as she had.

❄

The next morning Mary woke up before dawn. She felt the familiar awakening to work. Going somewhere with purpose energized her. She dressed in the dark, not wanting to disturb Ward who would sleep for another couple hours. She ate a quick breakfast and then set out for the nursing home.

It had snowed several inches in the night, and she walked through the dark, quiet streets, hers the first footprints in the snow. It felt good to be alone in the early morning, to feel the peculiar hush after a storm, to see everything that had been dull and gray before now pristine with the coat of new snow.

Claire was there to let her in when she arrived. Mary's high spirits were checked when she saw Claire did not welcome her good mood.

"I'll show you where to find your uniform," Claire said without a greeting as she set off down the brightly lit hall. If the world outside was still sleeping, the nursing home was abuzz with lights and noise. As she passed the cafeteria, Mary could hear dishes and pots clanging and kitchen workers talking above the sound of running water. The tables were already set for breakfast and a few residents had been parked in their chairs where they now sat, their heads drooping onto their chests, waiting for the food to appear.

Theresa was at the nurses' station. Unlike Claire, she was cheerful. She seemed genuinely surprised to see Mary, though. "Good morning. I thought maybe you wouldn't show up after seeing this place yesterday." She left no time for Mary to respond as she pointed toward a new uniform. "Go on. Get dressed, and we'll get you started here."

When Mary returned from the bathroom wearing her uniform and carrying in her arms her street clothes, Theresa and Claire were standing together in Theresa's office. Mary saw them through the office window, and although she could not hear their conversation, she could see they were arguing.

When she left Theresa's office, Claire noticed Mary standing behind the counter, still holding the clothes she had worn that morning. Without stopping, she said, "Just leave your stuff under the counter and come with me."

Mary hurried behind the counter, left her things, and ran to catch up with Claire who was already halfway down the hall. Mary caught her just as she entered one of the rooms.

"Walter, you old monster, how are you this morning?" Claire was saying as Mary joined her. On the bed was a man clearly missing a leg. Mary recognized immediately Walter was one of the residents Mildred and the other women had been talking about that night of the revival meeting. He was propped up in his bed now, his stump exposed. He didn't look at Mary as she entered the room. Instead, his bright, cold eyes were fixed on Claire who was bending to help lift him into a wheelchair.

"Goddamn you, you bitch," he said.

"Top of the world to you, too, Walter," Claire said as she continued to lift him.

"I don't want to eat with all those slobbering imbeciles," he said. "Makes me want to puke watching them drool all over themselves."

"Too bad. You're going."

Walter did nothing to cooperate with Claire, but despite this she easily lifted him into the chair. Mary marveled at Claire's strength and persistence. She didn't think she could have managed him so well.

Walter decided to acknowledge Mary's presence. "Who the hell are you?"

"I'm Mary."

Walter looked her up and down slowly, and Mary felt mortified by his gaze. "You're a gimp, too," he finally said. Mary laughed nervously. "How'd it happen?" Walter asked.

"Car accident."

He nodded. "Tractor fell on me. Laid under the sonuvabitch for five hours before anyone found me." He smiled suddenly. "So are you a nice woman or a bitch?"

"I'm . . ." Mary started.

"She's a bitch, Walter," Claire interrupted. "We're all bitches. She isn't going to cooperate with your little schemes, so don't go getting your hopes up."

"She's a gimp, ain't she?"

"It isn't a club she wants to join, Walter."

Walter didn't answer and Mary silently followed Claire as she pushed his chair out of the room and into the cafeteria. After he had been pushed up to the one of the tables, Mary followed Claire out of the room.

Once they were away from the cafeteria, Claire burst into laughter. "That old bugger is the only reason I can face this job every morning." Claire went on to explain. "He's a scoundrel, an absolute scoundrel, and I love him for it. He's always scamming for someone to bring him whiskey. He won't socialize with the other residents—and who can blame him—they're zombies. Someone keeps bringing him booze. I'd do it for him in a heartbeat, except the poor guy's a hopeless diabetic. That's how he lost his leg. He was lying about the tractor." She laughed again. "When I tell him I won't bring him his booze because of his diabetes, he tells me, 'what am I saving my health for?' Sometimes I have to admit, it's a good question. It's hard to say no to Walter." She glanced at Mary then. "You won't have any trouble with that, though, will you?"

"I wouldn't bring him whiskey, if that's what you're asking."

"That's only part of it. He wants you to bring him sweets too. Candy, cake, pie. He loves it all. And it's poison to him."

"If it's against the rules, I wouldn't do it," Mary said.

Claire stepped back a bit and took a long view of Mary. "You're a real rule person, aren't you?"

"I suppose I haven't thought about it."

"That's what I mean."

Mary felt herself bristle. "If breaking the rules hurts someone, then yes, I suppose I'm a rule person."

Claire waved Mary's comment away. "I didn't mean to get your back up. It's not the worst thing to be someone who goes by the rules. I'm not saying that. It's just, well, look at you, the minister's wife, right? You're a good girl down to your toes." Mary wasn't about to discuss her life with Claire and didn't respond. "Come on, we need to get Jessie up and get her out to breakfast," Claire said.

Throughout the morning, as Mary followed Claire on what she called the breakfast rounds, she admired how adept Claire was at shifting registers from patient to patient. She seemed to know exactly what each person needed to get motivated and out of his or her room. With Jessie, she was firm and motherly, with Kathryn gentle and polite, with Oscar, teasing. Mary had concluded by 8:30 AM as they were returning the residents to their rooms that as Theresa had said, Claire really was an exceptional nurse.

"You're really good at this."

"Don't tell Theresa. I wouldn't want her getting any ideas and giving me a raise."

"How long have you worked here?" Mary asked.

"Four years. Since I graduated from nursing school."

"Did you go to Custer City High?"

"Yep. Crusty City. My dear old alma mater. You?"

"Anselmo-Merna."

"Oh yeah? You one of those ranch kids from up there?"

Mary nodded.

"That explains a lot."

"What do you mean by that?"

"Hey, I don't mean to rile you. I seem to be doing that a lot this morning. It's just that you're different, that's all."

"Maybe it's you who's different."

Claire laughed at this. "I'm glad to see a little spunk from you, but it's too early in the morning for me to be laughing, okay? I've got a hell of a hangover, so you'll forgive me if I'm off my game a bit. I'll get nicer by this afternoon."

"Right," Mary said, surprising herself with her sarcasm.

Claire laughed. "I think there's hope for you, Mary Hamilton," she said with the first genuine smile Mary had seen from her. "I think we might even become friends."

By lunchtime, Claire and Mary had spent enough time together to have fallen into a rhythm. Mary pitched in to get residents into the cafeteria for lunch. When she later saw Claire stop by to talk to Theresa, it was obvious they were discussing her, and based on their smiles, Mary could tell they were pleased with her work.

"Let's go eat," Claire said after she'd returned from Theresa's office.

The cafeteria staff served them with a grumpy good humor, Claire teasing everyone along the way.

"Did you notice the guy washing dishes in the back?" Claire asked as they set down their trays. To Mary's nod, Claire continued, "What I wouldn't give to get in his pants." Mary glanced into the cafeteria again and noticed that even with his hair tucked under a silly white kerchief, he was a handsome young man. "He's just here for a few weeks, staying with his folks before he starts law school second semester." Claire shook her head and took a drink of cranberry juice. "This town is in short supply of hot guys. Have you noticed that?" Mary shook her head. "You're kidding," Claire said. Mary shook her head again.

"God, you've got to quit being Little Bo Peep. Don't you ever get horny?" Mary felt herself blush. "Don't tell me even if you're married you don't notice other guys," Claire said without waiting for an answer. "I don't buy it."

Mary was tempted by Claire's challenge to tell her everything about Ward, about how much she still missed Brian, but she didn't know Claire, and she'd already seen how quickly word spread in Custer City. There wasn't a thing she had done or said that hadn't gotten back to the church people. They'd expressed their disapproval of the new curtains she'd hung in the living room ("spending money like that") or visiting too much with Julie ("she's a Methodist, you know") or taking long walks alone around town ("it isn't seemly wandering like that") or going to the sale barn ("if you have time for that, you have time to take an extra turn cleaning the church"). Claire could think whatever she wanted to. Mary knew her life was on public display, and it had created a new guardedness in her.

"I love sex myself," Claire went on undisturbed by Mary's silence. "I don't think I'm a nympho or anything. I don't like that designation anyway, do you? If men like sex they're just considered normal, but let a woman say she likes sex and suddenly there's something wrong with her. I don't subscribe to things like that, and I don't let anybody else tell me what I'm doing is wrong." She glanced at Mary. "How is it being married to a minister?"

Mary's mouth was full, and she used that as an excuse not to answer immediately. She swallowed finally and shrugged, slightly overwhelmed by Claire's personality.

Claire shook her head again. "You going to keep this up for long, this mute thing? Because I'm going to hate working with you if you do."

"I'm sorry," Mary said. "It's just that I'm not used to people asking me questions like that. I'm not comfortable answering them right now, not without knowing you better."

Claire laughed. "There's not much to know about me, and you'll figure that out quick enough. I like to have a good time. I work here to pay the bills and because no one expects me to give up my soul to this place. Hell, most of the time nobody notices if I'm awake or not. So, it's good for that. The morning shift is the shits, though, and Theresa pulls that on me all the time, likes to make me suffer. That's the only thing that causes me grief here. Otherwise, I like these poor old suckers. They aren't hurting anybody, and I try to make them a little more comfortable."

By the end of their conversation that day, Mary had learned Claire adopted and then abandoned beliefs in the same way she did men, the way other women changed their wardrobe to reflect a new style. She had in the past been a Buddhist, a Christian Scientist, and a pagan. She had believed in the *I Ching*, tarot cards, the power of pyramids, and the Tao all to the same degree. At one point in their conversation she said, "No matter what else I am, I'm a hedonist, basically." Mary had to look up the word hedonist later in the dictionary in Ward's office.

By the time she left the rest home at three that first day, Mary was exhausted, but she felt satisfied, too. Claire had stuck with her the entire day, and some of her earlier testiness had given way to a more comradely silence. Mary sensed that Claire felt she had to perform her toughness, and that with time they would become more companionable. Now as they walked out the door together, Claire asked what she had planned for the evening.

"I'm going to go home and start making supper," Mary said. "What about you?"

"I'm taking a nap. That's the first thing. Then I'll head out to the Sage Brush to dance a little and meet some friends."

Mary wasn't watching later as she turned onto her block and so didn't see Kent Needham sitting in a green Ford pickup in front of her house until he hollered at her.

"What are you doing here?"

"I'm working in town now. Thought I'd stop by and say hello. I was just getting ready to leave you a note."

"I can't believe it. You're not on the ranch?" Kent shook his head. "Come on in and give me all the details."

Kent looked at his watch. "I have some time before I have to get back."

Though neither spoke of it, Kent could not hide his troubled expression at seeing inside the parsonage.

When they were settled at the kitchen table, Mary said, "Gus actually let you leave the ranch?"

Kent shrugged. "Larry can stay around there if he wants to, but I had to get out. Had a chance to buy in over here at Treegers, and I did. Dad and Mom weren't too happy, I'll guarantee you of that, but I decided that was their problem."

"Good for you," Mary said as she finished making a pot of coffee. The last she had heard from the Needhams was right before she married Ward when she had received a note from Iris.

"Dear Mary," the note had said, "I've just heard a rumor that you're getting married again. I was shocked by the news. I can't help but feel you've moved on too quickly. It makes me think maybe you never really loved Brian after all."

For some reason, most likely related to her reason for keeping the dark note she'd received from Mrs. Klein when she was in the hospital, Mary had kept Iris's letter. She wondered now as she looked at her former brother-in-law across the kitchen table if she didn't have a perverse wish to be scolded.

"So tell me about Treegers."

Mary noticed how Kent's eyes brightened as he began to talk about his work. "We're bringing in cattle from as far away as Canada, Texas, and Mexico in cheap lots. We use every new technology we have for feeding out fast—high-protein additives, work with the packing plants direct."

"I still can't quite see you off the ranch."

"I couldn't either, but things are changing. It isn't enough to just work hard anymore. You have to work smart. Dad thinks I'm a fool for getting involved in it, but I tell you, Mary, I have a good feeling. I couldn't've stay on the ranch, not the way it was. Dad can't let anything go, and he's only getting worse. Has to make all the decisions, and frankly some of them aren't all that smart anymore. He just refinanced to buy a new combine. He's already in debt up to his eyeballs and still keeps buying what the bankers tell him . . . Oh well. I don't need to be telling you any of this."

"You have good partners where you are?"

"The best. Paul and Walt Treeger. Their dad owned several hundred acres out here west of town. That's where we're developing the feedlots."

They were both quiet for a few minutes. "I'm really glad you stopped by, Kent. I've missed all of you."

Kent suddenly seemed uncomfortable. "How're you doing?" he said. "Are you doing okay, Mary?"

"I'm fine," she said, hearing something forced in her own voice. She looked away. Outside the kitchen window, the bare branches of the little hawthorn tree were covered with snow. The squalid backyard was now mercifully masked under the snow. With Berl's help she had drawn on graph paper a plan for a backyard garden. There wasn't anything there yet to indicate those plans, but she was itching for spring when they would start flower beds and make walkways and plant trees and bushes. She turned back to Kent. He was waiting. "I suppose I don't ask myself such questions," she finally said and then smiled. "I just started a new job today." She pointed to the paper bag by the front door. My new uniform's in there. I'm a nurse's aide at the rest home."

Kent laughed in spite of himself. "I'm having something of a hard time picturing you taking care of a bunch of old people, Mary."

Mary laughed too. "It's a far cry from what I figured I'd be doing."

Kent grew sober. "I bet you'll be terrific at it, but I came here hoping maybe I could talk you into coming to work for us at Treegers when we get our feet under us."

"Doing what?"

"What you do better than anyone I know—judge cattle. We'll need good pickers to sort the herd for the packers. There's an art to that."

Mary nodded. "I'd really like that. Let me know when you're ready. It feels good having something to do. I was getting pretty cooped up in this place."

"You finding some friends here in town?"

Mary shrugged. "A few possibilities, but no real friends yet."

"Your new husband?" Kent's voice caught a bit on the word husband. "He's a minister, we hear."

"Yes."

"That makes you a minister's wife."

Mary laughed. "I guess it does. I'm full of surprises these days."

Kent shook his head. "Who would have figured."

"Not me."

"You okay, really, Mary? Are you?"

Mary bit her bottom lip, startled by the sudden pressure of tears. She leaned her head back and blinked them away. "Oh, Kent, please quit asking me things like that."

"I'm sorry, Mary. I didn't mean to push."

"It's not you. I'm not up to answering that kind of question. I'm how I am. That's all."

"Sure. That's all right," Kent said.

"You ready for that cup of coffee?" Mary jumped up from the table, glad to change the subject.

They talked the rest of the hour about the other boys. Jeffrey was planning to go to Colorado to veterinary school. Billy would graduate from high school the following year. Larry seemed stuck on the ranch while Gus continued to fail and Iris played the role of placater.

After his second cup of coffee, Kent pushed back his chair from the table. "It's been a real pleasure catching up with you, Mary, but I need to get going. I've already taken more of a break than I expected."

"Would you like to meet Ward? He'll be home soon. You're welcome to stay for supper."

"You cooking?" Kent asked with a laugh. Then, before she could respond, he looked down quickly, and said, "No offense, Mary, but I don't think I'm ready to meet him just yet. I'm not saying I wouldn't want to one of these days, but not right now."

"I understand."

As she let him out the door, Mary saw the snow that had accumulated that morning had begun to melt through the afternoon. Now as the sky grew dark and the temperatures fell again, the slush had started to freeze.

"It's a nasty old day," Kent said as he headed toward his truck. "Makes me glad to have a job that keeps me mostly inside. You ever miss the ranch, Mary?"

"Every single day," she said. "There isn't a day I wouldn't rather be on the ranch."

Kent nodded. "I kind of thought you might say that. You always were the real cowboy. We all knew that. Even Dad. He'd never have told you, of course."

Mary watched from the porch as his truck disappeared down the street. Already the streetlights had started to come on. She felt a little let down when she lost sight of Kent's truck, but as she walked back inside she noticed the bag holding her uniform sitting by the front door. She'd wash the uniform this evening so it'd be ready to wear again the day after next. Maybe the job wasn't much by other people's standards, even by her own standards from the past, but it was more than she'd had a week ago.

≡CHAPTER 13

≡Christmas music played softly through the intercom system of the nursing home. In the corner, white lights blinked on an artificial Christmas tree. Outside, a string of colored lights hung across the window of the snowy courtyard. The wind blew them so they tapped against the glass, making Mary feel colder than she actually was. It was the week before Christmas and Mary and Claire were sitting together in the empty cafeteria drinking weak coffee. A few minutes earlier, Norma, one of the residents, had wheeled herself over to their table. Her fine white hair stood on end, and her red-rimmed eyes roved the room wildly. Finally, her gaze had locked on Mary, and she seized Mary's arm hard in her bony hand. "Call the sheriff," Norma had said urgently. "He needs to get me out of here."

Claire had gotten out of her chair and gently peeled Norma's fingers away from Mary's arm. "Norma, we'll call the sheriff right away, but you need to relax and wait now." Claire wheeled her across the room. "Get me out of here," Norma said again. "Get me out of here." Claire had nodded and stroked Norma's hair until she calmed down.

For the past week, Claire had been avoiding the cafeteria as much as possible, not wanting to see the guy she'd had her eye on Mary's first day. She'd gotten what she wanted from him, and now she was ready to move on, but he was stuck on her. He was even talking about putting off law school for another semester and wanted Claire to move with him to Lincoln in the summer.

"I don't know what I'm going to do about that loser Jeremy. He's driving me crazy." Claire shook her head and rolled her eyes before taking another sip of coffee. She came to work without much concern for her appearance. The polyester nurse's uniform didn't flatter anyone's figure, her hair was barely combed most days, yet it was obvious she had all the attributes most men would find attractive. Mary was quiet as she waited for Claire to continue, but Claire grew quiet too.

They sat in companionable silence watching now as Jim, the maintenance man, swept haphazardly around the room with his big rag mop. He was an odd man, someone Mary would never have guessed lived in Custer City, someone who might have frightened her a little if she hadn't known him. Claire had told Mary to be careful not to make any sudden moves or loud noises around him. "He's shell-shocked," she had explained. "Cracked up in Vietnam. That place ruined him." Claire described how once when a stack of chairs had toppled, making a tremendous racket, they'd found Jim cowering under one of the cafeteria tables. "Poor guy. He was freaked out, and there was nothing we could do to help him. Theresa finally had to crawl under the table and talk him out."

Mary watched Jim now out of the corner of her eye. He was a large man, made soft over the years. His skin was gray and saggy. He wouldn't meet anyone's eyes, and he moved silently among the residents and the staff like a ghost. No one bothered him here. He seemed not to notice her and Claire, even as he swept around them.

"How you doing, Jim?" Claire said.

Jim grunted without looking up.

Claire waited until he had moved on to ask, "What are you doing for Christmas, Mary?"

"We're going to visit Ward's mother in Indiana."

"You driving?"

"Yeah."

"Do you like his mother?"

"I don't really know her." Mary didn't go on to say her heart was breaking to have to be away from her family, that she felt homesick even thinking about that long car trip with Ward, let alone spending all of Christmas with only his mother. She glanced at her watch and took a quick sip of coffee. "I've got to get going," she said then. "I promised Julie I'd watch Molly this evening."

Mary had recently asked Theresa about increasing her hours. She was finding a social life here among what she thought of as Custer City's castoffs. She felt she fit with them better than she would ever fit with the church members. The good thing about the job was that it didn't contradict what was appropriate for her. By taking care of the elderly, she had found a job above reproach, perhaps the only job besides teaching elementary school children or being a nurse at the hospital that silenced the criticism of the church members. Ward still didn't approve, but Mary had been firm in her refusal to discuss it. She worked harder than ever to be sure she fulfilled all of her obligations for the church so there'd be nothing to criticize.

As she walked home, Mary thought about the dark, empty parsonage. She couldn't face it. Not yet anyway. Ward was at a funeral in Callaway and wouldn't be home until late. By the time she reached the back door, she was so averse to entering that she instead headed straight for the church. There, in the darkening light of late afternoon, she felt immediately at peace. She had been negligent of her piano lessons lately. That's what she told herself as she approached the piano. She'd just play through this week's pieces and then be out of there. As soon as she laid her hands on the keys, though, she felt a surge of excitement. The doors were closed. Ward was nowhere nearby. No one else was within earshot. She could play as she wished.

Her hands crashed onto the keys in a huge breaking chord. From there she rolled off in both directions, feeling the clash of emotions inside her brought into sound. She felt herself start to breathe easier as she played, and with the expression of each chord some stricture on her chest seemed to loosen. She hadn't realized she was crying until a tear splashed onto one of the keys and startled her out of her reverie. She stopped suddenly. The tumultuous sounds she had made reverberated across the sanctuary as she lifted her hands from the keys. How long had she been playing? She checked her watch and was shocked to discover she had been playing for an hour. It didn't leave her much time to get out of her uniform and over to Julie's house, but she felt cleansed by the experience, tired but rejuvenated.

She ran to the parsonage and stumbled out of her uniform and into a pair of jeans and a sweater. She wasn't hungry, felt a little queasy in fact, as she headed next door to Julie's house.

After Julie had left and Mary was watching Molly crawl about among her toys on the living room floor, she was startled by more tears. She hadn't been able to tell anyone about how unhappy she was. Who would care if she was unhappy? She was being self-indulgent to think only of herself, and with each wave of despair she upbraided herself harshly for acting like a child.

❋

The next day the car was loaded, and Ward was waiting on her to finish wrapping one last present before they took off. He was excited, she could see, to be going home, and she felt a twinge of guilt for her dread of the week. She had packed things for lunch and supper since they planned to make it in one day to Bloomington. She had only been as far east as Omaha, and the drive through Missouri, Illinois, and Indiana interested her. From what Ward had told her, it was a very different place from the Sandhills.

Already by the time they had reached Missouri, she was seeing the difference. Trees everywhere. She tried to picture all of it in summer when the trees would be in full leaf. She thought she might not like it then, for even now without the foliage she felt hemmed in by the view, a little claustrophobic not being able to see to the far horizon.

They had planned to arrive at Mother Hamilton's house at around eight that evening, but midway through Illinois the car ran out of gas on the interstate. An hour before it happened, Mary had noticed the gas gauge was running low.

She asked about it, but Ward didn't respond. As they came upon a gas station, he glanced at the marquee and kept going. Only when they had passed did he say, "We'll find it cheaper ahead."

He said this again and again as they passed station after station. And while it seemed there were many gas stations along the way, time was passing and Mary grew increasingly conscious of the dropping needle of the gas gauge and the raw cold outside. Her suggestions finally gave way to commands, all of which Ward calmly ignored. He assured her he knew the road, and of course he did. She regretted her nagging, only to begin again as he passed yet another gas pump.

"Mary," Ward finally said, "we'll be fine. Trust me. You don't need to worry."

She was chastened and had finally settled back into her seat when the car started to sputter. Ward kept the car going for another mile before finally pulling onto the shoulder and flipping on the emergency flashers.

"Ward!" she said, meaning, how could you? What were you thinking?

Ward didn't seem concerned, which made her own anger seem childish, hysterical even.

"It'll be all right," Ward said again, pulling his coat from the back seat. "We'll flag down a trucker. There's another station just ahead."

Mary wanted to say something in response to this, but she

didn't know what. Are you crazy? came to mind. Is it just me? Who are you? But his calm demeanor as he slipped on his gloves silenced such criticisms.

"You want to come along or wait?"

Mary couldn't bear to wait alone in the car as evening began to fall; she reached for her own coat and followed Ward out into the cold. They waited longer than Ward had anticipated by the side of the road.

"It doesn't usually take this long," he said at one point.

"This has happened before?"

"A few times."

Finally, a trucker out of Hanover, Kansas, stopped for them. "Do you know what's wrong?" the trucker asked after Ward and Mary had crawled into the cab.

Mary noticed Ward didn't answer. The driver noticed it, too. He looked at Ward and past him to Mary before turning his attention back to the road.

"I'll have to drop you here," he said as he turned into a Texaco station. "Someone'll get you back to your car." He looked at Mary again with that same puzzled expression. He was an older man. He'd told them he had a family. She thought he looked at her the way her father would have if he'd found her in this situation. She was pretty sure she was never going to tell her father this story.

The wait for a ride back to the car turned out to also be longer than Ward had expected. The man running the place was nice.

"I'm alone tonight," he said, "or I'd take you back myself."

He pulled out two stools from a back room so they'd have a place to sit while they waited, and he'd taken it upon himself to ask customers if they could give Mary and Ward a lift back to their car. Mary watched as patrons slowly turned to look at them in their predicament. Person after person shook their head no to helping them. She and Ward didn't talk about what had happened. Instead, as if wanting to keep up her spirits, Ward told her about Bloomington. He was in the middle of a story about how in the winter all the neighborhood kids gathered with their sleds at one steep hill unofficially designated for sledding when another trucker offered to take them to their car.

Ward stood up and shook the man's hand then introduced Mary. Unlike the previous trucker who had reminded her of her father, this man was of a distinctly different cast. His eyes roved quickly up and down Mary's body. She felt his gaze viscerally. She was relieved Ward was there, but if he noticed the man's interest in her, he gave no indication of it, continuing to talk blithely as they headed for the truck.

The trucker opened the passenger-side door and gestured for Mary to get in first. She hung back, hoping Ward would take the hint.

"Go on up, Mary," Ward said, holding the gas can they'd borrowed at his side.

"I'd rather . . . ," she started.

"Go on, honey. Don't be so timid."

In the end, she sat in the middle but kept herself as far from the trucker as she could, all the while feeling his eyes on her and now and then how he accidentally let his hand brush her leg.

❈

After they had returned the gas can and filled the tank, they drove for a few more hours before Ward pulled into a rest stop. "I'm so sleepy, Mary," he said. "I've got to take a little break here." He looked at her and hesitated before asking, "I don't suppose there's any way you could try to drive?"

Mary hadn't driven for almost three years. "I don't know," she said, her palms suddenly damp. "I suppose I could try."

"Good girl," Ward said. "The traffic isn't too bad right now. This might not be the worst time to get back into the swing of it."

Mary found his remark a bit glib, but she compliantly opened her car door. She needed to get over this silliness, and this was as good a time as any. She was determined to succeed as she slid behind the steering wheel and waited for Ward to get into the passenger side.

Once he had buckled his seat belt, she laid her hands on the steering wheel. She took a deep breath and turned the key. At the same time she felt the engine catch, she heard a bone-crushing noise. Her hands flew off the steering wheel. Stricken, she looked toward Ward who returned her glance with a look of confusion.

"What is it, Mary?"

"That noise. What was that terrible noise?" Her heart raced, and she felt herself breathing rapidly.

"There was no noise."

"Yes there was."

Ward didn't say anything for a few seconds. "Believe me, Mary," he finally said. "There was no noise."

She hesitated before raising her hands again to the steering wheel. Once more, as soon as the engine caught, she heard the loud, metallic sound. This time, she didn't say anything to Ward. She simply got out and waited by the passenger side.

"I can't do it," she said after Ward opened his door with a puzzled expression. "I'm sorry."

He didn't try to cajole her into trying again, nor did he ask her what had happened. In fact, he seemed undisturbed as he got out of the car, saying only that he needed a fifteen-minute nap and then he'd be fine to drive again.

The cold had already started to seep into the car. Mary pulled the blanket she had brought along out of the back seat and spread it over their legs as Ward laid his seat back to sleep. While Ward slept beside her, Mary sat bolt upright, wide awake, peering into the darkness beyond the windshield.

❈

Mother Hamilton greeted them when they arrived at her door at 2:00 AM, long after they had promised. The house was dim as they entered, and Mary's first glimpse of it was in the shadows. It smelled of some flowery scent. There were small tables everywhere covered by doilies upon which sat little figurines; paintings covered every wall. Plastic runners covered the carpet in high-traffic areas, and plastic also covered the couch and the chairs in the living room. The house looked like a museum, and Mary guessed nothing had changed in all the years Mother Hamilton had lived there.

Unlike Ward, Mother Hamilton was very tiny. When she answered the door, she was wearing a hairnet over her white hair. Ward kissed her. Then Mary pressed her own cold lips against Mother Hamilton's dry, soft cheek before she ushered them upstairs to the guest bedroom where they would be staying. Mary had wondered why the guest room instead of Ward's room, but she later understood when she saw Ward's old bedroom had not been changed since he had left home.

The twin bed was still covered by a chenille bedspread, looking as though he had just left it that morning. On the walls were posters reflecting his adolescent interests: a banner from his high school, his letter from basketball, awards for debate team, and winning medals for speech contests. On a stand was a chessboard with pieces in midplay. This was meaningful, she later learned, as it had been a game begun with a friend who later committed suicide, a monument to Ward's friend's failure to want to live, and a symbol for when he'd decided to become a minister like his father. "Until then," he told her, "I'd been living only for myself. I saw I was headed for trouble when Gene killed himself. I committed myself to living for Jesus, prayed for forgiveness, and felt the power of the Lord wash over me. That very night I committed my life to the Lord. I went to the map." He gestured to a U.S. map on the wall. "Closed my eyes and pointed. Wherever I landed, that's where I pledged to the Lord I'd go." He smiled and nodded at the memory. "My finger fell on the Sandhills of Nebraska, and the nearest town was Custer City. I kept that town in my mind and in my prayers all through Bible College and seminary, and whenever I was tempted to go elsewhere, I reminded myself of my promise to the Lord."

As Mary listened to his story, she had the eerie feeling his meeting her fit into the same pattern of prayer before random pointing. She felt unsettled by his method of decision making, though she couldn't say how it was all that different from her own instinctual decisions of the past.

That first morning Mother Hamilton was already up when they both came down to the kitchen. She was dressed in a blouse, skirt, hose, and heels. This was her uniform. Through the week to come, Mary would discover that Mother Hamilton even cleaned the house in these clothes. She was as tidy a woman as Mary knew, both in her person and in maintenance of her house. Every closet was perfectly orderly, every drawer uncluttered. Mary snooped. Nothing was out of place. Mother Hamilton had her hair professionally styled once a week, and she slept on a special pillow to keep it from flattening overnight.

Despite the tidy dress and the tidy personal habits, Mother Hamilton was one of the homeliest women Mary had ever seen. Her face was pinched and narrow, her nose and chin sharp. She looked, and Mary hated to admit it even to herself, like a sourpuss. Mother Hamilton's face seemed to reflect some bitterness of heart that Mary could only guess at. She was pretty certain she would never learn the cause from Mother Hamilton, for if Ward was closed, his mother was even more reserved.

In a wedding picture Mary found hanging on one of the walls, she saw that Ward took after his father, who had been tall, broad shouldered, and fair. In the photograph, Ward's father was smiling an easy, open smile while in contrast the young Mother Hamilton looked bewildered, uncertain. Even in the photograph it seemed Ward's father took no notice of her. They were not touching. They seemed to inhabit parallel space as though the photograph had been doctored, bringing together two separate photographs into one. Mary studied the picture longer than was appropriate, and through the week of their stay, she came to understand part of her fascination with the picture was her desire to understand her own marriage.

"It's your turn, Mary," Ward prodded. She looked at the tiles on the table, the letters swimming together, no word forming. Finally, Ward leaned over and sorted the tiles briskly with his index finger. He didn't say anything, but he smiled at her as she looked from the word he'd formed—"pet"—and back to his face. She picked up the three letters and laid them in the little tray.

This was the second night of playing Scrabble. Ward and his mother loved the game. Ward told Mary it had filled many lonely evenings after his father had died.

"You rascal," Mother Hamilton said now, jolting Mary alert again. Ward laughed and rubbed his hands together. "You absolute rascal," Mother Hamilton repeated, looking about as happy as Mary had seen her. They tried to explain to Mary something about an "x." Ward had obviously won the game. They kept careful scores.

"Mary, you're doing better," Ward said as he tallied up the totals. "Just fine for a beginner. I'll bet by the end of the week you'll be a contender."

"I think I'll bow out from now on."

Ward looked at her quickly. "Come on now, Mary. Don't be a poor sport." He had put on his most jocular voice. "Don't give up so easily."

"It's not that." Mary felt herself flush with anger. "I don't enjoy it. It isn't fun for me." At this, Ward glanced at his mother, and Mary saw her raise her eyebrows quickly. Still another way Mary was misbehaving. She had a sudden violent wish to sweep the game pieces off the card table and storm out of the room. She let the vision pass and tried to make a joke. "I wouldn't want to embarrass you by winning too soon." The joke fell flat, but Ward tried to compensate for her lack of social grace by laughing heartily at it. Mary felt as though she could have strangled him. She pushed away from the table. They'd start another game this evening, she knew, but she wouldn't be there. For the remainder of the week, she decided, she wouldn't be there.

It was on one of those evenings while Ward and Mother Hamilton played Scrabble that Mary discovered Ward's father's library in a small upstairs study. She browsed the shelves, recognizing some of the same Bible commentaries Ward had. She saw many of the same books Ward had leant her only a year before. She pulled some of them off the shelf but they couldn't sustain her interest.

For their entire stay, Mary never once heard Mother Hamilton again laugh after that game of Scrabble. She rarely saw levity of any sort in her, not even as they opened gifts on Christmas morning. Everything Mary could see of her was there on the surface, and nothing in her house contradicted that appearance. She wasn't a hypocrite, Mary finally concluded, but if before she thought she hated hypocrites, she now found she despised almost as much the person for whom all her beliefs were so true and so real that she denied doubt and confusion.

CHAPTER 14

⇒"That feels so good," Zoe Hendricks was saying as Mary brushed her long white hair. Once a week, Mary washed, brushed out, braided, and pinned up Zoe's hair. "You're such a good nurse, Mary," Zoe added.

"I'm not a nurse. I'm only a nurse's aide."

"That doesn't matter to me," Zoe said. "All I know is when you turn me it doesn't hurt so much, and when you comb my hair, I feel cared for." Zoe sighed with pleasure again. "Have you ever thought about becoming a nurse, Mary?"

Mary didn't respond as she continued to brush the silky white hair that fell to the middle of Zoe's back. Zoe, who had been bed-fast for almost a decade, was now in the final stages of Parkinson's. At ninety-four, she had been in the nursing home longer than any other current resident. For all those years the staff had tried to convince Zoe to cut her hair, but she had adamantly refused. The defining passions of her life had been left behind, everything except her hair. Her hair represented something of her former beauty, her independence, who she had been, who she was.

Today Zoe started to tell a story Mary had never heard before about a boy she'd once loved.

"My father didn't approve of him," Zoe said. She laughed, but her laugh sounded a little forced.

"Tell me about him." Mary concentrated as she drew a comb down the middle of Zoe's head and separated the two halves of her hair in preparation to braid.

Mary paused and looked at Zoe. Her face had grown wistful, and her eyes took on a faraway look that had become familiar to Mary since working at the nursing home. "Oh, he was handsome," Zoe said finally. "He was as blonde as I was dark. And tall. My, was he tall. I was crazy over him." She smiled to herself for a second. "He was a great one for competing. Everyone knew Harvey Edwards. He never lost at anything. And he could sing. Oh, could he sing. We were always cast opposite one other in all the school plays." She laughed suddenly, then looked at Mary. "He was famous for being afraid of snakes, and everyone teased him no end for that. Even the teacher got in on it. Any time she'd find a snake in the schoolhouse, she'd ask Harvey to take it outside." Mary must have looked a little startled, for Zoe went on to explain, "Those old country schools, you know. Nothing to keep out the outside." She paused. "Now that I think back it was cruel to pick on him like that, but he was such a clown, and we thought it was so much fun." A smile lingered on her face for a few seconds. She seemed suddenly far away from the clamor of the nursing home with its lights and buzzers and sighs and moans.

"What happened?" Mary finally asked, and Zoe's smile slipped away. She looked at Mary, and her face grew stern.

"Why, it's the oldest story in the book. My father broke us up. Harvey wanted to run away after we'd finished school. He knew my father would never give his approval if we asked, but I was afraid to disappoint my father." A pained expression passed behind her eyes, and she sighed. "I just couldn't disappoint my father, not even for the sake of my own happiness."

Unlike her other stories, this story Zoe did not embroider, and Mary sensed it was this story that most defined her regrets, that it was the story she could never really tell. She knew not to prod. Zoe would say no more about Harvey. She had noticed Zoe never talked about her late husband. She was polite about answering all of Mary's questions about her past life, but she always side-stepped her husband, making the story of Harvey now all the more compelling.

The story bothered Mary all day as she worked. Zoe had allowed the fear of her father's judgment to determine the course of her life, and Mary felt lurking behind what Zoe hadn't said was the senti-ment that now, at the end of her life, such judgments didn't matter, and they shouldn't have mattered then, that her love was her only gift and she had squandered it.

Mary guessed she was adding to Zoe's story her own story. She couldn't at all say what Zoe's story really meant, but she saw that her interpretation was what mattered. It was her own life that seemed stunted, wrongheaded, and things had been adding up to no good since coming back from Mother Hamilton's two weeks earlier. She had tried her usual regimen of focusing on the good things and working hard, but she couldn't seem to move beyond her feelings of foreboding. She couldn't seem to find a way to get past how deeply unhappy she felt. Some days she had such a pow-erful urge to flee that she actually picked up the phone intending to call her parents to come get her, but each time before she could dial the number, she caught herself and hung up.

As Claire had hoped, the cafeteria guy had given up and moved to Lincoln so she and Mary were free to take their morning coffee breaks in the cafeteria again. Today, the winter sun streamed through the large windows facing the inner courtyard. In winter the courtyard was a woebegone place with abandoned benches and dormant flowers. Mary guessed that come spring it might be a place where she would enjoy spending an hour some afternoon, but she couldn't imagine any of the residents entered it.

"I met someone you know last night," Claire said after they sat down.

"Oh, who was that?"

"Kent Needham."

"Where'd you meet Kent?"

"At the Sage Brush. He's cute. Why didn't you tell me about him?"

Knowing Claire's ways with men, Mary suddenly felt protective of Kent. She didn't think he was quite savvy enough to be the victor in Claire's games.

Claire laughed. "You should see your face. Don't worry. He's not my type." She took a sip of coffee, then set her cup down slowly. "Kent and his partners are building quite a little business out there at Treegers. He invited us to come visit sometime, see what they're doing. Would you want to do that?"

"Sure. He stopped by to tell me about it when he first moved to town, but I haven't seen him since."

"Kent told me some interesting things about you. Why didn't you ever tell me about Brian?"

"How do you start a conversation like that?"

"There were plenty of times you could have told me." When Mary did not respond, Claire went on. "So, that's what happened to your leg?"

"Yes."

"I want to be your friend, Mary," Claire said. She said it with such unexpected sincerity that Mary felt flustered. She felt as though she hadn't had a friend for a very long time, and Claire's declaration both rattled and warmed her.

Perhaps it was this conversation that led Mary a week later to come to Claire with a request. It was an impulse, much like picking up the phone to call her parents, but this time she didn't stop herself. She blurted out without preamble one day in the cafeteria, "Could I stay with you for a few weeks until I find my own place?"

"Of course," Claire said with only a hint of surprise. "What's going on?"

"I just need to get away. I need a little time to think."

"Are you all right? Ward hasn't hurt you, has he?"

"No. It's nothing like that. It's not him. It's me. I'm confused and I need time to sort things out." She didn't want to tell Claire the real reason for her decision to leave, the three men Ward had brought home after a meeting in Broken Bow the night before. They'd been sleeping in their car, and he'd wanted to shelter them for the night. The three men all gave Mary the same creepy feeling she'd had toward the truck driver in Illinois, and like that time, Ward was oblivious to her discomfort. She had tried to explain herself, but Ward wouldn't hear it. She'd asked, "Why don't we put them up at the hotel, let the church's Macedonian fund pay for it? That's what it's for." Ward had frowned at this. "That's ridiculous, Mary, when we have plenty of room." Although she had relented, she'd laid awake all night, listening, imagining all the ways they might be putting themselves at risk.

"Whenever," Claire said now. "I have an extra bedroom, and you're more than welcome to stay for a while." Claire paused. "It'd be nice to have company."

"Thanks, Claire. I haven't decided when, but soon."

"You look miserable," Claire said.

"I feel miserable. It's a terrible thing to leave a marriage."

"I don't mean to be critical, Mary, but you take things way too much to heart."

"That's not true. I haven't been very thoughtful about my life at all."

Claire's face brightened. "Hey, why don't we plan to do something on Saturday, get you out of the house a little, clear your head? You up for a drive to Treegers to visit Kent?"

"Why not?"

"Do you want to drive or should I?"

"I don't drive."

"You don't drive?" Claire leaned back and looked at her. "I'd be glad to teach . . ."

"No, it isn't that. I don't . . . I don't feel comfortable driving."

"Because of your leg?"

Mary paused. "I guess, yes."

"No problem. I'll pick you up around one."

❄

When Claire arrived on Saturday, Mary was waiting for her on the front stoop of the parsonage. They headed south of town on Highway 21 toward Treegers. Mary hadn't been on this highway since the night of the accident. She couldn't imagine how she had avoided it so long. She watched as the highway wound up and down the hills. The dead grass lining the shoulders of the highway had bleached to a pale yellow. The wind blew, hitting the car hard from the northwest. Mary was grateful to Claire's chatter for the time it took to get to the entrance of the feedlot.

At the turnoff, a large wooden sign straddled the dirt drive. "Treegers" had been burned into the wood in cursive letters. Claire turned onto the road. Halfway into the compound, they arrived at a padlocked gate.

A voice came over a speaker mounted on a wooden pole. "Who is it?"

"Claire Rowe and Mary Hamilton," Claire said.

There was a short pause before the speaker burped on again. "Come on in." Apparently attached to a remote entry, the gate opened on its own and Claire drove through. As soon as their car had cleared it, the gate swung back into a locked position. Mary shuddered slightly, but Claire drove through the gate as though nothing was out of the ordinary.

As they rounded the first hill, Mary noticed large metal corrals. Beyond those were more corrals being constructed with built-in feeding troughs and watering units. A large building stood at the near end, and Claire drove directly toward it. Kent came out of the office, pulling on gloves as he walked toward the car.

"Hey," he said when Claire rolled down the driver's side window.

"Good to see the two of you. You can park over there." He gestured toward a parking lot filled with cars.

After Claire had parked, Kent gave them a quick tour of the office. Monitors with up-to-the-minute cattle futures lined one wall. Newspapers and books lay stacked on tables and credenzas. Three men were engrossed in telephone conversations Mary guessed were sales calls. As Kent took them out into the yard, he directed them toward a golf cart, which he steered expertly around the corrals.

Beyond the first hill, more corrals were being built, all of them still empty. In the corrals toward the back Mary finally saw several hundred head of cattle. They were packed into tight corners and standing on frozen mud and manure. Despite the cold, she could smell the dark odor of animals confined in a small space.

"How long do you keep them here?" she asked.

"It depends. We take anything from weaned calves to feed out to market to three-year-olds needing to be finished. We discourage ranging, and we've been working with the university to develop a high-protein feed to develop the carcass we want."

Mary didn't want to say anything to Kent, but she was horrified by what she saw. The animals seemed droopy, their eyes glazed. Many were lying in their own waste. She couldn't quite imagine working in this environment. She noticed then another corral to the west that held half a dozen horses. "So you're moving them with horses?"

"Sometimes. We haven't decided yet if it's cost-effective, but some of the guys would rather work with horses, so we've kept them on. We're finding the three-wheelers work best, though."

Mary had wandered closer to the horses, and she saw the corral was choked with dead weeds: thistle, dock, pigweed, and nettles. Kent noticed what must have been her look of disgust for he said quickly, "We're planning to get that cleaned up soon." She didn't acknowledge his reassurance. She couldn't quite believe the Kent she knew could go along with any of this.

Later, as they drove back to the office, Kent pressed her for her opinion. "What do you think?"

"It's different."

He was clearly not satisfied by this answer. "I know it's different, but what's your impression?"

"Oh, Kent, I haven't thought about raising cattle for almost three years. I suppose, like you said before, this is a smart business move for you. How can you fight the inevitable?" She paused. "But, of course, it seems odd to me, unnatural, you know. It isn't how cows are meant to live." She laughed at herself. "But then, none of what we do raising cattle is natural."

Mary could see Kent still wasn't satisfied by her answer, but he let it go.

Claire, who had no experience with ranching, had said little during their tour. Now as they told Kent good-bye, she said, "Thanks for giving me a little glimpse into the world of high-tech cattle production."

Before they pulled away Kent came over to Mary's side of the car. She rolled down her window and he leaned in to hug her briefly with one arm. "Take care of yourself," he said. "It sure means a lot to me that you came today, Mary."

After they left Kent, Claire drove in silence for a few minutes. "Brian must have really loved you," she finally said.

"What would make you say that?"

"The way his brother is so gentle toward you. I can see it."

Mary didn't say anything to this, but as they pulled back onto the highway she suddenly felt overcome with nausea. Claire abruptly pulled onto the shoulder and Mary barely got out of the car before doubling over.

"What's gotten into you?" Claire asked after Mary had wiped her mouth and climbed back into the car.

"I don't know. I must be coming down with something," Mary said, though she harbored the thought that she had been sickened by what she had seen at Treegers. Something was very wrong with that scene, and even with Kent's enthusiastic backing she didn't get it.

A Sandhills Ballad ◁ 141

Mary was a few minutes late for Bible Study the next night. She'd had to cover while a nurse on the night shift found a backup babysitter for her three kids. Ward was already well into the lesson by the time she came into the church basement. He and Ed Lundgren were discussing man's dominion over the earth. They were in passionate agreement about man's sovereign responsibility to restore the nation to its "godly roots." Ed had been the one to take such offense at Mary's inept answer at the first Bible Study she'd attended, and she could tell he still didn't like her much.

"Things are off kilter in this culture and nature's responding," Ed was saying. "It's God's way of punishing us for our sins. The nation's founders never intended this." He went on in this vein for several minutes. Mary had noticed since joining the church that Ed's tendency to talk about social issues more than the Bible bothered some of the members of the congregation, especially Lana who spoke up now to say, "Could we just discuss the book of Acts, Ed?"

"We are talking about Acts," Ed fired back.

Instead of steering the discussion in a less heated direction, Ward said, "Ed's right, Lana. We're citizens of a once-great nation that respected God's Word. We're in the End Times now, and all of us have to be more vigilant. We have to resist the culture of corruption that is the spirit of this age."

A satisfied expression settled on Ed's face at Ward's defense of him. Lana, who was sitting across from Mary, stiffened at Ward's admonition.

As soon as the Bible Study ended that night, Mary left the church, not even waiting to talk to Lana like she usually would. She felt something ominous that night, something she couldn't explain but that she felt like a physical threat, making her more certain she had to leave Ward and move in with Claire.

Two days later when Mary came into work, she heard a terrible racket in the west wing. Walter was ranting and throwing things from his room. As she came closer, Mary saw Theresa standing in the hallway, dodging flying objects. Already a pile of whatever Walter had been able to lay his hands on cluttered the hallway, including shattered glass. Walter was calling Theresa every filthy name he could think of, many of which Mary had never heard before, while Claire calmly sat behind the counter, updating the monthly medical records. She seemed unimpressed with the tantrum.

"What's going on?" Mary whispered.

Claire shrugged. "The usual. Theresa found a fifth of whiskey under his mattress, and she took it away. Like I told you before, it happens about three times a year."

Mary thought she understood something about Walter's rage. She wished she was so uninhibited that she could throw things and call names.

When it was clear Walter was finished, Mary helped Theresa clean up the mess in the hallway. No one spoke of Walter's tantrum, but later that day, after her shift ended, Mary went to Walter's room. She sat silently in the chair beside his bed.

"What do you want?" he finally asked, still surly.

"I don't want a thing," she said. Behind her, Mary felt the sun setting outside the window. Together they sat in silence as shadows gathered in the room.

"Walter," she said finally, "I understand that you don't necessarily want to keep living, so our arguments against the alcohol aren't helping." Walter didn't respond. She continued. "I can't bring you booze, but chocolate. How would it be if I brought you chocolate on the sly?"

Walter seemed to think seriously about her question for a few minutes. Finally, he stuck out his hand. It was a gnarled hand, made hard by years of work, and despite his weakened state, it was still a strong hand as it grasped Mary's. "Deal," he said. Walter was silent for a few more seconds. "Why are you doing this?" he finally asked.

Mary didn't respond for a while. She let the silence of the room soak into her bones before saying, "Because I've just lost control of my life and I'm starting to understand your anger." This answer seemed to satisfy Walter. Without saying good-bye, Mary left him sitting in the darkness. As she left by way of the familiar halls of the nursing home, Mary felt momentarily lost, as though she were seeing the place for the first time. Everything seemed foreign to her. She felt a confusion of emotions so clamorous she could hardly concentrate. She had no choice, she felt, but to accept her fate. Maybe Ward had been right. Maybe God did have a plan for her that didn't involve what she wanted at all. Something about her life felt destined. She was no closer to understanding what any of it meant, but she felt fate had a grip on her. Was she supposed to be learning something here about the dangers of selfishness, the risk or thinking only of her own happiness?

PART TWO

≡CHAPTER 15

≡A cold wind roamed about the house, trying each window before moving on. Mary shivered a little at the sound even though she was warm under the quilts dogpiled on the bed. Her new titanium prosthesis was propped in the corner. Adjacent to the bed stood her crutches in case she needed to get up in the night. Ward was gone for the evening, as he often was. Beside her, in a cradle against the wall, the new baby stirred, nestling deeper into sleep, making the snuffling, grunting noises she knew so well.

Three other children slept in the room beside hers, and this, the newest—a boy named David—was three months old. Her body was still recovering from an unexpectedly difficult delivery. Claire had been her birthing coach this time, as she had been with the other children, Ward never trusting his busy schedule to be a reliable birthing partner. Neither Mary nor Ward had known much about modern birthing practices until she was pregnant with their first child. Claire had been the one to share that information. Where Ward had been reluctant, Claire had been eager to assist, and Mary had been grateful through the years for her friendship. Few people in Mary's life had felt the fourth pregnancy was a good idea.

"What are you thinking, Mary?" Claire had said when she first heard. "You know you can't afford all these kids."

"One thing I know by now is how to be poor," Mary had said with a laugh.

Claire looked at her like she'd lost her mind. "That isn't funny. Besides, I'm not just talking about money. Ward's never home, and you're left alone too much with the kids."

Although Mary hadn't said anything to Claire, she had felt something radical happen to her after she'd learned about her pregnancy with David. Although she loved that baby sleeping in his crib beside the bed, she felt she couldn't face another pregnancy and keep her sanity. The kids were a marvel to her, though, and she spent every evening before sleep thinking back on their antics through the day. It was a bitterly cold January. Frost had coated the interior side of the windows with intricate patterns, and tonight she was remembering how they had run from window to window that morning scratching designs and words into the frost.

Joseph, the oldest, was a petite boy. His dark hair curled about his fine, pale face. A smattering of freckles covered his nose. Thick eyebrows formed a strong, straight line above his clear blue eyes. He often drew his brows together in concentration or worry. At nine he was a serious boy, fretful at times, given to living in his imagination. He liked to draw and make up stories. In his room, he was building an elaborate city out of cardboard, wood scraps, and fabric remnants. When he laughed, he laughed with his whole body, doubling up, sometimes falling to the floor, a surprising contrast to his otherwise serious nature.

Deborah was six and just starting school. She had Ward's sturdy frame and his blonde hair and blue eyes. Less imaginative than Joseph, she was sometimes frustrated by his self-contained preoccupation. When she was younger, she had occasionally sabotaged his careful creations, provoking him to rage. She showed an early interest in music and was in her second year of piano lessons with Mrs. Lesley. To Mrs. Lesley's approval, she had quickly surpassed

Mary's ability to read music. Deborah was endlessly aware of what was happening in the house and knew the contents of every drawer and every closet. Always watchful, Mary and Ward had to be careful about what they said in her presence and what they left lying out because she had an uncanny ability to puzzle out secrets.

Three-year-old Priscilla was a towheaded sprite. She danced and sang and listened with wide-eyed wonder to every word of stories and songs. She drew strange and compelling pictures, and expressed frustration when the family couldn't see her intentions. She often played happily alone in her room where she could be heard talking to her dolls and stuffed animals, carrying on elaborate conversations with them. She was often the confused butt of Joseph and Deborah's jokes, and yet wanted nothing so much as to fit in with them. She had an imaginary friend named Siggy, and when she was especially disappointed, she retreated into her closed world with Siggy. She had admitted to Mary soberly that she knew Siggy was "just pretend," but that she sometimes needed him.

Even at this early age, it was clear David had Ward's features, but unlike the older three he had the red hair and ruddy complexion of John's side of the family. He was a quiet, contented baby, and his eyes followed the antics of his siblings with precocious watchfulness.

Now, as Mary thought her evening was coming to an end, Joseph appeared at her bedroom door. His sensitive face was creased in worry and he seemed more like a wizened old man than a carefree little boy. Seeing him standing in the doorway wearing the Ninja Turtle pajamas he had gotten from his Aunt Judy for Christmas, Mary felt she could not begin to address Joseph's anxieties. He didn't speak of his fears like the girls did. Besides, their fears were all those Mary expected of children: spiders, monsters, bad dreams. Joseph's fears seemed darker, more complicated, and she couldn't help but feel that he was the child who bore the burden of the unspoken sadness at the center of their family. Although she put on a mask of happiness, no matter how much Mary thought she was hiding things, Joseph seemed to mirror her sadness back to her, to wear visibly upon his face her resignation.

"Come here," she said now, and he walked to the bed, his bare feet shushing on the linoleum floor. "Why didn't you put on your slippers?" Joseph shrugged, and she opened the blankets to let him into the bed beside her. "Your feet are like ice, mister." Mary tickled him, and he giggled. She was relieved for a second by his laughter.

After all these years of living in the parsonage, Mary had never come to feel at home there, nor had the church made any effort to make the house more livable. Every year, the new coat of yellow paint in the kitchen failed to arrest the slow creep of mildew up the walls, the ancient kitchen countertops defied her efforts at scrubbing them clean and retained a thick layer of intractable grime. The outside walls were thin and uninsulated. The unglazed windows rattled with every gust of wind, but the old wooden storm windows were in such bad shape they couldn't be used and gathered dust where they were stacked in the lopsided garage facing the alley.

Whenever Mary asked Ward to request from the church board something as simple as to replace the storm windows so the house wouldn't be drafty and cold, or to fix the dripping bathroom faucet, or to add new gutters, he always insisted that the church had no money for frivolous expenses. It pained Mary that he would think of her comfort and that of his children as frivolous.

If the interior defied her efforts, together she and Berl had created a backyard garden that was a marvel to the neighborhood. Now in winter it was hard sometimes to remember the pleasure of her garden in summer, but through each winter she read gardening books, anticipating the first nice days in spring when she could start to work the ground.

Even if Ward still questioned her Christian commitment, he hadn't been able to fault her skills as an organizer. She had played her role in those ways over the years without complaint, and no matter what her changing circumstances, she had met all of the congregation's expectations for service. Still, she knew they weren't entirely pleased with her. She had never managed to become the obliging minister's wife she'd understood early on was their ideal.

Unlike Ward had predicted, she had thrived in her work at the nursing home. So much so that she had almost earned her RN degree. In the early years of their marriage, especially when Joseph and Deborah were babies, she and Ward had frequently argued about her choice to work and go to school, but the fights had not deterred her. She had lost the battle over the house but she had won those over work and school. Now and then her father and Max came to do routine maintenance: patch the roof, clean gutters, oil hinges, replace gaskets on faucets, change the furnace filter, and put up plastic to help seal the windows a little against the cold. Despite the plastic, the windows shook every few minutes tonight as the wind pounded them, and a persistent draft rustled the curtains.

The wind gusted hard again, and Mary shuddered as she listened to it prowl around the house. She was suddenly grateful for Joseph there beside her. He leaned his head against her shoulder, and they sat together in companionable silence for a few minutes listening to a song Mary could not identify on the radio.

"Did you have a bad dream, Joe?" she asked finally.

He nodded.

"You want to talk about it?" He shook his head, and Mary hugged him a little closer. "I'm sorry."

"That's okay," Joseph answered. "Mommy," he said, "tell me a story about the Egg People." The Egg People stories had originated with an egg hatching project gone wrong when Joseph was in kindergarten. To counter his disappointment after the eggs didn't hatch, Mary had made up stories about the tiny men and women who had hatched in the middle of the night and still lived in their house. They were silly stories, but the children liked them, and they often wanted updates on what the Egg People were doing.

Tonight, as she told it, the Egg People had made pea soup in the kitchen after everyone had gone to bed and they were now sleeping in the afghan on the couch. Joseph smiled as Mary described them. They'd gone to sleep with their faces and hands unwashed, and they'd used the afghan as a napkin.

"Tell me another story," Joseph said. "Tell me a story about when you were little."

Mary thought for a while. She'd already told him all the stories she could remember from when she was little, so she told him a story about summer, about how when she was a teenager she and her friends had made a boat out of an old horse tank. The tank was large enough to hold a few chairs, and they had used it to float down the Middle Loup River near the Stiles ranch on hot summer days. She described all of her friends: Janna and Katie, Art and Jim, and crazy Eddie and Kevin. Joseph knew the names of her old friends; she'd talked about them all before. She didn't go on to tell Joseph about how they had also concocted a crate to hold a case of beer they could pull along and keep cool in the water. Nor did she mention how when the sun grew too warm and they'd had a few of those beers, they skinny-dipped in the river. She smiled to herself, remembering what fun it had been. She told instead about how Art always tried to spear fish summer after summer even though he never caught a single fish that way. And how Eddie had once claimed to have seen a sea monster—"big as a house"—and how all one summer he was on the lookout for another glimpse of that fabulous monster.

When she finished with her story, Joseph pulled away and smiled at her. "Did Eddie really see a big fish?" he asked.

"Maybe," Mary said. "We acted like we didn't believe him, but we always went with him to the river to look for it." Joseph laid his head back against her shoulder without comment. They sat like that until they heard the door open in the front of the house.

Joseph sat up then. "Goodnight, Mommy," he said in his dusky voice.

"Good night, Joe."

Joseph was already in his room by the time Ward found his way to the back of the house.

"I'm surprised to see you still up," he said, unknotting his tie and hanging it on the knob of the closet door.

"You just caught me before I drifted off."

Ward nodded. He asked politely about her day, listened as she recapped what the children had done. "There are leftovers in the refrigerator if you want."

"Thanks. I ate before the meeting." He was referring to the meeting of the CCCA, a group for whom he served as spokesperson: Concerned Citizens for Clean Air.

As with most evenings in Custer City for the past seven years, the smell emanating from Treegers seeped in through the closed windows. Outside, she knew the smell would be vile. In the summer it was worse. If the weather was dry, dust was a problem. If it was damp, the smell was almost overpowering. During the spring thaw there were times when the air seemed hazy with the stench. Still, Mary was philosophical about it most of the time. If you made a living raising animals, there was bound to be an odor. It was a natural by-product of the business that formed the core of the area's economy. The people of Custer City could deny their association because most of them didn't actually raise, feed, herd, or slaughter the cattle, but their fortunes were tied to the cattle market nevertheless.

Several years earlier Kent Needham had bought out the interests of the Treeger brothers, and had brought into the business not only Larry but Jeffrey—Jeffrey having finished his degree in veterinary medicine. The CCCA had been formed by townspeople who claimed Treegers's proximity to town was compromising their quality of life and endangering Custer City's ability to attract other businesses to the area. They wanted Treegers to move the operation to another town, and seemed indifferent to the fact that Treegers also employed more than eighty people and paid them better than any other business in the area. They were unmoved when the executives of Treegers argued that they made every effort to regulate the smell.

Since its founding five years earlier, the CCCA had been successful in getting state legislators to pay attention to the town's plight. During the years of the CCCA's activities there had been a decline in the town's population. The CCCA regularly used these statistics to bolster support for their argument that Treegers needed to close. Mary sometimes felt the failure to attract businesses, and the declining population, had as much to do with the widespread exaggerations by the CCCA about the town's bad air as the quality of the air itself.

The CCCA had been formed by an original group of four: Polly Krueger, a beautician; Lyle Benton, a banker; Bill Carlisle, the owner of Custer City's biggest hardware store; and Peter Collins, a rancher over by Sargent. Like some other ranchers in the region, Pete was disgruntled with Treegers's practice of bringing in cattle from other states instead of contracting with local ranchers. Mary knew, though, that the local bank had refused to loan Treegers money when they first started to expand, and most area ranchers had refused to bring them their cattle, preferring instead to continue to ship to feedlots in Illinois and Indiana as they always had. Now, belatedly, some area ranchers were offended that Treegers did not show a preference for local beef.

A year into it, the founding four members of the CCCA had approached Ward about becoming the spokesperson for the new organization. They'd heard him speak when he'd been on the city council, and they thought he was someone who could help them promote their cause, someone who could be persuasive to lawmakers.

Ward had not asked Mary's opinion when the CCCA first made the invitation to him, but she'd felt so strongly about the issue she'd offered it anyway. "I don't think it's smart for you to mix this kind of thing with your ministry," she had said. "There are bound to be conflicts you haven't thought about." Ward at first dismissed her concerns, going so far at one point as to say, "Mary, if I wanted your opinion, I'd have asked for it," but since its founding, her prediction had come to bear many times over. There had been tense church meetings where members who held different opinions—some of whom even worked at Treegers—either threatened to leave the church because of Ward's high-profile involvement in the organization or did in fact leave, among them some of Mary's favorites in the congregation. Her best friend in the church, Lana Perkins, had left long before the controversy over the CCCA, explaining to Mary that Ward's theology had become too conservative for her.

For every family that left the church, though, there was a new family eager to join because of Ward's profile in the community. Other church members whose political views weren't necessarily in conflict with the organization nonetheless felt that Ward's energies were unfairly split and that too often the church came out in last place. If Mary had been asked, she would have argued it was the family that came last with Ward.

As the CCCA grew in membership and increasingly gained attention from the state government, Mary had seen Ward's loyalties shift. She felt he rather liked rubbing elbows with state legislators and enjoyed the spotlight as occasionally he was quoted in the *Lincoln Journal Star* or *The Omaha World Herald*. He was featured regularly in the *Custer Weekly*. Ward had received help and encouragement from national Christian organizations. Leaders in those groups were clearly interested in Ward's ability to galvanize public opinion, and although he never spoke about it to her, Mary suspected they were grooming him for other purposes.

He'd said to her once shortly after they were married, during his first run for city council, "We're going to get elected to city councils and school boards." His use of the collective "we" had chilled her, though she didn't ask and Ward hadn't offered who "we" was exactly.

"How was your meeting?" she asked Ward now.

"Fine," he said but did not elaborate. Mary's connection to the Needham family had come up in one of the recent meetings of the CCCA, and Mary had noticed Ward's reserve with her. Perhaps he was right to distrust her; after all, only a few months before, while still very pregnant with David, she had gotten a phone call from Kent Needham, their first contact in a long time.

The phone call had been Kent's attempt to find out if she had any influence with Ward. Treegers was suffering from the growing strength of the CCCA's lobbying efforts. "Are you in support of all this, Mary?" he had asked, his voice sounding hurt.

"No," Mary had said, resenting his accusatory tone.

"We're under a lot of pressure out here."

"I'm sure you are."

"I wonder if there's any way you could help us get the CCCA to meet and discuss our differences, try to come to some compromise without the politicians?"

She knew Kent had made several attempts to get Ward to meet with him and his brothers, but each time Ward had refused. Kent said now, "What's Ward's problem with just sitting down with us? Why can't we just talk? We all live in the same town for crying out loud."

"I wish I could help you, Kent. I really do. Honestly, there isn't anything I can do. I don't have any influence over Ward."

"I find that hard to believe."

"Well, it's the truth," Mary said, but she could tell by Kent's good-bye he hadn't believed her.

Early on, while Ward was still weighing the decision about whether to accept the position as spokesperson for the group, Mary had told him, "There aren't a lot of rules out here, and the rules there are aren't written anywhere. You've got to tread carefully, Ward. You're an outsider. You'll be an outsider until the day you die because not only were your parents not born here, but your grandparents weren't born here."

Ward had scoffed at her characterization of Custer City. "You're awfully condescending toward these people, aren't you? Don't you think they're more sophisticated than that?"

"This isn't a question of sophistication. It's a question of deep loyalties, and believe me, if you're an outsider, you stand to lose a lot more than if you're someone whose family has been in the area for years."

Ward had turned that argument against her. "Why don't you join us, then? You have the roots I lack, and people here would sit up and take notice if you backed us."

She shook her head. "They might not turn on me in the same way they'll turn on you, but my joining wouldn't help anything. Besides, I can't go along with the goals of the CCCA. I'm from a ranch family, don't forget. If Treegers offered local ranchers a discount on contracts, then trust me, they wouldn't be so critical."

"The ranchers had good reasons for not contracting with Treegers out of the gate," Ward said.

"I'm sure they did, but they're also bullheaded. They don't like change, and they don't like to compromise."

"Why are you being so harsh, Mary?"

Mary had felt a flush of anger at Ward's scolding. "I know ranchers a whole lot better than you do, Ward. I may not be able to say that about many things, but I can say it about this. Besides, my folks were among the first ranchers here to contract with Treegers, and they've been pleased with the work they do." Their conversation ended on that note, and a week later Ward had announced his decision to accept the role as spokesman. The only question Mary raised at that point was about compensation.

"Mary, it's a fledgling organization," Ward had said. "There's no way they can compensate me for my time. Maybe eventually."

Four years later, he was still putting in the equivalent of a full week's work for the CCCA without pay.

Tonight, as Ward got into his pajamas, Mary said, "Joe and Debbie have a school program next week. Do you think you could make it?"

"Oh, Mary." Ward sounded aggrieved. "There isn't any way I can find time next week. We're booked every night. You know we're getting ready for the governor's visit."

Mary sighed softly. "It'd mean a lot to them if their father could be in the audience."

Ward smiled as though their wanting him there was some special sign of their affection for him. "Claire will go with you. They love having her around."

"Of course they enjoy Claire, but she isn't their daddy."

"Mary, don't make me feel bad about doing what I have to do."

"Do you? Do you really have to do it?"

"It's only for a short time."

"That's what you've been saying for four years. It's always something."

"But it's true. We're making real headway here, and it isn't going to last forever."

"Neither is this time with your kids."

"I'm here every night, aren't I? Don't act like I'm not interested in my family. That's why I'm doing this, and it's not fair of you to try to make me feel guilty for doing good and necessary work."

Mary knew she should just drop the issue, but she pushed anyway. "You make it sound as though no one else could speak in your place. Why is it that you have to be there all the time?"

"You know very well why I need to be there, especially now when we're so close to getting legislation to tighten regulations. It's not just us anymore either; it's becoming a national issue."

As if to appease her now, Ward bent over to kiss her lightly on the cheek. He paused, and later she guessed he had been debating about whether to tell her what he said next. "We came up with something tonight." His eyes gleamed as he spoke. "We're going to look into the possibility of suing Treegers on behalf of the town." Seeming not to notice her shocked response, Ward went on to explain. "We've contacted a lawyer, and he's going to let us know if we can build a case against them."

Mary didn't respond. The idea was so bizarre and divisive she couldn't quite get her mind around it. Ward then said, "If you want to stay awake for a while, that's all right. You can keep the light on."

How unfailingly polite he was. How unfailingly did he seem to do the right thing, and yet she so often felt wronged by him.

Before turning out the light, Mary reached for her crutches and went to check on the older kids. A nightlight lit the hallway so if they woke they'd have no trouble finding their way to her. Joseph had gone back to sleep, and the girls were still sleeping soundly. Mary stood in the doorway to their room, listening to their breathing, watching their sleeping faces. Didn't she have everything she needed for happiness? What more did she want from her life? A little more money. A decent house. But otherwise, what was she really lacking? There were so many worse off in the world: people being killed for what they believed, children starving right in front of their parents' eyes, families thrown out of their houses.

Whenever she expressed such thoughts to Claire, Claire said, "Why do you have to reach so far to feel better about your life? Sure there are people starving and people dying. So? What does that have to do with you?"

Mary's situation had been the subject of their most heated arguments. Claire wasn't given to martyrdom, and she frequently accused Mary of wallowing in it. "You have real reasons to be unhappy, Mary," Claire said now and then, but instead of making Mary feel better, such comments only made her feel worse. She felt she was giving in to her worst impulses by allowing herself to be affirmed in her unhappiness by Claire's objections. After all, Claire was still a self-proclaimed hedonist. Sometimes, like tonight, as Mary walked back into the bedroom to see that Ward was already deep in sleep, she felt contrite about her complaints with him. More than anything in the world, she loved her children. She believed in keeping their lives safe and happy. Whatever her dissatisfactions with Ward—and they were many—for the sake of her children she opted not to dwell on them.

≡CHAPTER 16

≡Claire pulled up to the curb promptly at nine on Saturday morning. Inside the house, Mary wrestled the three older children into their coats while David wailed in his car seat.

"I can't believe it," Mary said as Claire walked in the door.

"I said I'd be here at nine."

"But on a Saturday morning? I didn't think it was possible."

Claire smiled as she lifted David out of his car seat. "Hey little fella. What's all the fuss? You waiting for Aunt Claire?" In her arms, David settled down, hiccupping slightly as she rocked him. "What can I do to help?"

Mary pushed her hair out of her eyes and looked around the living room, which was cluttered with the kids' things. "Could you get David into his snowsuit? I'll grab the suitcases and shoo the other kids out to the car."

Within a few minutes they were all buckled in, the baby on the bench seat between Mary and Claire, the three other kids in the back seat. Their suitcases were stowed in the trunk and the cherry pie Mary had made sat on the floor between her feet. She turned to Claire as Claire started the ignition. "Are you sorry you agreed to do this?"

"I will be, but I'm not yet."

Mary laughed. In the back seat, Deborah and Priscilla began to squabble before they had even reached the edge of town. The sun's glare was diffused behind a thick veneer of clouds, turning the sky the color of galvanized metal. In the distance, the hills were gray. They encountered no traffic between Custer City and the Rasmussen ranch as Claire's Pontiac Bonneville roared down the highway.

Before the house came into view Mary saw smoke coming from the chimney. At the sight, she could imagine what the house smelled like. She knew Lydia would be busy making the big noon meal in honor of Mary's visit home, her first in the new year of 1990. John and Fresia would be out checking the cattle, making sure the water in the tanks was open, but they would head back in time for lunch. Although she lived only thirty-five miles away, she rarely got home to the ranch, and her refusal to drive only partly accounted for it. She was busy, and the problems of getting four kids organized for a weekend visit made it easier to stay put. In the past, John or Fresia usually came to get her and the kids. Sometimes Ward drove her out. Judy, a proponent of what she called tough love, was still critical of Mary's unwillingness to drive. She refused to take Mary to the ranch and wouldn't allow Max to either. This time Claire had been good enough to offer.

It was cold to the bone as later she and Claire began to unload the kids from the car. Lydia came to the kitchen door. She wore a white apron over her jeans and she held her thick-veined hands up in greeting as the three oldest children ran to hug her. "Oh my. Look who's come to visit." Lydia stooped to kiss each eager face. "And look who else is here." She walked out into the cold without her coat to see the baby. Mary flicked back the blanket briefly to reveal David's face. He had fallen asleep on the drive and she had succeeded in not disturbing him when she took him out of his car seat. "Goodness, he's sure changed, hasn't he?" Lydia glanced at Mary and put an arm around her. "How's my girl?"

"I'm fine, Grandma. Do you remember Claire?"

"Of course I do. I'm glad you could make it."

✳

As Mary anticipated, Lydia had been baking. On the counter, cloverleaf rolls were cooling alongside a triple-layer chocolate cake and pumpkin and pecan pies.

"I brought a pie, but it looks like you've already got dessert, so you can put it in the freezer and eat it later if you want."

"You know this family can't get enough dessert. Three pies and a cake will make your grandpa very happy. Shorty's here, too, and you know how he likes sweets." Shorty was one of the hands who had worked for Gerald and Cal for years and years. As a child Mary had loved him. Although gruff like all of those old ranch hands, he had always gone out of his way to do kind things for Mary and Judy when they were little girls: whittling tiny animals out of sticks, finding arrowheads in the pastures, anything he thought might delight a child. He was a quiet man, given to punctuating conversations with single-syllable words, usually swear words, which he drew out so they became at least three syllables long. He came to stand in the doorway to the kitchen and leaned against the doorjamb. Mary noticed how he hobbled on his ruined knees. His skin was leathery and thick. His hands gnarled and stiff, his fingernails hornlike.

"Well, I'll be," Mary said, and went to hug him with one arm, holding the baby out with the other arm for him to see.

"D-a-a-a-mn," Shorty said with a shake of his head as he looked from the baby to Mary. He shook his head again for emphasis.

Mary looked around for the other kids, but they had already scattered. "I'll introduce you to the other kids later."

"D-a-a-a-mn," he said again.

"I know," Mary said. "It's hard to believe, isn't it?"

He grinned, revealing a few missing teeth.

Cal emerged from the bathroom. It was clear from his pink cheeks he had just finished shaving. His mustache was still wet from being shampooed. Like Lydia, he made over the children, saving David for last. Cal had become an old man in the past year, and Mary couldn't help but notice how his hand trembled as he touched David's face. "This one's a keeper," he said as he smiled at Mary.

Any visit home was as fraught with reminders of how much had changed over the years as it was a confirmation of what had stayed the same. Will and Mark had both married young, Will now living and working in Grand Island and Mark in Kearney. Max and Judy had two daughters about the same ages as Joseph and Deborah. Max was a deputy sheriff and had been for six years. He'd given ranching a try but barely broke even, and rather than risk his family and his financial future, when he'd heard about an opening in the sheriff's department he'd jumped at the opportunity. Now and then he stopped by to see Mary in Custer City since the sheriff's office was in town.

Judy was the president of the school PTA and on the organizing committee for Anselmo's annual summer festival. A born leader, she managed her house like a well-run business, overseeing Max and her daughters like employees. Mary knew for a fact Judy ironed Max's underwear.

In high school both Will and Mark had been star athletes. By the time they'd graduated, it was clear neither of them would stay on the ranch. Their lack of interest spelled trouble for the future of the ranch, and although no one mentioned it, she knew John and Fresia worried about what would happen when they were too old to continue. Mary couldn't bear to think too long about the possibility that the ranch might pass out of the family.

Whenever possible, she still liked nothing more than to ride out into the pastures to the herd. Blue had died a few years earlier and now if she rode, she had to choose between three of the older saddle horses patient enough to tolerate her unusual mount. Other times she rode along with Fresia or John in the truck as they checked on the herd. She always hoped they'd cut the engine and let the cattle slowly mill around. There was nothing else in the world to her as calming as sitting quietly among cattle.

While Mary had been talking to Lydia in the kitchen, the three older kids had made straight for the cache of toys Fresia kept in the closet off the living room. They had pulled out the entire box and sorted through to find their favorites. Among the familiar toys were always new additions, and Priscilla ran to Mary now holding a new toy, her eyes wide.

"Mommy," she said as she held the doll out to her, "a princess."

"Isn't she pretty?" Mary admired Priscilla's find for a few seconds before Priscilla wandered off again, her attention still riveted in wonder upon the doll.

Mary caught her grandmother's eye. "That one sure reminds me of you when you were a little girl," Lydia said.

"Oh," Claire said in a mocking tone of voice. "Weren't you sweet, though."

Lydia's eyes hardened slightly. "Yes she was." Mary saw then her grandmother didn't much like Claire.

Mary laughed to hide the awkwardness. "So there. My grandmother says so. Come on and help me unload the car."

Together she and Claire walked back out into the cold, a startling contrast after the snugness of the woodstove. In spite of the cold, Mary loved to be outdoors in winter. She loved the sharp, dry smell of the red cedar trees, the dusty smell of dormant grass, the slight odor of old manure coming from the corral, smoke from the chimney. While she would have been up for a walk around the place, it was clear Claire was eager to get the suitcases out of the car and back into the warm house. If she wouldn't have felt guilty for foisting responsibility for the kids onto Claire and Lydia right before lunch, Mary would have gone by herself.

❉

Later, at lunch, the table was laden with the makings for a feast: smoked ham, dressing, mashed potatoes and gravy, raspberry Jell-O with cream cheese topping, sweet potatoes with brown sugar and pecans, cloverleaf rolls, Lydia's homemade chokecherry and gooseberry jellies, green beans, creamed corn, mandarin orange and walnut salad. They all passed the dishes amid teasing and talk. Deborah was sitting next to Mary. She caught Mary's eye at one point and smiled. She liked family get-togethers, routines, and rituals.

After lunch, while everyone was still gathered at the large round table in the dining room, the kids went off to play, and Max began to describe a situation that had come up recently in the sheriff's office.

"A woman from over north of Merna called up the other morning, said her husband's been missing for two days. We hadn't gotten any other calls on this guy, so we start looking around, finally find the guy's car. His billfold's there on the seat. His jacket. Nothing else. We don't find any prints; no sign of a struggle. The car was unlocked. No note inside. We looked high and low for him. Sent out a search team, even though there wasn't anything suspicious about the scene. The woman was convinced he'd been killed or kidnapped. Then yesterday the guy calls his wife collect from Texas. Texas! Collect? He's down somewhere near Lubbock. He's crying, says he wants to come home. He'd meant to leave her but couldn't do it. Admitted he'd created a new identity. Just like that, he was going to leave everything behind, make it look like maybe he'd been abducted or something."

"What'd the wife do?" Claire asked.

Max laughed. "Silly woman took him back."

Judy shook her head. "Well, I sure wouldn't do that." Everyone laughed at her vehemence, no one doubting what she would do.

"Neither would I," Claire agreed.

"I don't know," Fresia added slowly. "If you've been married a long time, it'd be hard, but I'd like to think I'd take him back."

John chuckled. "Honey, I'm sure glad to know you'd be so loyal, but you ought to know right now, I wouldn't be that loyal to you."

"Really?" Fresia asked, seeming genuinely hurt. "Really, John?"

"Yep," he said. "I can't even pretend just to make you feel better. That'd be it for me."

"H-e-e-e-ll," Shorty said with a chuckle.

"My, my. What a conversation," Lydia said and pushed her chair back from the table and began to clear the plates.

"Where'd you go just now?" Claire whispered to Mary.

"Oh." Mary laughed to cover her lapse, embarrassed to be caught daydreaming.

"I always tell you not to bring up this stuff, Max," Judy said. "It's a job hazard," she said to the others. "He sees so much awful stuff it's easy to start thinking everyone is a rat."

Max grew quiet before finally saying, "I guess maybe given the right circumstances, I think everybody is capable of doing things they wouldn't think they could."

"My land, Max, you can't mean that," Lydia said. "This conversation's too much. I think it's time for dessert. Sweeten things up here." Lydia headed back to the kitchen and Mary stood to help.

When they returned to the table with the pies and cake, the conversation had turned in another direction. Claire seemed to be settling in with Mary's family, and the subject had shifted to Mary, whom Claire was comfortably discussing with Judy.

They were comparing notes about Mary's tendency to hoard. "Have you seen her pantry?" Judy said.

"The paper sacks."

"Exactly. And the twist ties and rubber bands in the drawers."

"She's like a little old lady."

"Hey," Lydia said. "I take offense at that."

"So do I," Mary joked.

Judy and Claire quit their joking as soon as the plates were distributed and the coffee poured. John got up to add another log to the fire, and as he did so, he winked at Mary conspiratorially.

She thought back over the years and saw again and again the evidence of how her father had tried to understand her. Sometimes, when he was in Custer City alone, buying a farm implement or going to a sale, he stopped by and picked her up to go to the City Café for a treat. He always insisted they find someone to watch the kids so it would just be the two of them, and at those times as she sat across the booth from him, she always felt like his little girl again. He'd talk seriously with her about the herd and the ranch operation. On a recent visit, he'd thanked her for her foresight years ago about avoiding the rush to selective breeding for larger Herefords and Angus. "Temperamental heifers. Coming in open if you don't treat them just right. Everyone thinking about that extra few pounds and not thinking about the cost of inputs. Well, now they're thinking about it all right. Now there's lots of interest in our stock, all of them trying to correct a mistake in breeding. Grandpa said to me just the other day, 'How on earth did that little pipsqueak know this was going to happen?'" John shook his head. He always took off his cowboy hat and laid it on the seat of the booth beside him, his hair plastered against his head the way she liked it. Like now. He looked like a man taking a break from his work, not a man of leisure at all, but a man with pressing business always at hand.

Suddenly Mary felt a sharp pinch of nostalgia. She missed riding out with her father, separating to drive the herd into new pasture or moving it into the corrals during spring roundup. She missed working in concert with someone with whom whole days could pass with barely a sentence uttered. In those silent days, she and her father—and later, she and Brian—had communicated more completely than she had ever communicated with anyone since.

"The Kruegers are selling out," Mary heard Cal say then.

"You sure about that?" John asked, and Mary couldn't mistake the concern in his voice. This was the fourth neighboring ranch to fold its operation.

Cal nodded. "I wish we could buy that southwest pasture of theirs." He shook his head again, his mouth in a grim line. "Now isn't the time to be buying." Cal looked at Max. "You interested, Max?"

"Not a chance." Max didn't hesitate before answering. He'd had all he wanted of the foibles of trying to make it in modern ranching.

"I sort of figured you'd say that," Cal said.

"You know anything about what's happening with the Needham place, Mary?" John asked. "We've heard rumors they're close to selling."

Mary hadn't heard this news. She couldn't say she was shocked by it, but she felt her heart sink a little. "I haven't heard anything," she said finally.

"No, I don't suppose with all the trouble Ward's group's giving their boys they'd be calling you much." This from Lydia.

No one pursued this line of conversation. The family had expressed their reservations about Ward's actions plenty of times in the past. No one blamed Mary for what was going on.

Instead, Cal shook his head in obvious frustration. "Things start looking bad, and the bank calls in the loan," he said. "Every time. And yet we keep trustin' those buggers. Same thing over and over. It's the whole history of this western country."

"And those damned politicians and their farm bills," John said.

"Farm bills my ass. Corporation bills. Agribusiness bills." Cal growled.

"Sh-i-i-i-i-t," Shorty added, and Judy laughed.

"Now you two, mind yourselves at the table," Fresia said.

"Well, it's true, and you know it," Cal said. "They've got the farmer and rancher by the balls already, but they won't be happy 'til we're sharecroppers on our own land. Pretty soon the only people who'll own any land out here will be some rich asshole or another."

"H-e-e-e-c-k," Shorty said, then ducked his head and looked meekly at Fresia. Fresia smiled in spite of herself.

Lydia sighed. Even though Mary knew it disturbed Lydia to talk about politics at the table, she couldn't conceal her own worry.

"What I don't understand," Fresia said, "is why we keep putting politicians in office who time after time vote against our interests."

Lydia abruptly stood up. "We all know the reasons why. Let's not ruin our digestion with all this angry talk." She began to clear the dessert dishes from the table. "Would anyone like more coffee?"

By the time night fell, the temperatures outside had dropped to below zero. The wind buffeted the old house. Lydia shivered as she sat beside the stove crocheting a table runner.

"Makes you glad to be inside on a night like this."

Cal read in his recliner, a glass of whiskey on the stand beside him. Shorty had gone to the bunkhouse to turn in. John, in stocking feet, dozed on the couch while Fresia talked quietly to Mary and Claire. The older kids were all sleeping in the upstairs rooms, and Mary was nursing the baby.

"He's sure a sweet little guy," Fresia said, admiring her grandson.

Mary looked down at David. "He really is."

"Aren't you interested in having children of your own, Claire?" Lydia said. Her question startled Mary. Mary and Claire never spoke about such things. For some reason, Claire's commitment to noncommitment always seemed to preclude those questions, meaning there were a lot of areas of Claire's life off-limits to Mary, or at least that's how Mary felt about it. Lydia hadn't meant to be rude, and Mary hoped Claire wouldn't interpret it that way. She need not have worried. Claire was anything but fragile.

She joked now, "I never met a man I thought was as good looking as I am, and I'm not interested in having ugly babies."

As expected, her response made Lydia laugh. "Oh, Claire."

Claire never seemed to lack for male companionship, though Mary had to wonder sometimes what sort of companionship it was. That same pattern she had observed during the first weeks of their friendship had kept repeating in the years since. Half of the time she was chasing someone she'd just met and had to have, and the other half she was trying to figure out how to get rid of him. Like Claire had told Mary the first day they met, men always seemed to fall for her, but she never could stand the thought of being with one man for very long. Mary was used to this behavior from Claire, but tonight she thought she saw something sad behind Claire's eyes after she'd answered Lydia's question, and she wondered why their friendship wouldn't allow for the sort of conversation Lydia had tried to initiate.

✤

One of the things Mary loved best about visiting the ranch was that she didn't have to go to church on Sunday morning. Fresia sometimes went alone, but she never suggested Mary should go with her. This Sunday morning, they had all slept in. Even the baby slept until seven thirty, snuggling against Mary under the blankets and dozing off for another half hour. Then the three older kids were there, jumping on the bed and crawling in beside her, their cold bare feet against her.

"Settle down now," she finally said as they began to wrestle with each other. "Time to head downstairs." They were off in a flash, all three of them, their feet on the stairs so loud it sounded as though they were falling rather than running. After their noisy exit, David looked at Mary in bewilderment.

"Don't mind them," she whispered to him. "That's just the three stooges." He smiled at her then, his first smile.

✤

The weekend passed much too quickly. The temperature had stayed below zero, and now on Sunday afternoon as Claire went to start her car it refused to turn over. John got out the jumper cables and he and Shorty charged the battery. Later, as they all bundled into the car, Mary could see her parents were worried that they might have problems down the road.

"Maybe I ought to follow you on into town," John said.

"We'll be all right, Daddy."

"This is a good old car," Claire added. "It'll be fine now that it's warmed up."

"Will you call us first thing to let us know you made it?" Fresia said, stomping her feet to keep warm, her face white with the cold.

"Yes," Mary said out the car window. "Get inside, all of you, before you freeze."

Cal and Shorty stood in the yard and Lydia waved from the open doorway. As Claire drove away, Fresia blew a kiss while John paced a bit before finally waving as well. Mary watched as the others headed back into the house while John headed toward the barn instead. She was sure no chore took him there, only his need to be away from the family for a few minutes. She knew he struggled with a private grief, and she guessed it probably had to do with her at least some of the time. She didn't know how to reassure him that she was all right. She wasn't sure she could reassure herself of that, for the truth was she felt her heart sink as they pulled onto the highway toward Custer City and the parsonage. Home was still the ranch, not the parsonage, and she felt, as she always did when leaving her family, that she had to turn off some part of herself to reenter the world where she now lived.

Halfway back to Custer City, David, who had been contented for the entire weekend visit, inexplicably started to wail in his car seat. Mary tried everything she could think of to soothe him.

"Just pick him up," Claire said finally, clearly reaching the end of her patience with the noise. The older kids grew quiet in the back.

Deborah concurred with Claire. "Mommy, just pick him up," she said in a commanding tone.

"I can't, sweetie. It isn't safe."

Claire kept glancing away from the road toward the howling baby.

"Should I stop?"

"I'm not sure. Maybe something's pinching him. Do you mind?"

In answer, Claire pulled abruptly onto the narrow shoulder of the highway. Mary unfastened the car seat and pulled the screaming baby out. Almost immediately he quieted in her arms. Mary checked him carefully to make sure nothing had been causing him discomfort. His diaper was dry. There was no evidence anything had been pinching him. He had been fed right before they had left so she knew he couldn't be hungry. David was smiling and cooing at Deborah who had unfastened her seat belt and was leaning over the seat talking to him.

"Okay, little mother," Mary said to Deborah. "Time to get back into your seat belt. And you," she said to David, "are going back into your car seat."

As soon as she had buckled him in, he began to shriek again. Mary shrugged as Claire cast her a despairing glance. "I don't know what else to do," she said. "Let's just get home as quickly as possible."

They drove the remaining miles to the accompaniment of David's screams. When Claire dropped them off, they were all exhausted.

"I don't know how you do it," Claire said after the last of the bags had been carried inside.

≡CHAPTER 17

≡At night, they listened for the exceptional sound that would signal a problem, silence being the most alarming of all exceptions. Mary liked best those hours when all the residents had been bathed and tucked into their beds for the night, the hall lights dimmed, the nurses talking quietly between making hourly rounds. No night passed without some event, and it was never a true quiet, filled as it was with moans, grunts, screams, and shouts, but after ten years Mary had grown so accustomed to this tapestry of noise, she no longer heard it.

Over the years there had been changes. Staff turnover was high, and aside from Claire and Theresa, Mary now had the most staff seniority. The biggest change was in ownership of the home. Fred Carpenter, one of the wealthiest men in Custer City and owner of an international construction firm, had sold his business and bought the nursing home after his wife, Elizabeth, became a resident. Elizabeth suffered from Alzheimer's, and Fred had managed her care at home for years before being forced to give up.

Every day Fred was in his office wearing an impeccable suit, shined shoes, a flashy tie, and cufflinks. In his late sixties, he was still tall and fit. His reddish hair was thinning and he combed it over a pink bald spot. His long face was freckled and pale. He seemed a little slick to Mary, and she had been uncertain how she felt about him until one evening when after regular office hours she caught him in an unguarded moment with Elizabeth.

Every week he brought in someone to do Elizabeth's hair and makeup. She must have been a beautiful woman at one time, and in her dementia she still clung to the trappings of her former beauty. Fred was in her room one night after Elizabeth's hair had been done. She was admiring herself in the mirror. She wore a dark blue suit that Mary knew without being told had been very expensive, and her dyed blonde hair lay in ringlets down her back, a concession perhaps to a preferred hairstyle from the distant past, definitely inappropriate for her now. From the back, Elizabeth still appeared to be a young woman, her figure untouched by the years, but the face looking back from the mirror was a wreck, and the makeup only accentuated the disastrous effects of her disease. In that unguarded moment, Fred looked at his wife with loving eyes, remembering her—it seemed to Mary from where she stood undetected in the hallway—as she had once been. Fred gently led Elizabeth back to her bed after she finished admiring herself, and Mary saw in his tender gesture how much he must have loved her. After that night Mary never joined with the staff members who regularly criticized Fred's administrative decisions, chastened by her memory of that glimpse into his relationship with Elizabeth.

Within the first year of her work at the nursing home, Theresa had talked to Mary about getting an LPN license at Kearney State College. After completing that degree, Mary had started working on her RN. Each semester she had managed to find rides with people from Custer City who were also taking classes in Kearney. Her grandparents had come up with the tuition money, and Julie, who had never had any children other than Molly, had watched Mary's children for years while Mary worked and went to school. Most times it felt like everything Mary earned at the nursing home went toward helping with gas money to and from Kearney and paying for childcare, but she was committed to finishing her degree.

All these years, Mary had withdrawn from the rest of the nursing staff at this quiet time of the evening to study. Homework pressed every free minute she had at home as well. Now that Joseph and Deborah were in school they better understood the concept of homework, and Joseph sometimes checked with her to see if she had finished hers.

Tonight she was having a hard time focusing on her studies, and it wasn't just Berl Frakes's frequent moans. Berl, whose tender care of the church's privet hedge she had admired so long ago— who had helped her make a backyard garden so fabulous that each summer people came to look—had been a resident at the nursing home for two years, quickly becoming a favorite of the staff. Mary now understood Berl had severe osteoporosis. After two strokes he was paralyzed as well. He was dying, and, like nerves connected to a central nervous system, the entire nursing staff was attuned to his suffering. Mary sensed that once he stopped moaning they would all instantly notice the silence and know he was gone. Although everyone on the nursing staff agreed death would be merciful for Berl, Mary felt that losing him would be akin to losing a family member.

The real reason for Mary's distraction tonight, though, was the news Ward had delivered when he had come home for lunch earlier that day. Acting on their threat, the CCCA had hired a lawyer and formally filed a lawsuit on behalf of Custer City against Treegers. Mary had hoped for weeks that their plan would not materialize. She feared everyone in town would think she supported it, that she somehow agreed with their nonsense, when the truth was she didn't like this sort of trouble, felt sickened by it. She dreaded the ways it would divide Custer City.

Giddy with his plan, Ward had talked more openly with her than usual. He and Ed Lundgren, who acted as his second in command for the CCCA, had been in touch with someone Ward referred to as Galahad. Thinking she had misheard the name, Mary said with a smile, "Galahad?"

"It's not his real name," Ward said offhandedly.

Mary remembered then the envelopes Ward sometimes received with a return address of Warriors for Jesus. She thought now how she'd once overheard him refer to himself to someone on the other end of the telephone as Tedrick. While it had all seemed slightly laughable to her before, now as shadows gathered in the empty cafeteria where she sat, she felt something dark pass through her heart. As she'd long suspected, this wasn't about Treegers at all. She'd said as much to Ed Lundgren once.

"The battle is for the Lord," Ed had said.

"You think God cares about things like this?"

"You're too cynical for your own good, Mary," Ed had replied. "There's going to come a time when you won't be so glib." He'd said this with such authority that Mary had been momentarily swayed by him.

✳

Since the visit to the ranch, Mary had seen little of Claire. In fact, Claire had seemed glum all week. She guessed it was some trouble with a man, as usual, but after making her hourly rounds at 9:00 PM, when Mary stopped by the nurses' station Claire still wasn't around.

"I haven't seen hide nor hair of her all night," Theresa said and rolled her eyes.

Ordinarily Mary wouldn't have bothered looking, but tonight she decided she wasn't studying anyway and might as well talk to Claire. She finally found her in the empty solarium. It was cold out there, and it was evident Claire wasn't happy to be found. She barely acknowledged Mary's greeting as she came into the dark room.

It was Claire who broke the silence. "So what's eating you tonight, Princess?" Claire often teased Mary like this, and while before Mary had always understood it as affectionate, tonight she thought she detected an edge to the teasing.

"Berl," Mary said.

Claire paused. "Yeah. Me too."

They were silent for a few minutes before Mary told Claire about the lawsuit. Claire had known all along about the idea and agreed with Mary that it would be bad for the town.

"That's a bummer," Claire said, but her voice sounded flat and thick. Mary thought she heard a quiet sniffle as well.

"Claire, you're crying. What's the matter?"

"I told you. It's Berl."

"Come on."

Claire wiped her cheeks with the backs of her hands, acknowledging at last she had been weeping. "Would you say I'm one of your best friends, Mary?"

"You know you are." Claire was quiet again, and Mary prodded. "What's going on?"

Claire shifted in her chair so that she was facing Mary. Even in the dim light from the hallway, Mary could see tears shining on Claire's cheeks. "I need your help, Mary."

"Of course. Whatever you need."

"Don't answer so fast there, sister. The one thing I need is the very thing you can't do."

"What's that?"

Another sniffle from Claire. "I have to go to Lex next week. I have an appointment. I can drive there, but I won't be able to drive myself back afterward." Claire looked at Mary. "You're the only person I trust to do this for me."

Mary had never seen Claire this serious before. She swallowed hard. Of all the things to ask of her. "But there are plenty of people you could trust to drive your car," she finally said. "Why does it have to be . . ."

"Not drive my car, stupid. I'm not worrying about that, Mary." Claire suddenly grabbed Mary's hands. "You have to do this for me. I've been trying to think of a way to ask you for the past week."

"There's no one else who can do it?"

Claire shook her head. "No one I trust."

"Anyone else would be more trustworthy behind the wheel of a car than I would, Claire. I . . ." Mary started. She hated to admit her refusal to drive so blatantly.

Claire was quiet for a few seconds. She twisted hard a red band she wore on her wrist. She had tried to explain to Mary once what the bracelet meant, something about spiritual energy and healing. When she finally spoke again, her voice was terse. "Stop being so dense, would you, Mary? I'm telling you, it's not the driving I'm worried about. It's the kind of procedure I . . ."

It took Mary a second to finally understand. "Oh . . . you're . . ."

"Yes."

"Oh, dear." Mary did not ask Claire if she was sure. She did not ask if there might be another way, if together they couldn't figure out an alternative. After all her years of friendship with Claire, if Mary had learned nothing else, she had learned Claire always knew exactly what she thought. She was always in possession of herself, certain about what she did or did not want.

Mary had never seen her like this before, though. "I'll do it," she said.

"You will?" Claire was obviously unprepared for her answer, for she impulsively hugged her. "Oh, Mary. You've solved a huge problem for me. I know I can trust you not to tell anyone about this."

Claire was right. Mary would never tell anyone. It was Claire's business, and it would remain Claire's business. Still, Mary didn't know how she could possibly do what she had promised. She couldn't imagine how she would drive again just like that, but she decided in that cold, dark solarium she would do whatever she had to help her friend. She'd find a way to do it.

The next week Mary made arrangements with Julie to watch the two younger kids. Early that Wednesday morning, Claire pulled up in front of the house, and Mary, who had been watching, met her at the curb. They exchanged a tense greeting. It was February, and there had been snow earlier in the week. The highway was cleared, but the plowed snow stood banked against the shoulder, blackened by the slush thrown by passing cars. Though the sun was out when they started, the farther west they drove, the more overcast grew the sky.

"Would you like to talk about it?" Mary finally ventured.

"Nope."

And that was that. The door was officially closed on the subject. The miles passed as each of them silently focused on her own thoughts. Mary was thinking about Berl. He had died on Mary's shift three nights earlier, leaving this earth as gently as he had lived upon it. The funeral was to be held this morning, and Mary had felt torn not to be there and guilty for wishing to be anywhere else but with Claire.

Berl had wanted so little from his life, it seemed to Mary. He had been a sort of model for finding the good in what he had been given. No one would have described Berl's life as easy—widowed young, crippled by a debilitating disease, in the end, bedfast and alone. No one except Berl, who could still laugh at himself, still smile at the nurses each morning and each night, still celebrate the changing seasons, the birds and the squirrels, the leaves coming on and falling from the branches of the Norway maple he treasured outside the window of his room. Berl had told Mary once that the tree was like a friend to him. He had laughed when he said it, as though anticipating Mary's skepticism, but Mary understood well how Berl thought. The natural world was the place where he best understood God's role on the earth, a place of near worship for him, and it was his simple faith she most wished she could emulate.

Still thinking he needed to explain, though, Berl had said, "Things in nature can be our companions." He told her how he had spent his days studying that tree so deeply over so many years that he almost felt like he could make an argument for it having a soul, "a type of soul," he had hurried to add. "If you watch anything close enough, over a long enough time, you're bound to come to care about it. It's our nature to make things meaningful."

Mary thought about that conversation now. She thought about how that same need to study and curate could become a bad thing, too, like how she herself had avoided this same highway, Highway 21, for almost a dozen years, how she had made it a monument to her fear. She was thirty-three years old, and she had been avoiding her life, refusing to take responsibility. Today she forced herself to take note of this refusal, especially in light of Berl's still reaching out against the most impossible strictures. When they came upon it, she was going to make herself look at the spot where she knew Brian had died. She was determined that what had happened on the road to Indiana that Christmas so long ago would not happen to her today when she got behind the wheel of Claire's car. It couldn't happen. Claire was counting on her, and Mary didn't have a choice but to make sure she got Claire safely back home after . . .

Mary didn't know how she felt about what Claire was doing. It wasn't something she thought she could do herself. At least she didn't think so. But she couldn't be sure. That was the thing. She wasn't like Claire. She was never quite sure what she thought.

She glanced at Claire now. Claire wore a steely expression, and she never took her eyes away from the road, clearly taken up by her own thoughts. Mary was glad to be left to hers as they came upon the fatal intersection near the turnoff to Oconto. She noticed as they passed it that her right leg was tensed, her foot pushing hard against the floor of the car, as if stomping on an imaginary brake. Her body seemed to harbor some memory of that March night, and she felt herself begin to tremble. Embarrassed by her tremors, she exaggerated a shiver to suggest she was cold instead, and Claire turned up the heater, the only indication that she had noticed Mary's presence.

By the time they reached the outskirts of Lexington, Mary had calmed down. Claire drove straight to the clinic, a flat-roofed stucco building in a nondescript area on the fringe of the business district. There was a large gravel parking lot around the building, and a chain link fence surrounding it. In the parking lot were three other cars. Several people milled around the open gate. Some were holding signs depicting graphic images and urgent pleas meant to cause the women entering the clinic to reconsider. Standing closer to the gate were people wearing green vests. One of them beckoned for Claire to drive through. Mary heard a groan from Claire as she maneuvered through the gauntlet of protesters, and they pressed upon the windows of the car.

"Get away," she shouted. "Get the fuck away." They continued to throng about the car, shouting for her to reconsider as Claire finally cleared the gate. Her hands were shaking as she parked, and Mary suddenly felt anxious for her.

Claire seemed to feel it, too, for she looked a little pale now as she turned off the car. "It's now or never." She reached for her purse on the seat between them.

Mary laid her hand over Claire's, forcing Claire to meet her eyes. She didn't speak but she squeezed Claire's hand briefly before letting it go. Claire hastily grabbed her purse, and swiped at her eyes as she got out of the car while Mary followed more slowly. They both did their best to ignore the shouts from the crowd and followed one of the green-vested volunteers into the clinic.

Mary was glad she had brought along her homework. She was taking a clinical this semester that was challenging all of her fortitude for nursing. While she waited she wanted to have something to distract her. In the lobby, two other women sat on black vinyl office chairs. Out-of-date magazines—their covers either torn or completely gone—were piled onto end tables. The floor was clean, but the white linoleum had been badly worn in the high-traffic areas, leaving a path toward the back of the clinic, like a cow path, Mary thought, and then regretted it. A young receptionist smiled at them, and Mary sat down while Claire checked in.

When Claire came back to sit beside Mary, she immediately reached for a magazine, flipping quickly through the pages, stopping occasionally to read the caption beneath a photograph until a nurse wearing a pale pink uniform called her name.

"Wish me well," Claire said under her breath, sounding for a second almost like her old self.

"Good luck," Mary whispered a split second too late for Claire to hear as she was already walking away, following the nurse down the gray path.

❉

How much later was it? An hour? A half hour? Three hours? Mary had lost track of time and didn't check her watch when the nurse brought Claire out to meet her. Claire was pale, but she smiled when she saw Mary. The nurse handed Mary a bottle of pain killers, a box of heavy-duty Kotex, and a brochure with postprocedure instructions, all of which Mary took automatically without really paying attention. She shoved the things into her bookbag before taking Claire's arm and steering her out the door and toward the car, a little surprised when Claire did not resist her help. When they got to the car, Claire immediately headed for the back seat where she gingerly sat and then laid down. The protesters and volunteers had all left their post at the gate, and the parking lot was empty.

"You mind if I sleep?" Claire said.

"Are you all right?"

"Yes."

"Okay." Mary heard the doubtful tone in her own voice. "I'll get you home as quickly as I can." She swallowed hard as she opened the front door. She piled together her purse, her bookbag, and Claire's purse on the seat beside her, paused for a few seconds, then put the key into the ignition, cringing slightly as she did so, expecting the same cacophonous sound from before. Instead she heard only the engine's smooth purr. She swallowed again, checked the back seat where it was clear Claire was already nearly asleep, and slowly put the car into reverse. Her hands felt clammy and her heart raced, but she tapped the gas pedal and felt the car respond. She carefully steered out of the parking place.

Somehow this small success was enough, and Mary knew everything would be all right. Still, she was thankful for light traffic as she pulled onto the street. She was surprised at how quickly and naturally driving came back to her. For a second, she could almost remember being that confident twenty-one-year-old girl she had once been.

Claire slept and Mary drove. Time passed, and with it, Mary's fears. It had begun to snow softly, and she watched as the first flakes melted against the windshield. She searched the dashboard until she found the knob for the windshield wipers. The wipers leapt up and cleared the glass. Just that quickly she wasn't afraid. She was no longer afraid.

Claire did not wake up even when Mary pulled into the parking space in front of her apartment building, and Mary shook her gently. Claire seemed to swim up out of sleep. Through half-closed eyes, she acknowledged Mary.

"We're home," Mary said. "Can you walk on your own?"

Claire nodded groggily. She took a few seconds to pull herself into a sitting position, rested for a few more seconds, then moved with a wince toward the car door.

"Here. Let me help." Mary offered her arm, and together they walked to Claire's door. The snow was falling fast and Claire looked up once, the snowflakes causing her to blink.

"It's snowing," she said. "How'd it go? Driving?"

"Just fine. It went fine."

"I don't know how to thank you, Mary," Claire said once they were inside the apartment.

"Don't worry about it. I was glad to help." Mary didn't go on to explain that it had been the best thing to happen to her in a very long time. She was puzzled why no one, not Ward, not anyone in her family, had insisted before this that she drive. Judy had tried, but even bossy Judy had failed.

Mary remembered the things from the clinic. She pulled them out of her bookbag and laid them on the kitchen table after helping Claire lay down on the couch.

"You going to be able to make your way home?"

Mary ignored Claire's question. She lived four blocks away. How could she not make it home? "What could I get you to eat before I leave?"

"Nothing. I'm not hungry."

"Are you going to be okay here alone?"

"Yes. I just want to sleep a little more."

Mary watched as Claire started to drift off again. "I'll check on you later tonight."

Claire roused herself. "You don't have to. Really."

"Yes I do. Really."

"Whatever." Already Claire's eyelids were dropping, and before Mary made it to the door she knew Claire was asleep.

Four blocks wasn't far enough to walk. Instead, Mary chose to go the longest way home, around the south part of town, up into the hills where the nicer houses were. She didn't care that her tennis shoes were getting wet in the slushy snow, or that the flakes melting in her hair were starting to drip onto her face. In fact, she lifted her face to greet the falling snow, to welcome the cold.

A rabbit, startled by her passing, shot out from beneath a bush where it had been hiding. It ran across a lawn, leaving its prints in the snow. The shock of the rabbit's quick movement seemed to jolt something loose in Mary's mind. All these years she'd believed God had somehow singled her out, that she had been chosen, for some reason she couldn't discern, to learn a hard lesson, but there was no lesson. And just as she had earlier that day shrugged away her fear, she felt herself stop believing in the vindictive God she had fabricated in the hospital.

She hardly felt her cold foot or her dripping hair or her wet face as she began to run in her lurching way home to her children. She didn't care if any of the church people saw her. For the first time since marrying Ward and moving to Custer City, she didn't care what Ward would say if one of the church people told him about her unseemly behavior.

CHAPTER 18

The snow fell for a week, fourteen inches total, the biggest snowfall of the winter. Despite the cold and the dark, every evening after supper, the three older kids begged to go back outside to play. Mary zipped them into their snowsuits and sent them into the backyard. The porch light provided only a small pool of light past which Mary could barely see them as she peered frequently out the kitchen window. She was never satisfied until she had accounted for all three of their shadows, hard to see sometimes for the snow-covered young evergreens and the dormant bushes bordering the walks. The children had built a snowman their first night out. Each night thereafter, they had a snowball fight, missing one another now and then so that Mary heard an occasional muffled thud against the side of the house. Although she never saw them in the act, in the morning she would see the hint of snow angels already filling in with new snow.

At three months, David's eyes followed Mary hungrily. If she happened to catch his eye, he burst into such a delighted laugh, she couldn't help but laugh in response. If she neglected to pay attention to him for a few minutes, he coughed crankily to get her attention again. The intensity of his gaze made her think at times he was only playing at infancy, that he could talk if he only chose to. How early her children seemed to have been marked in their personalities, down to the point of their gestures, so distinct that she had early on concluded personality had to be as genetically coded as eye color or height.

Mary had missed two nights of work this week because Julie was sick. At first, Mary had been afraid Julie's illness might be a fabrication, a way to let Mary and Ward know she didn't approve of the lawsuit. Although in this instance Mary's fears had turned out to be false, she knew in other situations she had in fact been slighted, in some cases outright snubbed. As she had predicted when Ward first proposed the lawsuit, some members of the church were openly distressed about his involvement in the controversy. It had proven to be the most divisive point in the church's recent history, and there was no small worry that at least three more families would leave because of it, among them Mary's favorite couples, Alice and Delbert and Kelly and Greg. Ward appeared not to be concerned about these divisions in the congregation. It was a side of him Mary didn't recognize. She had spent over a decade living a life constrained by his preoccupations about the approval of the church members, and now she was confused to see him throwing over their concerns for so flimsy a cause.

When she questioned his decision, Ward shrugged her off. Ironically, despite these departures, the church was actually growing. Ward's profile in the community and his strong stand as an activist against Treegers had attracted attention. With this growth in attendance had come various improvements, starting with getting rid of the old hymnals, those musty old things that Mary had loved, and buying an expensive machine that projected the words to simple songs on a screen in the front of the church. A band with a guitar, drums, and a keyboard now played rather than Mrs. Lesley at the piano.

Emboldened by his success, Ward discussed openly from the

pulpit issues regarding the CCCA and the pending lawsuit. He'd turned the battle with Treegers into a metaphor for the battle between good and evil, believers and unbelievers. Mary had expected the congregation to resist such displays, but instead they seemed to revel in their role as persecuted believers. Ward's sermons grew more and more strident as he talked about God's retribution against evildoers and how Christians had been given not only the right but the obligation—a mandate—to take the country back from those who had corrupted it. Mary was puzzled as to how Treegers fit this description.

The children were at the back door now, their eyes bright and their cheeks rosy. Their clothes were wet, but they all looked happy as she let them inside.

"Mommy," Joseph said to her, "did you see what we did?"

"No." She stooped to help Priscilla out of her boots so she could take off her snowsuit.

"You'll like it," Deborah said.

Joseph shook his head. "You'll hate it."

"Oh, you think so?"

They both nodded their heads.

"I'll take the flashlight out and look once your things are all hung up." Mary hung Priscilla's snowsuit on a hook inside the back door before reaching for Joseph and Deborah's things to hang.

"Is Dad home yet?" Joseph asked, his voice suddenly gruff.

"No. He won't be home until late again tonight."

"He's never home."

"Daddy's busy, Joe. Do you want me to tell him something?"

"We want him to see what we made," Priscilla said, wiping the back of her hand across her runny nose.

"Use a Kleenex, Pris," Mary said. "I guess I'd better go out and see what you three did out there." After she'd put the baby in his swing in the living room, she slipped on her boots and pulled her coat off the hook. On a ledge above the door was a flashlight, and she took it with her as she walked out into the cold. The air was very still as the snow continued to fall fast and even. Already the kid's footprints had started to fill in on the back steps. The image filled Mary with a sudden sadness.

It turned out they had built a snow dog. They'd been asking for a puppy, and here, apparently, was another attempt to call attention to their request. Before she turned to go back inside, she noticed a detail that had escaped her at first glance. They'd used a stick to create the effect of the dog lifting his leg to pee on the snowman. Joseph's doing, no doubt. His irreverent humor struck Mary so funny she laughed aloud. She looked toward the kitchen window, where she could see the kids were all watching her. She was still laughing as she shone the flashlight toward them, hoping to signal that she'd seen the snow dog.

When she opened the back door Deborah asked, "Did you see it?"

"I did."

"We made her go potty," Priscilla said.

"Are you sure it's a she?"

Priscilla looked momentarily confused by the question.

"Priscilla's just dumb," Joe said. "Me and Deborah know it's a boy dog."

"Don't call your sister dumb, Joe."

Joseph mumbled a half-hearted apology to Priscilla.

"Will Daddy like it? Will he let us get a puppy now?" Deborah asked.

"He'll hate it," Joseph said.

"Of course he won't hate it, Joe. What's gotten into you all of a sudden?"

Joseph frowned but didn't answer Mary.

"Joseph's dumb," Priscilla said.

"Prissie. What's with all of you tonight? Being so mean to each other. If this is how you're going to act after you play outside, I won't let you go out again tomorrow."

"We'll be good," Deborah said and pushed Joe. Joe pushed her back. Mary put her hands on her hips and waited until Priscilla finally nodded her head, and Deborah solemnly said, "We'll be good." Joseph hung his head but refused to look at her, and Mary knew not to push.

"I know you'll be good," she said finally, and replaced the flashlight and hung her coat. "It's time to get your baths and into your pajamas."

In the living room, Mary heard David start to grumble in his swing. She hoped he could last until she had the other kids in bed.

❄

Ward came home after the three older kids were asleep and Mary was rocking the baby. He bent to kiss her and looked at David for a few seconds. "Let me get warmed up and then I'd like to hold that little man for a while."

"There's soup warm on the stove if you're hungry."

"That sounds good." He took off his coat and draped it over the couch. "I don't think it's going to quit snowing anytime soon."

"Did you happen to talk to Linda tonight about what she needs done for the children's program?"

"They want an original play again this year, with music. She wants you to set it up." Mary nodded. She'd expected as much. He went on. "And they need you to head up the food donation drive this year."

"Oh, Ward," Mary said. "I'm so busy right now with the baby. I don't know that I can do it."

Ward didn't respond to this. His policy of never getting involved with committee work at the church meant he would never intercede for her.

She paused before asking, "How'd it go tonight?"

"Fine. I know you don't believe it, but we really are seeing an end in sight."

Mary didn't respond. After years of this she knew one thing ended in time for another to begin. Tonight, though, she was worried about Joseph. "Is there any way you could make a little time to spend with Joe?"

He sighed deeply. "I'll try to make it home a little early tomorrow night from the church so I can eat with the kids. How would that be?"

"That'd be something."

Ward looked offended. "What does that mean?"

"Don't read into it, Ward. It means what I said. It's something." She paused for a second. "Joe seems bothered about not seeing you more."

Ward didn't answer her. Instead, he went into the kitchen where Mary heard him dishing up a bowl of soup. He didn't come back into the living room immediately. When he did, he changed the subject back to the lawsuit.

"We're going to get some media coverage over this."

"I know. You told me that already."

"No, I mean *real* coverage. Someone from the AP contacted *The Weekly* wanting more details. They're planning to send a crew out to cover the preliminary hearings and again for the trial."

Mary nodded. She looked down into David's sleeping face. She couldn't quite bear to look at Ward right then. When she glanced back up, he had finished his soup. He laid the bowl on the end table, stood up, and silently reached for the baby. Mary handed him over. She watched as Ward carried David back to the couch. She had a vivid memory then of the first hours after Joseph was born when she and Ward were alone in the hospital room and Ward had lifted Joseph from her arms before settling into a chair. She could picture that scene now, the window with the morning sun starting to rise behind Ward, the yellow chair where he sat for the next hour as he quoted from the Gospel of John. He'd been memorizing the gospels. That was how they spent their first hour together as a family before a nurse had come to take the baby for more tests. Mary recalled how the nurse had seemed puzzled by the scene, suggesting perhaps that "mom needed to get some rest" while the baby was gone, and that "maybe dad needed to get some rest too." Ward had taken the nurse's advice and had left the hospital to take a nap.

※

For reasons Mary did not entirely understand herself, she hadn't mentioned anything to Ward about having driven Claire's car. Since then, though, she had begun to make a plan. Her parents had an old Ford Escort they rarely drove, and she had a hunch they would be willing to let her use it. If she could start driving herself to classes in Kearney, she could go full-time and try to finish her program sooner. Just that morning she had looked at the course catalogs and figured out she could graduate in six months with her RN. That was, if everything went well: if Cal and Lydia were willing to continue to pay for her tuition; if Julie was willing to babysit more hours; if Ward went along with it; if she could manage the extra homework in addition to her hours at the nursing home, and her work with the church.

Mary had told no one, not even Claire, about what had happened to her after the drive home from Lexington. She felt Claire of all people would understand it least. Claire wouldn't understand at all someone thinking like Mary had. She would wonder what the big deal was in Mary's realization that there was no God judging her. Claire had never felt otherwise. At least until now.

Since the day at the clinic, they hadn't spoken about what happened, and Mary guessed they never would. In the same way, they had not discussed Claire's recent meetings with Ward. The first time Claire showed up at the parsonage and Ward answered the door, telling Mary as he did so that he had a counseling appointment, Mary thought it was a misunderstanding. She had joked with Claire about it, the laugh dying on her lips when neither Claire nor Ward laughed along.

"You're the appointment?" she finally said. Claire nodded. "But why?"

"I just have a few questions. I've been reading the Bible . . . and I have some questions."

Mary's face must have registered her complete bewilderment for Claire said, "I do read, Mary. I'm interested in these things."

Mary wanted to say, "Since when?" but she stopped herself. Claire had dabbled in one new belief after another. How could Mary now be surprised that Christianity might be among her interests?

Mary looked over at the couch where Ward was still holding the baby. David was soundly sleeping and Ward had started to nod off himself. Mary stood up, nudged Ward, and took the baby.

"You need to get to bed."

Once she had settled David into his crib, she checked on the other kids where they slept. The drafty house worried her sometimes, but the kids never complained about being cold. By the time she got into their bedroom, Ward was already asleep. She started to undress but stopped herself. She wasn't sleepy; she felt restless, a little agitated tonight. She closed the bedroom door and walked back into the kitchen where she looked out the window into the backyard. The snow still fell fast. Now that the kitchen was dark she could see the snowman and the snow dog in the backyard. The moon was a smear of light behind thick clouds. Around her, the town was hushed, and Mary felt a moment of deep contentment, as she guessed every mother must, to know her children were safe at home, but she couldn't seem to settle down to sleep herself.

For an hour she wandered through the rooms of her strange house, the steps up and down to its various additions, by now so familiar that she could move about in the darkness without difficulty. She had become accustomed to the house's awkwardness, its ugliness, its chill, but tonight sleep would not come, and she found the house a burden in a way that was new to her. She couldn't stand to stay a minute longer, and for the first time since Joseph's birth, she decided to leave the house without asking permission.

She felt almost giddy as she put on her boots and her coat and walked out the front door, locking it behind her. She glanced back once after she reached the sidewalk to make sure no lights came on, but the house remained dark. She had no particular destination in mind, and she headed to the place where habit took her. As a senior member of the staff, she had a key to the back door of the nursing home, and she let herself in. She had planned to go see Claire and Theresa, but when she noticed Berl's empty room on her way to the nursing station, she paused and went inside.

The bed was tightly made with new bedding. Everything had been freshly cleaned and deodorized, waiting for the next occupant. In the darkness, Mary sat on the edge of the bed as she had so many times when Berl was still there. She looked outside at the tree he had loved, its naked branches lit eerily from below by the foundation lights, looking to Mary tonight like arms raised in grief.

She remembered how Berl had told her about when he was a little boy living north of the Birdwood River, how in the prairie surrounding their house there had been a solitary tree that was a landmark for him in his childhood. One day when he was walking home from school, the tree he had counted on as a compass in that vast landscape was gone, and he remembered feeling momentarily lost. Later, he had rushed into the house frantic with the news of the missing tree, a devastating loss to him. After all these years he had forgotten what had happened to the tree, but he had never forgotten the sting of his father's laughter at his grief.

"Jesus, you scared me," Claire said from the hallway, startling Mary from her memories. "What on earth are you doing here?" Claire laughed. "Sorry I startled you. For a minute I thought you were Berl."

Mary stood up. "I was just coming to talk to you and got sidetracked."

"Now? Where are the kids?"

"They're asleep. Ward's home with them." Claire looked at Mary a bit dubiously, and Mary didn't blame her. This was odd behavior for her. She shrugged as if anticipating all of Claire's questions, and Claire let it drop.

"What are you doing sitting in the dark? It's creepy." Mary followed Claire reluctantly, not wanting quite yet to leave her memories of Berl. "Come with me for a final swing down the west wing," Claire was saying, "and then I'll take a break."

As they walked, she told Claire about her plans for the car. When she had finished, Claire stopped and looked back at her. "That's good, Mary." Before she turned to walk away, she added under her breath, "All because I made you drive from Lexington the other day?"

"Yes," Mary said. "It was good for me. It was the best thing . . ."

Claire's back stiffened. "Well, I'm glad something good came of it."

They were silent as they passed the remainder of the dark rooms in the west wing.

As if their previous conversation had not occurred, Claire said lightly, "All's quiet. They're either asleep or dead." This was the sort of sardonic humor Mary had grown used to. In a place where death was all too real, the staff had to find ways to joke about it in order to distance themselves. Mary had broken an unwritten rule by becoming too close to Berl. Still, everyone knew Mary and Berl had been friends long before he became a resident. Theresa had tried to warn her about it when Berl moved in, but even Theresa had to admit that with some residents it was impossible not to get attached. If the nurses were doing their jobs right they would mourn the death of a "client." Theresa always insisted on using the administration's terse terminology.

"Did Ward have any news tonight about the lawsuit?" Claire asked once they sat down in the cafeteria.

"No," Mary said. She wondered again about Claire's new interest in Ward's activities. It would have been the right time to bring up again what had now become her regular meetings with him, but Mary knew Claire would only deflect the question. As strange as it all was to Mary, she couldn't seem to confront Claire a second time.

＊

Later that night as Mary walked slowly back home, moonlight filtered through the clouds. It would be spring soon. Even with a foot of snow on the ground and snow still falling through the cold, cold air, Mary could feel spring was very near. She and Berl were alike in that way. They were both children of this place, and they understood the loneliness of living with animals more than with people, living closer to the sky and the earth than with the things people had made. Even a town as small as Custer City still seemed confining to her, and although she had learned to live close to the sounds and smells of other people, she had never truly become comfortable with it.

That night when she finally slept she dreamed; it was a glorious dream. She was dancing with Brian at a country fair. Fiddles played a lively tune. As they danced, they laughed. They danced, their feet so nimble it seemed as though they were not so much dancing as flying. As the dream continued, the faces of her dance partners changed: first her father; then her grandfather and Max; Will and Mark; all the boys of her childhood and the boys of her adolescence; Gus and the Needham boys; every man she had ever loved, all of them laughing as they moved across the room with her. When she woke from the dream she was laughing out loud. The dream had filled her with joy, and she smiled into the darkness for a long time thinking about it. Ward, undisturbed, slept beside her. Only then did she recall he had not been among the dancers in the dream.

≡CHAPTER 19

≡Three weeks later, when John and Fresia dropped off the Ford Escort at the parsonage, the snow was gone and the grass had started to green. There was still a chill in the air, but the birds were singing, and the path of the sun had changed. In two weeks it would officially be spring. Judy had followed in the Chevy pickup, and everyone was now standing in the driveway of the parsonage as John described the car's quirks to Mary. Fresia held David while the older kids climbed in and out of the car, crowding close to Grandpa as he opened the hood and showed Mary the oil cap.

"Hey, Skinny," Judy had said when she first greeted Mary. "What on earth suddenly made you decide you could drive again?"

"I don't know. I just decided it was time."

Judy shook her head. "A little late, if you ask me." She picked up a strand of Mary's hair and let it drop back to her shoulder. "You need a haircut. You look like you're twelve years old with that long hair."

"I don't have time for haircuts."

"Why don't you take it around the block?" John said. "I'll ride along with you."

Mary got into the driver's side and adjusted the seat for her height. She tentatively turned on the ignition. The little car coughed but finally started. She took a few minutes to locate the headlights, switched on and off again the windshield wipers and the hazard blinkers. John got into the passenger seat, and Mary looked at him quickly. She waited for the kids to move off the driveway before she backed onto the street. Neither she nor John spoke for several minutes as she concentrated on getting a feel for how the car handled.

"I'm real proud of you, Mary," John finally said.

"Don't be, Daddy. I should have done this a long time ago. It's crazy to be proud of someone for finally starting to act normal. You can be proud of me when I graduate with my RN degree. But this is a shame, all of it."

"You're being a little hard on yourself, aren't you?"

"No," Mary said and glanced across the seat at him again before turning her eyes back to the street. "I've been sleepwalking, and it's time I woke up."

John changed the subject. "Speaking of your degree, Grandma and Grandpa said, 'Tell Mary the tuition money's in the bank.' They're glad to hear you're going to try to finish soon. We all are."

Mary nodded. She pulled onto Highway 2 and depressed the gas pedal. The car responded sluggishly but eventually got up to speed.

"It isn't the punchiest car," John said, "but it'll get you there and back. If you have problems, let us know." He paused. "We want to help you, Mary."

By the time she pulled back into the driveway, Ward had come home for lunch. His face registered not only his surprise at seeing Mary behind the wheel of a car, but his disappointment that she was driving and it appeared he was the last one to know it. Mary couldn't say why she hadn't told him.

Ward's initial confusion was quickly replaced by his usual politeness. "Well, well. What's this?" he said as he approached the driver's side door. Mary was trying to get out and didn't immediately acknowledge him.

"Mama and Daddy are giving me this car so I can drive myself to classes," she finally said.

Ward continued to nod. "That's nice of you," he said first to John over the top of the car, then to Mary, "I didn't know you were driving again. When did this happen?"

"I don't know." Mary heard her own impatience. "I just decided it was time."

Ward laughed thinly.

"Where are the kids?" Mary said.

"They're in the house with Judy and your mom."

John had moved to the back of the car from where he now beckoned to Mary. "You've got jumper cables here, a tool kit, a winter emergency kit, and here's your jack and everything for changing tires."

"Thanks again, Daddy."

Ward had followed Mary, and he reached out to take John's hand now. "This is sure generous of you."

John hesitated a split second before taking Ward's hand. He didn't respond to Ward's thanks, but as he hugged Mary to him with one arm, he said softly, "Anything for my girl."

Fresia had brought sandwich fixings, and Judy hollered from the doorway that lunch was ready.

The older kids were eating lunch when they entered the kitchen. "Mambma brought cake," Priscilla said, her mouth full.

"Chew your food before you talk." Mary noticed the cake, one of her grandmother's triple-layer chocolate cakes. "Oh, Grandma Lydia sent one of her special cakes."

Priscilla nodded, her eyes bright, her mouth firmly closed and chewing even though Mary knew it cost her all of her self-restraint not to speak.

"Can we ride in the car with you, Mommy?" Joseph asked.

"We'll go for a ride when Grandma and Grandpa leave."

Mary sensed as she spoke that all the adults in the room were looking at her oddly. She understood none of them could account for why after a dozen years of refusing to drive she had so suddenly decided she could.

Ward had good reason to wonder why she hadn't told him about the request for the car, why he was the last one to know about the breakthrough. Mary sensed his hurt. His relationship with her family had never improved over the years. Not even the births of the children had helped. In fact, it had only created new opportunities for her parents to criticize since they had noticed that Ward was so seldom at home. Today, Ward ate a quick sandwich and went on to explain he had a wedding to perform in Sargent the next day and he had to oversee the rehearsal this afternoon. Ward never complained about how busy his life was. Mary felt a momentary sadness for him. He seemed both half formed and admirable, and she was confused about her feelings. He wasn't a bad man. She certainly didn't hate him. If anything, she felt indifferent toward him much of the time. Her life with him was a habit. Since her pregnancy with Joseph, she'd never thought she had any choice except to stay with him. But if she were free to choose again—and this was something new, asking herself such dangerous questions—she knew without a second's hesitation that she most certainly would not have chosen Ward Hamilton as her life partner.

She must have been preoccupied for a few minutes, for Ward interrupted her with a quick kiss. "I'll be late."

"Okay," she said.

"I'll put David's car seat in the Escort so you can take the kids for a drive later." He stooped to kiss each of the kids before leaving. He shook John's hand again and stiffly hugged Judy and Fresia.

Once the lunch dishes had been cleaned up and the two little ones laid down for naps, John said, "Why don't you take some time and drive a little on your own?"

"Go ahead, honey," Fresia said. "We'll be fine here. Take the afternoon."

Even Judy encouraged her. To Mary's question about her own

kids at home, Judy replied, "I don't get into town that often. I might just run out and do a little shopping."

"Maybe we'll both do some shopping," Fresia said, glancing at John to make certain he'd be willing to babysit.

"Why are you looking at me like that? I'm fine to stay here. Joe and I can keep an eye on things, can't we?"

Joseph, who was playing with LEGO blocks on the floor, looked up at his grandfather and smiled.

Mary, suddenly liberated, hardly knew what to do with the gift of time. She picked up the car keys. "I think I will go out for a while. Thanks."

"I mean it now, Mary. Take some time and get used to the car," John said.

"Okay." Even as she spoke, Mary knew where she wanted to go. She wanted to drive along the back roads south of Highway 2, west of Mason City to the Rasmussen family homesteads near where the town of Algernon had once been, where John's family had all lived and died. Mary hadn't seen those homestead places for years. When she'd last seen them, they were already in serious decline. In the family cemetery, bridal wreath spirea and lilacs grew wild, and the stones marking the graves of her ancestors were either toppled or eroding. She had always loved that remote place, though, where diamond willows and Russian olives grew along sloughs and draws between craggy hills.

❋

When later she pulled onto her grandparents' homestead, she would have known the property anywhere. Even though the house and barn were gone, and only the windmill and the stock tank remained, the spruce trees she remembered from her childhood still stood, and in her memory she could see again the two-story house and the corral and barn down the hill, the orchard in back, the chicken coop and the granaries, the shelterbelt to the north.

The new owner had converted the property to pasture, and a herd of mixed cattle milled around the old stock tank.

Mary headed farther west to the places where her great-aunts and great-uncles homesteaded. It had been over a decade since she had last been here, and she barely recognized the sites covered by fields of soybeans and corn.

She saved for last the house where her great-grandparents had lived, and where John's demented great-great-grandfather had spent his last days. In his final years, the old man had taken to running away, so they had built a ten-foot-high fence around the property to keep him in. The fence was long gone, but the house was still standing. Its weathered wood siding peeped from behind overgrown mulberry and hedge apple trees, and the farmyard was surrounded by an ill-kept pasture. The house had not been occupied by anyone since her great-grandparents had died. Mary stopped the car and got out to walk around. An old outhouse in the back leaned to the east. Ragweed and ironweed grew tall in the front yard. Old farm implements rusted in the back, their tines and tongues and scoops like the bones of prehistoric animals.

Since her father's most vivid childhood stories were those of his great-grandfather's attempts at escape, Mary found it oddly amusing that she now worked with people who regularly tried to escape their confines. Although John had loved his grandparents, he had admitted to Mary that in those final years of his great-grandfather's life, he had hated to visit them. The old man scared him as a child, with his wild, bloodshot eyes and his long, matted hair. In his dementia, he often tore off his clothes. John had told Mary that although the old man never tried to climb the fence, when he tried to dig his way out underneath it, the solution had been to dig a trench around the fence and fill it with fresh cow manure. John recalled his grandparents laughing as they described the old man shaking the manure from his hands and saying in his guttural accent, "Ahck, ahck." John had felt both terrified of and sorry for the old man.

Mary felt connected to this place because of her father's stories, but it now seemed like a dead branch of her family. All the Rasmussens were gone except John, her siblings, and herself. Her father's family was alive only in memory, and even the memories that kept them alive were fading. Mary had never brought her own children here, and she doubted she ever would. She didn't talk to Judy or her brothers about the Rasmussen clan, and she didn't think any of them had the same preoccupation with the past she did.

The last time she had visited Algernon was right before she married Brian. She had brought him to see where her people had lived and died. He had understood the gesture for what it was, an invitation for him to understand her whole life, and he had reciprocated by taking her to the cemetery at Rose. She felt a sudden sharp pang at the memory. She hadn't been back to the place where Brian was buried since the Needhams had taken her to his grave the November after he died. She'd like to see his grave again in springtime. She felt a tiny flutter of excitement; she was driving again, and she could go where she wanted.

❉

By the time Mary got home it was late afternoon. The Escort had almost gotten stuck on the muddy, rutted back roads a few times, but in the end the car had handled well, and she was pleased with it. The morning sun had been replaced with overcast skies, and it looked as though it might rain before evening.

The lights were on in the living room. Mary knew her family would be waiting for her as she parked in the driveway, but she didn't immediately get out of the car. Instead, she sat for a few minutes and let the silence settle around her until the kids burst out of the front door.

"Mommy, did you go for a drive?" Joseph asked.

"I did."

"Where did you go?" Priscilla said, stepping back to make room for her as Mary got out of the car.

"I went to see a place where my grandparents and my great-grandparents used to live."

"Algernon?" Deborah said.

"Yes." Mary looked at her quickly, startled by how much she always noticed.

"David's hungry," Deborah added, and it was obvious by her tone she was a bit miffed at Mary for all the fuss.

"I'll feed him as soon as I get inside. He'll be okay, little mother."

Deborah frowned slightly and looked away. Priscilla took Mary's hand, and Deborah finally took her other hand. Joseph followed.

"How'd she run for you?" John asked when she came inside.

"Great. I took it out to the old place."

"You drove on those roads around Algernon?" Fresia said. "It's a wonder you didn't get stuck."

"I did get stuck a few times, but that little thing maneuvered its way out of it."

John smiled, and Mary could tell he was pleased not only by her driving but by seeing something of her old spirit again. She remembered all the times in the past when he had looked at her with concern and skepticism. How difficult it must be, she thought, to watch your children flail. She didn't know where the word *flail* had come from, but she felt it suited her. She didn't want to be flailing anymore. She was going to do her darnedest not to.

"We need to get home to the horses," John was saying now. "You call if you have problems with the car, you hear?"

"I will." Mary hugged her parents and Judy good-bye. As they were going out the door Mary noticed the packages her mother and Judy picked up. "You weren't kidding about shopping, I see."

"We don't spend an afternoon in Custer City just every day," Fresia said. "We have to take advantage of it when we can."

❋

"What shall I feed you all?" she said to the kids after her family had left.

"Grandma left some meat in the refrigerator." Deborah pulled Mary by the hand to see that indeed her parents had brought several cuts of beef.

The kids were elated when after supper Mary loaded them into the car. She struggled for a few minutes to find the old seat belts lost behind the back seats. "Joe, you'll have to sit in the front with me, all right?" Joseph nodded. "And Debbie, can you watch Prissie and David in the back seat?" Deborah nodded.

The sun had set by the time Mary got everyone belted in. "Let's see if these headlights work." The lights came on, and Joseph sighed with audible relief. "What shall we do?" she asked, guessing already the answer she got in unison from the older three. "Ice cream."

She smiled and put the car in reverse. "Ice cream it is." She backed down the drive. She had imagined she might balk with the kids in the car, but she didn't. Her confidence never wavered even as she pulled onto the highway and drove to Dairy Queen.

"Aunt Claire's here," Joseph said, sitting up straighter as Mary parked.

"Where?"

"There's her car." Joseph pointed.

"She'll think it's funny to see us, won't she?" Mary said.

The kids squealed with the excitement of creating a surprise. Even little David chortled. Mary laughed too.

"Don't run off," Mary scolded once Joseph and Deborah got out of the car. "You wait for me to get Prissie and David out."

"She can't see us," Mary heard Deborah tell Joseph. Mary glanced inside and saw Claire sitting in a booth across from an older man. It took a few seconds for Mary to realize the man was Fred Carpenter, the nursing home administrator. She stood up and looked more closely. As she watched, Fred leaned forward and something about the gesture led Mary to conclude he was the one. The one Claire had made clear she would never reveal to Mary.

Mary's amazement at the discovery had more to do with how she felt about Fred than any sort of moral judgment. He was clearly devoted to his wife, despite her long, slow decline. Mary didn't judge Fred for looking for and finding companionship after all these years, but he was almost forty years older than Claire. Even as she thought this, Mary knew it wasn't the age difference that bothered her.

Mary was not in the mood to be spotted by either of them, but she didn't know quite how to get out of the predicament she was in with the kids. They would be terribly disappointed if she made them leave without their ice cream, yet she felt strongly she shouldn't embarrass or compromise Fred and Claire. Why had they chosen to meet in such a public place anyway?

"Joe and Debbie," she said, "do you think you two could get ice cream cones for yourselves and for Prissie? Mommy's going to stay outside here with her and David."

Priscilla's eyes immediately filled with tears. "Why can't I go, Mommy? I've been good."

Mary hugged her. "Of course you have. It's not that. I need you to stay and help me with David." Priscilla looked longingly at the Dairy Queen. "I'll bring you another time. I promise," Mary said. "Just you and me, okay?"

Priscilla set her mouth. "Okay, Mommy," she finally said with resignation.

"That's my girl." Mary turned to Joseph and Deborah. "Let's not bother Aunt Claire this time, all right? She's in an important meeting, and we don't want to interrupt." Mary hoped that Joseph and Deborah could get in and out without Claire noticing them. From the engrossed look on Claire's face, Mary thought it might be possible. Mary knew Claire well enough to see even from the parking lot that she was angry. Fred was clearly not responding in a way that pleased her. Mary could only see Fred's back, his impeccable suit, the fringe of reddish hair, the ruddy color of his neck and the bald patch on the back of his head, but it was enough to convey his tension.

She handed Joseph and Deborah a five-dollar bill and watched as they went inside. The girl behind the counter recognized them, and Mary saw her glance out toward the parking lot to confirm the story they were telling. Mary waved and the girl waved back.

Custer City was a small town, and it was well known that Mary Hamilton, the pastor's wife at the Church of Christ, had not driven for many years. Those who knew her could guess the reason, but over the years the rumor mill had manufactured extravagant stories. This new turn of events would be all over town by tomorrow, Mary thought with a sinking heart. She lived in a world where a small decision reverberated and circled back again and again, always with new variations.

"We got 'em, Mommy," Joseph said when he returned to the car holding carefully both his cone and Priscilla's. He handed Priscilla hers. "You want a lick?" he asked Mary after he had handed her the change.

"Just one. Thanks." Mary licked the dripping ice cream at the rim of the cone. "It's starting to get nippy out here," she said when she finished.

Priscilla nodded, her face already smeared with ice cream. "Nippy," she repeated. From his car seat David began to make cranky sounds.

"Mr. Cranky Pants," Deborah said and crawled into the back seat. "He can't have ice cream, can he?"

"No, he's too little for so much sugar."

Priscilla nodded again. "Too little," she repeated.

Mary didn't think Claire had noticed them, but as she finished buckling the kids into the car, she wondered why she was in such a panic to keep Claire's secrets. Why was she feeling so responsible for Claire? Besides, this was a public place, and if Claire didn't want to be seen, she shouldn't be in public. As she was grumbling to herself, Mary realized it was she who didn't want to be seen. She who didn't want to know the truth. She couldn't bear to hear the whole story of Claire's life. They were best friends. Everyone knew that. But there were significant things that divided them. Mary had always known this in theory, but seeing Claire with Fred, someone Claire had never even hinted at knowing beyond the nursing home, made it real, and Mary couldn't shake the feeling that her friendship with Claire, like so many other things in her life, was evidence of how much of the world was a mystery to her, how superficially she experienced life.

≡CHAPTER 20

≡Claire was the fun one. Mary never tired of seeing the kids run to greet her when she came to visit. For the first few minutes after each arrival Claire devoted herself entirely to them, lifting and swinging, romping and growling, then attentively listening as each of the older three in turn told about their week. Even baby David was old enough now to appreciate the significance of a visit from Aunt Claire and impatiently waited his turn to be held.

"He's rolling over!" Claire said as David's turn came. "When did this happen?" She scooped him up and tickled him.

"Say, 'last week, Aunt Claire,'" Mary said.

"You little monkey, you." Claire danced him around the room.

All was well until later in the evening when Claire grew quiet, her earlier buoyancy giving way to one of her sour moods. Mary was used to Claire's ups and downs and ignored her as she went about getting the older kids to bed while Claire held David in the rocker. When she returned, Mary saw Claire had already changed David's diaper and put him into his sleeper. Bedtime always went better if Claire was there to help.

Claire didn't say anything as Mary took David and sat down to nurse him, but Mary glanced up just as David's mouth clamped down and she intercepted a dark, fleeting glance from Claire. The expression was so bitter, it startled Mary. David lost the nipple and fussed crankily. By the time she'd readjusted and looked up again, the expression had passed and Claire was leafing through a magazine. Mary would have forgotten all about it if as Claire was leaving for the evening she hadn't said, "Well, Old Mother Hubbard, this barren wasteland is leaving." She had obviously intended it to be funny, but the tone was wrong, and Mary recalled again the cold look she had intercepted earlier.

There was no time for Mary to stew about what might be bothering Claire. They had work to do. Mary had been assigned to organize a fund-raiser for the CCCA to help with legal expenses, and Claire had volunteered to help. The date had been set for the weekend of Memorial Day, in hopes, Mary knew, of cashing in on the God and country aspects of the holiday. She and Claire had already advertised and started to line up the volunteers to bring food and provide talent. Women from the community had offered to help. Understandably, the church women felt divided in their loyalties and most of them, in spite of their views on the issue, felt they didn't want to be involved in anything that would offend the pro-Treegers church members. Mary hadn't wanted to be involved either, but Ward had made it clear he was counting on her.

The lawsuit filed by the CCCA made impossible demands. They wanted nothing short of Treegers closing down, and Treegers had finally dug in their heels, hiring a high-profile lawyer from Omaha to defend them. Now, with their business at risk, they would not back down from the fight at hand. Time had only exacerbated tensions in Custer City between the opposing camps in the lawsuit. Some who were pro-Treegers took out their resentment toward Ward and the CCCA by openly scorning Mary. Even the children were affected by it, and it was not only other children influenced by the views of their parents, but also teachers who vented their anger on Joseph and Deborah.

Earlier in the week Mary had impulsively called Kent Needham and asked him and Larry to meet her for lunch in Overton.

"I'm glad you called, Mar," Kent said, using their old nickname for her. They agreed to meet at the Landmark the next day, where, without his saying it, they hoped they wouldn't be seen together.

When she called, Mary had hoped a meeting with the Needham boys could bring about a resolution, but tonight as she contemplated their meeting the next day she wondered why she was looking for someone or something to rescue all of them from the thing that held them in its grip when she knew such rescue was not really possible.

⁜

Kent and Larry were already at the Landmark when she arrived. It had been twelve years since Brian had died, and she had seen little of them during those years. Not since her visit to the cemetery in Rose had she seen them together. They both looked older—Kent stouter than he had been as a young man, his belly straining against the buttons of his striped western-cut shirt and the buckle of his wide belt. Larry, still thin, resembled Gus more with age. Across the table, Mary noticed how haggard his face looked, the pale skin seeming to hang off his high cheekbones, his hair the same pale color as his skin. Mary guessed they thought she looked older too. Both of them had married local girls and had children younger than hers, though Mary had never formally met their families. They did not speak about the troubles on the Needham ranch, but she knew it was the reason Kent had been able to recruit Larry and Jeffrey to the business.

Kent and Larry seemed nervous as they looked over the menu, and Mary suddenly felt sad for them. The days they had shared together were long in the past and they were strangers to one another. Unlike the past, none of them knew quite what they could ask for or count on from one another. After they had placed their orders, both men shifted slightly in their chairs.

Finally, Kent cleared his throat. "You seem tired, Mary."

"I am tired, Kent," she said, a little surprised by her own sternness. "I have a lot of reasons to be tired." She hesitated a second before adding, "One of the things that's really making me tired is watching you guys screw up."

Both men seemed surprised by her confrontation. Larry glanced at Kent and then back to Mary. "Now wait a . . ."

Kent interrupted. "What do you mean we're screwing up? We didn't start all this. We haven't done anything wrong." He paused before saying, "It's your husband's who's hitting below the belt."

Larry nodded. "This is the deal. Even if we win the lawsuit, which we're going to do, the company is still slandered. What are we supposed to do? We've put everything into making things go at Treegers, and it . . ."

"Oh, stop being so pathetic," Mary said. "You both act like you're helpless." There were few people in this world she would talk to so candidly. They might feel shy with one another, but she knew these men.

Kent glanced at Larry. He picked up his spoon, gently tapping it twice on the table before he caught himself and dropped it. He looked quickly around the restaurant before saying, "I think maybe you don't . . ."

"You think I don't understand? Is that it? It's too complicated for someone like me to understand?"

They didn't answer immediately, and Kent finally said, "It would really help matters along if you could talk to Ward for us. Tell him to back off, or at least get him to talk to us."

Mary sighed loudly and sat back against her chair. "That's not why I suggested we meet. I've told you before, I can't tell Ward to do anything."

Larry laughed. "That's a little hard to believe. We know how persuasive you can be. Brian would have done anything for you. Heck, all of us would have."

Mary winced at the reference to Brian. "Ward isn't Brian."

Their food arrived and Mary used the diversion to pull herself together. It wouldn't do any good to argue with the Needham boys. After a few minutes of quiet while they salted their food and pressed their napkins into their laps, Mary finally said, "The truth is, the CCCA isn't your problem. It's the public you need to be worrying about."

"What makes you think we aren't worried about that?" Kent said, leaning forward, his mouth full of mashed potatoes, and in that instant Mary saw him again as she had seen him that first night at the Needhams' dinner table. She glanced at Larry and saw again the young man he had been. Her face must have softened, for they, too, seemed to be seeing her in memory. Suddenly, they were back on the ranch, eating together as they had so many meals, working together every day, discussing how to tackle one problem or another on the ranch.

Mary set down her fork. "It doesn't matter what the CCCA says. You've let them distract you, and you've been overestimating people, thinking they'll figure things out for themselves, but they haven't, and they won't. Not like this, anyway."

Larry sat up straighter. "She might have something there," he said to Kent. Then to Mary, "But so what?"

She took a bite and swallowed it quickly. "Here's what. You need to talk to the newspapers. Start talking to the reporters, you guys. You act downright retarded sometimes, thinking it's all going to go away. That's backfired on you. You need to work with these people, explain how you comply with EPA standards. You go beyond them, I bet. Right?"

"That's what we keep saying, but no one listens," Kent said.

"No, you don't keep saying it," Mary interrupted. "You're saying it to yourselves maybe, or to people who agree with you, but you aren't saying it to the people in Custer City who are darned fed up with the stench around here." Kent grimaced at this, but Mary went on. "You need someone who can remind people that you have more than eighty employees from the area. You pay a living wage.

You guys live here. People forget that. You were raised around here; you're raising your own families in Custer City. Why can't you find a way to make it clear you don't want to foul your own nest?" She stopped then, a little embarrassed by her vehemence and the articulation of ideas she didn't know she had. The guys were silent. She shrugged finally. "I won't lie to you. I don't like what you're doing. I don't like it at all. I've never been able to come to terms with it. I love both of you, but I hate your business. I hate how close you built to town." She paused. "But I figure feedlots aren't going away, so you somehow have to help people figure that out. If they drive you out the problem isn't going to go away. Am I right about that?"

"Yes," Larry said. "That isn't just you talking. Someone will come along behind us if we leave." He was quiet for a few seconds before he finally looked at Mary with a tired smile. "What you're saying makes sense to me, but I don't know. How do we start doing those things?"

"It's pretty clear you can't, so you need to hire someone who can. You guys come across like you have something to hide because you won't talk to anyone."

"Damn." Kent laughed. He nodded. "Same old Mary. You want to come work for us, be that person who knows how to talk?"

This wasn't the first time Kent had offered her a job at Treegers. Over the years he'd called Mary several times to ask if she'd come be a picker for them. Mary had been tempted many times by his offers, but she'd never felt right about accepting.

Mary smiled and shook her head. "You'll have no problem finding someone." She grew serious. "You're both smart men, and you're good men. I know that about you. I know you're trying to do things on the up and up. I know it even without seeing inside Treegers." As they finished the rest of their meal, they discussed ways to work with the media.

Later, as they waited for the bill to come, Kent said, "I think you're right about our not having trouble finding someone to be our spokesperson, but, you know, Mary, we always need someone to cut out the finished cattle for the packers. Would you reconsider coming to work with us?" Mary laughed, but Kent persisted, suddenly serious. "Don't laugh. I know you still love it. I hear all the time from people how you're over at the sale barn every week."

Mary felt herself flush. "I do still love it, but . . ."

"Is it just because of Ward?" Larry said, "Because . . ."

She brought her head up quickly. "No. It's not Ward. It's me. My life's different now. Everything's different. The truth is, and you can think it's silly if you want to, I want to be a nurse. It's what I really want, what I've been working for."

Both men nodded soberly. "That isn't silly, Mary," Kent said finally. "But you ever change your mind, we'll have a job waiting for you."

When they parted that afternoon, Mary said good-bye to Kent, and Larry walked her to her car. Before she got inside, Larry kissed her lightly on the cheek and then hugged her. She was a bit unnerved when she pulled away to see church members Esther and Elmer Kleinsasser watching her from their car parked a few rows down.

She hadn't noticed them in the restaurant and guessed they'd just pulled into the lot. She could see by the stricken, judgmental looks on their faces that they'd seen, and she felt her heart flutter and drop with a thud. There was no way to explain, for the truth of her meeting with Larry and Kent Needham was as much a betrayal to Ward as a suspected infidelity. She could see that perhaps she was growing reckless. As she drove back to Custer City, she knew she had crossed a line. She'd known it as soon as she'd decided to come to the aid of the Needhams against her husband.

❈

That evening at work, shortly after she'd gotten herself situated at one of the tables in the empty cafeteria to study for finals, she heard the start of an argument between Theresa and Walter. After all these years, Walter was still alive and fighting with the staff. He boasted in his debatably better moods that he was too mean to die, and Mary figured sometimes that might not be far from the truth. As usual, he was verbally assaulting Theresa for the administration's rules barring him from one vice or another, all the things he claimed would make his miserable life a little more meaningful. No one had believed he would live as long as he had, and his longevity had only added to his argument that the things he loved would not necessarily endanger his life as much as they all claimed they would. "You're just afraid if I die you won't get that fat check every month," Mary heard him say tonight.

Despite her empathy for him, when it came to Walter's tantrums Mary was squarely on the side of the nursing staff. After all, she'd been on the receiving end of his diatribes. Over the years he'd abused all the nurses at one time or another. Tonight, though, Mary allowed herself to be distracted from *Principles of Surgical Technique* to listen closer to Walter's argument. She'd become immune to the violence and vulgarity of his language, so she could filter it to hear only the core of his logic. And this is what she finally understood. He wanted them to see that he was a man, not a child, not a dimwit. He'd spent fifteen years of his life in this "hellhole" on their terms. How dare they try to preserve and lengthen his already needlessly long life by inflicting upon him their arbitrary rules meant for no other reason than to prolong life? Who were the knotheads in charge here, anyway? He understood he'd have to smoke outside, but the fact that they wouldn't let him smoke at all without him sneaking around about it made no sense. He was no longer ambulatory, and he was frustrated to madness about having to beg and manipulate to find someone to take him outside for a smoke. Just a smoke! He wasn't looking to commit a crime. These things had so enraged him that over the years he had become someone he didn't recognize, someone he didn't like. He'd been a decent man once, but he'd been reduced now to this maniacal bullying because of the tyranny of the administration and its minions.

She listened as Theresa denied Walter not only the things he wanted but the right to express his desire for them, and even the right to hold the opinion he had of the administration's rules. And Mary knew in that moment that if Walter had been a younger man in full health, dressed in a suit and tie, in full possession of himself, none of them would have dared speak to him as they routinely did, as though he were a naughty child. Walter was right about them. She saw how any one of them could be driven to the same fits of rage they saw from Walter if someone treated them with such condescension.

As Mary listened that night, she found herself weeping. She was relieved there was no one there to see her. She wished she were weeping in empathy with Walter, but that wasn't it at all. Not really. She felt he was describing something about her own life. Walter's dilemma of being trapped and at the mercy of a group and a place that couldn't understand or respect what he needed seemed like the most poignant of all dilemmas, the worst conceivable outcome of a life. So what if he died of alcohol poisoning or lung cancer or a heart attack? At ninety-eight wasn't it time to die of something? So what if she wanted to meet someone from her past, to have a life of her own that didn't involve the scrutiny of a bunch of backward, out-of-touch, ignorant people?

※

After Theresa had been back at the nurses' station for an hour or two, Mary went to sit with her behind the desk. She knew how it felt to be savaged by Walter. No matter how many times it happened, you never became accustomed to it. Mary could see it in Theresa's whole affect. Usually tough and resilient, Theresa was slightly sunken now. Mary guessed Theresa felt like she did that it shouldn't be any big deal to let Walter live his life as he wished, but she had a job to do. Whatever resolve Mary might have had earlier to defend Walter, it had been lost as soon as she'd seen Theresa's face. It seemed like no one could cut anyone slack; they were always following orders in some way, mindlessly following orders.

Her resolve seemed to have failed her twice in one day, for as much as Mary wanted to stand up to Ward and to the CCCA, to speak out against how they had backed Treegers into an impossible corner, leaving them no way out, no useful compromise, she felt as though she couldn't quite bring herself to do it. She knew Ward wouldn't listen to her, and she knew, too, that the CCCA had already gone too far with their plan to revise it now. And it wasn't as though she had no sympathy for the CCCA's side of things. After all, this evening the stench from Treegers filled the nursing home. No one needed to smell such a foul odor. It was the CCCA's absolute unwillingness to compromise that Mary found most troubling. Like Walter's suspicions about the nursing home's motives, she had become suspicious about the CCCA's motives. It felt to her as though they didn't really want to solve the town's problem but to continue to justify their own existence.

⇛CHAPTER 21

⇛Within a week of her meeting with the Needhams, Mary noticed a Gretchen Miles issuing statements to the press on behalf of Treegers. It was clear to Mary she was positioning Treegers so the operation no longer seemed defensive or devious but instead like a concerned business. Ward had also noticed. Accustomed to being depicted as the good guy, Ward seemed to realize he might have to vie for the continued goodwill of the newspapers' readers.

"Did you have something to do with this?" he asked Mary after he'd read the second article in which Gretchen Miles was quoted.

"What would I have to do with it?"

"You've been spending a lot of time with the Needhams lately." Until then Mary hadn't known if the Kleinsassers had said anything to Ward about seeing her with Larry Needham. Now she knew they had, and it shouldn't have surprised her as much as it did.

Ward turned his attention back to the article, plotting, Mary figured, how he would counterattack. She concluded that she had nothing to fear from Ward because he didn't take her seriously. He didn't really believe it was possible for her to have had an idea like a PR person. Mary understood that Ward knew the CCCA wouldn't win the lawsuit, but winning wasn't what they were after.

❋

What had she done with her watch? She'd been looking for a week without success. Finally in frustration, as soon as the semester ended in May, she went to the little jewelry store downtown.

"Betty, I've lost my watch. I need the cheapest thing you have."

"Cheap does as cheap is, Mary," Betty said.

"I imagine you're right about that, but cheap is all I can afford."

Betty laughed. "I'll tell you what. Since it's you, I'll make a deal." She bent to open a drawer behind the counter and brought out a tray of watches. She laid it on the counter between them and looked up. "I'll give you whatever you want here for twenty dollars. Is that cheap enough?"

Mary gestured downward with her thumb.

Betty shook her head with a chuckle. "I need to talk to that Theresa O'Gorman about paying you a little better." She paused. "All right. Tell you what I'll do." She picked up five of the watches and handed them to her. "Ten bucks. Whichever one you want. That's the best I can do."

Mary smiled. She laid the watches on the counter. As she studied her choices, Betty went to ring up another customer. Mary glanced up briefly to see a handsome man wearing a rumpled white shirt, khaki pants, and red Converse sneakers. His curly hair was unkempt.

"Your wife will like these," Betty was saying as she wrapped a pair of silver earrings in the shape of tiny bucking broncos.

The man laughed. "They're for my boss. She likes a souvenir when I travel."

He noticed Mary and smiled, a smile so guileless and disarming she couldn't help but smile in return. As Betty wrapped the earrings, the man leaned closer to look at Mary's choices. He pointed suddenly to a watch with a small square face and a thin black leather band. "That one suits you best," he said and smiled again.

Mary looked and saw he was right. She nodded. "I'll take this one, Betty."

Betty glanced up from the where she was working. "Yep. That'll do it."

The spring day was warm, and for a few seconds Mary was tempted to work in her garden instead of going to the sale barn like she usually did on Thursday mornings. The ranchers all nodded as she made her way to the spot she liked high in the back. She had just gotten settled when she noticed the man she'd seen earlier in the jewelry store come into the arena. He scanned the crowd, noticed her in the back, and climbed up the steep concrete stairs to sit beside her.

"Are you following me?" Mary asked as he sat down.

"I was about to ask you the same thing. We seem to be doing the same touristy things. What brings you to this backwater?"

Mary felt herself stiffen at this characterization of Custer City. "I'm from here."

"Whoops." He laughed without apparent embarrassment. "Where are you living now?"

"I live here."

The man turned to look at her more closely. "Really? I wouldn't have pegged you as a local."

Mary shrugged. She turned to watch as they brought out several cull cows: one blind in one eye; another bony and swaybacked; yet another lame in its right front leg. Once they sold, the hands brought in several broke-mouth cows, which went a little higher than the cull cows had. After that came the calves.

The man beside Mary gestured toward one, a Charolais bull calf. "That's a pretty little calf. I'd bid on him if I had a farm."

Mary paused. "I wouldn't touch that calf if you gave him to me."

She could see the man was a little startled by her assertion. "Why's that?"

"For one thing, I'm interested in maternal breeding, not terminal breeding. The exotics are overrated." She gestured with her chin then. "Now that little black Angus there on the left." She indicated a compact calf near the gate. "She's got a little tarentaise in her, but that's all right. I'd start with her." She scanned the lot again. "I'd add that brockle-faced one, and that other Angus there in the back. I'd bid on that little red bull." She began to build a herd in her mind then and was, for a few minutes, so focused on what she was doing she didn't notice the man was watching her.

"You're serious," he finally interrupted.

Mary laughed, embarrassed suddenly at having forgotten herself. "Not really. I just do this sometimes for fun."

"You come to the sale barn and build imaginary herds? For fun?" He raised his eyebrows. "So how do you know how to do that?" He gestured toward the sale ring. "Seems a little witchy, if you ask me."

Mary laughed. "I've been called worse." She glanced at her new watch. "I need to get going."

"See you," the man said in a tone of voice that indicated he hoped not.

❋

At the end of that week Mary entered the dim sanctuary of the church. It was a beautiful May morning, and she couldn't bring herself to close the doors, not with the sun shining so sweetly outside. She propped open the door before she sat down to play the piano. The birds were singing and a breeze came into the sanctuary. She could smell newly mown grass. For once she couldn't smell Treegers at all.

She laid her fingers on the keys for a few seconds, feeling the ivory cool against her fingertips. Then she began to play. She started out respectfully enough, playing scales and simple songs in just the way Ward would have liked had he walked in. Even after she began to play as she dreamed, she concentrated on playing softly, but she quickly forgot that intention and eventually let her fingers fly over the keys. As she played, she felt transported as if she were riding on top of the music, rising high above the keyboard.

At some point well into it, she sensed a human presence in the church and abruptly stopped, already mumbling an apology to Ward, or Mrs. Lesley, or Linda Turner, or whoever it was. In her flustered state, she awkwardly tried to extricate herself from the piano bench when a masculine voice interrupted her. "Don't stop playing." She paused and looked to the back of the sanctuary. The sun was so bright all she could see was a silhouette in the open doorway. "Don't stop," the man repeated. "That was amazing."

"Oh, no," Mary said, and tried again to stand up.

"Please," he said, moving now toward the front. "I'd like to hear more."

Mary had no intention of playing more, but she finally gave up her attempts to stand and settled back onto the piano bench. She waited as the man came to the front of the sanctuary and stopped near the piano. She saw then it was the man she'd seen earlier in the week, still wearing the same khaki pants, white rumpled shirt, and red Converses. They laughed as they recognized each other.

He pointed to her watch. "I was right. It suits you."

Mary nodded. "Thanks for the advice."

Though his clothes made him seem boyish, small wrinkles around his eyes and mouth led Mary to guess he was older than he looked. When he laughed, as he just had, his face lit up and his brown eyes sparkled.

"What was that you were playing?" he asked.

Mary felt herself flush, embarrassed all over again. "It was nothing."

He laughed as though he thought she was being funny. "It was obviously something. We both heard it."

"It's just something I made up, that's all."

His face grew sober. "You composed that?" His question made Mary self-conscious. "Did you write that piece?" he asked again.

"Oh no. I don't read music. Not really. I couldn't begin to write it."

"And yet you play like that?"

"Yes, well, I apologize. I shouldn't have. I get carried away sometimes."

"Stop apologizing. It was amazing," he said, and then he did something that struck Mary as very peculiar. He sat down, not on a pew but on the floor. She noticed he had been carrying what looked like a heavy bag, which he laid to one side. "It's high time we introduced ourselves," he said. "I'm Michael. Michael Reitz."

"I'm Mary."

Michael smiled. "Nice to meet you again, Mary. So, Mary, do you just hear that music and play it?" She nodded. "I'll be darned," he said almost to himself. He looked around the church. "Is this your church?"

"Sort of."

He shook his head. "You're a little goofy. I'm not sure I get you. How is this *sort of* your church?"

"It's my husband's. He's the pastor."

Michael raised his eyebrows. "His name wouldn't be Ward Hamilton, would it?"

"Yes. How did you know?"

"I'm here with the AP, covering the preliminary hearings in the Treegers case." He pointed to the bag as though it offered proof of what he had said.

Mary was suddenly suspicious that he had known all along who she was. Maybe he really had been following her earlier in the week.

"I know what you're thinking, and the answer is no. I had no idea who you were. You don't exactly look like a preacher's wife, at least not the preachers' wives I knew when I was growing up in Iowa."

The morning sun had risen higher and it shone now into the church. It seemed to illuminate Michael Reitz where he sat on the floor. Mary looked toward the doorway, and Michael followed her gaze there. Before he turned back to her, he looked around the decaying sanctuary. "This place is spectacular," he said when his eyes returned to hers. Mary smiled and nodded.

"I've always liked empty churches," he went on. "I can't say I much like a church when the people are there, but . . ." he stopped himself. "I'm sorry. I didn't mean to be insulting. I know it's not how other people . . ."

"No . . . I agree," Mary said in a rush. "There's something holy about the church when it's empty that I never feel when there are services." She looked down, embarrassed about having shared so much.

Michael tipped his head and looked at her quizzically. "You're a weird one, but I like weird people."

They were silent, and the stillness of the church fell palpably over them. Michael eventually stirred to get more comfortable on the floor, and it roused Mary from her stupor. When it seemed he was about to speak again, Mary braced herself, wary of what he might ask. She was so relieved when instead of asking about the lawsuit he asked about the Sandhills that she was downright verbose describing the place where she had grown up.

"Could you take a break and walk with me for a while?" Michael asked after she'd finished.

"Yes, but I can't be gone long. My kids are with a neighbor, and I don't want to take advantage of her."

"No problem." Michael got to his feet with an agility that Mary envied. He picked up his bag. "Do you mind if I snap a picture of you before we go?"

"I'm not a part of the story with the CCCA and Treegers," she said. "I'd really rather not be brought into all that."

Michael frowned. "That isn't why I want to take your picture. The sun is nice coming in here right now, and there by the piano, the light; it would be a good shot. It'll remind me of your whacked-out piano playing."

Mary stood up as Michael took his camera from the bag. She felt herself flush, but she posed stiffly beside the piano and smiled as Michael raised the camera to his eye.

He lowered the camera. "Just relax, Mary. You don't have to look at the camera. Think about the music you were playing earlier." When he mentioned the music, Mary felt herself grimace slightly, then relax, distracted for a few seconds until she heard the click of the camera. "That's it," Michael said softly. "Thanks."

Mary closed the church door tightly behind them as they left. The sun was warm, and she took off her jacket. Michael asked questions about the town. He didn't ask about Treegers or the CCCA. It was Mary finally who brought it up.

"So are you writing the story about Treegers as well as photographing?" Mary asked.

"No. I'm not a reporter, but I have a personal interest. I wasn't kidding when I said I was from Iowa. My folks still own a farm there. They're facing the same problems with the big feedlots."

Mary nodded. "The situation here is very complicated."

"It's complicated everywhere."

"From what I've read, though, Treegers seems to take a bit more responsibility than some places where no one even knows who the owners are. The owners are local and Treegers is the town's biggest employer, and times are hard for people out . . ." She trailed off, regretting she had told Michael things he already undoubtedly knew.

"That's exactly what interests me," Michael said. "It's why I asked for this assignment. I understand things better when I see them in photographs." He paused. "I don't know why that is. I've always been more focused on what I see than what I hear or what I read."

Mary didn't feel obliged to comment, and they walked in comfortable silence for several blocks. Michael, to her relief, didn't snap any more pictures after the one he'd taken of her in the church. He'd tucked his camera back into his bag and walked now with his hands swinging by his sides. He seemed genuinely interested in the town, commenting on the new library and asking about some of the abandoned buildings.

"I have to admire how little towns like this try to hang on, but I'm still puzzled by you. You don't seem like someone who would have stayed here."

Mary shrugged. "Born and raised, I guess."

They walked another couple of blocks before Mary said, "I have to get my kids, but you're welcome to eat lunch with us. Nothing fancy, but you're welcome if you can put up with four little ones."

"I wouldn't want to be a problem."

Mary laughed. "How could you be a problem compared to four kids?"

As soon as Mary walked into Julie's house, the three older kids came running. They had been making clay figures. "The clay's baking, Mommy," Priscilla said, only casting a quick glance at Michael before dragging Mary to the kitchen to look into the oven where the figures they had made were slowly drying.

"I'll bring them over after they're finished," Julie said after Mary had quickly introduced her to Michael.

"So you're here to cover the biggest news to happen in this town ever?" Julie said. Michael smiled. "Why so early? The trial date hasn't even been set yet, has it?"

"We're covering the preliminary hearing to start building interest in the trial."

"It doesn't seem like the sort of thing that would interest the national media," Julie said.

"It's a perfect news story. The big company, the little town, the company changes the entire climate of the town without there being any discussion about it, and the town fights back. David and Goliath."

Julie nodded. She glanced at Mary and raised an eyebrow so quickly Mary doubted Michael saw it. She knew immediately what Julie was signaling, that he didn't have a clue about the complexity of the issue. Mary indicated by an equally subtle shrug that she had talked to him enough to know that he was being facetious in what he had just told Julie and that he understood more than he was letting on.

All the while Julie and Michael were talking, Mary had been quietly gathering the children's things, and she was waiting now by the door holding David and the diaper bag.

"Who are you?" Joseph said to Michael.

Michael smiled. "I'm a friend of your mom's. My name's Michael."

Joseph seemed satisfied with his answer and headed to the door, but Deborah lingered for a few seconds, seeming to take measure of Michael, narrowing her eyes slightly before following Joseph. Priscilla was still preoccupied with her clay figures, and Julie was promising her that she would bring them over as soon as they were ready. Michael took the diaper bag from Mary's shoulder, and he helped Priscilla down the front steps.

When they arrived at the house, Mary paused for a second at the front door, dreading as she always did to let someone inside for the first time. Michael had complimented the flowers in the front yard: iris, poppy, a few fading tulips. The lilac bushes, viburnum, crab apple, and serviceberry were all in bloom, and the redbuds had just started to lose their blossoms. His silence as he took in the interior of the house seemed more puzzled than pitying. She and Ward had never bought new furniture, and the same castoffs that had been there when she arrived still remained. The floors were still covered in the same peeling linoleum she'd encountered on her first visit, and although she had painted the kitchen cupboards, there was no hiding they were a hodgepodge. The mildew stain on the kitchen wall had started to bleed through yet another annual coat of yellow paint.

"Let's go pick some greens for lunch," Mary said, and the kids headed to the backyard.

Michael followed. He stopped at the back door and took a few seconds to look around. "Did you do this?" he finally asked.

"With some help from my friend Berl, and the kids have helped too."

Michael walked to the middle of the brick patio and took in the walks, the arbor, the trees, the little fountain, the bushes, the perennials, and ground covers. "It's really something, Mary, a little paradise. Who would have guessed it?"

While she and the kids went to a back corner of the yard where she kept a fenced-in vegetable garden, she glimpsed Michael wandering among the walks.

"See," Deborah said, holding out the colander of greens, spinach, snow peas, and radishes to Michael when she emerged from the vegetable plot, a signal she'd accepted him.

"Are those for lunch?"

Deborah nodded soberly.

Inside, Mary quickly cooked grilled cheese sandwiches and made a salad of greens and spinach garnished with radishes and snow peas. Michael didn't follow her inside but stayed in the backyard with Priscilla and Joseph. When she went outside to call them in to eat, Michael said, "It's so peaceful back here."

"Do you want to eat outside?"

"Could we?"

"Of course. Joseph, will you help Deborah and me carry things out? Michael, could you get the baby's high chair, please?"

Between them, they quickly set the picnic table. A mourning dove cooed from a telephone line above them, and robins and cardinals darted between the trees and bushes.

"It's perfect here," Michael said, looking around the yard again. The sun was warm. The sky a robin's egg blue. Fat white clouds drifted in the windless sky, the water in the fountain gurgled.

She nodded. "It's perfect in Nebraska for one week in May and one week in September."

Michael laughed. "Sounds a lot like Iowa."

At the end of the table, Priscilla had started to entertain the older kids. She liked to clown, and when she was on a roll, like now, there was no telling what she'd do for a laugh. She had a mouthful of salad, and she was squeezing the green mush between her teeth. Joseph and Deborah giggled.

"Prissie. Food in your mouth," Mary said.

Priscilla closed her mouth and chewed deliberately. Still clowning, she rolled her eyes dramatically. More laughter from the older kids. Joseph was so tickled by Priscilla's antics he held his stomach as if in pain. Even David crowed, platting his hands flat against his high chair tray. Mary felt the beginning of a giggle herself. She glanced at Michael, who like her was trying not to laugh. Suddenly they were both laughing with the kids. After their laughter had subsided, Mary wiped tears from her eyes. She led a guarded life, and when with anyone except her children or her own family, she regularly hid behind the second self she'd created all those years ago when Ward baptized her, but it was odd how with Michael she'd been completely herself. Even Claire hadn't won her trust in quite this way.

Mary let this thought pass as Priscilla, finished with her clowning, said earnestly to Michael, "Did you know the dishes in our kitchen know how to talk? At night while we're asleep they come alive and dance."

"No, I didn't know that," Michael said. "How do you know? Have you seen them?"

She shook her head. "The Egg People told us. They see them."

"The Egg People?" Michael looked questioningly from Priscilla to Mary. Mary nodded back to him and Priscilla answered.

"The Egg People live in our house. They're very little." She indicated their tininess by pinching her fingers together tightly. "They wake up at night. Mommy knows the stories."

Michael smiled at Priscilla and then at Mary. "Your Mommy knows them, huh?"

Joseph nodded. "She knows good stories."

"Maybe she'll tell us a story," Michael said.

"Yeah, Mommy, please."

"Not right now," Mary said. "Maybe later."

The children quickly got over their disappointment and finished their meal.

❋

Later, as Michael helped Mary carry the dishes inside, he said, "You have happy kids, Mary."

"That's nice to hear," she said. "It's the hardest job I've ever done."

"You're obviously doing something right."

After helping with the dishes, Michael wandered around the house. Mary was a little surprised by his familiarity, but she wasn't offended. Nor did she try to explain about the parsonage. He stayed for a short time after lunch, content to sit in the yard with her and watch the kids play.

Julie brought the clay figures over just as he was leaving. Once he was gone, she asked Mary, "How did you meet him?"

"I've run into him a few times around town, and then today he wandered into the church while I was playing the piano."

Julie looked at the door as though she thought she might still see Michael standing there. "We don't see guys like that around here very often."

"No, we don't."

"Seems nice."

"He is nice."

Julie paused. "Are you worried he's using you?"

"It crossed my mind," Mary said. Julie looked a little doubtful. "Don't worry. I didn't say anything I wouldn't want repeated."

As if to change the subject, Julie glanced toward the kids. Priscilla was admiring her new clay figures. Joseph was playing with his marbles, and the baby was sleeping. Deborah had come to stand beside Mary, taking her hand as she said good-bye to Julie.

Not fifteen minutes after Michael had left the phone rang. Linda Turner. "I couldn't help but notice you had a visitor this afternoon."

"Yes."

After a long pause, Linda, clearly disappointed about not getting any details from Mary, said a little petulantly, "All right then. I wanted to make sure everything was okay over there."

"Never better."

CHAPTER 22

"Hey, thanks for lunch yesterday." It was Michael on the phone.

"We put on quite a show for you, I'm afraid."

Michael laughed and went on to tell her about how he had spent the previous evening discovering the City Café and later wandering out to the Sage Brush to check out Custer City's night life.

"What'd you think?"

He laughed again. "Let me put it this way. If I were into dirty dancing, I'd have hit the jackpot." He went on to describe how one woman mimicked—he hesitated—"performing a sexual act on her partner." He then compared the scene to a couple of movies, stopping himself midway through his commentary. "You don't know what I'm talking about, do you?"

"Not a clue. I don't see many movies."

"No need to sound so apologetic." He paused. "Actually, it's sort of refreshing to meet someone who doesn't know all that shit."

Mary was relieved when he didn't follow up with a hasty apology for his language like most people she knew would, singling her out as the minister's wife.

They talked for an hour, during which Mary frequently had to interrupt the conversation to monitor or help one of the kids. Each time, Michael asked for details about what had happened. At one point, she'd had to break up a fight between Deborah and Priscilla. "They're supposed to be drying the breakfast dishes," Mary said when she came back on the line, "but I look over and there's Debbie with her hands around Prissie's neck, shaking her like a little rag doll." Michael chuckled, and Mary went on. "Jeepers, these kids are testing me this morning."

This sent Michael into a spasm of laughter. "I haven't heard anyone say 'jeepers' since I left Iowa."

He called again the next day with more news. He'd spent the previous day driving in the Sandhills. "Where did you grow up?" he asked.

"North of Anselmo, there along the Middle Loup."

"I drove through Anselmo and on to Callaway, took the Garfield Table Road, and on to Arnold, up there in those canyons. My God. Who would have guessed? In Nebraska?"

"You found the Garfield Table Road?"

"I had a little help from the people who run the hotel."

He called every morning that week, and each time after she hung up the phone Mary wondered how they had found so much to say to each other. He'd met Morrie Stevens, the man who mowed the cemetery, and Evelyn Elsberry, the woman who managed the little historical museum downtown. He'd met Clyde Schweitzer, the local alcoholic, as close to a street person as Custer City had, and Ben Jenkins, the most eccentric man in town, who, rumor had it, was worth a fortune but lived in a tiny rundown house outside the city limits. It was said he knew governors, congressmen, and celebrities. Michael told Mary, "I have friends in Seattle who know Ben. They told me I had to look him up while I was here. He's something else," he said.

"How so?" Mary asked.

"Hard to explain. My friends think he's a genius. You really should get to know him."

At the end of the week, before he ended the conversation, Michael said, "I'm going to North Platte tomorrow, and I want to visit Cody's ranch."

"Really? Why?"

"Why? Because I like Buffalo Bill. Would you and the kids want to come along?"

"I don't know."

"Come on. It won't be as much fun for me to go alone, and I don't know anyone else in town. It's a Saturday, so the kids won't have school." Mary still hesitated, leading Michael finally to ask, "Is it that bad a place?"

"Oh, no. It's not that. Scout's Rest is a fine place, and there's a little park there in town, too, Cody Park. It's just . . ."

"You've been there a hundred times and the kids are bored with it."

"No. They've never been . . ."

"What? That settles it. They need to go. It's a local attraction. I'll bring stuff for a picnic."

Mary wondered briefly what Ward would think, but she figured he'd be busy as usual and wouldn't even notice they were gone. "Okay," she finally said. "Why not? What time should we be ready?"

✳

When she and the kids pulled up in front of the Grand Hotel the next morning in the crowded Escort, Michael was waiting out front. He opened the back door of the car and pretended to try to squeeze into the back seat.

"There isn't enough room for you," Joseph said.

"I can sit on your lap, can't I?" Michael said to Deborah.

"You need to have a seat belt," she said with alarm.

"I'm big. I don't need a seat belt."

"You do too," Joseph scolded.

"Do too," Priscilla repeated.

Michael mimed a crestfallen expression so absurd the older kids doubled up in laughter. David, in his car seat in front, made cranky noises at missing out on the fun. Michael maintained the expression for a few more seconds before finally snapping his fingers and beaming with a solution. "Okay. Mommy can stay here and we'll go alone."

"No!" Priscilla said. "Mommy has to come."

Deborah laughed nervously. "You can't leave Mommy."

Michael appeared to think a little longer. By this time, the older kids were completely enthralled, waiting to see what he would say next.

He pointed then. "You see that car over there?"

They looked. "It holds six." He looked back at them. "I don't think the owner will mind if we borrow it."

Joseph looked doubtfully at Mary, gauging her response to this. She smiled and shrugged.

"Are you going to ask first?" Joseph said.

"Naw."

"You have to ask," Deborah said and Priscilla nodded.

"So, it'd be bad if I took it without asking?" Michael said. The children nodded. He bit his bottom lip. "All right. I'm going to go inside and ask."

"Don't forget to ask for the keys," Deborah said.

"That's good. Thanks for the reminder."

For the few minutes Michael was away, the children sat as if spellbound, waiting for the answer. When he came out, he wasn't smiling and Mary felt their dismay. Only then did Michael smile and wave the keys, leading the three older kids to erupt with excitement.

Mary couldn't help but laugh at their elation. They were going on an adventure. They hadn't even started and they were already enchanted.

❋

Tall cottonwoods surrounded the white Second Empire–style house where Bill Cody had lived. The wide lawn was green now with new grass. Evergreens bordered Ducklake Pond and junipers lined the foundation of the house. They toured the inside of the house first. Michael exclaimed over the furniture made of horn, the cowhide rug, the horsehair sofa and chairs, the horseshoe chairs on the front porch. "I like how this guy just kills something and comes up with a new piece of furniture." He looked closely at all the framed photographs of the Wild West show, Buffalo Bill posing with the Indian actors in various venues across the United States and Europe.

In the huge red barn, Mary lingered over the vintage tack, the restored coach Buffalo Bill had used, the posters from the shows, the bison and elk heads and hides, the horns from longhorn cattle. "I love this guy," Michael said at one point after looking at a few more framed photographs of Cody.

After their tour of Scout's Rest, they drove across town to Cody Park. The kids had been a little subdued at Scout's Rest but here they came into their own, running to look at the elk, deer, peacock, donkey, and geese in pens lining the drive.

When Michael saw the carousel, the swimming pool, and the little amusement park, he was disappointed that they wouldn't open for another week. The kids didn't seem to mind as they played on the playground equipment and looked at the animals. Michael had asked Mary to bring a blanket for a picnic. Now, as she spread the blanket on the grass, Michael and Joseph carried the picnic things from the trunk.

Michael set down a box of fried chicken. "Are you having a good time, Mary?"

"Of course."

He smiled and looked at the kids. Joseph had run off to join the girls who were watching an albino peacock. "They're really cool kids," he said.

※

As they pulled into the parking space in front of the hotel late that afternoon, the kids were all asleep. Michael cut the engine and looked first at David in his car seat between him and Mary and then through the rearview mirror at the three older kids in the back seat. She glanced at them where they were slumped together in sleep.

She met Michael's eye and they exchanged a smile. "They're completely worn out," Mary whispered. "They've had so much fun today. Thanks so much, Michael. They'll be talking about this for days."

"No one had more fun than me." Mary thought about Michael's unrestrained joy in playing with the kids and guessed he might be right.

The next morning at breakfast, the kids talked excitedly about their trip the day before.

"You went to Cody Park?" Ward said.

Mary nodded. "Yesterday."

"He was funny," Priscilla said. She started laughing with the memory, and Deborah and Joseph laughed with her.

Ward smiled quizzically at their hilarity. "Buffalo Bill?" he asked Priscilla.

"No, *him*," Priscilla said and stood up then to mimic how Michael had chased them, acting like a monster dragging one lifeless leg and arm. This imitation set them off into peals of laughter, Joseph falling out of his chair. This time Ward directed his questioning glance toward Mary.

Still smiling at the kids' laughter, she said, "We went with . . ."

Ward snapped his fingers then and cut her off. "I almost forgot. I saw Mabel last night. They're going to need you for Vacation Bible School after all. They need you to teach third . . ."

"I can't this year, Ward," Mary said in dismay. "I told you that I start my last classes the week before VBS, and there's no way I can get away during the day."

"It seems to me you have your priorities a bit mixed up," Ward said. "But don't involve me, Mary. You'll have to take this up with the VBS Committee yourself." Ward frowned. "Linda mentioned she'd seen some guy hanging around. Has that AP reporter been out here asking you questions?"

"No," Mary said, deciding that technically she was telling the truth. Michael wasn't a reporter, and he hadn't asked her any questions.

"Well, if anyone does come snooping around, don't be wading into any of this yourself. Make sure you send them to me."

Mary resisted the urge to roll her eyes. "Gotcha," she said.

※

Michael didn't call on Sunday, but when the phone rang on Monday morning, Mary knew it would be him. Shortly into their conversation, he said, "I need you to do me a favor," and Mary felt her heart drop briefly. Here it came. What she'd been dreading—his request for information about the CCCA.

"Okay," she said, hearing the guardedness in her voice.

"Rebecca, my editor, wants me to get a few shots of a facility in Lexington," Michael said. "Kip," who Mary knew was the reporter, "interviewed some people down there yesterday and they think it might be a good contrast to the Custer City story." Mary waited, still wondering about the nature of his request. "So, could you ride along and help me find this place?" he said. Mary laughed, as much with relief as at the absurdity of his request. "Lexington isn't exactly a big city. You'd find your way, no problem."

"Yes, but being lost takes time." He paused. "Besides, I'd like your company." Mary didn't respond immediately, and Michael went on. "It's the kids, right? Can you find a babysitter on late notice?"

After another pause, Mary finally said, "I think Julie could probably do it."

"I'd want to pay her," Michael said. "You'd be doing me a favor and I wouldn't expect . . ."

"Let me give her a call. If she's free, then . . . sure, I'll go."

Even before she hung up the phone, Mary was planning. The

older kids were already in school. The baby had been fed, but he wasn't dressed yet.

"You must be really busy with the fund-raiser coming up," Julie said when Mary called her later. Mary felt a twinge of guilt for letting Julie believe she needed her because of the fund-raiser.

As she got David ready he seemed cranky. Mary checked his temperature. Although it was normal, she felt a niggling worry as she hurried through dressing him. He tried to smile at her in spite of his tears. She'd ask Julie to keep an eye on him. If he developed a fever, she trusted her to know what to do. What was she thinking, going off with Michael? That twinge of guilt she'd felt before wouldn't quite leave her, but she also saw in herself an unexpected willfulness. She wanted to go to Lexington with him. She wanted the adventure of it, the opportunity of it, even though she wasn't sure what she meant by opportunity and adventure. When she thought of it in those ways, she thought she was being a fool.

❋

As soon as he pulled up to the curb, Mary jumped into Michael's car, hoping no one noticed them, or if they did, that they'd assume he was one of the people she still sometimes carpooled with to Kearney for class.

"You seem nervous," he said as she buckled herself into the passenger seat.

"Just go."

"Am I putting you in a bad spot, Mary?"

"I'm putting myself in a bad spot."

"I forget what life's like in a small town."

"People talk. That's all they do. Don't worry about it," Mary said.

Once they were on the highway Michael's rental car was smooth and quiet, so unlike her little Ford, and Mary settled into the plush seat as the car spun down Highway 21. The car curved around the hills, dipping and climbing effortlessly. As they drove, Mary thought about the layers and layers of stories this highway held for her. So many stories she couldn't begin to tell anyone. She couldn't imagine how she would ever have the energy to tell another person all her stories.

Michael interrupted her thoughts. "I like it out here."

"What's Seattle like?"

"It's a great city. You've never been there?"

"No. I haven't traveled."

Michael nodded. "I've lived there about ten years now, and I love it, but to be honest, and don't laugh, there are things I miss about living in the middle of the country."

Mary didn't laugh. "Like what?"

"I don't know. Buying a house you can afford, having a yard, not having to drive in traffic all the time."

"You must like the excitement of the city, though."

Michael shrugged. He kept his eyes on the road as he talked. "I do, but the truth is, I don't really take advantage of what's there that much. And my job . . . I used to love all the travel. It was great when I was in my twenties, but now," he chuckled, "now, I fantasize about being the sort of guy I was trying to avoid being when I left Iowa."

"And what kind of guy was that?"

"The kind of guy who comes home and mows his lawn, or shovels his walk, nods to the neighbors, eats dinner, drinks a beer, and watches TV."

Mary laughed and looked across the seat at him. "I can't quite see you being that guy."

Michael met her eyes and smiled before turning back to the road. "You'd be surprised. My work can get fairly boring. Waiting in airports, hanging around other journalists in hotels. After a while everything starts to look the same." He interrupted himself with a laugh, and Mary saw he was blushing. "I've just answered your question with the biggest journalistic clichés there are."

He glanced at Mary briefly before looking back to the road. "Before coming out here, I'd decided that when I get back home after this assignment, I'm going to start looking around for something else, try to find work with a newspaper, maybe even in Iowa. Especially in Iowa." He looked at her and smiled again. As their eyes met this time, Mary felt something like a line snap between them across the seat. Whatever happened, she knew Michael felt it, too, for he seemed flustered and looked away quickly. Neither of them spoke for a while. Desire, like a third presence, joined them in their silence.

She had a sudden memory of David, and she fiercely regretted having left him. She must have looked as miserable as she felt, for Michael looked at her and slowed down. "Are you all right, Mary?"

She smiled, ashamed of her worries. "I'm all right. I was just thinking about the baby. He wasn't himself this morning when I left."

Michael slowed the car further. "Do you want me to turn around?"

"I'm sure I'm worrying for nothing."

She felt Michael look at her across the seat, but she didn't meet his eyes. "I mean it, Mary," he said, slowing the car even more.

She paused but finally said, "No. It's all right. I'm just being silly. I'll get past it."

Michael hesitated a second before he sped up again. They were quiet for a few minutes. Miles passed. Michael pointed wordlessly once at a deer standing near the side of the road.

"You must have complicated memories after living in the same place all your life," he said, finally breaking the silence.

Mary glanced at him briefly before turning back to look out the side window. "Yes," she said, thinking he didn't know the half of it. To change the subject, she asked, "Tell me about some of your travels. I'm so envious of you coming and going like that."

Until they reached Lexington, Michael told her about the places where he had been sent on assignment. To her, he seemed to be describing a fairy-tale life, the most glamorous life imaginable.

"No wonder you called Custer City a backwater," she said as they pulled onto Highway 30 and headed for downtown Lexington.

"Don't hold that against me. Besides, there are a lot of remote places in this country. Within a few hours of every major city are places so insular you can hardly believe they exist in this century." He glanced at Mary. "There's nothing wrong with a place being out of the way."

She didn't know if he had changed his mind, or if was he saying these things now to protect her feelings. Either way, she had spent all her life thinking she was no one living in the middle of nowhere. She sat up straighter and watched as they approached their turn-off. She gave Michael directions to the feedout facility, though she wouldn't have needed to bother. The smell was direction enough. The feedlot was about fifteen miles out of town, and the closer they got, the more overpowering the odor.

Unlike Treegers, there was no automated gate at the end of the drive. Instead, they were met by a burly man wearing the customary western uniform: Levi's, a western shirt, boots, and a hat.

"You the fella from the papers?"

"Yes," Michael said.

The man's glance fell on Mary and lingered for a second. She seemed to have passed his appraisal. He straightened up and gestured for Michael to park.

"Talkative fellow," Michael said as he pulled into the lot.

"I'm surprised they'll let you in here at all."

"I would be too if I didn't know my editor. She could charm dirt into dill."

Mary laughed. "What kind of saying is that?"

"That's a Grandma Snell saying, that's what that is."

They watched as another man walked toward the car. Clearly one of the executives, he wore a tie and a button-down blue shirt and dark pants. Though his sleeves were rolled up, he didn't look as though he'd been working outside.

He smiled as Mary and Michael got out of the car, extending his hand first to Michael and then to Mary. Mary noticed his gold watch against the dark hair on his forearm as he shook her hand.

"Matt Broder."

"Michael Reitz." Michael gestured toward Mary. "My colleague Mary."

"I'll be showing the two of you around today," Matt said. Mary's first response to Matt Broder was to pull back, to grow reticent with her suspicion, but she noticed how Michael now matched Matt's easy persona. She saw immediately how he was able to put Matt at ease.

For the next hour, Matt drove them through the facility in a golf cart, pointing out recent improvements and talking in general terms about the state of the industry. Michael asked to stop occasionally while he snapped a photo. During these stops, Mary looked closely at the cattle while Matt attempted to make conversation with her. She observed their glazed eyes, their sluggish movements, how they stood with their heads drooping. She played along with Michael's introduction of her as an AP employee, hoping she'd never see Matt Broder again. She'd decided she respected Michael for being able to play along, to do his job so well, but she knew she would never be able to do it.

After half an hour of driving through a small section of the feedlot, Matt parked the vehicle and Michael shook his hand. "Thanks for all your help, Matt."

Matt took out a business card and handed it to him. "Give me a call if you need anything, buddy."

"Sure thing, man."

Neither Michael nor Mary spoke after they got into the car. Matt watched as Michael backed out of the parking space and continued to watch as they left the compound.

"Jesus," Michael said once they'd driven through the checkpoint with a final wave to the guard. He looked at Mary, the personable demeanor replaced now with a troubled expression. "What'd you think?" he finally said.

Mary shook her head.

In response, Michael shuddered slightly.

"Were you able to get some good shots? Our good friend Matt was keeping you on a tight leash."

"I think so. I was on zoom focus most of the time, so if the film turns out, I got a few things Matt probably wouldn't expect."

They drove for several minutes in silence until they reached the outskirts of Lexington again. "Do you have time to eat lunch with me, Mary?"

She hesitated a second before nodding.

"Someplace nice. Let's go someplace nice."

"Okay." Mary thought for a minute. "There aren't a lot of nice places around here. You'd have to go to North Platte or Kearney to find something a little fancy, but there's a restaurant out toward Johnson Lake. Are you up for a drive?"

"Sounds good. So what's this Johnson Lake?"

"It's a lake," Mary said and laughed at herself.

Michael laughed too. "Could we go there after we eat?"

"I suppose." Mary was suddenly uncomfortable with how long she was staying away from home.

"Do you need to call the sitter to let her know?"

"I do."

Mary gave directions, and as they drove Michael said, "I think people from Custer City should come out here and see this place if they think Treegers is bad. It might give them some perspective." Mary didn't say anything. So much that was wrong in the world was made acceptable by that kind of reasoning, she thought. Michael apparently misunderstood her silence, for he apologized now. "I'm sorry. I don't mean to offend you."

"Why would you think that?"

"Well, you have a personal interest. The CCCA. I didn't mean to impose my . . ." Through all of their phone conversations the previous week, Mary had expected him to talk about the lawsuit, and she had been relieved when it hadn't come up. Now she understood it had been out of deference to her.

"The truth is," she interrupted him, "I don't agree with what the CCCA is doing." She hadn't intended to confess this so openly, but now that she had started she wanted to explain. "I think the lawsuit is ridiculous."

If Michael was put off by her stridency, he didn't let on. He nodded slowly but didn't say anything.

Mary continued, feeling somehow liberated by it. "I hate what the CCCA is doing to Custer City. It's no way to solve the problem."

After a pause, Michael said, "It must be hard for you."

She swallowed slowly and was surprised to feel tears gather. She blinked them back. It had been harder than she'd let herself realize. "I try to stay out of it as much as I can, but I end up getting involved anyway. Like this fund-raiser tomorrow night; I'm in charge of putting together the program for that." She looked out the window for a few seconds. They were driving slowly, and she had kept her window down so the spring air filled the car. The ditches were full of wildflowers. Red-winged blackbirds flitted from fence post to fence post. "It's horrible to keep doing things you don't feel right about," she said under her breath before adding, "Oh, don't listen to me. I'm just complaining."

Michael looked at her quickly. "You have a right to your feelings."

"You think so?"

He frowned. "I know so." He seemed about to say something more before he caught himself. "There's the place," Mary interrupted, pointing to the distance where a small white building stood alone on the prairie.

"Perfect," Michael said as he parked the car in the gravel lot.

After they had been seated, Mary excused herself to go call Julie. The restaurant was dim as she made her way back to the table where Michael was waiting. It was early afternoon, past the noon rush, and there were hardly any other patrons. The blinds had been drawn against the bright sun outside.

Michael had ordered coffee for both of them, and as Mary sat down the waitress handed them menus.

"Everything all right?" he asked.

"Fine."

"Can Julie keep them awhile longer?"

"Yes."

"Great. Maybe we can go to the lake later and walk a little if that sounds good to you."

"It sounds wonderful." Mary's voice caught as she spoke, and to hide her embarrassment she looked intently at the menu.

After they'd ordered, Michael looked at her frankly across the table. "Tell me what happened to your leg, Mary."

"Oh," was all she managed to say. People didn't usually ask so directly.

"Is it hard for you to talk about it?"

"No. It's not that." She smiled and shrugged. "I forget it's so noticeable."

Michael returned her smile, and Mary went on to tell him briefly about the accident.

"That's tough, Mary."

She paused before saying, "My first husband died in the accident; I was driving." She had never before admitted this to anyone.

Michael didn't speak for several seconds. Finally, he reached across the table and picked up her hand. He laid it gently in his palm and looked at it as though it were a precious thing. When he glanced up again, his eyes were soft. "I see." That was all he said, but in those few words, she felt he really did see, and she was comforted in a way she had not been for all the years since the accident. The desire she had felt earlier in the car was there again between them. A palpable presence, and she felt herself flush.

"We're in a pickle, aren't we?"

"We're in a pickle."

Their order came, and they avoided talking about their situation until after the bill had been paid. Before leaving the restaurant, Michael picked up her hand again. "Listen, I'm going to be back in a month once the trial begins. I want to see you again. That'll give us some time to think."

Mary had been nodding, the reality of her life eclipsed for a few minutes, but now she felt a thud in her chest where remorse settled. What was she doing here with Michael? What was she thinking?

"Think about what?" she said and shook her head. "Michael, I'm sorry. I was wrong to let something get started between us. I don't know what got into me. I really don't. I have four kids. There's no way on earth I'd do anything to hurt them, and here I've acted like they don't matter."

"But how can you stand it?" Michael said with more vehemence than Mary expected. "How can you stand to live with that man?" He looked away. "I'm sorry. I shouldn't have said that, but knowing what I know about you . . . and seeing and hearing Ward . . . I can't see how you've managed it all this time."

"Ward's not that bad."

Michael looked at Mary. He paused and pressed his lips tightly together before deciding to speak. "I don't mean to insult you, but your husband's about as empty a human being as I've ever met. There's nothing there, Mary." Mary didn't respond, and Michael seemed contrite once more for having spoken so openly against Ward. "We need to get you home," he said finally.

The drive home was sober. Neither of them said much, and Michael seemed especially quiet. As they approached the outskirts of Custer City, he reached for her hand. "Mary, promise me you'll think about what I said earlier, that I'll see you again when I come back next month."

When she finally met his eyes, Michael was waiting, the expression on his face so open and vulnerable that despite the impossibility of it all, Mary felt she had to trust him.

"I promise," she said finally. Michael nodded. Before he stopped at the curb in front of the parsonage, he squeezed her hand briefly without looking at her. "Next month."

"Next month," she echoed, feeling a little giddy at the promise she was making. She jumped out of the car and forced herself not to look back in case someone was watching.

The parsonage looked more bleak to her than ever and Michael's words came back to her. "How do you stand it?" How had she stood it? She saw her answer to that question as soon as she opened the door to Julie's house and Priscilla ran to greet her with news of her day. David chortled from where he was on his hands and knees on the floor. He was full of smiles for her as he rocked back and forth. "He's trying to crawl!"

Julie was smiling. "He just started doing that this afternoon."

Mary swept David up in her arms and nuzzled the soft part of his neck where it met his shoulder. "Are you trying to crawl, you little booger you?" David giggled, arching his back with delight as she tickled him.

"He's a precocious one," Julie said, still beaming at David.

"I really appreciate your doing this on such late notice, Julie."

"I don't mind at all."

Only then did Mary stop to wonder about her appearance. Did she look flushed? Guilty? If so, Julie didn't let on.

As Mary opened her purse to pay Julie, she found there on top two twenty-dollar bills. Michael must have left them. She couldn't imagine when he had done it, and something about his having opened her purse and laid those bills inside seemed so intimate to her that Mary felt herself blush slightly. She finally recovered enough to pick them up. What did it mean, his paying like that? The gesture confused her for a few seconds, but more than anything she felt gratitude for his understanding that she didn't have the money to spare for extra babysitting.

"This is way too much, Mary," Julie said after Mary had handed her the money.

"Just think of it as a little extra for the inconvenience of being asked at the last minute and keeping them so long." Julie still hesitated and Mary pressed. "Really," she said. "I can't do it very often, but I want to this time."

"Thank you," Julie said. "I really don't mind having them, you know.

It gets quiet around here when Molly's in school." Mary glanced into the kitchen where Priscilla had gone back to her coloring.

"Okay, kiddo," Mary said, "we need to get going."

"Mommy, please. Can't I stay just a little longer?" Priscilla said. She wasn't finished with her picture and didn't want to leave it.

"I'll tear that page out for you, Prissie." Julie carefully tore out the page and handed it to Priscilla who carried it gingerly with both hands over to Mary.

"Thank you," Mary mouthed to Julie above Priscilla's head. Then to Priscilla, "You can finish this at home." When Mary opened the door to the parsonage and Priscilla ran inside ahead of her, she filled that dreary space with joy and life. Had it not been for that, she would have found it unbearable to enter.

That night Mary woke from another vivid dream. She had dreamt she was in a strange country, nowhere she recognized. In a moment of terror at the beginning of the dream, she learned there had been a military coup. Foreigners were being arrested and she knew she was in great danger. She was in a barracks of some sort when she heard the news, and as she ran out of the building she knew she was running for her life. She ended up in a large parking lot alone. From there, she could hear gunshots and people screaming. She was paralyzed by terror, unable to move on her own, when a man she didn't know grabbed her arm and told her to follow him. They ran together, the man pulling her along with him. They had not gone far before a female soldier stopped them with a pointed rifle. Mary had known with certainty the woman was about to shoot them both. It was then Mary felt something warm and wet on her leg. She looked down to see the strange man relieving himself against her. Shocked, she drew away. The soldier was shocked, too, and lowered her gun with a sound of disgust, seeming to decide in that moment both Mary and the strange man were mad and not worth bothering with. She gestured with her gun for them to go. As they fled, the man didn't speak of what he had done, but even in the dream Mary understood, as surely as she had ever understood anything in her life, that the man's deliberate and repulsive action had saved both of their lives.

When she woke in the night, she still felt the sense of terror and ultimate relief of the dream. Beside her in the darkness of their bedroom, Ward's breathing was shallow and fast and Mary knew he was dreaming, too. In all the years of their marriage, he had never shared a single one of his dreams with her. She could not begin to imagine what beings and places inhabited them. She remembered what Michael had said about Ward being empty. She didn't know if that was true, but she knew there was a gulf between them. She had never found a way to cross it, nor had Ward found a way to cross over to her.

⟫CHAPTER 23

⟫The morning of the CCCA fund-raiser began early for Mary as she and the women she had enlisted set up the hall. Claire was there first thing that morning to help. Tequila Sunrise—a local old-style country band—arrived early to do a sound check while the women set up tables and decorated. One of the ranch women, Lila Gates, had brought a large American flag. Her husband Earl dragged in several straw bales.

"I thought these might make a nice backdrop for the program," Lila explained as Earl brought in the last of the bales.

"Sure," Mary said. Earl moved all the bales to the stage. Already the morning was hot, and Earl's face shone with perspiration. Mary thanked him when he had finished. He smiled and gallantly touched the brim of his cowboy hat.

"Glad to help."

Later, Mary and Claire arranged the bales while the guys in the band—most of them men in their sixties—took a break from their sound check to hold up the flag so Claire and Mary could tack it to the wall. The men were careful not to let the flag touch the floor and scolded Mary a couple times for being careless. Once the flag was up and the bales arranged as they liked, Claire came back from her car with two bleached horse skulls she usually kept at her apartment and arranged them along with a few Indian baskets on the bales of hay. Mary wasn't sure what sort of vision all this expressed, but as they stepped back to survey their work, she and Claire were pleased with the results.

Raymond James, the band's fiddle player, liked the effect too. "I feel like I'm on the set of *Hee Haw*."

Boyd Harrison, the band's drummer, spoke up. "So when are you two going to get into your skimpy costumes?"

"You'll have to wait and see," Claire said, egging them on a little. Mary said nothing, but she smiled at their antics. She felt tired, muted, wobbly. No matter how much she tried to be upbeat and energetic, she couldn't quite pull it off. Claire noticed, and after the band members had left—promising to return an hour before the event started—and the other women were busy starting the pork barbecue, she beckoned Mary outside.

Already by noon, it was unbearably hot, unusual for May. An oppressive stillness suggested a storm brewing somewhere, and neither of them was surprised to hear later a tornado watch was in effect for most of the day.

In a pavilion beside the community center a roping contest was in full swing. Claire and Mary stopped and watched the horses and their riders chasing, roping, and wrangling the calves. At the end of each performance, an announcer proclaimed the time and reminded the audience how that particular participant was ranked in the competition so far.

"Did you do that?" Claire asked.

"Not for competition," Mary said. She didn't elaborate. It felt like such a long time ago, like someone else's life in fact.

They sat down at a picnic table under an oak tree. The shade of the tree provided scant relief from the sun's heat.

"Are you feeling all right, Mary?" Claire said after they sat down. "I can take over here if you need to go home."

"I'm all right. I'm just off today."

Claire looked at her. "You've been more than just off. What's up?" This was the first time in weeks that Claire had seemed like her old self. Since the trip to the clinic in February their friendship had not been the same, but any time Mary tried to address the problem between them, Claire made a joke or in some way steered the conversation in another direction.

Claire's unexpected kindness, the heat, her exhaustion—later Mary couldn't explain why she suddenly told Claire about Michael. She knew as soon as she started she was making a serious mistake, and even though she stopped short of telling Claire everything, it was still too much.

Claire looked at her, mouth open in surprise. "Are you crazy?" Mary didn't respond, and Claire frowned and turned away, refusing to look at her for a few seconds. "I don't get you, Mary," she finally said. Mary hadn't expected Claire to understand necessarily, but neither had she reckoned on this judgmental response. After all, if anyone knew and understood how lonely her marriage was, it was Claire. Through the years, she had often been critical of Ward. Despite that, in addition to her weekly Bible studies with him, Claire had started attending church regularly on Sunday mornings. It still startled Mary to see her there, so out of context, always sitting near the back of the sanctuary. But who knew better than Mary how if you were experiencing doubt in your life, there was no one like Ward to make you feel you'd come to the right person to find salvation. Mary assumed this new Christian kick would run its course like all of Claire's other fad beliefs had through the years.

"Don't do anything stupid, Mary," Claire said. "You don't know anything about this guy. You've made a mistake, but just let it go now and don't let yourself be tempted again."

Mary nodded, though she found it ironic that Claire—who had never in her life, as far as Mary could see, resisted any temptation, had in fact courted temptation at every turn—was lecturing her on temperance. Mary decided she would have to back away from the story, try to find some way to undo the damage she had done in telling Claire.

Mary wiped her brow and lifted her ponytail off her sweaty neck. Not a breeze stirred. She was finished talking to Claire.

Claire wasn't finished with her, though, and she said, playing into Mary's greatest fear, "You've got no right to think about doing anything that would put those four kids at risk." She paused for a second. "I'm glad you told me; it's good to get these things out into the open where you can see them for what they are." Mary nodded again, both chastened by what Claire had said and angry at her for scolding as if Mary didn't care about her own children.

Unlike Claire had said, though, talking about Michael and bringing him into the open had only made him more real to her. To this point, he had seemed little more than a figment of her imagination, but having said his name aloud to someone else, making another person a witness to what had happened between them, she finally felt Michael was real. It was as though she had been keeping him in a secret chamber of her heart, sealed away, a fantasy, but in confessing she had let him out into the whole of her heart.

That night, Ward was emcee for the fund-raiser. Outside, the wind raged, and rain intermittently drummed on the building's metal roof. In the kitchen of the community center the staff kept a radio on in case they would need to take cover. Ward stood behind the microphone and announced the various musical acts, talking between numbers about the mission of the CCCA and their need now more than ever for financial support. He described the hotshot lawyer Treegers had hired, and walked a fine line between dismissing his abilities in the face of the greater power of the Lord—who he made clear was on the side of the CCCA—and creating the sense of imminent threat from the man. This was a fund-raiser, after all. The fluorescent lights made Ward's pale skin look slightly waxy. He was perspiring beneath the lights. The air-conditioner only did so much to cool the cavernous building now that it was filled with people.

Ward was still a striking man, tall, broad shouldered, and fit. In recent years he had started wearing a mustache, and his hair was still thick. Mary saw that most people must think of him as handsome. He had adopted certain aspects of western wear, and tonight he was wearing a white short-sleeved button-down shirt and a bolo tie. He was most comfortable in front of a crowd, most alive at those moments when he had an audience at his command.

The majority of people in the audience were simple folks. Many came from what the residents of Custer City called "the hills." Treegers had little impact on their quality of life, but the company represented everything they had over the years come to despise about the rich and powerful. They wanted someone to blame for the ways they felt their prospects always diminished—and Mary couldn't fault them for their fears—but she knew it was not Treegers that was the real threat to them. It was a combination of things so complex and contentious that few people seemed able to sort it out, and she was disgusted by the way Ward's simplistic answers manipulated the fear and ignorance of the people gathered here.

What a reassuring presence he was for them, though. Eloquent and knowledgeable. He could rattle off statistics and acronyms for government agencies, and various federal policies and all the ways the CCCA could appeal to such agencies for help. "In God's name," he always reminded everyone. He made them feel they had someone smart on their side. Tonight, as the fund-raiser drew to a close, Ward asked everyone to close their eyes and bow their heads.

Before beginning his prayer, Ward spread his legs wide and clasped his hands at his crotch. With his head bowed and his eyes clenched tight, he nodded in emphasis with each impassioned plea of his prayer. "Let us submit ourselves to the God of the universe," he said, "and lift our hearts in petition to the Almighty Lord on behalf of the town of Custer City, for he has promised that his wrath will be poured out upon the tyrant and the oppressor."

Mary did not bow her head. Rather, she watched Ward, his face contorting as he earnestly prayed. She stole a glance at Claire, expecting to meet her eye with a wink and a smile. Instead, Claire kept her head lowered, her eyes closed. In fact, she nodded her head in agreement with what Ward was saying. Mary shivered. She felt she could no longer stand to be among this group and abruptly left the building in the middle of Ward's prayer.

Outside, although the rain had stopped, clouds still roiled in the dark sky as she walked through the quiet grounds. The calf roping competition had ended, but the large corral was still filled with calves milling about in the unfamiliar darkness. They rustled and lowed softly. Horse trailers, campers, and trucks belonging to the ranchers who had come in for the competition that day were parked around the periphery of the pavilion. Despite the bad weather, most of the people were sitting outside their campers and tents. A few truck radios were on as the campers monitored the storm's progress. Horses staked beside their trailers grazed on the thin grass of the parkway. They stamped impatiently as Mary passed. They swished their long tails and whinnied softly, their great heads nodding. She was tempted to stroke their noses, to scratch between their ears. She imagined climbing up on one of those broad bare backs, wheeling the horse around, and riding out of the pavilion grounds onto the gravel road and finally into the dark plains beyond. For a few seconds, she could almost feel the wind in her hair as she sped across the hills.

As if in sympathy for her mood, the stump of her left leg began to ache. This pain was new to her, a throbbing ache she felt she could never soothe. She walked slowly through the muddy grounds, dreading her return to the brightly lit community center. Ward would be talkative and exuberant, full of his success. The children would be clingy and cranky. She didn't know what she would say to the suddenly self-righteous Claire, and then there were all those well-meaning, ignorant people who would never in all their dreams prosper as they hoped, despite Ward's promises for blessings from on high.

But she did go back, and it was as she had anticipated. David was asleep and Priscilla close to it. Mary told Ward she needed to get the kids home to bed. Filled with magnanimous generosity, he said, "Take the car. I'll catch a ride later."

He would be late getting home, and Mary didn't mind. After she had put the kids to bed, she went into the backyard and looked up at the sky. The humid night air was thick and the wind had died down so now an eerie stillness rested over the town. Despite the haze, a few stars glowed toward the eastern horizon. The stars didn't seem cold or indifferent to her. Long ago she had irrationally decided that Brian was somewhere among them, and that he still looked down upon her with interest. She felt his presence that night, and understood that for a long time she had made Brian a sort of substitute for God. He was no longer the husband of her youth; he had been transmuted into a place that transcended human frailty. She felt his love for her as something unconditional, his interest in her undiminished with time. She hadn't really thought about it until tonight, but it was to Brian she prayed when she prayed, and she asked him now for guidance, telling him about her fears for her children.

Under the troubled sky, Mary poured out her feelings. She was no longer the girl she had been when she met and fell in love with Brian. She couldn't say if she knew what love was anymore, or even if it mattered, but she knew her life depended on tracking her thoughts carefully, pursuing them to a conclusion of sorts. This was her one and only life. This short life. And she didn't want to live for another forty years as she now was. If she'd learned nothing more from the residents of the nursing home, it was that. She couldn't let herself be derailed by her guilt. She needed to think. What was it she wanted? What did Michael mean to her? What did he represent?

She decided Michael represented escape from her life with Ward. She forced herself to stay with it. The *real* question before her was her freedom. This was progress. She could do this. She could think it through carefully. What she needed was a plan for a future where she could be happy.

The sky rumbled and the clouds stirred again in the west. Before going in, she decided on a plan: after her summer school classes, she could graduate in August. She'd be in a position then to get a job with decent pay and benefits. Her heart raced slightly at the thought of such independence, serious income of her own. She'd find a little house to rent in Custer City, hire a babysitter full-time, and still have money to spare. Ward would be upset at first, of course he would, but he'd eventually come to accept the decision. He couldn't stay angry, and they'd work it out together. After all, she wasn't the only one unhappy in their relationship; she felt certain Ward would feel liberated too. If she made the first move, if she played the hard part, he could blame her and still maintain his status in the community and with the church. If taking all the responsibility for the failure of the marriage was the price of being free, she was more than willing to accept it.

Clouds churned across the dark sky. All the conditions were right for a tornado, but, peering into the darkness, Mary knew there would be no storm that night. She heard the slam of a car door. Ward would think it was weird if he found her wandering around in the backyard. She'd play her role for a while longer, buy herself time to formulate the details of her plan without Ward becoming suspicious. As she hurried back inside the house, she felt something click into place.

≡CHAPTER 24

≡For years *The Custer Weekly* had regularly published short articles about the conflict between the CCCA and Treegers, but once the lawsuit was filed, the paper began to print feature-length pieces each week. Initially, the articles had played up the Wild West aspects of the case, the CCCA cast in the role of vigilante justice forcing the law to pay attention to the abuses of the hostile gang at Treegers. Previous articles, no matter how short, had always included a photograph of Ward. If *The Weekly's* photographer didn't have a candid shot of him for a particular article, the paper reprinted a formal photograph from its archives taken when he graduated from seminary. Ward was photogenic and even if the articles hadn't made him out to be the good guy, the photographs would have.

Prior to their hiring Gretchen Miles, the Needhams had refused to allow the paper's photographer access to Treegers, so photographs were taken from the distance through the chain link fence, giving the impression the place was a cult or a penitentiary rather than a business. The antagonistic relationship between Treegers and the newspaper had ended only recently when articles began to include Treegers's point of view. As often as not now, the Needhams were depicted as representatives of progress, embattled and hindered by forces of fear and ignorance. Studio photographs of the Needham brothers accompanied the recent articles. While not as photogenic as Ward, they had the distinct advantage of looking like local guys, men the area residents recognized as their own, no longer the sinister, unseen, evil geniuses they had been for some readers in years past.

The recent articles had led many readers to conclude they may have misjudged Treegers, and Mary heard more than one person admit they now saw the Needhams as concerned businessmen. Each week they cited some new initiative underway to address Custer City's concerns about air quality. When interviewed, the brothers appeared to be knowledgeable and up to date, quoting at length from new research findings from the Ag Department at the University of Nebraska, leading James Hayman, the reporter who had been covering the story for years, to interview some of those university researchers, all of whom confirmed Treegers was among the most reputable and far-seeing of the large feedout units in the state.

Whether Treegers was truly as benign as it was now being depicted in the articles wasn't clear to Mary, but as she'd told Larry and Kent, hiring Gretchen had allowed the company the opportunity to present its side of the controversy, and Mary sensed the tide of public opinion had begun to shift.

The Needhams noticed the change in the media coverage, too, leading Jeff to call her one day shortly after Gretchen had started working for them. Mary recognized his voice instantly. All the Needham boys had a similar timber of voice, and it was their voices more than their appearance that reminded her of Brian.

"I just wanted to tell you how thankful we are for your suggestion, Mary. Gretchen's worked wonders for us. Have you been reading the paper?"

"Of course."

"I won't keep you," Jeff said. "I just wanted to let you know we appreciate it. And we appreciate you, Mary. Don't think we don't know how . . . how things are for you."

Mary wondered later what they knew about her and resented anew how the CCCA's extremism had forced her to defend Treegers as she had.

Ward was not one to express anger, but Mary could see he was angered by this turn of events. He'd been counting on public opinion staying on the side of the CCCA, and it was a potential disaster if favor shifted away from them when they were only weeks away from the trial.

He didn't talk to Mary about his worries, but she couldn't help but overhear when he talked on the telephone to Ed and other members of the CCCA. She knew from those conversations they were trying to come up with new strategies to keep the good citizens of the county outraged. As if to mock the CCCA, the smell from Treegers was less offensive than usual. Without the stench, the fight was an abstraction, and Mary guessed some of the more religious members of the CCCA might in fact be praying for the worst odor to return.

This morning's article, however, was a triumph for Ward and the CCCA. Ward had been caught in a dynamic pose during the previous evening's fund-raiser, and the backdrop of the flag and the countrified setting leant him an air of populist authority that Mary knew would have broad appeal for the readers of *The Weekly*.

Claire came over first thing that morning, bursting in through the front door. "Did you see the paper? Isn't it terrific?"

Minutes before Claire's arrival, Mary had gotten Joseph and Deborah out the door for school, and she had less than half an hour to get the younger two off to Julie's house before she had to be at work. David still needed to be fed. She was responsible for contributing a salad to a church gathering later that evening, and she hadn't yet finished putting it together. David was under the kitchen table crawling through a puddle of orange juice Priscilla had spilled only a few minutes before Claire showed up, while Priscilla was throwing a tantrum in her bedroom because Mary had insisted she change her clothes after the accident with the orange juice.

Mary had clearly not given Claire the response she expected, and in addition to everything else, Claire now seemed put out with her. "Are you still mooning around?" Claire said as Mary ducked under the table with a wet cloth. Mary didn't answer, but she was irritated enough by Claire's question that she lifted her head too quickly and hit it against the bottom of the table.

Claire didn't seem to notice. Without waiting for an answer from Mary, she went on. "You should be proud of Ward." Mary sensed rather than saw that Claire was holding the newspaper out for her to see, and she had the distinct impression Claire thought she was hiding under the table rather than trying to clean up a mess.

"I am proud of him," Mary said, "but I have a lot to do before I have to leave for work. Could you give me a hand?"

As if coming to her senses, Claire said, "Sure. What do you need?"

Mary felt another wave of impatience. Why was it so hard for people to see what needed to be done? Why was it that she always had to orchestrate everything?

She sighed. "It's Prissie. She's mad because she wanted to wear her pink sweater, but she . . ."

"Gotcha," Claire said, and Mary heard her move into the other room where from the distance she heard her say, "Prissie, we need to get you into some clean clothes." Mary couldn't hear Priscilla's answer, but she heard in the plaintive tone of her voice she wasn't cooperating. "I know," Claire said in response, "but Mommy needs you to be a big girl now." This was the Claire Mary knew from the nursing home, the Claire who could cajole a dissatisfied resident into or out of doing anything. She was a miracle worker here too. By the time Mary was rinsing the dirty rag out in the sink, Priscilla had returned to the kitchen in a clean outfit.

"Thanks, Claire," Mary said as she stripped David out of his pajamas and set him in his diaper and T-shirt in the high chair to feed him. He opened his mouth wide for each bite.

After a few minutes of silently watching, Claire said, "You aren't still thinking of doing something stupid, are you?" The suddenness of her question startled Mary. She had foolishly hoped Claire might have forgotten about yesterday's conversation.

"Claire, I don't know what you're talking about. I'm not thinking about *doing* anything except getting through my day. Could we talk about something else, please?" She looked significantly toward Priscilla, who although playing in the other room was within earshot.

"I don't get you, that's all," Claire persisted. Mary felt a flush of anger, and David, seeming to pick up on her agitation, began to fuss, turning his head away from the spoon where before he had been eating eagerly.

"Today's paper is full of praise for Ward," Claire said.

"I know. It's a great story."

"Isn't the photo layout something? Did you see us? Look!" Claire pushed the paper under Mary's nose, and there was the photograph Mary had seen earlier of herself and Claire standing together behind the food table. Mary hadn't really paid attention to the photograph before, but, as she looked closer, she noticed she looked tired. Claire said as much as she pulled the paper back toward herself again. "It's not the best picture of you; I don't mind it of me, though." She added under her breath then, "Guilt doesn't sit well with you." She delivered this admonition in a casual tone, but the directness of the statement hit Mary like a physical blow. She almost questioned if in fact Claire had spoken until she looked up and saw the same cold expression in her eyes she had intercepted weeks earlier when she had been nursing David. The expression that time had been so fleeting Mary had dismissed it, but this time Claire's loathing was transparent.

Mary recoiled. "What's that look for?"

Claire adjusted her face. "Nothing. I just don't understand you anymore."

"You don't understand me?" Mary said before she could catch

herself. "I don't have a clue what's going on in your head, Claire." There. She'd said it. Whatever was happening between them needed to be confronted.

"I guess that makes two of us."

"Okay then. Let's start here," Mary said. "What's up with all the Bible studies and your coming to church every Sunday? Since when have you been so pious?"

"Since I decided I needed to make some changes in my life." Claire looked away from Mary briefly before she continued. "I've been living for myself too long, and I need friends who will remind me of the right path."

Mary nodded. What could she say? Even if she had wanted to pursue the conversation, she didn't have time. David's earlier fussing was now full-fledged crying. His breakfast was unfinished and Mary still wasn't ready for work. Whatever rift there was between her and Claire seemed much too big to tackle under these circumstances.

About Ward, she knew Claire was right. If Mary were a proper wife she would be not only supportive of Ward's efforts but proud of him. After years of work, his vision was finally paying off, but unlike Claire seemed to think, Mary wasn't comparing Ward to someone else. She wasn't interested in choosing between two men. As she'd realized the night before, this was about owning up to a mistake, acknowledging she had taken the wrong path a long time ago, and having the courage finally—though she knew some would undoubtedly say selfishly—to own up to it and correct the course of her life before she was like Zoe or any of the other residents in the nursing home who regretted the lives they had lived and wondered with bewilderment now what they had feared so much in life that had kept them from realizing their desire. Mary thought with a twinge of sadness there had been a time when she could have talked to Claire about what she was thinking. Although their conversation did not last long that morning, Mary knew she hadn't done enough to appease Claire's suspicions. When she returned to the kitchen after dressing David, Claire was gone.

A week after this confrontation, Claire stopped by the house again. For a few minutes it seemed almost like old times as they shared a cup of coffee at the kitchen table. Claire was tickling David, and he was shrieking with laughter. Claire's face was so joyous and beautiful in that moment Mary thought she loved her as much as she loved anyone in the world. Then David, in his spasmodic delight, reared back and bumped his head hard on the kitchen wall. His laughter quickly turned to hiccupping sobs. Claire tried to console him, but David refused to be comforted, urgently reaching instead for Mary.

"It's naptime, isn't it, sleepy boy?" Mary said as she lifted David from Claire's arms. Had she imagined it, or did Claire cling to him a bit longer than normal, giving Mary the momentary sense of having to wrestle him away? She had forgotten the incident when she returned after depositing David in his crib with a bottle, but as soon as she sat down to her coffee again, she saw by Claire's expression something was wrong.

"You should have talked me out of it," Claire said.

"Talked you out of what?" Mary set her cup down slowly.

"You know."

Mary did know, but for reasons she did not entirely understand herself, she wanted Claire to say it out loud.

"The abortion," Claire said.

"Talk you out of it? I couldn't have talked you out of anything, Claire, and you know it."

"That isn't true. You should have been a real friend to me." Claire's eyes welled up. "You should have known I wasn't in a position to be making a decision like that on my own."

"But that's insane, Claire. You've always been so confident," Mary said feebly. "I figured if anyone knew what she wanted, it was you. If you'll recall, though, I did try. You didn't want to talk."

Claire's face closed, and the conversation ended.

＊

It was almost June, and Joseph and Deborah would be finished with the school year in another week. Since the night of the fund-raiser and the vision she had seen for her life, Mary had begun to make a timetable for leaving Ward. By late summer she'd start looking for a place to live so she could move the kids and get them settled before the school year began. She had already talked to her professors about jobs in the area. A nursing shortage more severe than any shortage in memory meant a good job market. Her professors assured Mary that she'd have her choice of jobs if she was willing to commute. She ranked among the top three in her graduating class. Some of her professors had even hinted that they thought she should pursue work in a specialized unit at a large hospital. They spoke of hospitals in Lincoln, Omaha, and Denver. More than one of them encouraged her to continue her education and pursue a master's degree.

Her success as a student had come upon Mary suddenly. After years of struggling as a part-timer torn between her many commitments, she had barely had time to complete her class requirements, let alone feel there was anything remarkable about what she had done. Only now, at the end of her program, was she aware of her accomplishment.

In the meantime, Claire took every opportunity to belittle Mary about Michael. She was clearly fishing for information, and she hit a nerve when one night at work she said, "I can't believe you would buy into the sort of cheap trick this guy played on you. Do you really think someone like him would be interested in a woman like you? You have four kids, for Pete's sake. You live in Custer City, Nebraska. You're no one to him. He meets glamorous women all the time."

What Claire said echoed Mary's own fears. Since the first flush of happiness, she'd begun to have doubts, and Claire's comment that seducing naive women was a challenge to guys like Michael had hurt. He'd gotten to her, and Mary sensed now her vulnerability, her gullibility to predatory men. How had Claire put it? "Guys like Michael rack up as many women as they can as their travel trophies." And she had concluded with the verdict: "He's bad news, Mary." She supposed Claire was right. After all, she'd seen him switch registers first with her and later with Matt Broder, becoming someone she didn't recognize. What assurance did she have that he was being genuine with her? Still, no matter how she tried, Mary couldn't forget how Michael had looked at her as he'd picked up her hand that afternoon in Lexington. She didn't know how someone could fake a look like that.

✻

When it arrived, the letter caused no suspicion. The address was typed, the return address blandly official. She opened the envelope, absently assuming it was a piece of junk mail when a handwritten letter fell out along with a photograph. She had forgotten about the photo Michael had taken that first day in the church, and she was startled by the attractive woman she saw looking back at her.

"Dear Mary, I imagine you're sitting at your kitchen table," the letter began. Michael's handwriting, though unfamiliar to her, seemed right. The letter went on. "Summer must be full-born there by now, and I'm guessing the big kids are playing outside in the garden. How I wish I could be there again. Maybe the little spooder is crawling at your feet as you read this," as in fact David was. "I'm not a big one for words," the letter went on. "You'll have to forgive me that. Like I told you, I understand things better in photographs. I can't express everything I'm feeling, but Mary I've been looking for you for a long time, and now that I've found you, I can't stop thinking about you. Maybe the pic will explain it. Who would have imagined it—not me, that's for sure—that I'd find the woman of my dreams in the middle of Nebraska? But I did. Love, Michael."

Mary looked at the photograph again. As Michael had said, it told her everything she needed to know. She thought she could finally see herself as Michael had seen her that day, and she felt a glimmer of that same sweet emotion she had felt when telling Claire about him. She wasn't giddy with it. No, it wasn't like that, but she felt a deep, slow happiness, an emotion she hadn't known for a long time.

How was it possible that it had only been two weeks since he'd left town? She couldn't think about what was happening logically. Nothing made sense in that way, but this was hers to decide, hers to make of what she wanted. She gave herself permission to make her choice. She wished things were otherwise. She wished she wasn't in a position to hurt Ward, to disappoint her parents, to frighten her children. Still, she felt a funny sort of confidence growing in her. Later she folded Michael's letter carefully and stuck it in the lining of the little-used jewelry box she kept on her dresser.

Within a week of the first letter, a second one arrived, anticipating her questions. At one point, Michael wrote, "I know you think I live an exciting life, but it isn't how you think. It's hard to meet people when you're on the road all the time. Maybe I'm a little off that way, a little at odds with myself, but for the first time in a long time, meeting you, I felt comfortable with someone. With you, Mary."

⁂

Ward was not a moody man, but for days he had been in a funk. Mary was unaccustomed to having to deal with his personality this overtly. He was subdued, not his usual buoyant self. She heard him speaking in low tones on the telephone sometimes late at night, conferring with the lawyers and Ed and with other key members of the CCCA. They were out on a limb, and they'd come too far to have things go badly for them.

She saw a darker side of Ward, too, a place where his usual competitiveness became obsession, pushing him to do anything it took to win. She felt him plotting. After hanging up the phone, he stayed up late writing what she assumed were plans to continue the fight with Treegers. The struggle, as she had suspected for some time, had long ago stopped being about air quality and had become a personal vendetta. Treegers was the enemy and they needed to be annihilated. Sometime over the years of the fight, a line had been crossed, the civic dispute taking the form in Ward's mind of a spiritual battle, a battle with Treegers over the town's salvation.

If she felt it had been her right to help the Needhams, if she felt she had only been exercising her own opinions or that they could have thought of the public relations aspect of the dispute on their own, she had only to think about how she would feel if Ward knew the content of her meeting with them to know it was not that simple. She had been disloyal to Ward. Their whole life together she had been disloyal to him. She didn't value what he valued. She couldn't subscribe to his view of anything, let alone his view of the world or how God worked in the world. They weren't partners in any sense of the word. They weren't even good partners in raising their four children together.

≡CHAPTER 25

⇒By the end of June, the days were still unseasonably hot, temperatures over one hundred degrees for a week without a break. The school year ended and Joseph and Deborah brought home boxes of papers and art projects that Mary stacked in their bedrooms to sort later. Ward was tense with preparations for the trial and spent more time than usual in his office. Mary washed and ironed all of his best shirts; she shined his good wingtip shoes and sent his two suits to the cleaners. Ward had timed his haircut a week in advance of the first day of the trial. He trimmed his nails carefully. It felt to Mary as she watched him that he was preparing for battle.

She, meanwhile, looked all undone. She hadn't had a haircut since before David was born, instead pulling her hair back into a ragged ponytail rather than bothering with any sort of style. She had no particular reason to dress up and hadn't bought new clothes in years, still preferring to buy vintage clothes at the secondhand stores in North Platte and Kearney as an afterthought while buying clothes for the kids. Her mother always complimented her on her thriftiness. "You do so well, considering . . ." But with Ward's preparations she felt her own shabbiness in a new way.

She was frantic as she started her last summer school classes. In addition to the classes, the nursing home had lost two nurse's aides, and Theresa had not yet replaced them, so Mary was scheduled for more hours than usual. The church was planning its Vacation Bible School for the middle of July, and while Mary had been able to talk her way out of being the director and out of teaching the third graders, she was still chair of the planning committee and was expected to help contribute food for each day's lunch.

She was distracted that morning the day before the trial was to begin when she answered the phone, and she felt her heart catch the moment she heard Michael's voice.

"I need to see you, Mary."

She paused, but her hesitation felt dishonest to her, for her first impulse upon hearing his voice had been to drop the phone, to drop everything facing her in the busy day ahead, and run to him.

"Please," Michael said, and Mary was impressed by his assertiveness. Unlike her, he didn't seem confused. Was that a good or a bad thing that he wasn't confused? He had little to risk here, while she . . . she had everything to lose. She had children to think about. She stopped herself. Who was she telling this to? Who did she need to convince? She swallowed hard. No matter what else she did, she decided to be honest with Michael. Lying to him, even in the form of denying what she had felt in May, seemed like a serious violation. She didn't care that the church folks, Ward, or Custer City's gossips would not share her reasoning.

"Can you meet me in North Platte? I have a clinical there at the hospital this morning."

The relief was obvious in Michael's voice. "Just say where and what time."

"La Cocina at three o'clock, there on Highway 30 coming into town."

"I'll be there."

As she hung up the telephone, Mary had the distinct feeling of having set something into motion, a sensation not unlike the effect of toppling dominoes. For a split second, the feeling was so vivid and overpowering, she caught her breath. More melodrama, she thought, as she quickly shifted her attention back to her day, beginning with getting the kids dressed and ready to go to Julie's. What would she do without Julie?

When later that morning she drove out of town toward North Platte, she felt her own heightened mood mirrored by all the activity in town. The court case was a big deal. Marquees in front of various businesses reflected the particular loyalties of their owners. The hotel welcomed everyone, careful not to appear to take sides, as did the restaurants. The steakhouse was advertising for a big barbecue that night, and already on this steamy Monday morning, Bob Kelly, the chef/owner was outside on the street tending to the huge cast-iron smoker, which Mary knew he would have started in the wee morning hours.

As she left town heading west on Highway 2, Mary was overcome again by another odd sensation. Through the rearview mirror, the unspooling highway seemed suddenly to speed up and the town to recede and for a moment to disappear altogether from her view. When she looked again everything was normal. The experience was so disturbing that she worried for a moment for her mental health. Her nursing studies had taught her that stress could do strange things to the mind. She felt keenly that Monday morning in June that something was coming her way, that in fact whatever was coming had already been done. With this thought, she felt a catch in her throat. She blinked quickly, took a deep breath, and forced herself to concentrate on the road and the clinical ahead. Like pulling a shade to mute a too-bright sun, she put Michael out of her mind.

By the time her clinical ended at two thirty, she had recovered from her morning jitters. Still, when she entered La Cocina and saw Michael sitting on a stool by the front door waiting for her, she was not prepared for the force of her emotion. He was more hand-some than she remembered. He wore his customary white shirt, khakis, and red Converses, but his hair looked longer and lighter, his skin darker. He had clearly been in the sun during the month of their separation. His eyes held hers. Then he smiled. She forgot herself as she returned the smile and followed him, as though mes-merized, to a table in the back of the restaurant.

A dirty fish tank, its filter gurgling, stood against the back wall near where they sat. Mary was distracted by the sound of traffic on the highway outside the window, the way the heat rose off the asphalt. She scanned the menu but couldn't stop sneaking looks at Michael across the table. He was similarly distracted by her. As her eyes scanned her choices—fish taco, bean burrito, chile rel-leno, enchilada—she chose the tacos, an iced tea, and Michael. She chose Michael.

After they had ordered, Michael took her hand beneath the table. Neither of them spoke for several minutes. Finally he broke the silence. "I know it's insane, but I can't stop thinking about you, Mary." He shook his head slightly and smiled ruefully, suggesting bewilderment over his predicament. "It's the damnedest thing. You've bewitched me." He laughed before going on. "One day I'm a regular, self-contained guy, the next I'm a scattered mess, and the only cure for putting me together again is you." He went on. "I want you to know I'm not prone to this kind of impulsive thing. I'm like my dad. I don't like messes, but here you are, sweet, beauti-ful Mary. That day in the sale barn when you told me you wouldn't take that bull calf if someone gave him to you . . ." He laughed. "I'd never heard anything like that. And the way you played the piano, like a crazy genius. And your magical garden and your kids . . ." He shook his head again. "You're the weirdest, most wonderful person I've ever met."

The waitress returned with their plates and Michael didn't finish his thought. Nor did they speak of it again. Instead, they fell into a dreamy suspension of time, the condition Claire had referred to as moony. Even being reminded of Claire's criticism couldn't dampen Mary's feelings. She thought she could fall into this state of being with Michael, this mooniness, and never willingly extricate herself, never return to the real world where she eventually remembered she had real children with a real babysitter, and a real VBS meeting later that night.

By the time she thought to check her watch it was already six. Somehow she managed to tell Michael she had to go. In fact, she had to leave immediately. The dream state continued until she pulled up in front of the parsonage. Until then, she hadn't noticed the cars parked in front and what appeared to be reporters standing on the parsonage lawn. Ward stood in front of the cameras answering questions. She realized Michael had probably given up being at this news conference to meet her, and she wondered fleetingly what that might have cost him. Not wanting to get caught up in any of the pretrial publicity, she cut across the church lawn and approached Julie's house from the alley.

As she stepped onto the porch, Mary was reminded of the month before when she had first been with Michael. Unlike before, she now knew she was too far gone to second-guess her intentions. If her faculties through the afternoon had been scattered, once she focused, she felt acutely aware of everything. The smell of the grass was intoxicating. A breeze had sprung up, and she thought she could almost hear a song in the wind sighing through the trees. Her children, when they ran to greet her, were so alive and beautiful they left her breathless. She felt as though she had been seeing life in black and white before and suddenly she was seeing in color. How had she missed so much? Michael hadn't stolen anything. He'd given her back the world. There was more room in her heart now, not less.

She kneeled and opened her arms and the kids came to her. She nuzzled against their warm necks, tempted for a minute to weep against their small shoulders, but she caught herself. When she finally looked up, Julie was watching her carefully. Mary stood, lifted the baby, and held him against her. The intensity of Julie's gaze was almost too much, and Mary feared she might blurt out everything. She'd experienced something remarkable. After all these years, she'd been given another chance at happiness. That was how she thought of it, but the experience with Claire had taught her to keep it to herself. She would have to do this alone.

Afterward, she couldn't hope anyone would harbor a generous thought for her. Everyone in this small town would turn against her. It was as clear as if it had been scripted. If she broke the rules, broke ranks, refused the role she'd been assigned, she'd meet not with understanding but with hostility. That was the price she'd pay. If not for the kids, Mary knew, she would have gone to the parsonage—to that crooked house where she had spent so many miserable years—packed a bag, and left. She would have run to Michael at the Grand Hotel, knocked on his door, and sought sanctuary with him until they could leave together. For a split second she indulged in the fantasy of the ease of that flight.

Mary continued to use David as a shield to avoid Julie's questioning eyes, and she somehow managed to get the children organized and out the door, herding them down the alley and toward the back door of the parsonage.

"Who are all those people?" Priscilla asked when she saw the cameras on the front lawn.

"Those are the filmers," Deborah said. "They're here to film Daddy."

"You mean reporters," Mary said absently.

"No," Joseph said. "They're making a film about Dad. Someone's making a film."

"How do you know that?"

"Dad told us," Joseph said.

"He told you that?"

"Joseph," Deborah scolded. "Daddy said Mommy wouldn't like it. You weren't supposed to tell."

"Why would he think that?" Mary asked. Deborah shrugged, and Joseph looked away. "Joseph?"

Joseph shrugged. "He said it was the money."

"The money?" Mary said, wondering why she seemed incapable of anything except repeating what she heard. She slowed her steps, feeling as though part of her reasoning had fled. It seemed she wasn't the only one who had secrets in their family.

"He's giving the money to the CCCA, and he said you wouldn't like it if you knew," Joseph said, and it was obvious he was disgusted with himself for betraying Ward's confidence.

Mary was tempted to say, "He'd be right. I wouldn't like it." Instead, she said nothing and picked up the pace as they crossed the yard. By the time they reached the back door she didn't care what Ward did. Ward's business was his. His decisions, which he had always led her to understand were his alone even if they affected her, truly were his. All the illogical, pecuniary, small-minded decisions he made, Mary suddenly realized with astonishing relief, were his own. She wouldn't have to suffer them anymore. She was almost in a good mood again by the time she shooed the kids into the house.

⁂

It was this ebullient mood that she later blamed for what happened. They were in the kitchen that evening, Ward lingering over a late supper, the kids already in bed, Mary drinking a cup of tea.

"So, what was all the ruckus outside this evening?" she asked, feigning ignorance. Ward shrugged but didn't answer. Mary could see he was tired. She paused for a second before pushing further. "The kids said someone is making a documentary about the court case."

At this, Ward jerked up his head. Mary guessed he was startled to learn the children had betrayed his secret to her, and some part of her was satisfied that he had to doubt himself a little. "Why didn't you tell me yourself?"

"I didn't think you'd be interested, Mary." He didn't say it defensively. In fact, his tone was so resigned she felt herself wavering.

What kind of monster was she that her husband couldn't interest her in his life? Perhaps if he'd said nothing after this, perhaps if he'd simply gone on to describe the documentary . . .

Much later she would replay what happened next and wonder why it had gone as precipitously as it had. Whatever sincerity she had seen in Ward's face earlier was gone. "Are you going to run to the Needhams and tell them about this?"

Mary figured Ward had a right to be angry at her. It wasn't his anger and disappointment that stunned her; it was the expression of pure scorn on his face. He'd unmasked himself, something she'd never seen, and she didn't like the man she saw before her.

Mary didn't say anything to this. Instead, she took a few seconds to finish her tea before standing up to clear the table. She turned her back to Ward and as she turned on the water to start the dishes she said softly, "This isn't working."

"The water?" Ward said. She glanced around. The expression she'd seen on his face earlier was gone. His question seemed logical enough, but for reasons she couldn't entirely explain to herself it enraged her. She felt her knuckles tighten on the dishcloth.

"No, not the water, Ward. Us. We aren't working."

"What are you talking about? Look at me."

Mary wrung out the dishcloth, then slowly turned around and leaned against the sink with weariness or insolence, she couldn't say which for certain.

"Mary, what's going on here?"

"Nothing's going on. That's the problem. You're so little a part of our lives, the kids and me . . . days go by before we even notice you're gone." She paused and laid the dishcloth on the counter. "You've been critical of me over the years, Ward. I've never quite lived up to what you expect or need. I'm not a good minister's wife. I'm not the kind of mother you want for the children, not supportive enough of your work in the church or the CCCA. I've never been able to transform this . . ."—she gestured then toward the house—"this disaster into a gracious home." Her voice broke and she turned away.

"Don't look away," Ward said, not unkindly. "Finish what you were going to say."

She sighed but she didn't turn back to him immediately. Instead, she bowed her head over the sink where she had turned the water back on. She watched it run into the sink and turned off the spigot before saying without turning around, "I used to think it was all me, that it was me failing you." She paused, picked up the dishcloth again, and began to wash a glass. "But I don't think that anymore. I don't think it's just me. I think it's me *and* you. We made a mistake."

"Do you honestly believe that, Mary?"

"I want a divorce, Ward." She was stunned to hear herself say it, startled by the word *divorce*, a word she realized she had never actually ever said aloud. She hadn't planned to say it now. Everything was happening in the wrong way. She wasn't ready for this yet. She heard Ward's chair scrape on the floor behind her, and she glanced over her shoulder. What she saw shocked her. Ward's face was livid. His lips formed a severe line. His hands shook so where he held the back of the chair that the chair's legs rattled against the floor. He seemed incapable of controlling the shaking, and for a moment Mary felt crushed by the extent of his emotion. She wanted suddenly to retract everything she had said. She wanted to erase the harshness of her words, but before she could speak Ward pushed the chair away.

"You do whatever you like, Mary, but don't think you're going to take my children."

"My children," echoed in the room. "My children. My children." His assertion, which erased her from the equation, suddenly symbolized all of her complaints with him. She was the adjunct, the handmaiden, the accessory, the servant to his dreams and desires. What had he called her after they were first married? His helpmeet. She was of no use to him as a full partner; her dreams were not important. Her role as mother was of no significance to him. In his mind the children were entirely his.

What had gotten into her, though? Why, on the eve of the trial, had she initiated this conversation? She wanted to believe it was only a coincidence, an accident of bad timing, but in some secret corner of her heart, she wasn't sure she believed her own self-justification. What she had said, though, about both of them having made a mistake, both of them failing, that felt true to her.

Ward left the kitchen before Mary could answer him, and she felt something solid and geometric slide into place in her mind. The marriage was over. What remained were the details to be worked out.

CHAPTER 26

≡The world tilts. Words change everything. Waking in a different bed makes the familiar house strange. Mary woke in the living room where she had slept on the foldout couch. She heard Ward in the kitchen making coffee, and when she went out she saw he was already dressed except for his jacket and tie.

"Ward . . ."

"Do you know where my good tie clip is?" he said.

Mary looked up quickly from where she had been leaning on the doorjamb, still in her robe. Ward didn't meet her eyes as he continued his coffee preparation.

"Did you look in the box on your dresser?"

"Yes."

"I'll look later." She walked over to the counter. "Here, let me finish that. You'll spill on your good shirt." Ward stepped away and let her into the spot where he had been standing.

"Ward . . ."

"I think I'll just take it off until I'm ready to go."

Mary sighed softly. "That's a good idea." She caught his eye briefly and the muted rage she saw there was the only sign he recalled their conversation from the night before.

After Ward left the kitchen, Mary put on water to boil for oatmeal. In the back of the house she heard the older kids rustling and the murmur of Ward's voice. While the water came to a boil she woke David and changed his diaper. By the time she got back to the kitchen, the older kids were seated around the table waiting for their breakfast.

Such was the power of habit that in spite of their lives coming apart, Mary and Ward started their day as they always had. Mary poured juice into glasses, put bread in the toaster, and stirred the oatmeal. From where she stood at the stove, she listened to the children's sleepy morning chatter. Today they seemed subdued. Ward had brought his notes for the trial to the table and they were respectful of his need to concentrate. Mary filled bowls with oatmeal, milk, and raisins. She buttered slices of toast before bringing everything to the table. Once she had set the breakfast things out, Ward pushed his notes to the side of his bowl and bowed his head for prayer. Around the table the older children followed his example. Only David and Mary did not bow their heads. Mary watched as David gaily clapped his hands in his high chair, attempting to get everyone's attention. Mary quietly shushed him.

"Father in heaven," Ward began, "we thank you for this food, for giving us a good night's rest. We thank you, Lord, for your great love for us, a love that endures despite our selfishness and our weakness." Ward was given to long prayers, but this was shaping up to be an especially long one. Mary glanced up and noticed the older kids were also watching Ward curiously. He continued as if unaware of their questioning. "I ask you especially, Lord, to help me overcome the Devil's distractions, to resist those who would wish me harm. And, Lord, just as Adam should have resisted Eve's temptation to evil, give me courage to stand up to those in Satan's control who would cause me to stumble." Mary stiffened. The children squirmed as their breakfast grew cold. Still, he went on.

Finally, Priscilla said, "Daddy, say 'amen.'" Ward stopped, and as if only then remembering where he was, closed his prayer. He pulled his notes back toward himself and read through them as he ate his meal in silence.

When Ward had finished eating, he stood up. He didn't look at Mary where she fed David. Joe and Priscilla chattered, seemingly oblivious to their parents. Only Deborah looked first at Ward and then sharply at Mary. "Bye, Daddy," she said. "Do good today at the trial."

Ward smiled and dipped his head to kiss her forehead. "Thank you, sweetie."

Priscilla echoed, "Do good, Daddy."

Ward smiled and kissed her as well.

"Dad," Joseph said, his voice husky, "will you know today if you win?"

Ward composed himself slightly and matched Joseph's serious mood. "I don't think so, son."

Joseph nodded soberly, though Mary doubted he fully understood. She regretted her hasty judgment as he added, "You've got a lot of good evidence against them." He said it as though it were a fact, as though the evidence were so compelling the CCCA couldn't help but win its case.

"That's exactly right, Joe. We've got a strong case or this wouldn't have come to trial." Ward raised his hands and folded them in front of him as if in prayer. "Pray for me," he said to the older kids. They all nodded soberly. Mary recalled what she had heard the night before about Ward taking them into his confidence, telling them about the film, asking them to keep a secret from her. It was clear to her now that he had been talking to the kids at length about the lawsuit as well, worrying them, burdening them, she felt.

"Good-bye, Mary," Ward said. She mumbled a good-bye without looking at him. His grand pretense grated on her nerves.

As she was finishing the breakfast dishes, the phone rang.

"Is Ward gone?" Michael sounded a little out of breath.

"Yes."

"Good. I don't want to put you in a bad spot." Mary suppressed the urge to laugh at this. "Are you in the middle of something?"

"Just breakfast dishes."

"I can't talk long. I'm on my way over to the courthouse in Brewster. Can I see you tonight?"

"I'm working the late shift." Mary said. "Maybe you could come by for my break."

"What time is that?"

"Nine."

"I'll be there." Michael was quiet for a minute before adding, "Mary, what will we do?"

Something in his raw appeal was more convincing to her than any declaration of love.

"I have no idea."

"Do you think Ward suspects anything?" His question peeved her slightly. She didn't like playing the childish role of hiding something from Ward.

"He doesn't know anything about you, but," she paused, "I asked him for a divorce last night."

Mary heard Michael let out a slow breath. He was quiet for so long she grew anxious. She hurried to say, "It isn't because of you. . . . It's not you. . . . It's . . . I'm not saying this right. You didn't make this happen; it's been coming for a long time; it's needed to happen." She stopped then, ashamed of her blathering.

Michael cut in. "Mary, I don't know what to say. I don't want to influence you to do something before you're ready."

Mary felt irritated again. "You aren't in a position to talk me into something this big."

Michael noticed her testiness. "Good," he said and laughed. "Is this our first fight?"

Mary smiled in spite of herself, but she didn't answer him right away. "Things aren't happening the way I'd planned, but I'm not sorry. Not for me, anyway. I'm sad for the kids." She felt her throat constrict painfully when she mentioned the kids. "I wish I could do this without hurting them."

She saw herself then as Michael must see her, foolish and flighty. The life she had imagined apart from Ward continued in Custer City. This was the life familiar to her children. They needed their school and their friends. Now, thinking about Michael, she couldn't imagine how all those pieces could possibly come together to include him. She couldn't imagine him making a life in Custer City, nor could she imagine taking her children away from their home. She was as stuck in Custer City as if she were a tree planted there.

As if sensing her dismay and the reason for it, Michael said with a chuckle, "I told you I was looking for a change. Hell, they're advertising for a janitor here at the hotel."

Mary laughed.

"I'll see you at nine," he said.

"Meet me outside," Mary rushed to say. "There's an alley in back."

Later that morning, Mary turned on the television to the local cable station. While the children played, she watched the start of the court proceedings. Ward looked sober sitting at the plaintiff's bench with the CCCA's lawyer. On the other side, Larry and Kent Needham also looked sober, dressed in suits, sitting with their counsel. She recognized almost everyone in the courtroom, but instead of watching the trial, she was hoping for a glimpse of Michael. Now and then the camera caught him as he moved about the room either snapping photographs or looking for an angle. Each time, Mary felt her whole body go tense, every muscle, it seemed, absorbed in trying to force the camera lens to follow him instead of the trial at hand. She couldn't concentrate on the testimony and the arguments each side laid out before the judge. Perhaps more than anyone in Custer City, she was invested in the court's judgment, but she no longer cared about its outcome.

At nine that evening, Michael was not in the alley when Mary got there. She glanced around. Nothing. No sound indicated his approach, and she felt her heart plummet as she stood there alone. In those few seconds all of Claire's warnings that Michael was only using her in a perverse contest ambushed her. It seemed not only possible but true, and Mary felt the weight of her foolishness crash down upon her. How could she have allowed herself to come this far on such a thoughtless course? As daylight began to dissolve around her, she felt as if she were a spectacle on a stage. Surely there were people watching in the shadows, laughing at the joke played on her, enjoying her humiliation. This wild accumulation of thoughts caught her off guard, not only for its vicious self-loathing, but for how rapidly it played across her mind as though she had been waiting for any excuse to begin the assault against herself.

She realized later she hadn't waited a minute before she heard footsteps. Even in the darkness she knew it was Michael, but why had he not been there waiting for her? Why was he late? Her jealous demands were strange to her.

"I'm sorry I'm late," he said while still a few feet away, and Mary shushed him, nervous someone from inside would see them together. Michael waited until he was standing beside her before whispering his apology again. "I had trouble getting my film sent out this evening."

"Is everything all right?" Mary came back into her right mind again, relieved to see him, forgetting everything but his presence.

"Yes," Michael said but didn't elaborate. Mary was grateful. She was interested in his work but was glad he could leave it behind. They had so little time together she didn't want to be a sounding board.

Michael glanced around the alley. He smiled as his gaze came back to her. "Do you feel safe here?"

Mary nodded.

He took her into his arms and kissed her. She felt herself resist slightly that first kiss, conscious of crossing a line she'd long respected of fidelity to her marriage, but the kiss felt so natural, so much like a homecoming, that she gave in to it. Michael pulled away once to look at her before drawing her close again. The next time he pulled away, he was not so casual. "Can you leave? Can you come back to the hotel with me?" Something rustled near the garbage cans down the alley from them. Birds cooed and chirruped as they settled in the trees. Just like that, it was night. A few stars glinted in the pale indigo sky.

Mary nodded and wordlessly walked back into the nursing home where she told Theresa she wasn't feeling well and needed to go home.

"You look flushed, Mary," Theresa said. "I hope you aren't coming down with something serious. I can't spare you for long."

Guilt washed over her briefly at Theresa's words, but Mary didn't hesitate as she left the building and went to find Michael in the alley. "Let's go," she said.

"My car's down the street here. Do you want to walk with me, or should I pick you up?"

"I'll walk with you, but I don't want to go to the hotel."

"Where to?" Michael asked after they got into the car.

Mary slouched in the passenger seat. "Stay on back streets," she said, directing him to a gravel road that took them north of town. The gravel quickly gave way to a dirt road winding through the hills, finally ending on a low-maintenance access road. Michael drove confidently on those dark roads with one hand on the wheel, the other hand holding hers. They didn't speak, though occasionally Michael squeezed her hand as if to convince himself she was real.

Finally, Mary pointed to the long driveway of an abandoned house. There had been no cars following them, nor had they met anyone on the way up. Michael cut the lights but left the engine running. All traces of daylight were gone. The sky was thick with stars. A half-moon hovered near the eastern horizon, peeping between the branches of the old Scotch pines that had once formed a shelter-belt. Mary nodded and Michael turned off the car. They sat together in silence for a few seconds, peering into the darkness through the windshield. She felt silly all of a sudden for not going to the hotel with Michael like a grown-up.

Michael didn't seem bothered. "I have a car blanket in the trunk," he said. "Are you okay with that?"

Mary nodded. She got out with him and waited as he pulled out the blanket. He searched briefly for a level spot. Mary followed him and when the blanket was laid out, she sat down. Michael joined her. For a few minutes they laid together on the blanket looking up into the sky. Michael rested his head on folded arms. "I don't think I've ever seen so many stars."

They both looked into the sky before Michael finally turned on his side to face her, propping himself on his elbow. "This is nice. I'm glad you suggested coming here."

"I wish I could say it was because I was being romantic. I was afraid to go to the hotel, afraid we'd be seen."

Michael drew his brows together. "Don't apologize, Mary. You're risking a lot here."

She felt the sting of tears and bit her bottom lip. "Maybe too much," she said.

Michael kissed her eyelids one at a time. She felt a shiver deep inside. The moon had made its steady arc across the sky and now stood just above the trees. Mary trembled as Michael kissed her neck and caressed her shoulder. As he moved his hand down to circle her breast, she tensed.

"What is it?" Michael asked.

She sat up quickly. Her heart thudded hard against her chest and her palms had grown clammy. "I don't know what's the matter with me. I . . . I'm sorry, Michael. I'm acting like a foolish little girl, but I can't do this. There's too much happening all at once, too many things. . . . I shouldn't have come. It wasn't right of me."

Michael stayed where he was. He moved his arm down across

his eyes for a few seconds. He turned his head away, but Mary could see he was disgusted with her. She didn't blame him. She was an amateur at adultery.

After a few minutes, Michael got up. He held out his hand to help her up, and he folded the blanket quickly without speaking to her. Mary suppressed the urge to apologize again as she followed him to the car. Michael got in after returning the blanket to the trunk. He moved to start the engine but stopped himself.

"What are we doing here? Can you tell me that?"

Mary shook her head. She felt Michael looking at her, waiting for an answer, but she had none.

"I should go home." She heard the resignation in her own voice, felt her hopes deflate. They sat for several minutes in silence. The car windows were down and Mary could smell the damp earth outside.

"Oh, Mary," Michael said at last. His face crumbled. "I apologize. I'm frustrated. I won't lie to you about that. I'm angry. Seeing you again, everything's clear to me. If I had my way, I'd get this story reassigned, and we'd run away from here tonight. And it would be an incredibly stupid thing to do."

Mary nodded. She didn't allow herself to wonder about the life they might make for themselves, the real life and how it might disappoint both of them. She looked into the darkness. The moon lit the abandoned house and the fields on either side of them. Someone had lived here at one time. People had loved one another, or they hadn't. They'd made promises to one another. They'd lied to one another. She wasn't a girl any longer. After losing Brian, she'd come to know she couldn't ever completely depend on someone else again, not like she once had. She was maybe damaged in that way, but she knew she'd never again give up the whole of her heart to another person.

"I'm impatient with this situation," Michael went on, "but you've never tried to fool me. You were always who you are. I let myself get involved." Mary wished she could say something to console him. She wished there was a solution.

"Things are moving too fast for me. That's all."

In the darkness she could feel Michael thinking. "We'll do this on your terms, Mary."

Mary caught her bottom lip briefly, startled by his words, but not saying what she felt. There had never been any other terms for her. She didn't feel caught up in something too big to resist. Her life included her kids. There were no other terms than those.

"Can I see you tomorrow?" Michael interrupted her thoughts.

"I don't know if I can manage it. I'll . . ."

"You don't need to explain. If you can make it, you know where I'll be."

She nodded.

"I'd better get you home." He started the car and began to back down the long driveway.

His choice amused her. "You could have turned around in the yard," she said once he reached the road.

Michael smiled. "We've done everything else backward, so why change now?"

Mary laughed, relieved suddenly to be talking about something less fraught. "That's true. I don't know anything about you, Michael. Not really."

"Like what?"

"Your mother's name, for instance."

"Is that important?" Michael's smiled in confusion, and then without waiting for her answer said, "Elizabeth. Her name's Elizabeth."

"I don't know your birthday."

"April fourth."

"Or if you have brothers and sisters?"

"Two sisters. Mary, why are you doing this? These are just the facts of my life. They're the things anyone can know."

Mary was quiet for a few seconds. "We didn't even talk about the trial," she finally said.

"Does that surprise you?"

"Everyone else in town is buzzing about it, but it's been the last thing on my mind."

Michael laughed.

Mary tipped her head, and Michael answered her unspoken question. "The CCCA did all right, but the Needhams will win this lawsuit. Without a doubt."

Mary was quiet. She bowed her head briefly. "I suppose I should mention one of those 'facts' you mentioned earlier . . . I'm sure you've already learned by now, the Needhams are my former brothers-in-law. Brian's broth . . ."

Michael's mouth fell open. He slowed the car and stared at her across the seat. Mary had assumed he would have discovered this already during the course of his work, but he seemed genuinely shocked. After he sped up the car again he finally said, "That explains a lot."

"It's just another example of how complicated things are for me and why we can't get swept away here."

"Mary." Michael looked at her. "I'm way past that. I'm already out to sea with you. Can't you see that?"

CHAPTER 27

≡The trial ended after a week, with the judge's decision coming back quickly—too quickly, according to Ward. The CCCA was not entirely unprepared when the judge found in Treegers's favor—detailing in his statement that they had clearly been in compliance with EPA standards and that they didn't owe damages to Custer City—but the judge's ruling that the CCCA should cover Treegers's legal expenses was a blow. Some members of the CCCA were embittered by the decision, Ed Lundgren chief among those who had been key supporters and had now begun to question Ward's leadership. Within a few days of the trial, Ed sent a letter signed by several key members, accusing Ward of misleading the group, holding him accountable for the judge's findings and the financial obligations now required by the court.

Ward stood alone. No one from the group seemed willing to step forward to defend him. He seemed undaunted, though, as he fought on, using the judge's ruling as a rallying cry for the CCCA to push further with its protest. Within hours of the trial, he'd begun to lay out a plan to appeal the decision to the District Court of Appeals. So far, there was no evidence the group would cohere around his new plan; instead, Ed seemed to be fomenting a movement against Ward that Mary could see might well jeopardize his ministry.

That week of the trial Michael had called every day. He called to tell her about the details of the trial, and he called to make her laugh. One night he called the nursing home and talked to Theresa. He told her he was checking out nursing homes for his ailing father and had heard about a marvelous nurse—Maria Hamilton. Could he speak with this Maria Hamilton? The other nurses buzzed about this for days. Mary found on her rearview mirror one morning a picture of a Hereford steer, an attached thought bubble containing the words "Chooooose me." In the garden the children found one morning three tiny baskets filled with small candies. "From the Egg People," a tiny card read. And for Mary, a mixed tape of musicians she'd never heard of before: Arvo Pärt, the Lounge Lizards, Tom Waits, The Clash, the Pixies. She played it over and over on high volume as she drove to and from her classes.

Michael's ability to make her laugh that week counteracted sharply with what seemed like Ward's lack of perspective about the lawsuit, as early into the hearings it had become obvious things weren't going as hoped. Ward's was a black-and-white view of things, and he clearly considered compromise a form of weakness. His competitiveness, so far limited only to the fight with Treegers, Mary now understood could be a liability for her leaving as easily as she had earlier hoped. Through the week of the trial, he had hinted more than once that he was not someone to tangle with, repeating that if she left it would be without the children.

Although Ward never again mentioned her request for a divorce, she understood his point. And if she had missed his meaning through the week, the sermon he preached the Sunday after the trial was an indictment against the traitor, the disloyal, the weak. He talked about Peter and Judas abandoning the Savior in his hour of need. While most in the congregation might have thought at first he was referring to Ed Lundgren and other members of the CCCA, the harsh gaze Ward leveled at Mary throughout the sermon led her to understand the sermon was meant for her.

What Mary had earlier observed about Ward's obsession with the lawsuit was only magnified now. He seemed like a crazed man. While others in the CCCA were calling for moderation, asking that they step back and reassess, Ward was insistent that they continue a full-on fight. Any suggestion otherwise seemed only to add to his determination, and he had begun to divide people into two categories: those who were with him, and those who were against him. Mary watched as formerly loyal members of the CCCA seemed to grow wary of him.

※

Michael left quietly on the Monday morning after the trial. Mary hadn't told him about the sermon or the other ways Ward had let her know he was serious about his threat to fight for the kids. There was nothing Michael could do to help her, and Mary hadn't wanted to waste their time together worrying or complaining. They'd made arrangements for her to open a post office box so Michael could send letters to her. It was still risky in this small town for her to be receiving such letters, but he had promised to send them as inconspicuously as possible.

"We'll keep in touch," he said on the phone the morning he was leaving. "In a few weeks, once you have a job and a new place, we can be more open. I don't want to be a back door man," he added. "When I come back I want to use the front door."

After Michael left, some cast of light left with him. Mary felt jangly and nervous as she tried to focus on finishing her final classes. Her life was about to change. She felt it, and she felt a sense of dread so overpowering some mornings she could barely face the day. Each morning she woke, her body felt leaden. Her center of gravity seemed to have shifted, and she felt off kilter, not able to organize and keep everything in balance as she once had.

※

After three weeks of this, one afternoon as she picked up the kids at Julie's house, Julie met her at the door. "Could you stay for a few minutes, Mary?" Julie said this with such seriousness that Mary felt her skin prickle. She seemed to be waiting for bad news.

"Is it one of the kids?"

"No," Julie said, "but there is a problem."

"What is it?"

"Come in. We need to talk." Mary felt her heart seize again as she followed Julie into the house. Julie cut straight to it once they were seated at the kitchen table. "Did you know your friend Claire is coming to your house on Tuesday nights while you're at work? She's coming to pray with Ward."

Mary shook her head. Despite sounding a little odd, Mary had grown accustomed to Claire talking to Ward. She shrugged.

Julie went on. "She's praying with Ward and the kids. For *you*."

"For me?"

Mary could see Julie was agitated as she stood up to get the coffeepot. Without asking, she filled mugs for Mary and herself, then sat down again. "Molly was over there last night while you were gone. Ward and Claire insisted the kids all come into the living room. Molly told me this morning they were praying to keep you safe from the Devil. They said the Devil had ahold of you." Mary must have looked as surprised as she felt, for Julie went on. "I'm sorry to be the one telling you this, Mary, but I felt you should know."

Mary felt the room spin slightly.

"I'm not going to allow Molly to go over there anymore when you aren't around," Julie said. "I'm sorry, Mary."

Mary grabbed Julie's hands where they were resting on the table. "Oh, Julie, sometimes I think you're my only friend. Don't feel bad about telling me. I'm just surprised, that's all. I never suspected."

"Why would you?"

"Do you think it's happened before?" Mary asked, hating the

hopefulness in her own voice. "Maybe she just happened to be there like Molly was."

Julie shook her head regretfully. "I've seen her car over there three weeks now, always on Tuesday nights. She comes right after you leave for work. I didn't think anything about it, figured she was helping out with the kids—and maybe that's what she was doing, Mary," Julie rushed to say. "I shouldn't speculate."

Now it was Mary's turn to shake her head. "No, you're right." When Mary was honest with herself, she had known for a long time something was very wrong. She said, as if to herself, "I can't believe they involved the kids."

When her eyes finally met Julie's, Mary saw she was furious. "I don't know what I'd do if I knew my husband was making my kids question me like that. Molly was scared when she came home." Julie looked at Mary. "Scared of *you*, scared the Devil would take her away too." She set her jaw and looked away, clearly trying to get control of herself. "I talked to her, explained that there was nothing wrong with you, but still . . ." She broke off.

"Thank you, Julie." Mary cleared her throat softly. "I suppose since we're talking, I should be honest with you. I'm planning to leave Ward after I graduate this August. That's what this is about. He carries on as though nothing has changed, and it's allowed me to stay, thinking everything's all right when it's not." At this, Julie shuddered. "I know," Mary said in response. "It's creepy, but I've been so busy, it's been easy to ignore. I didn't want to do anything rash that would hurt the kids." She laughed at this, hearing the bitterness in her own voice. "Looks like I wouldn't have had to be so careful to spare their feelings." She felt tears of frustration well up and blinked them away. "I was hoping with time Ward would settle down and we'd start talking about how to sort things out."

Julie drew her lips into a straight line. "I don't get the feeling that's going to happen anytime soon."

"He'll come around eventually."

Julie looked at her levelly. Her eyes said she doubted Mary's confidence about the outcome. "Be careful," she said finally.

❋

The following Tuesday, Mary walked away from the house as she always did at a quarter to five. She felt more than a little ridiculous hiding in the alley, but she was determined to confront Ward and Claire. She waited only ten minutes before she heard Claire's car and waited another fifteen minutes before quietly entering the house through the back door. She listened from the kitchen long enough to determine they were already well into their prayer meeting and then strode into the living room.

Claire was sitting on the couch, Priscilla on her lap and Deborah beside her. Joseph was in his own chair, and David sat on Ward's lap in the rocking chair. The girls were undisturbed at seeing Mary, but Joseph was clearly uncomfortable, old enough to understand the difficult position he was in, and she understood then the slightly stricken expression she had been seeing on his face the past few weeks. They'd all been holding hands, their heads bowed, and they looked up at her as she entered the room, their heads still slightly lowered. At Mary's appearance, Ward and Claire quickly dropped hands and pulled away from each other.

Otherwise, Ward seemed unfazed at seeing Mary. He'd had a lot of practice thinking on his feet, while Claire was not so quick. She couldn't mask her flustered expression.

"Mary," Ward said jovially. "What brings you back? You're just in time to join us. Claire came over for counsel, and we were just praying together."

"Yes, I see that."

Ward didn't falter. "Here. We'll make room for you."

"That's all right," Mary said, deciding to use his dishonesty to buy herself a little time. She was not yet ready to confront Ward. But Claire was another story, and she intended to let Claire know where things stood.

"I'm not feeling well," Mary said. "I was coming home to call you, Claire, to see if you could take my place tonight."

Claire stammered for a few seconds before finally pulling herself together. "Sure. I'll go."

Mary nodded. "I need to get something to settle my stomach at the drugstore. Would you mind driving me there and back?"

"Mary, I'll be glad to get that for you," Ward offered.

"It's all right. You stay here with the kids. They seem to be settled in with you. Claire's going out anyway, so she can just take me, can't you, Claire?"

Mary wasn't fooling any of them, and she knew it. She could feel Claire's discomfort, but in the face of Ward's implacable act, there was no way for Claire to refuse. She stammered a bit now before finally saying, "Wouldn't it be easier if I went to get something for you and brought it back so you could go lie down?"

"No," Mary said. "I'm not sure what I want."

Once they were in the car, Mary turned to Claire. "Drive to your place."

Claire drove in silence the few blocks to her apartment. They got out of the car together and slowly walked to Claire's upstairs unit without speaking. When Claire moved to turn on the lights, Mary stopped her.

"I don't want to see your face."

"Mary," Claire started. She seemed jittery, dropping her purse and pacing a few steps into the living room before asking, "Do you want something to drink?"

"I don't want anything from you except that you sit down and listen." Claire slumped onto the couch, and Mary sat down in the big La-Z-Boy chair where she'd sat so many times over the years. She felt keenly and without sentimentality as she took in once more the familiar details of Claire's apartment that this would probably be the last time she would ever be inside it.

She remained absolutely still, hoping to unnerve Claire, assuming she would spill everything if Mary gave her enough time. Sure enough, Claire, who had been sitting tentatively on the edge of the couch, began to twist the bottom of her shorts and then began to confess. She admitted to telling Ward everything, starting with Mary's help with the abortion.

"I didn't *help* you with the abortion, Claire. I did you a favor and drove you home from the clinic."

"Same difference." Claire went on to explain that she had told Ward after the fund-raiser in May about Mary's interest in Michael.

"Oh, Claire. How could you have?"

Claire ignored her. "I told him about Michael's wanting you and the kids to go away with him."

"Claire, you know that isn't the truth. What's the matter with you? Why would you say something like that?"

Claire's face grew ugly. "I'm doing this to help you, Mary. Unlike you, I'm being a true friend. It's obvious you don't know what you're doing." She added, echoing what Mary knew were Ward's words, "The Devil has ahold of you, and Ward and I are trying to save you from yourself."

"Listen to yourself, Claire. This is insane. You know better. How could you let Ward manipulate you like this?"

Claire straightened her shoulders and wiped her eyes. Her answer shocked Mary. "If I was married and being tempted like you are, I'd be grateful if you'd come pray with my husband for me."

Mary shook her head. She laughed harshly. "I can't believe we're having this conversation. You wouldn't do anything of the kind. You'd do exactly what I'm going to do, Claire, and that is to tell you I don't ever want to see you in my house again. I never want to see you near my children again either."

Claire flinched slightly but she didn't lose her resolve. "You know, Ward has seen a lawyer about custody of the kids. The courts may be biased toward mothers, and your family may have the money to help you, but he's still going to fight. Anyway, no matter what the courts say, those kids don't belong only to you, Mary. And the house isn't yours at all."

"The house may not be mine, but the kids most certainly are, and I'll be making other arrangements for them while I'm gone in the future, along with strict instructions that you're not to be allowed near them." Mary stood to leave, but before she reached the door, she turned. "I know a lot about you, Claire. More than you think I do. I know about the abortion, and I know about Fred Carpenter." At Fred's name, Claire's face flushed, and Mary knew she had guessed correctly about their relationship the night she'd seen them together in the Dairy Queen. "Do you know what I'm going to do with everything I know about you?"

Claire paled.

"Nothing," Mary said. "I'm not going to do anything because that's the difference between us, Claire. I'm going to be a friend to you even if you don't deserve it, because I'm not like you."

※

That night after Mary walked home, she got into the Escort and drove. It was late, but she wasn't tired, and she couldn't face Ward. She drove out into the countryside. Before she realized where she was going, she found herself driving toward Algernon. The sun was beginning to set as she parked the car at the old Rasmussen homestead. She cut the engine and let the evening settle around her. The lightning bugs beckoned and the cicadae keened in the trees. While in the past these would have been comforting sounds, tonight they seemed somehow sinister. She couldn't seem to make sense of the once familiar world. Something felt slightly off track in her mind, and she felt she could no longer trust her version of reality. Algernon had always been a peaceful place for her, a place to come for solace, but tonight it didn't offer her peace. As darkness fell, she watched the dim shapes around her take on new and troubling aspects. A sickness seemed to play about the landscape, and she felt haunted, not consoled, by the past.

When she finally returned home after midnight, Ward was still awake. Claire had called him, of course, after Mary had left her apartment. The kids were all in bed and Mary could see by the way they were sleeping they had been asleep for some time.

"Would you like to go for a walk?" Ward asked. His voice seemed kind but his words struck a chill. He wasn't one to suggest taking walks, and he would never have suggested leaving the kids sleeping alone in the house. For the first time, Mary felt afraid of him, afraid of his self-control and the rage she felt seething beneath his placid facade. He seemed like a man whose smiling face masked the knife hidden behind his back.

"I'm really tired, Ward. I need to get to sleep." Since she'd asked for the divorce, she'd continued to sleep on the couch. Ward shrugged. As he looked at her, she saw one corner of his lip turn up in what looked like a sneer. When he left, she felt as though all the air had been sucked from the room and found herself gasping for breath. Was this her life?

She lay awake for a long time that night, listening to the clock ticking on the living room wall. The floors creaked and a night breeze rattled the blinds at the windows. She was startled from her sleep again and again by dreams she couldn't recall upon waking. She woke once, though, with a vivid memory. She didn't think it had been a dream. On the ranch one time, in the middle of the night, while she and Judy were still little girls, they had been awakened by the noise of company. Something about a fire on a neighboring ranch. The house had burned to the ground, and she'd thought even then she knew which house it was, a grand white house on a hill with a white fence around a large front lawn, not the typical western ranch. The only person Mary remembered from the family was a girl about her own age who wore her long dark hair in ringlets. Mary had thought the girl looked like a princess. She'd been wearing a white lace dress Mary had coveted deeply that night. At her waist was a blue ribbon. Black patent leather shoes. White lace socks. What time of year had it been? Why had the girl been dressed as she was, as if for a party, if the family had fled a burning house? Had she really seen the girl? What was she to make of such memories?

The next morning when Ward came into the living room at dawn, it was clear he hadn't slept all night. He sat down on the edge of the couch and leaned toward her in a confiding way. "So, tell me about Michael."

Still groggy, Mary was startled awake by his question. "He's a friend," she finally said.

"How did you meet?"

"At the church."

This threw Ward, she could see. "How was that?"

"He heard me playing the piano and came inside and introduced himself. Why are you asking me this?"

Ward ignored her. There was a long pause before he asked, "Have you touched Michael's penis?"

Mary abruptly pushed the sheet away and with her one leg awkwardly hopped up from the couch. "What's the matter with you?" she said. "Why would you ask something like that?" Suddenly all of Ward's eccentricities seemed like serious afflictions to her, and she saw Ward—as Michael must have seen him, as her family and the Needham brothers saw him—as a vain, cold, calculating, and weak man. She couldn't imagine any other man in the world asking if his wife had been unfaithful in quite that way. Where before she might have felt sympathy for him, she now felt revulsion. She couldn't say why his question had so offended her, only that it had.

While she was still standing, balanced on her one leg, Ward quoted a brief passage from one of Michael's letters, and Mary knew he must have spent the entire night searching through her things until he found the few letters Michael had sent, all still stashed in the lining of her jewelry box.

⇛CHAPTER 28

⇛Mary stubbornly marked time, following through with the letter of her plan, afraid if she deviated to adjust for these new revelations the whole thing would collapse about her. Hot winds blew every day. Each minute of the day felt as tightly wound as a spring. She'd managed to cut her hours at work, but she was still there three evenings a week. VBS was in full swing, and her classes were shaping up to be among the most demanding of her entire program. Julie had been unusually flexible during this last push, agreeing to watch the kids every day, Mary no longer willing to leave them alone with Ward while she was gone. The church people seemed more wary of her than usual, watching her closely as if questioning her sanity. No surprise, she guessed, that Ward had shared their troubles with them.

She was running late that evening, exhausted after a long day, when she picked up the kids a little after nine. As soon as Julie met her at the door, Mary knew something was wrong. The sun was setting, and the entire town seemed to vibrate with the throbbing of the cicadae. The cold blast of air-conditioning from the open door of Julie's house was both shocking and welcome. The baby was asleep, Julie told her, and Mary could see the older kids were so engrossed in a movie they hadn't even noticed her arrival.

"Let's sit outside for a minute," Julie said, looking back once more at the kids. Puzzled, Mary followed her to the deck on the back of the house, where in the stifling heat they sat in lounge chairs. Although Julie tried to sound casual, Mary knew her well enough to know something was bothering her. Julie crossed her legs and uncrossed them again, restless in the heat. As soon as she sat down, Mary felt the weight of her exhaustion fall over her.

"Have you seen the letters, Mary?" Julie asked. "The letters Ward's been sending?"

"Letters? For the CCCA?"

Julie shook her head, impatient. Despite the heat, Mary felt a shiver. Julie's jaw clenched. "He's saying terrible things about you. I don't know how you can stand it."

"Well," Mary said with a humorless laugh, "I don't know about it, so I guess there's been nothing to stand."

Julie ignored Mary's attempt at humor. "He's saying you've lost your mind, that you're endangering the lives of your kids." At this Julie blinked back tears before looking at Mary. "Mary, you're the best mother I know."

"Go on, Julie. Just tell me what he's saying."

"He's trying to raise money to fight for custody. He's saying your family's going to put up a bunch of money to help you fight." She paused. "He's saying you've been unfaithful."

Mary nodded. She felt a trickle of sweat move down her spine. She looked across Julie's back lawn. A sprinkler pulsed, and she felt a sudden urge to walk through it. "It's true that I've become involved with someone else," she finally said, her voice barely a whisper.

Julie flinched slightly, then said, "That guy from the AP?"

Mary nodded. "Not quite what Ward would have everyone believe, though. Not a torrid affair, but I'm not innocent." She looked down at her hands and back at Julie. "I'm sorry to involve you. It wasn't my intention."

"You didn't involve me. Ward did. Besides, it's none of my business." Julie's eyes held Mary's. "It isn't anyone's business but yours and Ward's. It's wrong what he's doing." She paused again. "He's telling people that if they don't help you, you won't be able to leave him."

"When did you get this letter?"

"He's sent out two. The second one came today."

"When did you get the first one?"

Julie thought for a few seconds. "Three days ago."

It was all about energy, Mary thought. She'd made a decision a long time ago, after those first hard lessons with the church people, that she couldn't fight them and their expectations of her. She couldn't win. Not that way. It had been her guiding principle to keep a low profile, not to provoke confrontation, not to stand out. As long as she stayed beneath their notice, she was able to be who she was without too much conflict. She'd succeeded by standing back and allowing the momentum of other people's energy and desire to take over. By deflecting attention, she'd been able to work and go to school and raise her children in the public way she had without compromising her own goals. The strategy had worked for her in the past, but she understood it wouldn't see her through this situation. Now, whether she wanted it or not, she was the center of attention. While before Ward's considerable energy and seemingly endless capacity for organizing and plotting had been directed elsewhere, it was now focused on her.

As Mary walked home with the kids later that night, she couldn't imagine how letters like this had gone out without her knowing about it. Who else had Ward sent them to? She hadn't thought to suspect that he might be fighting her in such an underhanded way. She hadn't thought to take him seriously, and she had no excuse for this oversight. After all, she'd watched him fight Treegers relentlessly for years. How had she underestimated him so badly?

After the kids were finally bathed and in bed, she found Ward in his study. Before, she would have assumed he was writing his weekly sermon, but now she knew otherwise.

"So what will you accuse me of in this letter?"

Ward hadn't noticed her there in the doorway, and he seemed startled for a second before settling his mouth into a frown.

"Did you really think I wouldn't hear about the letters you've been sending?"

"I'm just asking people to pray for our family."

"You're recruiting for your side in a family dispute. Can't you see this isn't like Treegers? It's the kids you'll hurt doing this. I'm their moth . . ."

"*I'm* the one hurting the kids, Mary? I like that. I'm not the one planning to leave the marriage. I'm not the one endangering them. That's exactly what I'm trying to stop here, the kids getting hurt. Don't talk to me about your concern for them."

Mary felt all her arguments drain away as she saw the extent of Ward's anger. She knew she didn't have what it took to stand up to him. Not yet. He seemed determined to make public their differences, and what could she do to defend herself? Send a letter of explanation? Take out an ad in the newspaper detailing her side of things? For a minute she wanted to laugh as she imagined such an ad. Good Mother Asks That Town Gossips See Her Side of Things. Or, perhaps this headline: Hey, Wait a Minute. What About My Side?

Fresia said as much when she called the next day. Ward had even sent the second letter to her family. "I thought at first he'd just sent it to us," Fresia said, "but then I was at the store in Arnold yesterday and a few people mentioned they were praying for you. Can you imagine? What would they be praying for exactly?"

"I feel terrible that he's put all of you in this position."

"Stop apologizing for him," Fresia said. "Ward's a shyster to pull a stunt like this. Your father's furious, I'll tell you that." She paused for a moment, before saying more quietly, "Why didn't you tell us?"

"I didn't want to worry any of you. I need to hang on here for another few weeks until I can finish my degree. Then the kids and I can move out."

"I'm not so sure that's a good idea."

"It's just a short time, Mama," Mary said. "He's still in activist mode after his fight with Treegers." But even as she reassured her mother, Mary wasn't sure she believed this herself.

"Your sister's on her high horse. She'll be calling you later, so be forewarned. She thinks you need to get out of that house with the kids, and now, but you do what you think is right, Mary. We'll trust you to know your own husband."

As Fresia had warned, Judy called later that day and Mary heard an earful. "Max is really worried," Judy said at one point, and this got Mary's attention.

"Why is Max worried?"

"He sees this sort of thing all the time. He's not like the rest of us who can avoid knowing the worst about people. He says Ward isn't handling this well, and he's worried things are escalating."

❉

With all her distractions, Mary had neglected the garden this summer. Each morning as she fixed breakfast, she looked out the window and saw what needed to be done. Some days, she felt a piercing grief for Berl, as though the loss were only yesterday. How she missed puttering about with him. Those mornings as she raced off to her various obligations, she itched to be pruning and weeding and deadheading instead. Already weeds had taken over the beans and onions in the vegetable garden.

Then the calls came, and the visits, and the letters.

It was obvious Ward was putting people up to it. A third letter had been mailed, and this one even Janna—her old friend from high school—received. Ward didn't know Mary's school friends, which meant he was using her address book.

Janna called to see if everything was all right. After being reassured by their telephone conversation, Janna said with a grim laugh, "I thought after reading your husband's letter, 'If she's that nuts, why isn't she locked up?'"

"Well, who's to say."

"You shouldn't joke about that," Janna said, "but look on the bright side. A hundred years ago Ward could have put you away."

Mary grew sober. "I think Ward regrets things aren't still like that."

"He's an angry man," Janna said.

The letters had even been sent to Lana Perkins, a woman Ward still held in low esteem since she'd left the church all those years ago. Lana called, too. "Hey, crazy," she said when Mary picked up.

Mary laughed, recognizing immediately Lana's voice and her tart sense of humor.

"They're letting you answer your own phone over there?" Lana said.

"It's a wonder, given my condition." It felt good to joke about what was happening.

"Just keep in mind they can kill you, but they can't eat you."

Mary laughed. Lana's voice grew serious. "You keep your head up, you hear me, Mary? Head up." After leaving their congregation, Lana had gone on to eschew her religious faith altogether, and she said in closing, "You've shaken the shit out of your life, Mary. Don't wilt now. You promise me?"

❉

The third letter finally led Max himself to stop by the house. He pulled up in front of the parsonage one afternoon in a county sheriff's car, wearing his brown deputy's uniform. He seemed so official coming in this way, Mary thought at first he might be bringing her bad news.

He took off his hat before stepping inside the house. "I'd like to talk to you for a minute, Mary. Do you have time?" He was so courteous and formal, Mary felt oddly shy as she invited him to sit down. She offered him iced tea, which he declined, and she sat down across from him and waited. "Are the kids nearby?" he finally asked.

"Prissie and David are taking naps. Debbie's visiting Molly, and Joe's playing out in the backyard."

Max nodded. "Good. I don't want to involve them." Mary wondered suddenly why Julie and now Max had both been so careful to make certain the kids didn't overhear anything that would upset them, when their own father seemed not only willing but eager to involve them in those things.

"Mary," Max cut into her thoughts, "in my line of work, you come across a lot of trouble in families." He blushed. "I don't mean to say there's anything wrong with your family—it's not like that—but, I've got to tell you, I'm concerned about Ward. He's not acting real stable right now."

Mary laughed bitterly. "You could say that."

Max went on, "This is the thing, Mary. It's not just me, it's your whole family. We respect what you're wanting to do, but we feel like you should get your things together and move with the kids out to your folks' house, finish your classes from there, let things simmer down a little."

Mary sat quietly for a few seconds, thinking over what Max had just told her. She lacked his experience recognizing the warning signs of trouble, but she didn't doubt for a minute his concern. It was clear on his face. While he waited for her response, he self-consciously twisted his hat between his hands, reminding her suddenly of how the Needham boys had stood that day at the foot of her hospital bed, pleating their cowboy hats between their work-roughened hands. She was transported so entirely to that moment it felt as though it had happened only yesterday.

She came back to the present after Max coughed politely. He was not a man to meddle, and she knew he had given this visit a great deal of thought.

"Max, I feel so darned tired all of a sudden."

Max nodded slowly. "I know you do, Mary. That's the way some people react to stress, and it's normal as can be. Your dad wants to come here on Monday with the pickup and load up your things. All we need is your go-ahead and for you to get things packed without Ward noticing. Could you do that?"

Mary looked out the window. She'd been looking out this window for what felt like her whole life. Was it this easy now to leave? Just say yes and everyone would come to her rescue? Max was watching her closely when her eyes traveled back to him. This was the second time she'd become distracted in their conversation, and she could see the worry in his eyes, the way he seemed to be questioning not only her physical but her mental well-being.

"Let me think about it."

"Don't put it off too long, Mary."

※

The next morning Mother Hamilton showed up at the front door with a large suitcase. Without telling Mary, Ward had invited her to come stay. She had come by bus, and Ward hadn't even bothered to meet her at the bus station downtown. Mary was so shocked to see her mother-in-law, she didn't open the door for a few seconds and instead stared at her through the screen.

"Mary," Mother Hamilton finally said, "I'd like to set these things down."

Mary opened the door, and neither of them said a word as without invitation Mother Hamilton walked through the house and into Joseph's room, where she always stayed when she visited. She changed clothes and reemerged a few minutes later, continuing to ignore Mary as she began to look through the refrigerator. She behaved as though Mary was gone and she needed to find things to start lunch. She cleaned the counters and started to set the table, so thoroughly ignoring Mary's presence that at one point she went so far as to start to hum to herself. Never before on a visit had Mother Hamilton acted in such a proprietary way, and Mary was completely baffled by her behavior, so disturbed by it, in fact, that for a split second she actually wondered if she had indeed disappeared. When she finally came to her senses again, Mary stepped in and firmly took over.

"Mother Hamilton, you must be tired from your trip." She took the stack of plates Mother Hamilton was holding. "Why don't you go rest and let me handle making the meal."

"Grandma?" Joseph said later when he came inside. "I didn't know you were coming."

"Your father thought maybe I could be of help." Joseph nodded soberly and glanced toward Mary.

So this was what Ward had in mind. His mother was here to take over housekeeping. Together, they would raise the children without her. Mary could tolerate a few more days in this crooked house; she could, for a few more days, tolerate the crooked man she was married to and his prayer meetings and his letters, but there was no way she would allow this dried-up woman to think she was going to raise her children.

She called Max that evening and told him she'd be ready to go Monday morning.

"I'm glad to hear it," he said. "Your sister will be happy too. We've all had to restrain her from running down there and packing up for you. You know Judy."

Mary smiled and felt a rush of gratitude for her sister. "Yes, I know Judy."

"We'll see you Monday."

"Monday," Mary whispered, feeling herself make a pact with the future.

As soon as she hung up the phone she began to think about how she would pack the kids' clothes into large garbage bags, hoping they would draw less attention than suitcases, should Ward by some strange chance look into the backs of their closets. She would pack only the few things she would need. Everything else would have to stay behind. She would leave the parsonage with little else than herself and the kids. All the wedding presents from her marriage to Brian and the things she had accumulated in her years with Ward didn't amount to anything. She felt clean and whole, pure in a way, leaving everything from her past behind. Come Monday she and the kids would be gone.

When she called her parents later that evening to let them know that Mother Hamilton was there, Max had already called them. "You make sure that woman is out of the house Monday when your dad comes," Fresia said. "We don't need her calling Ward and him showing up to make a scene."

"There isn't much to move."

"Still. You'll need to think up an errand for good Mother Hamilton."

$\equiv$CHAPTER 29

$\equiv$On Sunday there was a noticeable dwindling in church attendance. Since the trial, church members who had joined only
because of the controversy over Treegers had trickled away each
week. As Ward preached, he seemed distracted, desperate to figure
out how to stop the leaking. Mary watched and listened. She heard
now beneath the text of his sermon that he was blaming her for
everything that had gone wrong in his life. She was responsible
for ruining his ministry, for destroying the church, for unraveling the CCCA, for endangering the souls of the children. Mother
Hamilton sat in the front pew, her eyes never wavering from where
Ward stood behind the pulpit.

The next morning, John showed up in the truck, Max and Judy
following close behind in their car.

"Why's Papa here?" Priscilla asked when she spotted his truck
out the window.

Mary peeked out the front curtain and saw John, grim-faced,
opening the truck's tailgate. "He and Uncle Max are going to help
Mommy with a few things." She'd been scurrying all morning to
pull together the last details before they left. "You kids are going to

ride out to the ranch today with Aunt Judy. Won't that be fun to go see Grandma and Great-Grandma?"

Priscilla clasped her hands in excitement, but Mary intercepted a troubled glance exchanged by Joseph and Deborah. She felt their questioning in the pit of her stomach. There was no time now to worry about it. She'd have to work it out with them later. Right now she needed to help her father and Max load the truck with the bags she'd been packing all weekend.

At Mary's suggestion, Beulah Murphy had invited Mother Hamilton over for coffee, and Mother Hamilton had left earlier that morning with no sign of suspicion. Still, Mary felt anxious about actually getting away without any complications.

"You have everything ready?" John asked once the kids were gone.

Mary nodded. "I'll pull the bags out here to the front door while you two load. There isn't much."

Max watched nervously down the street as he loaded the garbage bags onto the truck. Mary joked at one point, "If anyone asks what we're doing, we'll just say we're taking away the trash."

Max and John didn't laugh with her. They seemed anxious to be finished and on the road. Max had taken the day off from work and looked more like himself in jeans and a button-down shirt. Under the best of circumstances, Max was a sober man, and he was not inclined now to laugh about a woman leaving her husband. John, too, seemed more grave than usual. Mary sensed they felt this was their duty to her, but it was not something either of them did lightly. Despite all her confidence the past few weeks about leaving Ward, Mary suddenly wondered if she could be doing it if her family had done as Ward had asked and not been willing to help her.

Before they left, Mary walked through the house one last time to make certain nothing would appear out of place to Mother Hamilton when she returned. Mother Hamilton would wonder where Mary and the kids were, but she wouldn't be alarmed. Not for a few hours, anyway. Mary had left a note for Ward in the bedroom telling him where they'd gone. She hoped this would buy her and her parents a little time to settle in with the kids before they had to deal with Ward.

Before they left, she wandered the brick paths in her garden and thought back on all the work she and Berl had done together, drawing their plans on graph paper and working to execute those plans. While it had always been an eccentric garden, this summer's neglect had made it truly wild. She was leaving the parsonage different than she'd found it, but she could imagine the dismay of the next occupant upon encountering this tangled yard. She sat a few minutes under the arbor Berl had built, a gift for her birthday one year. So much had changed since then. She suddenly felt she couldn't have been leaving if Berl were still alive. Not for the world could she have disappointed that old man. Even if he would have understood what she was doing, she couldn't have done it. But why did she think that? Why did she suppose he would do anything to hold her back? Could she really picture him among the others writing and calling at Ward's request?

The hot winds of the early morning gave way to an oppressive stillness by nine thirty. The sun was radiant, the blue skies almost cloudless as on that July day Mary followed John and Max to the ranch. The black garbage bags in the truck ahead and the nursing books stacked on the passenger seat beside her were the sum total of material possessions she had to begin her life again. When they later pulled into the ranch drive, Mary couldn't help but compare this homecoming to her homecoming after the long stay in the hospital so many years before. She had truly had nothing then, neither possessions nor responsibilities. She wished the girl she had been could have made different choices. She wasn't sure she was up to the task before her of being strong for those four children waiting in the house. She knew this, though: if she was going to make it, she couldn't keep feeling sorry for herself, and she couldn't indulge in regret for the past. Still, she felt momentarily crushed rather than optimistic about her future. Her glib plans for a job and a little house seemed inadequate for making a life for her children.

Inside the house, Cal and Lydia had been entertaining the kids. "Why don't you go on in," John said under his breath. "Max and I can get the load. Those kids need their mom."

Mary could see what John meant. The glimpse she had intercepted earlier of Joseph and Deborah's doubt she now saw as naked anxiety on their faces. Priscilla, too, seemed confused. Only baby David played happily and obliviously with Lydia. The older three suddenly looked to Mary like traumatized children. She knew she had to tell them immediately what was happening.

As if reading her mind, Fresia gestured with her eyes toward the kids. "We've been asking a lot of questions this morning. Maybe this would be a good time for a talk."

Mary thought she'd almost rather do anything else in the world than hurt those kids, but the time had come, and she couldn't postpone it. "Joe, Debbie, Prissie, why don't you come walk with me?" They stood up docilely. She felt their reluctance as she led them out a little-used front door off the living room so they wouldn't see the bags being unloaded through the kitchen door. At least she could save them the visual image of their lives being disrupted.

They walked out behind the house past the north corral and into the high pasture on the old Sherman place. Usually the kids would have been chattering, but today they walked beside her in silence. They watched without comment as a cowbird landed on a fence post nearby and a red-tailed hawk wheeled high above in the sky. Somewhere nearby, they could hear a meadowlark in the grass. She'd taught the kids the names of these birds, and under ordinary circumstances they would have taken pride in pointing them out to Mary.

The morning sun cast its shadows long across the tawny grass as they walked. Her shadow towered above theirs, and she felt the weight of her responsibility, as if she were holding up the sky for them. They didn't need all the details.

"You know Mommy and Daddy both love you very much?" The children nodded slowly. Joseph chewed the inside of his cheek nervously. "We'll always love you, you know that, right? Nothing can change that, but sometimes mommies and daddies don't live together anymore."

"Why not, Mommy?" Deborah said.

Before Mary could answer, Priscilla insisted, "Siggy doesn't like it when people don't live together." Her face was red with her passionate outburst.

"Why is that?" Mary asked.

"It isn't good. Siggy says it isn't good."

Mary thought for a second before saying, "Well, but if you get to see both Mommy and Daddy lots, will Siggy think that's all right?"

Priscilla frowned. Mary could almost see the thoughts moving around in her head. Still frowning, she nonetheless slowly nodded.

"Where will we live, Mom?" Joseph asked.

"Once I get a job at a hospital, we'll find a nice house to rent in Custer City, so you'll have your same friends and your same school. You'll be near Daddy."

"We'll still see Molly?" Deborah asked.

"Absolutely."

"But who will take care of Daddy?" Priscilla said.

"Daddy's a big person. He'll be all right," Mary said, relieved by their questions.

As they continued their walk, she could see whatever fears had been planted by Ward's prayer meetings, and who knows what else, had been in part assuaged by their talk. The familiar chatter she expected of them returned as they continued to walk. They grew excited when they noticed a bird they'd never seen before.

"It's a blue heron," Mary said.

"That heron has a funny neck," Priscilla said, trying out the strange word on her tongue.

If she could stay strong, Mary thought as they walked back, if she could get them through this rough patch, they would be all right. She noticed as they neared the house the truck was unloaded and parked in its usual spot, so she took them inside through the kitchen door.

The family had clearly been talking about her, for their conversation abruptly stopped as soon as they heard her and the kids at the door. Mary couldn't be sure what any of them were thinking. Max still seemed worried, and even Judy was uncharacteristically quiet. Mary knew everyone, like her, was waiting to see what Ward would do when he learned she was gone. For now, though, she felt only a enormous sense of relief. As soon as she had driven onto the ranch earlier that morning, despite her fears, she had felt the easing of a burden she hadn't realized she'd been carrying.

"We've got your rooms all fixed up for you," Fresia said. "You'll share with David; the two girls will take Will's old room, and Joe can have Mark's room."

"Why don't I help you start unpacking things," Judy volunteered. Mary was so accustomed to Judy's criticism, she felt almost uncomfortable with her blatant kindness. She need not have, though, for as soon as Judy saw the garbage bags piled in the upstairs hallway, she was back to her old self. "What kind of way is that to pack?"

"The way you pack when you don't want anyone knowing you're packing."

Chastened, Judy nodded. "You open the bags and tell me where to take them."

After several minutes of working together, they had sorted the bags by room. Later, as they folded the girls' clothes into the empty bureau drawers, Judy said quietly, "I'm glad you left. You should have listened to all of us in the first place," she continued, "but seeing that you didn't . . ." Judy hadn't looked at Mary as she spoke. Instead, she remained intent on folding one of Priscilla's little T-shirts.

Mary had nothing to say. This was as much support as she could expect from Judy, and it was enough. It was everything. Mary ducked her head and blinked back tears. No one could see her crying. That would be the limit of everyone's patience with this situation.

Ward came alone to the ranch after dusk had settled across the prairie. The kids had been bathed and were ready for bed. Mary was upstairs reading to them on the girls' bed when she heard Ward's car pull into the drive. The kids heard it too.

Joseph jumped up to look out the window. "Daddy's here," he announced to the girls. They immediately leapt from the bed and ran downstairs squealing together, "Daddy, Daddy."

"How are my kiddos?" Ward said as he knelt to hug them all. His cheery voice was an unsettling contrast to the cold look he cast toward Mary and her family over the shoulders of the three older kids. Mary held David in her arms. She felt her entire family behind her braced for Ward's anger. Instead, he maintained that same cheerful tone of voice, as though nothing were the matter, even as he continued to send hard looks at all of them. The effect was unnerving, and Mary saw once more an anxious expression on Joseph's face.

"I'd like to talk to the kids alone," Ward said.

"Why would you need to do that?" Mary kept her voice level, aware of how closely Joseph and Deborah were listening to everything.

"They're my children too," Ward said and Mary was softened by the pathos in his voice.

"I've already talked to them a little. I told them as much as I felt they should know."

Ward nodded, and Mary took this as a sign of agreement. He reached then for the baby. "Please, let me hold him."

Mary looked down at little David who was already reaching for his father. She felt a peculiar resistance to having him taken from her arms, but she let him go.

"I won't be long." Ward herded the children upstairs.

Mary joined her parents and grandparents where they all sat together in the living room. Mary shrugged when she came into the room and perched on the edge of a chair.

"He wanted to talk to them alone," she explained.

"Do you think that was a good idea?" Fresia asked.

"No, but what could I do? He's their father."

"You could have told him no," John said, his tone softer than his words implied.

Mary looked down briefly at her hands clenched tightly in her lap before she looked toward the ceiling as though she might be able to hear what was happening above her if she concentrated.

"It's okay," Lydia said. "Ward has a right to see them. He needs a little time to get used to things. You can't keep the kids from him."

"No, you can't," Fresia said to Mary, though Mary sensed she said it for John's sake more than for hers.

John didn't respond, and Mary could tell he didn't agree with everyone else's reasoning. She forced herself to sit back against the chair. Night had suddenly fallen and she looked out the window into the darkness. She could see her family reflected in the dark windows, their forms blurred and distorted. They seemed alien to her, people she didn't know. She noticed the way she was nervously plucking at the fabric on the arm of the chair where she sat and clasped her hands in her lap again, wishing suddenly for the knitting needles Lydia plied. In the quiet room the needles clicked softly.

"It's about time for the news," Cal said finally and reached for the remote control. The television flickered to life, and Mary came back to the family. They were all distracted by the opening credits for the nightly news. Later, that would be how they explained the fact that Ward had made it down the back staircase to the same little-used front door where Mary had taken the kids out earlier in the day (and how Mary would fixate on this fact later, the use twice in one day of that seldom-used door) and out into the waiting car before any of them noticed. John was the one who heard the engine and saw the tail lights flicker on.

He bolted from his chair. "Is he taking those kids?"

Everyone jerked to attention.

"Surely not," Lydia said.

"Goddamn sonuvabitch," Cal growled, standing up stiffly from his chair to look out the window.

"He most certainly is," John said from the kitchen door where he was frantically trying to pull on his boots.

Mary had followed him, and she ran out the door and into the night without her shoes. As the car headed down the driveway, she ran headlong after it screaming for the children. The last thing she saw as the car pulled away were the faces of the older three pressed against the rear window. She could hear them crying, and later she would guess it had been their cries that led Ward to momentarily tap on the brakes as though he might be persuaded to stop. Whatever hesitation that tap meant, though, the moment passed and Ward stomped on the gas pedal and the car's tires sprayed dust and gravel at Mary as she careened awkwardly down the drive. There was no chance she could catch that speeding car but she persisted anyway, even as she watched the faces of her children disappear from her into the darkness. When she finally turned to go back to the house, the bottom of her right foot was bruised and bleeding from the rocks in the driveway.

"That shit for brains," John said as he met Mary limping back to the house. His boots were on, and he had his keys ready; Fresia was already waiting in the truck.

"We're going after him," John said. "Get in the truck. Your mother has your shoes."

The shame Mary felt in those minutes of silence as she rode with her parents—her father driving the truck faster than she'd ever seen him drive—defied words. She felt she had brought dishonor to her family. Dishonor was not a word they ever said out loud, and yet her family had for generations been careful to guard their good reputation. In a small community, it was the most important asset they had. She felt something crumbling in front of her and an absolute powerlessness to stop it. She had no clue how she could hope to control a situation that had so clearly spun out of her grasp. No one said anything for a while, but it was peculiar to all of them that they hadn't spotted Ward's tail lights anywhere on the plain ahead of them.

"He must be driving like a lunatic," John finally said.

"I hope he's being careful with those kids in the car," Fresia added.

Without discussing it, John headed to the parsonage in Custer City. None of them expected to find Ward there, but they had to look anyway. The house was dark except for one lamp in the living room, where Mary found Mother Hamilton sitting alone.

"Where's Ward?"

Mother Hamilton looked genuinely surprised by the question. "Why, he went out to your parents' house."

"He came, but then he left. With the kids." For the split second it took before Mother Hamilton's face snapped shut, Mary could see that she was taken aback by this news.

"Good for him," she said.

Mary ignored the remark. "Where did he take them?"

"I don't have any idea, Mary, and if I did I wouldn't tell you."

Mary slammed the screen door behind her.

"He's not here," Mary said breathlessly as she crawled back into the passenger side of the truck. "Let's go by Claire's apartment." Even as she said it, Mary knew it was a pointless venture. Her apartment was dark as they drove by.

For over two hours, they drove up and down the streets of Custer City. They drove the country roads surrounding the town to the homes of all the church members and the members of the CCCA, anyone they thought might give Ward sanctuary. The houses were all dark and Ward's car was nowhere to be found. More than one porch light came on in response to a barking dog, but they saw no evidence of Ward and the children that night.

It was well after midnight by the time they returned to the ranch. Cal and Lydia were still waiting up, and Lydia met them at the door, visibly dismayed to see them return without the children. She shook her head and gathered Mary into her arms.

"We'll find those kids tomorrow."

Cal hugged Mary roughly, enveloped her in his huge arms. "Your grandma's right. We'll get those kids back tomorrow. That bastard ever shows his face around here again, I'll fill him full of buckshot as soon as look at him."

"First thing tomorrow I want you to be ready," John said to Mary. "We'll go see Bertie about filing for divorce and custody. Then we'll find those kids." He turned to go to bed.

"Thank you, Daddy," Mary said.

He turned back toward her. "No one hurts my daughter. No one." Mary shivered slightly at this remark.

Fresia exchanged a glance with Mary before hugging her. "Thank you, Mama," Mary murmured as her mother left for bed.

"This is what family is for," Fresia said.

The phrase echoed in Mary's ears as she slowly climbed the stairs to bed herself. The lights were still burning in the upstairs bedrooms, and on the unmade bed lay open the book she had been reading when Ward came. *Winnie the Pooh*. Mary picked it up to close it, but instead she pressed its pages against her breasts. The storybook characters—Pooh, Piglet, Eeyore, and Tigger—seemed suddenly so human and vulnerable to her that she felt she needed to hold them close, to protect them somehow.

She held the book through that long, sleepless night, staring into the darkness outside where she saw the looming shadow of the cottonwood tree. Where were her children? The night was stifling and still, not a leaf rustled outside her window. Whatever comfort the tree had been to her in the past, it couldn't comfort her tonight.

≡CHAPTER 30

≡By seven the next morning, John, Fresia, and Mary were headed to Custer City to see Bertie Lange. The stillness of the night had given way to a hot, dry wind. Strong gusts buffeted the truck and dust obscured everything but a small section of the road ahead.

Bertie was already in his office when they arrived at seven thirty. Long past retirement age, Bertie Lange was a lean, slope-shouldered man, as desiccated as a dry leaf. Today he wore his customary bolo tie, western-cut suit jacket, and cowboy boots. He'd been the Stiles family's tax attorney since Cal and Lydia had been young, but like most professionals in small towns, Bertie had to assume many roles, so it was not unusual that they had come to him to file for divorce and custody.

"We don't see much of this," Bertie said in his customary drawl that morning after he'd heard their story. "What I'd recommend in this case, though, is that you file for ex parte custody."

"What's that?" Mary interrupted.

"That's a special exception to the rule that in order to file for custody the children have to be in your—to use a legal term—possession. Since there are mitigating . . ."

"I see," Mary interrupted again. She couldn't seem to help herself. "Let's do that."

"All right then. I'll file first thing this morning over at the courthouse in Brewster." Bertie talked slowly, weighing each word. His movements were equally deliberate. Mary felt maddened by his ponderousness. In an attempt to get control of herself, she bounced her leg and looked away while Bertie methodically pulled out of a file cabinet the forms necessary to begin the legal process. He typed in a few details needed for the form, then stopped and said, "Tell me again the condition of the children when Ward left with them last night."

"They'd just had their baths," Mary said. "Their hair was still wet. They were in their pajamas, barefoot. He snuck out the door with them."

Bertie nodded as he typed. For several minutes there was no sound except the typewriter and the wind buffeting the office's south-facing windows.

Finally Bertie pulled the form from the typewriter. "You'll need to sign here," he instructed.

Mary leaned forward, scanned to the bottom of the document, and signed her name.

Bertie looked at her signature before folding the form and methodically stuffing it into an envelope. "I'll go file this right away," he said before sealing the envelope. "We'll want to make sure we get there before Mr. Hamilton does."

"Do you expect a problem, Bertie?" Fresia said.

"Well, speed is on our side in a situation like this."

"So you do expect a fight?" John absently tapped the brim of his hat where he held it in his lap.

Bertie nodded slowly, his expression regretful. "I'm afraid it's shaping up that way, but it'll go better if Ward has to contest custody rather than Mary."

Bertie finally sealed the envelope, and while she watched him, Mary recalled how when they had gone to the parsonage earlier that morning to see if perhaps late in the night Ward had returned, she had found Mother Hamilton sealing a letter. Ward hadn't come home in the night. Mary shivered now as she listened to the wind prowling around Bertie's small office building. The wind seemed sinister to her this morning. She remembered how she had dreamt about the wind before coming out of the coma after the accident. She hadn't thought about those dreams for years, but she recalled how the sand had drifted with the wind, how it had filled the rooms of a strange house, how the sand had drifted into the house. What was it about that memory? She replayed the dream again, and as she did, she felt as though someone had grabbed her by the throat. The strange house in the dream. It hadn't been Brian. She stood up abruptly, startling everyone, and interrupting Bertie Lange yet again.

"Mama, Daddy, we've got to go. Now." She didn't wait for them to answer as she headed to the door.

Her parents and Bertie looked after her in alarm. "What is it?" Fresia asked.

"It's Ward. He's hurt the kids."

"Mary, we're going to get those kids back," John said. "Ward isn't going to hurt them."

"We didn't believe he could take them last night either." At this, John paled. He stood up.

Bertie said nothing, but he listened politely, still holding the envelope he'd just sealed. Fresia, clearly embarrassed, stood up as well, explaining as she did, "She's been under a lot of pressure, Bertie."

"That's just fine," Bertie said in the same calm voice he'd used throughout the meeting. "You go do what you need to, and I'll get this over to Brewster."

"We'll settle up later, Bertie," John said.

And then they were all in the truck. "Drive to the house again," Mary said.

When they arrived, Mother Hamilton was still there alone.

"Tell me where the kids are." Mary thought half seriously about putting her hands around the old woman's throat and choking her until she told her the truth.

"I don't know where they are. Ward hasn't called me."

And something in her face led Mary to believe her. She knew it was futile to ask, but she had to. "Where could he have taken them?"

At this, Mother Hamilton began to cry. It was the first time Mary had ever seen her anything other than composed. "We've got to find him, Mother Hamilton. I'm afraid for the kids; I'm afraid Ward's hurt them."

Mother Hamilton's tears stopped, and her eyes snapped. "Ward wouldn't harm those children. You're the one they need to be protected from. He's been their only parent all these years while you were working and going to school." So that was the case Ward and his mother had begun to construct against her. Mary didn't answer the accusations and instead ran back to the truck.

Calls to the church office and the CCCA office went unanswered. No one had seen or heard from Ward. By nine, Mary was frantic. "We have to call Max."

"Do you really think we should involve the sheriff's department?" Fresia said, clearly timid about a public spectacle and apparently doubtful about Mary's worries.

John, who had always trusted Mary's instincts, was less hesitant. As the hour had passed with no sign of Ward or the children, he was, like Mary, far beyond any concern about public embarrassment. Mary would have welcomed such embarrassment if it meant her children would be returned safely.

"You two stay here," John said as they parked in front of the sheriff's office. Mary and Fresia said nothing as they waited, listening as the wind bullied the truck. Within a few minutes John returned. "Max was there. He said he'd do some checking. I told him we'd go on over to the café and wait."

They had barely gotten seated when Mary saw Max on the sidewalk out front. Even through the windows of the café, she saw the grave look on his face. She stood up and was waiting by the booth when he came in.

"Let's go outside for a few minutes," Max said. Mary trembled as she followed him out the door. John and Fresia were close behind. As soon as all of them were on the sidewalk out front, Max said, "Marvin Wright, farmer over in Custer county . . ." John and Fresia both nodded at this, "called earlier this morning. Reported an accident on one of the roads near his ranch." Max paused. "The car matches the description of Ward's." Mary gasped and Max laid a hand on her arm. "Mary, we don't know that it's anything. We've sent a car out to check on . . ."

The sound of the wind grew still, as did everything else. In the silence, Mary watched as a gum wrapper skidded along the sidewalk. She focused all her attention on that silver wrapper. She needed to sit down. She needed to concentrate. That was all. She needed to lean against the side of the café and pull her knees to her chest. She needed to turn her attention deep inside where she knew her children were safe. Then Max was trying to lift her. Her parents were fluttering and soothing. A piercing sound, and the wind again, the thrashing branches of the trees in the park across the street.

EPILOGUE

≡Mary stood up. She walked soundlessly across the plush carpet to a credenza in the back of the room where she filled a cup with coffee. Out the sixth-floor windows overlooking Omaha, young pear trees in bloom bent in the wind. A spring blizzard had swept across the city only an hour earlier. The sky was white with snow and Mary delayed returning to the meeting at hand to watch the storm.

After only a few short years in nursing she'd left to pursue graduate degrees in hospital administration. Her colleagues in Omaha still expressed surprise at having attracted her away from the hospital in Des Moines where she'd started her career as an administrator. She shared little with them about her private life, and they barely knew the names of her three children. If her co-workers noticed in the photos in her office the pale scar traversing Deborah's face, they were much too polite to ask. All they knew was she'd been married to Michael forever, that her youngest child, Priscilla, had just left for New York where she would be starting an MFA in acting at NYU, that the oldest child, Joseph, was finishing his PhD in engineering at Purdue, and the oldest daughter, Deborah, was married and taught music in a Denver high school.

If they had asked about her life, she would have avoided talking about the accident that had hospitalized Ward and the three older kids and had killed Claire Rowe and critically injured David, who had been sitting on Claire's lap at the time of the accident. She would not have told them about how the area ranchers had come together to help Mary with the staggering hospital bills as every effort had been made in vain to keep the baby alive. The Needham brothers single-handedly raised or contributed over half of what was needed. They'd been generous to her to the end, but she'd lost track even of them. Sometimes an article in *The World Herald* mentioned one of them. They'd become wealthy men and major benefactors to conservative causes across the state.

When after the accident the details were revealed of Ward's plan to leave the state with Claire and the kids, he had been asked to resign from his ministry and had moved with his mother back to Indiana after he was released from the hospital in Broken Bow. While at first he had made an effort to keep in touch with the kids, through time his interest had waned and it had been years since they'd had contact with him.

Cal and Lydia had both died in the same year, more than a decade before. John and Fresia had sold the ranch and moved to Custer City where John now worked at the tractor supply. Mary had refused to return for the sale of the ranch and when she returned to Arnold now to visit Judy and Max, she never drove out to see the ranch. It was part of the past she'd worked hard to leave behind.

She had returned to the parsonage only once after Ward left to retrieve her things. After the truck had been loaded, she wandered through the house, and the only thing remaining in the empty rooms was the black desk in Ward's office, reminding her pathetically of a caged animal doomed to wait out its imprisonment until the walls deteriorated around it. She saw her life at the time in those terms. Her sense of a malevolent force unleashed after her own accident had returned when David died, causing her to stumble once more into the debilitating depression of her younger self. The universe, or fate, or destiny—not God, as she no longer believed it was God tormenting her—seemed bent on doing harm to her and those she loved. For months, nothing anyone could say would dissuade her from this belief.

In the months following David's death, Mary felt her sanity was something separate from the rest of her like a cart attached with a weak hitch. Her mind was a small, skinless creature, all exposed nerves, and she spent what felt like all of her energy trying to protect that vulnerable self. The routines of daily life felt as violent as searing light or an arctic wind. She turned away from everything and everyone.

At night she could not sleep. If the moon was bright, she wandered outside into the pastures, oblivious to the rough grass and the uneven ground. Other nights, she paced the rooms of her parents' house while they slept. She wandered from doorway to doorway, from window to window, restlessly peering into the darkness. She spent hours watching the moon make its trek across the sky. She was haunted by a recurring dreamlike image of David lost in a snowstorm, crying for her while she searched desperately for him, blinded by the blizzard. He needed her but her efforts to find him were impeded again and again. Her helplessness to reach him was such a burden she wanted to shrug away her own mind, to rid herself of these thoughts by abandoning her own reason.

One night, her mother had found her wandering like this. Fresia had crossed the room and gathered Mary into her arms.

"Mama," Mary said. "I'm so lost. I can't find my way."

From where she leaned against her chest, Mary had felt the effort of a hard swallow in her mother's throat. "I know you are, but you have to come back to us, Mary. Please try to find some way back to us."

Her mother had led her to the sofa, and in the dark living room they sat together. Mary felt herself begin to rock, and while it had occurred to her that she should stop, she couldn't. Fresia hadn't said anything, but her arm tightened around Mary's shoulders, as if Mary were about to bolt and she was the only thing holding her to the earth and to this life. Fresia had been wearing a sleeveless nightgown. It was August and the house had been stifling, but still Fresia had held Mary close, even as sweat had trickled down against their sides.

❊

Mary became well acquainted with the little graveyard north of Arnold where the Stiles family had been buried for three generations. Cal and Lydia had already erected a headstone and reserved two plots for themselves. Behind Cal and Lydia's single large marker was the small headstone that marked David's grave. Mary had an overpowering urge to be near his grave, and each time she went she had compulsively left gifts and notes. Her behavior, she had known even then, bordered on the bizarre, but it was only there, at the place where he lay buried, that she had felt some reprieve from the panic she felt otherwise. Each time she returned, the notes she had left on previous visits had blown away; they were often stuck in the tough prairie grass on the edges of the cemetery fence or plastered against other gravestones. The toys were faded or water soaked.

That first Christmas Mary had felt like a shadow among the living. She had watched her three surviving children and her nieces and nephews, but unlike everyone had clearly hoped, she had not taken delight in their antics. Instead, the day only under-scored how their lives would go on while David's would not.

Everyone had done all they could to make the holiday more special than usual. Mary had understood the extra effort for what it was. She had wondered at her family's naiveté, though, to think celebrating could contain the loss. If they had been honest with themselves—and she had wondered desperately at the time why no one would be honest—none of them could have been happy that Christmas either. It had been an elaborate compensation, and the only good—a good she could not entirely begrudge—had been for the sake of the children still living in the family.

Inside, though, Mary was howling. She was inconsolable, and she knew then the image the world over of the grieving mother walking the earth, looking endlessly, restlessly for her lost children, was no mere metaphor. She felt her spirit raging, fierce and indefat-igable, separate from her, like an emissary sent into the world not for revenge but for restitution. She wanted her baby back. Nothing less than that. She had been startled sometimes that her pain was silent when inside, her grief deafened her.

From where she now stood looking out the windows in the boardroom of a major hospital, that woman she had been—Mary Hamilton—was almost incomprehensible to Mary Rasmussen, the woman she now was. She marveled sometimes at where her life had led her, how far she had come from being that troubled young woman. In her better moments, she recognized the two accidents bracketing her life with Ward as the metaphor it was.

Michael's patience with her still surprised even him. He'd persisted for months, undaunted by her refusal to return his calls and letters, the letters piling up so she finally closed the post office box they'd opened together before he had left that summer. She'd brought home the bag of unopened letters and put them high on a shelf in her bedroom. Their relationship felt tainted to her. She couldn't for a while help but think it had been the catalyst for a disaster.

The blizzard outside today had reminded her of how she'd finally come out of her long, puzzling trance and had made her way back into the world. While Mary preferred not to think about the past, at the sight of those trees bending in the blizzard, a vivid memory muscled its way into her mind.

❋

By morning on that day in early March it had been clear Fresia should not be leaving the ranch, but both Cal and Lydia had appointments scheduled with their specialists in Kearney. The appointments had been made months in advance, and there was no way to change them without turning it into another long wait. John insisted they take the four-wheel-drive pickup. All of them had noticed that morning the thin gray line on the western horizon in an otherwise perfectly blue sky, and although the radio news hadn't mentioned a storm, they all warily eyed the horizon while they ate breakfast together.

"You stay tonight," John said finally to Fresia. "If there's any chance of snow, you just stay put."

Fresia hadn't argued. If she had been making the trip alone, she might have scoffed, but with her elderly parents on board, there was no way she would risk being out in a plains blizzard. Mary had helped Lydia set the table, awkward with her crutches. She had not strapped on her leg that morning before breakfast. Those days, she often didn't bother putting it on in the morning, opting instead to use her crutches until later in the day. There were entire days when the leg had remained propped against her bedroom wall.

Before leaving that morning Fresia instructed Joseph and Deborah to watch out for Priscilla, and John went out to check on the cattle. As soon as he left the house, the weather abruptly changed. The sky bleached to a slightly more faded blue and the wind picked up. Within only a few minutes a northerly gust shouldered against the side of the house so hard it shook the windows. A piece of galvanized tin came loose on the roof of the toolshed and the wind banged it with a rhythmic defiance before finally tearing it away completely. Mary watched as the tin cartwheeled across the yard and finally came to rest in front of the house. The sky blanched.

At first, the sleet was so fine it was impossible to see except against the faded red barn and the dark opening into the granary. There Mary could see it blowing horizontally in the gale. She heard it ticking against the window glass. Within half an hour, the sleet turned to snow, flakes so large and thick they looked like the contents of a down pillow flying about wildly in the wind.

She didn't worry about John out in the pastures. He had seen all sorts of bad weather, though they would all agree spring blizzards were the worst. The cows were calving. John's nightly reports indicated there were several cows nearing term, and he had gone out that morning to the heavies' pasture to bring those nearest term to the corral.

By midmorning, Mary couldn't see the outbuildings for the blizzard. She went onto the porch where John kept a stack of firewood, loaded the sling, and awkwardly carried the wood back inside. The logs were dry and it took no time to get the fire stoked in the stove. The house seemed very empty, and Mary felt a sudden crazy urge to get into the car and drive somewhere, anywhere. Finally, the crackling fire comforted her. She had a vague sense the kids were in the house, but she didn't know where. For months, inexplicably and to the dismay of everyone around her, the surviving children had felt like ghosts to her.

An hour later she was heating a pot of chili for lunch when John banged into the house. The sound of the wind was so clamorous

Mary hadn't heard the tractor in the drive. Usually when John came inside, especially on days like this, he carefully removed his boots and hung his coat and hat on pegs in the mud porch where they wouldn't drip on the floor. Today, though, he had come right into the kitchen. He stood now in the middle of the room still in his boots and coat. He'd left both the porch door and the kitchen door open to the outside, so cold air and snow billowed into the house. The snow on his clothes was already melting in the heat, and Mary noted in a quick glance the puddle growing on the floor at his feet. His skin was patchy white with cold. His blue eyes looked steely beneath his ice-coated lashes and brows.

"I need your help, Mary," he said, out of breath. He'd hesitated when he first came inside, and Mary guessed he had been weighing his options, wondering if maybe he should try to make it down the road to the Reynolds' place for help. "There's no time to waste," he went on. "That little black heifer's down in the north pasture. She's going to need help right away, and I can't do it alone." He glanced around the room futilely as though he thought perhaps Fresia might have miraculously returned. Whereas in the past Mary's reflexes would have been immediate, she now stood as if paralyzed by his request.

"Mary." John tried to snap his fingers in his gloves. "Jesus. Wake up, girl. Get yourself ready. You can use your mother's coveralls." Mary recognized the distraught look on his face. She understood the perils to that heifer and her calf. She knew what needed to be done for them, and the high cost to the ranch if they lost both animals. She knew time was wasting, but still she remained rooted to the kitchen floor, her hand holding aloft the wooden spoon she had been using to stir the pot. What she didn't know anymore was where she belonged in all this. She didn't have the first clue why John seemed to insist she could help when she saw so clearly she couldn't.

"Mary, for Christ's sake. Get a grip on yourself." John was not a man to keep explaining himself, and although Mary had seen evidence of his kindness toward both humans and animals, she knew well his temper too. And even knowing this, seeing his jaw set tight, an expression she could only call livid in his eyes, she still couldn't seem to take the first step toward getting dressed. He waited.

"Daddy, I can't," she finally said.

John threw up his hands, too disgusted to speak, and left the kitchen. The slam of the kitchen door was followed shortly by the slam of the porch door, followed dimly by the slam of the tractor cab door. She remained fixed to the spot where John had left her, feeling a shame so deep it penetrated to her core, and beyond that to the bones of all of her ancestors who would never have sanctioned or understood such selfish ineptness.

Then, before Mary had a chance to recover herself, John banged back inside again. This time he strode across the kitchen floor. He laid his large gloved hands on her shoulders and looked into her eyes. He was not very much taller than she, but she felt the power in his broad shoulders, his thick arms. She saw the veins corded in his temples, but it was his eyes that pierced and held her.

"Goddamn it, Mary, I want you to get off your pity pot and start being a help around here. I'm tired of you dragging a dead body around with you. You're stinking up the place."

Mary must have looked as shocked as she felt, but he went on. "That's right. I said it. I'm not having a corpse under my roof. You hear me? I know you're suffering, but Mary, your mother and I are hurting too." He teared up slightly, and his voice broke for a moment before he went on as fiercely as before. "Your kids need you, Mary." He turned away slightly. "The difference for the rest of us is that there's no one around to indulge our self-pity." He turned back to her and in a gentler but no less firm voice said, "I need your help out there, sister, and I don't want to hear any maybes. You go upstairs and strap on your leg, and then put on your boots. I'll check on the kids and get you set up with the other things you'll need." He shook her slightly. She felt her face start to crumble; her bottom lip began to quiver. "No blubbering now,"

John said. "You can blubber later all you want. But not now . . . right now I need you to be my right-hand man."

❀

John steered the tractor through the deep snow into the pasture. A few times Mary felt him glance across the tractor's cab toward her, assessing, she supposed, her state of mind. Although she didn't meet his eyes, she must have reassured him she was all right, for she felt him finally turn his attention fully back to driving. Mary could make out a trace of the tire tracks from his former trip. In less than half an hour, the tracks had almost drifted closed. Visibility was minimal and when the wind gusted, they could see nothing, forcing John to slow the tractor to a creep.

Mary had felt sluggish when she first got into the tractor cab, but now with the cold she felt awake in a way she hadn't felt for a long time. Inside the trailer they hauled behind the tractor, John had thrown a few supplies—the calf puller, which they would likely need, army blankets, clips, scissors, rags, antibiotic, a syringe, and disinfectant.

In the distance, Mary thought she could make out the herd, their shadowy shapes shifting in and out of sight. Sensing Mary's question, John said, "That's them." She nodded. The wind buffeted the left side of the heavy tractor. The animals parted for the tractor and then came together again to follow behind. They milled around the cab when John finally stopped. He got out, closed the door, and shooed the cattle away with a sweeping motion. He had left the tractor running and the headlights on. Mary saw he had parked exactly as she had expected, to light the area and to block the wind as they worked on the heifer Mary noticed lying in the snow.

Already John had dropped to his knees by the animal's side. Her dark coat was covered with snow. Mary could see by her heaving side that the heifer was still alive but struggling to breathe. By the time Mary reached them, John had cleared away the ice that had formed on her face. The heifer's eyelashes were thick with frost as was the beard of her chin. She bawled softly once after John cleared her nostrils. Wordlessly, he moved to the other end where he lifted her tail gently. Even that light touch caused the heifer to groan deeply.

"There, girl," John said in the crooning voice he used with his cattle. Something in that familiar tone struck Mary to the heart. Her father was known even among other ranchers for his way with animals. In a business where ranchers routinely reacted to the stubborn, just plain thickheadedness of cattle with force—it was not unheard of for a frustrated rancher to hit a balking cow across the head with a two-by-four—John Rasmussen was different, and his cattle responded in kind. They followed him like dogs. In fact, as he kneeled behind the heifer, the herd he had shooed away had come back and circled around, lowing softly to one another.

John stripped off his gloves and his coat, quickly rolled up the shirt sleeve of his right arm, and pushed up the sleeve of his union suit. He applied disinfectant and inserted his bare arm into the heifer up to the elbow. In her heavy clothes, Mary awkwardly knelt at the cow's head. She talked soothingly to her. The heifer groaned again, and John grunted with exertion, his arm going deeper as he felt for the calf. The fog of his breath circled his head. Around them, the herd pressed closer still. Their breath formed a white fog that hung like a cloud above the scene. Steam rose from the heat of their bodies. The cattle shifted and stamped restlessly but didn't move otherwise. Mary glanced up into the ice-covered faces of the cattle, most of them white-faced Angus unlike the black Angus heifer lying at her knees. For a few seconds, looking at the herd, Mary felt something akin to happiness.

When John finally finished his examination, he pulled out his arm, slick with blood and mucus. Mary handed him a rag she had removed from the trailer. He stood and wiped his arm. "Calf's breech." He pulled his gloves back on and lifted the calf puller out of the trailer. "I'll need that syringe loaded." Mary nodded. She gathered the other things he would need too.

After John had looped the chain around the calf's back feet and he had glanced up to tell her what he would need next, Mary couldn't help but notice the relief in his eyes when he saw she was already prepared. They exchanged a quick glance. Mary gestured with her head toward the herd gathered around them. "We've got an audience."

John smiled, and for the first time in months, Mary felt she could almost laugh with real joy at those absurd cattle. She knew this would be a detail in the story John would tell her mother later about this day. It would be the story of a calf's delivery, but it would also be the story of Mary's return to the family, and it would be all that was said about it.

John stood and tightened the calf puller against the heifer's back end. He ratcheted the wench, gaining enough torque on the puller to begin to slowly extract the calf. After a few minutes, Mary saw the calf's black hooves and reached in to assist in the pulling.

In the end, the calf came easier than they hoped. They both knew, though, that even after all their intervention, chances were the calf might not survive. They dried him roughly with a blanket before wrapping him in another blanket and loading him into the trailer. At the sound of her calf's weak bleating, the heifer had scrambled to her feet. She lowered her head menacingly once toward John and Mary, associating them with her recent pain. They quickly loaded the gear back into the trailer, and John found and roped another cow he knew was close to delivering. He tied the cow's halter to the back of the trailer. He knew the heifer would follow behind without a lead as long as her calf was inside the trailer. As he drove slowly back toward the house, both cows followed, their heads bowed into the wind. Mary watched to make certain neither of them fell in the deep snow. Their breath quickly condensed to ice on their faces, but still they plodded along after the tractor.

Finally, John pulled into the driveway. He drove straight to the house where he unloaded the calf and carried him onto the mud porch. Mary followed and quickly went into the storeroom for old towels while John unwrapped the calf from the blanket. After Mary had rubbed him down with the towels, the calf stood up on wobbly legs, his hooves black and shiny, his eyelashes long as butterfly wings. Outside, the heifer paced in the snow, bawling loudly for her calf.

Mary sat with the calf while John went back outside. She could barely see him for the snow as she watched him halter the heifer and lead her and the cow to the barn. Until Mary lost sight of them in the whiteout, she could see John pulling hard on the heifer's lead as she resisted separation from her calf.

When he came back onto the porch, John dropped to one knee. "How's he doing?" he said and carefully felt the calf leg by leg before running his hands along its sides and back. He looked into the calf's eyes, pried open his mouth, and peered inside. "He's just fine," he finally answered himself. Mary nodded. "He's a dandy calf." John smiled. Mary was still bundled in her coveralls and hat. "Go on inside and get yourself warmed up," he said. "I think this little fella's all right to go out and join his mother."

"I'd like to go with you."

John paused. He looked at Mary closely. "All right." He stood up and lifted the calf at its middle, its long legs dangling while Mary held the door open. Together they walked through the storm toward the barn. Already the snow had drifted to their thighs. John grunted with the exertion of carrying the calf while lifting his feet out of the deep snow. The wind roared, and the snow still fell fast, so that by the time they reached it, the dim, dry barn was a welcome reprieve.

The heifer came to the edge of the holding pen and sniffed at her calf. John didn't need to tell Mary this was a good sign. Mary opened the gate, and John set the calf down inside the pen. The heifer continued to sniff and began to lick and to prod the calf with her nose. She lowed softly. Within seconds the calf had found a teat and was butting against the heifer's bag, wheezing and slobbering, eyes rolling in his eagerness to feed. Mary felt a surge of the same joy she had experienced earlier while watching the herd in the pasture.

Before they left the barn, John added a few forkfuls of new straw to the holding pen. He left feed and water for both the heifer and the cow, and he plugged in a small heat lamp above the calf. Before closing the door, John and Mary took one last look at the calf.

"We'll unload the trailer later," John said. "Let's get ourselves some lunch now."

❋

The fire in the woodstove had been stoked, and Mary and John sat in front of it, eating the chili Mary had quickly heated up again. They said little to each other as they watched the fire crackle. The kids, already finished eating, played quietly in the next room, while outside the blizzard showed no signs of abating. The wind continued to rage, blowing relentlessly against the north side of the house while snow fell steadily through the gale. Fresia had left a message saying they would stay the night in Kearney. She hoped to make it home tomorrow once the roads had been cleared. Both Mary and John knew how in these winds the snow would drift across the country roads. Mary shivered a little as she listened to the wind's howl. She pulled one of Lydia's afghans close around her.

John set his bowl aside finally. "That was good. Thank you."

Mary nodded. She continued to eat as John watched the fire.

"If it weren't for getting out in it, I wouldn't mind a good blizzard," he said.

Mary nodded again. John wasn't one for talking so much, and Mary guessed it was a sign he was a little unsure about what had happened between them earlier that day. As if to prove that point, he said now, "Mary, I . . ."

"Daddy, it's all right," Mary interrupted. "You were right."

He smiled sadly and nodded once. Although Mary felt he was still unconvinced, he said, "You were my right hand out there today."

After they washed their dishes, she and John put on their winter gear again and went back out to the barn to look in on the heifer and her calf. The calf was asleep on the straw. He didn't even raise his head when they came into the barn. The heifer, though, was standing guard over her new offspring. She watched John and Mary cautiously as they came to stand beside the pen. In the next stall the other cow paced.

"She'll deliver sometime tomorrow," John said after checking her quickly. He wasn't worried. She had birthed several calves over the years, and he doubted there would be complications.

"I should get back inside to the kids," Mary said.

John looked up in surprise. "I . . ." he started to say. He shook his head and looked away. "That's good," he finally said.

Their evening chores finished, Mary and John once again fought the drifts and the wind to walk back to the house. As they walked, Mary knew she would enroll in classes again, that she would finish the degree that had been interrupted by David's death. She could accept what John had said earlier about her being his right-hand man as the compliment he'd intended it to be, but as soon as he'd said it, she'd known she wanted her own place in the world, her own goals, her own power to judge. She'd never again be someone's right hand or someone's helpmeet. She'd find her own path. She knew she had a long road ahead of her. She was flawed in some way. She didn't know quite how, and it didn't matter. What she did know was she had a lot of work to do to become the woman she was determined to be.

Through the gloom, the lights of the house beckoned. Mary thought then that she could stand almost anything—the wind, the cold, the ice forming on her face—as long as she knew they would eventually reach home.